Jenny Jones was born
at Loughton County F
of York. She now lives in York and is married to a
musician. They have two children.

FLY BY NIGHT is her first novel.

Fly by Night

Volume One of
Flight Over Fire

Jenny Jones

First published in 1990
by HEADLINE BOOK PUBLISHING PLC

First published in paperback in 1991
by HEADLINE BOOK PUBLISHING PLC

A HEADLINE FEATURE paperback

10 9 8 7 6 5 4 3 2 1

ISBN 0 7472 3398 5

Typeset in 10/10¾ pt Plantin
by Colset Private Limited, Singapore

Printed and bound by
Collins Manufacturing, Glasgow

HEADLINE BOOK PUBLISHING PLC
Headline House,
79 Great Titchfield Street
London W1P 7FN

To the memory of Anne Ellen Farmer

Contents

List of Main Characters

The Benu Bird
Lycias – The Sun God
Astret – The Moon Goddess

Eleanor Knight

Peraldonians (followers of Lycias, the Sun God)

Dorian Toussaint – Emperor of Peraldon
Lucian Lefevre – Mage, scientist and High Priest to Lycias
Mariana – Lefevre's sister
Idas – Lefevre's lieutenant
Emile Blanchard – Warden of Peraldon
Phinian Blythe – a captain in the Warden's Watch
Karis – his wife
Uther – his servant
Jarek Duparc – his friend
Hamnet Lin – his uncle
Beavis – the Lock-keeper
Elfitt de Mowbray – governor of Cliokest
Marial – a musician
Sharrak – one of the Parid

Mortimer Reckert – renegade Peraldonian

Cavers (followers of Astret, the Moon Goddess)

Nerissa – High Priestess to Astret
Alaric Warde – her husband
Blaise – the Great Mage

Aylmer Alard – Mage
Thibaud Lye – Mage
Matthias Marling – Mage and scientist
Lukas Marling – his brother
Margat – sister to Matthias and Lukas
Fabian – Margat's son
Caspar – his twin brother
Letia Witten – foster-mother to Matthias, Lukas and Margaret
Niclaus – her husband
Stefan Pryse – Commander of the Guard
Haddon Derray – a warrior
Brendan Leafe – a warrior
Oswald Broune – widower of the priestess Richenda
Selene Derray – a refugee

The Jerenites – Allies to the Cavers

Martitia Merauld – their leader
Thurstan – her son
Powel Hewlin – a soldier
Albin Rede
Idony Waters
Jocasta Garraint
Siward Smisson – a doctor

Riders of the Northern Plains

Ingram Lapith – Archon
Coronis – his daughter

The Arrarat

Ash – the midnight hawk
Astrella
Asta
Arkemis

The Fosca – (dark angels) mercernaries

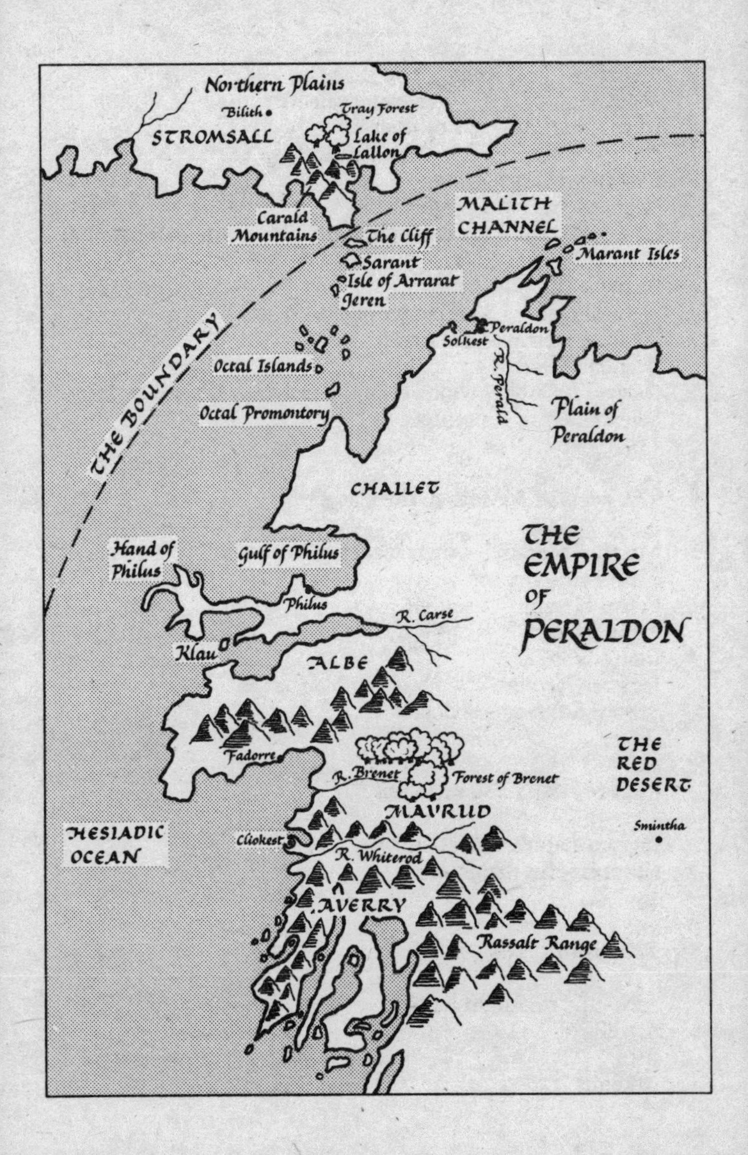

Northern Plains
Bilith
Tray Forest
STROMSALL
Lake of Lallon
Carald Mountains
MALITH CHANNEL
The Cliff
Sarant
Isle of Arrarat
Jeren
Marant Isles
Peraldon
Solkest
R. Perald
THE BOUNDARY
Octal Islands
Octal Promontory
Plain of Peraldon
CHALLET
THE EMPIRE OF PERALDON
Hand of Philus
Gulf of Philus
Philus
R. Carse
Klau
ALBE
Fadorre
R. Brenet
Forest of Brenet
THE RED DESERT
MAVRUD
Smintha
HESIADIC OCEAN
Cliokest
R. Whiterod
AVERRY
Rassalt Range

The Emperor

At the centre of his ringed palace, the Emperor lived alone amidst golden toys of great artifice. No one disturbed him. He touched a key and a bird sang, silken wings beating in time to the music.

As he watched, the little toy lifted from the jewelled tree and trilled round the high arching room, almost touching the starry ceiling.

He heard in the distance, over the song of the bird, the bell chiming for Veneration Mass. The High Priest, Lucian Lefevre, would be presiding over his favourite ceremony.

The Emperor never attended ceremonies. Never appeared in public at all, delegated all his official duties to subordinates, let all his fine robes hang in moth-balled cupboards. His empire held no interest for him.

The bird's mechanism was running down. He should guide it back to its perch, but some perverse prompting stayed his hand. He watched it flutter briefly against the painted constellations, and then its song ceased and it crashed, in a tinkle of fragmenting metal, to the floor.

Too late now. Too late and too far he had travelled, in the lost wastes of grief and guilt. There was no going back. Calmly he opened the door to the hidden stair which led to the High Priest's private quarters.

The stair was rarely used now. Long ago, Lefevre had spent much time with him, consoling and justifying what had happened. They rarely met now, for the Emperor preferred solitude.

Where his own rooms were filled with golden, enamelled and jewelled toys, silken cushions, deep carpets, the High Priest's private quarters were austere. Bare boards, plain walls, a hard bed. No relief, no softness. Except for the roses. Growing in tubs, from pots and boxes. Bowls of pink and white and gold and crimson stood on every surface. The scent was overwhelming.

Even the shrine was decked with flowers, the petals tumbling over onto the marble, the golden vases cold to the touch. Between them, resting in a crystal dish, lay a small, intricate, glowing centre of light.

The Emperor knew what it was. It held the key to everything; no more, no less. It reverberated with golden fire. He could scarcely bear to look at it, but he nerved himself to pick it up.

Cradling it in wondering hands, he walked through lonely corridors, down empty stairwells, through unguarded doors.

Who would stop the Emperor, within his own palace?

Out across the inner bridge, which vaulted over the trees and sweet-smelling flowers of his private gardens. Past the blank walls of the prisons, through the gate to the deep moat, the ring filled with swirling seawater, fed by the waters of the lagoon itself.

The bridge over the moat was also deserted. Quiet water lapped the struts, lapped against the high sides of sheer walls.

The water was very deep, only slightly disturbed by the movement of the tide. For a while he watched it, washing against the smooth marble sides. Then he looked from the small, golden secret in his cupped hands to the full Moon shining so far away.

'Forgive me.' What else could he say?

And then, with all his strength, he threw the golden secret high, up towards the Moon, far out over the quiet seawater moat towards the lagoon.

A faint splash as the depths received it.

A larger one as he followed it, ending his life of betrayal with a gesture to chance.

A hazard for the future, hope for the present.

PART ONE

Chapter One
The Party

'Why aren't you dancing?'

'It's too hot.' The girl pushed herself away from the wall, and walked out into the kitchen where the drinks were. The man followed her, frowning.

'I'd have got you a drink, if you'd said.'

'I'm quite capable of getting a drink myself, Rob. Go and make sheep's eyes at someone else. I've had enough of it.'

They were not alone in the kitchen; embarrassed, the others began to talk more loudly. Rob, a thin, hollow-shouldered young man, flushed and reached out a hand, catching her sleeve.

'Eleanor – please. Can't we just talk?'

She swung round, eyes flashing, red hair flying.

'Don't you understand plain English? I don't want to know any more. I've had enough. Go away.'

'You don't mean it! Don't say such things!'

'I certainly do mean it. Get lost, get stuffed, GO AWAY!'

'The hell with you, Eleanor Knight, for a spoilt bitch. Have it your own way. I hope it makes you happy!' His voice rose in a shout as she drifted out of the kitchen, back to the dance floor.

The man by the door clapped briefly. Tall, dark hair untidy, long mouth expressive, he gently nudged Rob's shoulder.

'Trouble is, she probably will be,' he said.

'What?' Rob was staring blankly into an empty glass.

'Happy. Your erstwhile lover. People that selfish usually manage to fall on their feet.' He paused. Rob wasn't listening, so he poured neat whisky into the empty tumbler, and put it into Rob's hand. 'Go and get drunk,' he recommended. 'It's a party, after all.'

'Did you have to do a lot to it?'

'Damp proof, rewire, new window frames, strip beams . . .' Caroline sighed and stared around the crowded room. 'The garden was even worse, like a wilderness.'

'Still, lucky you, to find this place. And all this lovely food and drink, you must have been at it for days. I don't know how you find the energy.' Debbie forked moussaka into her nicely painted mouth.

'Eleanor gave me a hand.' They both turned to watch the red-haired girl talking to a fair broad-shouldered man, expensively clothed.

'She's not all bad. And with parents like that, who can blame her?'

'They're not so unusual. How many marriages ever rate as happy after twenty-five years? You can't go on blaming your parents forever.' Debbie was severe. 'What's she doing with Lewis? I thought Rob was the flavour of the month.' She had lowered her voice and Caroline casually bent her head closer.

'Well, it's quite a story.' Caroline smiled secretly. 'He gave her this camera, a birthday present or something . . .'

'And the bloody bitch threw it out of the window! And it was no Kodak, I'd paid over nine hundred for it . . .'

'More fool you.' Dave poured whisky into his glass.

'That's not the worst of it! Then, she went downstairs, and got into the Porsche – my Porsche, what's more – and drove over it! Crushed it completely. Bloody bitch.'

'You're well out of it.'

'I know.'

'What are you looking so sad for, then? Have another drink.'

'Okay . . .'

'It's too hot in here.'

'The windows are open already. Let's go outside . . .'

Lewis Pritchard took her hand and led her out into the garden.

'What are you doing, bro?'

'Making a fire.' Mark stood up, swaying slightly. He gazed at them over the careful pile of twigs and paper.

'Why, for heaven's sake? It's hot enough without that.' Eleanor looked down her nose at him.

'I thought we could tidy up for Pat and Caro. Help them get rid of some of the rubbish.' His words were slurred, his intention impeccable. 'Give us a hand, will you?'

'You're nuts. All right then.' Amicably, Lewis began dragging dead wood from the hedge.

'Are you mad? What about your clothes?' Eleanor stared at him. 'Let's go and dance again.'

'See you later, sweetheart. Enjoy yourself.'

The party progressed, and the game prospered. The recently landscaped garden provided generous bonfire material, and the fire grew tall, raging into the night sky.

'These any use?' Adrian, with cluttered waste-paper baskets.

'Throw them on!' Mark was inspired.

'There's some tea chests in the garage – ' Rob, staggering a little, recovering.

'Get them!'

'What about these?' Juliet, her skirt held wide, filled with empties.

'No, no, don't be silly, girl, not bottles . . .'

'Still playing?' Acidly, Eleanor to Rob, through the flames.

'Join us?' Flushed with heat and alcohol, he was prepared to forgive.

'Forget it . . .'

'Why are you so bloody? Why can't you just join in like everyone else?'

'Why should I? Little children, playing . . .'

He seized a bottle from the discarded heap and suddenly flung it at her through the flames. Too surprised to think, she fielded it automatically, and held it briefly. Then she saw Lewis watching her, so she threw it high through the air to him, daring him to catch it.

He did, grinned at her, and then the game was on.

Bottles, green, gold and brown spun high, illuminated and flashing in the yellow flames. Laughter tinged with hysteria gripped them, and people came out of the house to join them. With reckless skill they hurled the bottles, higher, faster, less and less accurately.

The glass glinted and flashed, light caught through flame, sparkling and brilliant, and sparks flew through the air, leaping around them all. Sometimes they missed the catch, and the bottles slipped through sweaty hands to roll harmlessly on the grass or to shatter against stone. An exercise in nerve and dexterity, they were all too drunk not to make mistakes.

And then Rob found himself clutching an amber bottle, and pitched it high over the flames, laughing with exhilaration. At the highest point of its arc it met and shattered against another; jagged shards of glass showered into the fire, and everyone screamed with delight.

A small splinter caught Eleanor's arm.

Suddenly and inexplicably furious, she stepped back from the fire, dabbing at it with a scented handkerchief.

'Are you all right? Oh, I'm so sorry, Nell, let me see . . .' Rob, running to her side, all concern and worry.

She snatched her arm away and tossed the stained handkerchief into the fire. 'It's nothing. Don't fuss.'

'Do let me see . . .'

But she pushed him away, and flounced off down the garden, bad-tempered, into the dark.

'Eleanor – please, come back . . .'

'Let her be,' Dave said, cynically. 'She'd like another scene. It's not worth it. Come on, let's go in . . .'

But Rob stood there for a moment, staring down the long garden, and murmured under his breath, once, 'Oh, Eleanor . . .'

Chapter Two
Awakening

Eleanor walked quickly away from the bright flare of fire-light, out into the garden, sweat cooling on her face and hands in the light summer breeze.

Gravel crunched underfoot when she found the path. The scent of pinks wafted as her dress brushed by. Somewhere in the distance she heard a muffled rumble of thunder. The air became heavy, cloying.

Good temper returning, she smiled. It was a good party. Lewis would soon follow her. No one else had worn that shade of green. And, of course, she had at last got rid of Rob.

Such were Eleanor's principal concerns, that summer. Pampered, wealthy, only daughter of casually indulgent, preoccupied parents, she had scraped through school with the minimum of effort. She had acquired just enough skill to bluff her way into a well-paid job as an estate agent and found, rather to her own surprise, that she was good at the work and enjoyed it. A combination of social skills and a practised eye for assessing monetary worth served her well, at work and elsewhere.

She was enjoying herself that evening, glad to be at Pat and Caro's housewarming, glad that Lewis Pritchard was interested. Happy to be pretty, confident and free, wearing emerald green on a summer's evening at a party in Hertfordshire.

She continued down the quiet path deeper into the dark. Some steps led to a sunken rose garden. Narrow paths were lined with pansies and lavender, heavy scented in the still air. The full moon shone fleetingly between gathering clouds, casting into sharp relief the statue of an archer, moss stained and unlikely, bow raised to the stars, poised at a fountain's edge.

For a moment Eleanor gazed into the still water, but the image of the moon was blurred by clouds. Really, Caro did give good parties, and it was such a bonus to have a huge garden to explore as well. For the moment she was content to be on her own, free from the pressure of Rob's unhappiness, of Lewis's admiration.

She glanced about her to ensure she was still alone, and then lightly spun round, arms outstretched, face raised to the clouded moon, laughing to herself. She was not without a sense of the theatrical, however, and it occurred to her that dancing in a moonlit garden really required an audience. It would be rather a waste if Lewis did not follow her soon.

She looked back to the house, just able to see the glowing windows, the wide-flung doors, through the hedges and shrubs. A feeling of isolation, almost exclusion, caught her unawares. The party was well under way without her. At that moment there was another crack of thunder, much closer.

A storm. This was no time to be wandering alone in a rose garden. Lewis would be looking for her. She was about to return to the house, to the warmth of golden glowing windows, the noise and laughter. Through the dark rose trees she could see the fire, burning brightly.

And then time stood still.

In an instant that dismantled the universe and her life with it, the golden windows of the house closed. Like eyes blinking, shutters fell over the light, blocking it away. It was totally, unexpectedly dark. She hardly had time to wonder what had happened, why the house had shut its eyes, when the fire on the terrace flared up, flared wildly up into the sudden blackness.

And in the flaring of flames she saw huge wings beating, soaring over the fire, high over the flames, coming for her.

She stumbled back against roses, and the thorns caught in her dress and hair, holding her upright, offering her to the night. She was imprisoned there, struggling, seized with incredulous terror, watching the wings surging through the sky towards her.

A hawk, its claws cruelly curved, its eyes blank and empty as the night itself, reaching down to wrench her out of ordinary existence . . .

In sheer and dreadful panic she closed her eyes, fainting in the grip of thorns, and hardly felt the rush of air, the clutch of alien claws, the nausea of the ascent.

And as all order was devastated in the power of hawk-flight, as the world spun in a sickening gyre beneath her, she lost the last threads of self-awareness, of identity.

An unmeasured time later the world steadied around her, leaving her in an exhausted void of incomprehension and terror. Lacerated, flinching with dismay, she attempted to make some sense, find some reason.

For a long time it seemed that there was nothing in existence she could cling to, nothing to recognise or hold on to. She would have wept, but her body still seemed to be dispersed and fragmented. And all that presented itself to what remained of her mind, incongruously, was the cold clear outline of an archer, silhouetted against the moon, bow raised, arrow pointing.

Time passed – or didn't pass, she had no way of knowing. But at some stage, gasping for breath, she realised that she was lying on the ground, muddy earth beneath her fingers, cold damp air in her lungs. She seemed to have been flung there, abandoned, a leaf dropped by the wind.

At first she lay still, hardly daring to stir, simply grateful that the world had stopped spinning, that she was still inhabiting her body, still alive. Under her outstretched fingers the grass grew sparsely through sandy, poor soil . . . she began to assemble thoughts, to wonder what had happened.

There was a blank horror in her mind, an image of wings and claws, but it was already faint, fading fast. It was too unlikely, belonging to nightmares and dreams, not reality.

Had she passed out? Had a tree fallen, struck by lightning? Already, wincing, her mind was beginning to gloss over the shock. There were tears on her cheek, and her hands were shaking. She moved her head a little and rough cloth brushed her face. Not green silk. A grey wool blanket, flung over her.

She brought her hand up to touch it and the grainy texture of coarse fibres did a little to soothe her. Crossly, for she didn't like mysteries, and had already almost forgotten what had happened – what was there to remember? an unpleasant fainting fit? an extraordinary nightmare? – she pushed herself into a sitting position and looked down at her crumpled dirty dress, the blanket slipping off onto the grass.

Her arm was beginning to sting, where the flying glass from that stupid game had struck her. And where was Lewis anyway? This party wasn't turning out at all as she had planned. She was about to get up, fussily brushing the mud from the green silk, when she caught sight of the rain-drenched landscape in dreary half-light.

She drew in her breath, suddenly, the back of her hand pressed hard against her teeth. Rain, earth, grass, trees, yes; but where was the rose garden? The house? Who were these people?

Certainly not party guests, they were too old and their clothes were quite wrong. Some six or seven figures were gathered around the remains of a huge fire. It was still dimly spluttering, the smell of woodsmoke acrid in the damp air.

Where did the fire come from? Lightning? . . . but it was all wrong, this was a deliberately constructed bonfire, and there were coloured shards of glass lying at its perimeter.

And then, where the house should be, she saw the Cliff.

A huge black mass, looming out of the rain beyond the fire.

There are no cliffs in Hatfield Greenoak. None. No hills even, nothing like this. Standing there, a wall of rock, it was like a physical jolt, a blow to the body, a shudder in the mind. She could not take it in, not accept it.

It towered up into the clouds, solid and immutable, stretching away as far as she could see, lost in the twilight dark. Its presence was a denial of reason and logic, a vast insanity, a delusion, and her mind baulked at it, refusing it. She didn't know what it was. How could it exist? She stared at it, her mouth dropping.

She jumped. Something touched her shoulder.

A hand. Her head turned. For a moment the shape of the face above her, the hollows of the eyes, jutting nose and thin line of mouth were as meaningless to her as the wall of rock. A collection of shapes, shadows and surfaces. She was blank with shock.

The hand moved again, unthreateningly, gently insisting that she should react.

An old woman, her face half hidden by the hood of her cloak, holding out a hand to Eleanor, encouraging her to rise. She was gesturing silently to the fire, inviting her to share its warmth. She was dressed in rags of muddy undistinguished brown, layers upon layers, skirts, aprons, shawls, cloaks. Eleanor stared at the outstretched hand, and stayed where she was, her mind stultified with incomprehension. Where had the cliff come from? These people?

A delusion. A dream. She must be hallucinating, she thought, as she looked at them. They were all dressed in drab layers, the men in leather jerkins and leggings beneath concealing swathes of hood and cloak. Outlines were blurred, indistinct. Some crouching on heels, others standing, they seemed united in the urge to get warmer, but in little else. They were shouting, anger and disappointment crashing in the air, words hurled between them.

At first she could make nothing of their conversation, but gradually her ear became accustomed to a strange accent, the vowels blurred, the consonants accentuated.

'You're a bloody fool, Matthias!' A tall man, his voice hot with anger and exasperation, was shouting. 'A waste of time and resources. I told you it wouldn't work!'

'There's no reason to think that this is a failure. I would not leap to conclusions if I were you.' The second man's voice was quieter, but potent, energy contained.

'A woman! What possible use could she be to us? Cooks, housewives, seers, even sodding priestesses, sure, but no use anywhere else!'

'You blaspheme, Lukas! Take care, the women are no laughing matter!' An older man stepped out of the dark into the uncertain light of the fire. Not as tall as the first speaker, thickset, with a greying beard and hair, he spoke with the confidence of unquestioned authority.

'We sent the Guard out.' The tall man's voice was

measured in danger. 'Our friends and families are risking their lives. Some will die, may be dying even while we speak – '

'You could not have gone, Lukas, I needed you here – ' the quiet man broke in sharply.

'All *right*, we've been through that a thousand times before!' The tall man swept on. 'And the only result of all this effort, all this risk, is some damned female. Indeed, no laughing matter!' He glanced at the grey-haired man. 'No laughing matter at all.'

'It may have been all for the best,' the quiet man continued steadily. 'It's not clear yet, Lukas. We can have no idea what the outcome will be. The Sayer has not let us down before.'

The other looked at him for a moment in silence, his glance unreadable. Then, in a swirl of black cloak, he strode away from the fire towards Eleanor. She could just make out black hair flopping forward, startlingly white skin, deep-etched lines between nose and mouth. Sky-blue eyes hotly at variance with the long, sneering mouth, he glared at her.

'What are you looking like that for? You'll not be asked to do anything. You'll be chanting prayers, just like the rest of them. It'll all be easy for you.'

She stared at him, utterly bewildered. Why this hostility, this bitter anger? She stood up, brushing out the folds in her dress, turning her back on him, looking for the house.

Who were these people? They must have moved her somewhere while she was unconscious for some obscure reason. They were gypsies, uncouth and foreign. Perhaps they were going to hold her for ransom.

For a moment the panic returned. But at the same time, she knew it was ridiculous. Her parents weren't *that* rich. And no one was trying to restrain her. It was nothing like any kidnap shown on television or in the press. Nobody was even much interested in her. It was probably some stupid joke.

Strong resentment began to supplant the fear. She had had enough of this. She backed away from the tall man, retreating into the dusk.

He watched her, unmoving, making no effort to stop her.

It was only half dark, an uneasy twilight. Although the heavy rain obscured everything more than a few feet away, she felt sure that she would soon come across some familiar landmark, a road, a house, a signpost. As she moved away from the fire, her shoes began to sink in mud.

Dismayed, she stopped, bending to retrieve a slipper held fast in the squelching dirt. The man, damn him, was laughing.

'Where do you think you're going?' he said, his voice now alight with mockery. 'There's no way through over there. That particular quagmire is impassable to the north . . . you'd do better to stay here.'

Furious, frustrated, she managed at last to drag her slipper from the mud, and stood up, turning on him.

'What is this? Who are you anyway?' she said angrily. 'I didn't see you at the party.'

'This is no party.'

The words hung in the air, cold and unfriendly. The blue eyes were no longer bright with laughter but frowning in contempt. 'If it's parties you want, Peraldon is in that direction. If you fancy a long swim, that is.' He nodded over his shoulder, out into the dusk.

'What on earth are you talking about?' She was mystified and beginning to shudder in the chill wind. Surely this was unusual, even for an English June?

'You must be drunk,' she went on, dismissively. 'The coast's over forty miles away. If this is some kind of a joke, it's a pretty feeble one. Which way is the house? I should be getting back.' She was not really expecting a sensible answer, but it was worth trying anything to get out of this sea of mud.

He stared at her for a moment, as if weighing up methods of approach. Standing still, he was tall and gaunt in the half-light. She shivered suddenly, not only from cold.

Eventually, he reached a decision. Holding out a hand he pulled her back towards the fire.

'Come on,' he said, more gently, with a sudden, unexpected smile. 'You'd better put something warm on. I can't recommend catching cold here. An eternity of coughs and sneezes. Not attractive; no, not at all.'

He stopped, aware at last how little she was paying attention.

'I'm Lukas, Lukas Marling. Matthias is my brother. He can make the explanations. He is one of the Four, after all. It's his fault that you're here. We mean you no harm.'

He's mad, she thought. Mad, drunk or high – probably all three. Perhaps his brother or one of the others would show her the way back to Caro's house. She'd humour him, get warm by the fire, and then find out which way to go. For the moment, abandoning the dialogue of reason, she accepted a drab, rough woven cloak offered by one of the women round the fire. Moving towards its smouldering warmth, she ignored the others, who merely glanced at her, and muttered to each other.

There were rocks jutting from the muddy, sandy soil, but they were too jagged for comfort. She squatted on her heels, amongst the coloured glass shards, and held her hands out to the fire. A mug of something steaming hot, savoury, rich and unidentifiable, was passed to her. Sipping it, she felt suddenly cheered, fortified by its pungency.

Time to make a stand, she thought. This had gone on quite long enough. She didn't like feeling vulnerable, not in control. Besides, people were ignoring her. Even that tall man – what was his name? Lukas, or something – was talking to someone else.

'Right,' she said, standing up. 'I've had enough of this. I was invited to a party at Oaktree House –' she waved a hand vaguely over the quagmire. 'I don't know who you are or what you're doing here, but I think as a practical joke this is all in very bad taste. I really should be getting back . . .' She faltered slightly, aware that no one was paying much attention. 'I'd be grateful if someone could just point the way to the . . .' She trailed off, realising that now no one was looking at her at all.

Chapter Three
The Pendulum

They were all staring beyond her to a small party of women approaching the fire from the Cliff face. A silence had fallen. They watched warily as the black-cloaked figures drifted through the rain and arranged themselves in a ring round the fire and its attendants.

Curiously, Eleanor tried to see their faces, but the hoods of their cloaks fell forward, disguising and concealing. She wondered who they were. The party could wait. This was rather interesting.

After all, it had nothing to do with her.

One of the hooded women stepped out of the circle towards the older, authoritative man.

'You have failed.' There was no reproach in the stern, alto voice, only a bleak statement of fact.

'Nerissa –' he moved forward, and gently pushed back the hood, revealing a thin, sunken face, hard-etched with austerity. Black hair, unevenly streaked with grey, was scraped harshly back. Pale eyes, unblinking and passionate, gazed at him.

Hesitantly, he lifted his hand, as if to stroke her cheek, but she jerked her head away.

'Now will you believe?' She was intense. He paused, looking back to the others by the fire as if for guidance.

Sighing, the quiet man stepped forward to join them. He was smaller than the others, slight under a heavy black cloak. Its hood was thrown back, revealing dark, thoughtful eyes, a mouth weary with strain. He wore the same layers of clothing as the other men, the cloak over rough leggings and a loose shirt but, where the others carried knives and swords, he held only a wooden staff.

Strangely carved it was, reaching away through an elongated spiral into the dark beyond the level of his eyes.

'Nothing has been proved,' he said, patiently.

'But it didn't work, did it?' The woman spoke with a curious mixture of passion and satisfaction. 'Nothing has changed, the Stasis stands still as ever.'

Turning suddenly to the older man she said, 'You don't have to look so disappointed, Alaric! You must have known that heretical experiments would be worse than useless! Why else should Richenda have died? It was all in a wrong cause, and it killed her, the best and brightest of all our Sayers!'

She waved furiously at the remains of the fire. 'Prayer and faith are our only recourse! There is no other way!'

Are they lunatics? Eleanor wondered. Are they dangerous? She began to feel glad that they weren't paying any attention to her.

The older man continued, painfully, steadily. 'I think you are wrong, Nerissa. We have tried your way for a long time now, and there has been no change.'

'We have eternity to fill! The Goddess does not move to our petty time scales!'

'Too true,' said the man named Lukas, stepping forward, casting long shadows. 'She moves not at all . . .'

The smaller, quiet man, clearly Lukas's brother, put a restraining hand on his sleeve, but it was too late. The woman spun round, glaring with hatred.

'You! You and your brother have much to answer for, Lukas Marling! If it were not for you and your foolish experiments, your doubt and meddling, if it were not for those, our faith might have been enough to restore the Lady to Her throne!'

'Don't be so damn obsessive, Nerissa.' Lukas's voice was cool and dismissive. 'I'm not asking you to give up anything. Let us get on with what we have to do. It's not asking a lot.'

She took his coolness for deliberate provocation, and spat with fury. Like a cat, she spread her hands wide and hurled herself at him, the nails reaching for his eyes. The long mouth twisted with contempt. He stepped aside.

'Nerissa!' The older man, Alaric, caught her wrists and

clasped the thin body, trembling with rage, to his chest. 'My love! You mustn't!' Holding her tight, he frowned over the top of her head to Lukas. 'And you, Marling, are not a child to be making fun of our Priestess. We need to work together, for the Lady's sake! Disunity is ruinous to our purpose.'

'Too late, Alaric Warde, far too late . . .' murmured Lukas, and Eleanor, watching, was not sure that the older man had heard.

But his wife, twisting round, spoke with unexpected, powerful restraint. 'It is never too late, Lukas; our Lady will always forgive, and listen to those who genuinely repent.'

'But I don't repent, Nerissa, not at all,' said Lukas. 'In fact, I have every intention of exploring, experimenting, fighting back and generally causing as much trouble as I possibly can. There's no way I'm going to accept this bloody mess with a prayer and a hymn. And I'm damn sure I'm not alone in that!' He looked at Warde, a question in his eyes.

Nerissa had stepped away from her husband, and was holding out a hand to him. 'Come, Alaric,' she said. 'Come with me. There is peace in the way of the Lady, and honour, and love.'

What are they all talking about? Eleanor wondered. What lady? What mess? Anyway, it was nothing to do with her, and not at all helpful in getting her back to the party. She was about to remind them of her presence, when the older man looked directly at his wife, and Eleanor felt suddenly dumb, ashamed to be witness to so strong a passion.

'My dearest love,' he said, and she saw Nerissa flinch at the warmth of his tone. 'My dear, I respect your path, the way you have chosen, with all my heart. I know that prayer and faith give strength, comfort and courage, that all our hope must centre around the Faith. But –' and here, unwillingly, he caught Lukas's eye once more. 'But – faith changes nothing! It exists to lighten what we already have, it helps us to endure. But it reveals nothing new, brings about no alteration in this hellish Stasis. We have to try, and try again, other paths!'

'We have to accept the Lady's decree! If She has allowed our lives to stand still, there must be good reason for it! We only need faith and trust!'

'For heaven's sake, Nerissa, we need much more than that!' Lukas was exasperated. 'It may suit you to chant prayers for all eternity, secure in a bizarre belief that this' – he waved an expressive hand out at the rain-filled night – 'is the Lady's idea of a good time for all, but I'd like the chance to acquire a suntan, just once in my life!'

'You're a fool, Lukas Marling!' Alaric was stern. 'This is no time for levity.'

'It never is. No levity, no laughs, no joy. Ever. That's why I'm prepared to try anything – anything at all – to change things, and don't deny you feel the same, Alaric! I've no wish to interfere in whatever remains of your marriage, but must we always endure this perpetual nagging?'

'Enough!' Warde was shouting.

'Fine companions you have in your work!' hissed Nerissa to him. 'You forsake the Lady, and me, for this?'

'We have to attempt to break the Stasis, Nerissa. I can't give that up.' Grey hair, grey eyes, he stood steady as a rock.

'You will continue to use forbidden lore, then? Neglecting our Lady? Will you also go on fighting, wasting lives, risking what little peace we do have?'

'I have to.' The words were wrung out, from a depth of great misery.

'Blasphemer! Heretic! Evil and bedamned –' Shrieking, wild with disappointment and rejection, she backed away from him into the enfolding, concerned circle of black-cloaked women. Softly, quietly as a dream, they soothed her, drifting slowly back towards the Cliff, protecting, concealing.

Muttering, the other women round the fire gathered themselves together and followed after the group of priestesses. The one who had first drawn Eleanor towards the fire held out a hand to her again, just as before. She shrugged as Eleanor shook her head.

Against her will she had become interested in the conflict she had just witnessed. It was all inexplicable, of course, confusing and obscure, but there was something about the force of Nerissa's passion, and Lukas's wilful, almost malicious stirring, that had caught her curiosity. But the hysteria in Nerissa's voice revolted and repelled her, and besides, this was getting ridiculous. She was cold. She wanted to be getting back, and the Cliff was clearly the wrong direction.

She turned to the men at the fire, wondering which of them would be the most helpful. Alaric Warde was out of the question, staring bleakly into the flames, lost in painfilled thought. He was a loser, she thought. His wife held the power. Another dreary contentious marriage. For a moment two faces flickered in her mind, her mother careless with triumph, her father cold and calculating. This was just another boring power struggle. There would be no help there.

Lukas, moodily pacing up and down, was difficult and incalculable. She felt unequal to tackling him again.

She decided instead to try the man who held the wooden staff, Lukas's brother Matthias, who had silently watched the emotional turmoil of the others, frowning.

Determinedly, Eleanor planted herself in front of him.

'Please,' she said, uncharacteristically patient. 'Tell me which way to go, to get back to Oaktree House.'

He looked at her thoughtfully. He appeared to be weighing up something.

'Ah, yes. What did you say your name is?'

'I didn't, but it's Eleanor Knight.' She didn't know why she was telling him this, but his eyes were not unfriendly. 'Which way should I go?'

'I can only advise the Cliff, really. Perhaps you should have gone with Nerissa and the others. They'll look after you –'

'I don't want looking after! I just want to get back!' She almost stamped with frustration. Would no one understand?

'Well, it's a bit difficult to explain right now –' He was distracted. He turned towards Warde, concern in his eyes.

'Look, how do you feel about trying it again?' he said to the older man. 'The conditions are still right –'

Eleanor stared at him with disbelief. Was he really going to go on ignoring her? As if he knew her thoughts, he gave her a brief, warm smile, suddenly looking very much like his brother.

'Don't worry,' he said. 'I'll only be a moment or two. There's just something I need to sort out. Go and get warm, and I'll come and tell you all about what's happened in a minute.'

Deflated but obedient, for what choice was there, she went back to the fire, grateful for its dying warmth. It was the one comforting constant in the whole of this strange episode. Looking out into the chilling rain, she could not imagine straying far. If only she had the courage to tackle the dark, to find her way back. But she was not particularly brave, nor very used to taking initiatives in unfamiliar situations.

For the while she decided to wait, as Matthias had suggested, to keep warm against the constant drizzle and cold wind. She didn't notice the tall figure approaching, and jumped when he spoke.

'Staying here all night?' Lukas's flippancy imperfectly concealed something dangerous and worrying. She stared at him for a moment, and then surged to her feet.

'No, of course not! I've had absolutely enough of all this. I don't care if none of you will help, I'm getting out of here!'

Roughly she pushed past him and flounced off into the dark, but within a few steps her heels were beginning to sink into the mud again. Suddenly she was swung violently round by his grip on her shoulder.

'Listen!' He was almost shouting, obviously pushed beyond endurance. 'There is *no* party over there! No blasted house, nothing that you know! This is not your world, you're somewhere else, this is Chorolon. You've been brought here, Matthias knows how, I don't, because of a failure, a miscalculation. You're an accident, an experiment that went wrong, we don't need or want you at all . . .' He stopped.

Eleanor gazed at him, shocked.

The vivid blue eyes staring back at her seemed to comprehend everything about her. He paused, resignedly.

'It won't be easy,' he said more calmly, releasing her shoulder, 'but you'll have to trust us. We mean you no harm. Go to the Cliff now, the women will look after you.' He pushed her, not ungently, away from the fire towards the towering black wall.

'What do you mean, not my world? Then, where am

I? Who are you?' Her voice was tinged with hysteria.

The man sighed with irritation.

'Just do as I say.' He sounded tired. 'Go with the women, Matthias will explain later. Go on, go!' She found him suddenly frightening, with his intense eyes that understood so much and were so distant.

She was glad to get away from him. She began to walk slowly towards the Cliff. She was still not seriously frightened, for it all appeared to be a dream, a hallucination. Yes, that's what it is, she thought, clinging to the only possible explanation: if it's not a joke, then it has to be a dream. I'll go along with it for a while, there's no point in fighting these things. And then I'll wake up, probably with an almighty hangover, at Oaktree or at someone's flat, Lewis's, perhaps . . .

But she couldn't remember drinking much, and had refused the other drugs.

The Cliff loomed huge and black over the sodden landscape. Its top was lost in rainsoaked cloud, and water streamed down its uneven surface. As she drew closer, she saw it was honeycombed, flecked with myriad lights. A thousand caves fragmented its wall. Fires burnt brightly in the mouths of many of them, illuminating the entire rock face as it stretched away into the dark. It was a whole city of dwellings, perched precariously at the edge of a precipitous drop, offering some semblance of warmth and shelter against the bleak, wet dusk.

She didn't know where to go, where to try first. She stopped, hesitating in the rain.

A small group of hooded women emerged from the Cliff-face and came towards her across the muddy grass.

Nerissa Warde was at their head. She held out a thin hand to Eleanor, thin and pale. But it was steady, and her voice warm. The hysteria had passed.

'Welcome, friend,' she said. 'I'm sorry you were left out there with those renegades.' She sounded almost fond, almost teasing, Eleanor thought incredulously. As if she had not just been rejected by her husband, and her religion derided. Again, the impression of strength and power was undeniable.

'We thought you would follow us in,' she continued. 'But

perhaps we did not give enough consideration to your confusion.'

At last, thought Eleanor. At last someone has realised that I don't understand. She smiled gratefully at the older woman, who drew her into the shelter of a large cave mouth at ground level.

Eleanor relaxed a little, out of the wind and rain. It was a relief to be in the company of quiet, softly moving women, seriously welcoming her to their midst.

The cave mouth gave no indication of the size of the cavern within. Rough, cold rock soared hundreds of feet over their heads.

It was difficult to see in the flickering torchlight how far it extended back into the Cliff. There were deep shadows round the walls, shadows that moved, wavering with the light. Women, black-hooded, silent and watchful.

Eleanor's high heels echoed on the stone floor. Nerissa led her firmly to the centre of the space.

'I'm sure you would like to join us in giving thanks for your safe deliverance,' she said, confidently.

'Oh, but, I –' Eleanor's horrified protest was disregarded as the entire assembly of women knelt on the cold floor. Nerissa pulled her down until she too was on her knees. Hating this almost more than anything else that had happened to her, but unwilling to embarrass herself in front of so many strangers, Eleanor listened impatiently to an unfamiliar, puzzling prayer.

'We thank You, Oh Boundless Lady, who holds the cradle of Life forever still, for the safety of our sister from worlds beyond. We trust that in Your wisdom and power, You have sent us, through her, help to endure more courageously the mysteries of Your Rule. Dearest Lady, forget not Your handmaidens who here daily renew their pledge of obedience to Your Eternal Rule. Forget us not, we pray, forget us not . . .'

'Forget us not, we pray, forget us not . . .' The chant was taken up by the assembly, repeated softly over and over again. It was mournful, pathetic even. A strange conclusion to a prayer of thanksgiving, thought Eleanor, but then nothing here was at all familiar.

She could see no altar, no presiding priest or priestess. There was no focus for the eyes except an immense silvery pendulum that hung high above them all. It was motionless, still and steady in the chilly air.

They all appeared to be absorbed in lonely worship, chanting softly, heads cast down. Without hope or light. It was all rather desperate and Eleanor found it depressing. She began to long passionately for home.

Where was home? Where was this place? What was happening? Her nails were digging into her palms as incomprehension swept over her. Her thoughts were beginning to run wild again, but then, softly rustling, everyone around her stood up.

'You will need to rest now,' said Nerissa, 'and I'm sure there are many explanations which need to be made. But first, you must meet our sisterhood.'

Eleanor drew in a ragged breath. All she wanted was an answer or, better still, an awakening. But Nerissa did not seem someone to cross without good reason, and Eleanor was in no mood for confrontation. She stood passively at Nerissa's side and watched as all the women moved away from the walls. In single file they came to stand before her, one at a time.

At first Eleanor could not look away from their faces, for as each woman paused and threw back her hood, she gazed straight into Eleanor's eyes. Women of all ages, pale skinned, dark or grey-haired, they all stared at her, demanding a response, while Nerissa recited their names.

Eleanor could not decide what to do. A sociable smile was clearly inappropriate, and she had little else to offer. For all their differences in age, the women's faces were curiously similar: thin, intense, drawn, each one expressed an overwhelming and urgent need.

Such want made Eleanor uncomfortable. She looked away from their faces and instead watched their hands, clothes, hair, anything to avoid those beseeching eyes. The reassurance she had felt in the presence of so many women was illusory. These women had nothing to give her: they could only take.

It took hours. There were hundreds of them. Each

haunted face drove home that this was somewhere else, some other existence. Something she didn't understand, something foreign and alien. She was shaking by the end of it, trembling with inescapable realisations.

Get me out of this, let me go. I don't want this. Let me wake up, out of this nightmare. Please God, let this end.

She barely noticed when the stream of women had stopped. Nerissa turned to her with a sympathetic smile, offering food and rest. She accepted numbly, too weary to question, and began to follow her out of the cavern.

Before they had even traversed the length of it there was a hoarse, excited shout from outside. All the women ran out into the open, looking up into the rain-filled sky. Caught up in the rush, desperate and exhausted, Eleanor tried to find Nerissa, but she was lost in the crowd.

Cold again, lonely and confused, she felt tears of weakness and self-pity stinging in her eyes. She stood in the rain, amidst the black-shrouded and anxious women, and did not, party dress notwithstanding, look much different from them. Her tears began to fall, mixing with the rain.

Chapter Four
Karis

'Will you dance this evening?'

'Darling! No, really, it wouldn't be at all graceful!' Laughing she glanced down at her thickened waist, and the sun glinted on the golden comb in her hair. 'And besides, there'll be no music.'

'I could sing,' he offered.

'And that really would cause a riot. If you could sing even one note in tune, I'd dance a fandango for Lefevre himself!'

Amiably he flicked water from the jug across the table at her and then, as she dodged, stood up and moved to kiss her.

The scent of thyme growing in the cracks between the stones hung heavy over the terrace. The midday sun was almost at its zenith. The garden was bright with late roses, chrysanthemums and asters, and a blackbird sang in a fig tree. The air was still, sweetly warm and perfumed.

Her lips tasted of honey.

'I dare you,' she said at last, as he sat down again. 'We'll give them a shock.'

'I've never refused a dare yet, but your Doctor Tulliver is more than I can face.'

'Is this the gallant captain of the Warden's Watch I hear? Frightened of poor Doctor Tulliver, so earnest and pedantic? Phin, strive for a little courage! He won't even be there!'

'But his spies will be,' he said darkly.

'Your mother? Mine? The sisters, cousins and aunts, friends and busybodies of Peraldon, all gathered at Gallatley's great Mimosa Reception, specially to spy on poor pregnant Karis and her wicked husband? Let's give them all a thrill.' She leaned across the table towards him, eyes sparkling and lips slightly parted.

'I know,' she said. 'I'll sing, and you can dance!'

Later that day, while Karis was taking her afternoon rest, he worked in the garden, thinning out and digging over an overgrown border. It was work he enjoyed, hard and physical. He decided to build a bonfire to clear the rubbish.

He piled the branches high. The fire caught easily and flames danced in the air. Hot and sweaty, he was glad when Uther emerged from the house with some beer.

'That's going to take you a while.' Uther put the tray on the grass and nodded to the heap of garden rubbish stacked ready to burn.

'I know.' Phinian Blythe crouched down and poured a long drink. Uther had put two glasses on the tray, so he gave him one too. He glanced up at the sun. 'I've got until about seven. I suppose.'

'Any particular reason for the party, is there?'

'Not that I know of. But then I'm not part of Lefevre's inner circle. It's just an excuse for fine clothes, too much to eat and drink and yet more infernal dancing. You don't know what you're missing.' He kicked a branch back into the place, and watched it flare up. The smoke rose grey and swirling into the clear sky, flecked with orange-gold sparks, and the wood crackled in the silence.

'A big do, then.' Uther was faintly disapproving. 'Don't you think it might be too much for Lady Karis? Shouldn't she be resting a bit more, now?'

'Lord, don't you start too! You sound just like my mother. If Karis took all the advice she's been given she'd be demented with boredom by now. She actually likes this kind of thing. Anyway, there's still four months to go.'

'Hm. You can't be too careful.' Uther remained unconvinced.

'Don't worry, Uther. No one will take any chances with this baby.' He laughed, breaking a branch over his knee and throwing it onto the fire. 'My sister has even started a book on possible names for the poor infant.'

'Have you made up your minds yet?'

'We haven't decided. It rather depends what he – or she – is like, I suppose. Karis quite likes Annaliese or Guillem –'

'I like a plain name myself. Not one for the fancy stuff.' Uther looked severely at the leafy branch Blythe was thrusting into the vigorous blaze. 'That'll never catch.'

'Just watch.' Sure enough, the fire flamed incandescent around the dry wood.

'She's a great one for making work, your lady,' Uther said.

Blythe laughed, wiping one grimy, scratched hand over his brow. 'No, let's be fair, Uther. It was a joint decision to open up the view. And that old bay tree was really rather an eyesore.'

'Yes, but the Ferry's no improvement.'

'Well, we didn't know it would come to rest here,' he said reasonably. Frowning slightly, Blythe looked across the garden to the quayside which ran along its boundary to the lagoon beyond.

Floating there, unmoving on the still water, was an absurd, immense baroque creation, tier upon tier of tawdry, chipped paintwork, shabby deckchairs, and dusty curtains. The Ferry rose high out of the water, creating long shadows on the quayside, and undoubtedly spoilt the view.

He sighed. Sooner or later Lefevre would decide to have a spring again, and then it would be spruced up, refitted and repainted, and the jolly parties on the lagoon would start once more. Because of the frequent Caver raids, it was no longer used to transport supplies to the far Marant islands. Its only function now was as an unusual setting for the more extravagant celebrations of the Peraldonian aristocracy.

Phinian and Karis enjoyed the occasional parties on the Ferry, the music over the water, fireworks overhead. They'd have to leave the baby with a nanny or the grand-parents. Or they might decide to stay, quiet at home, the three of them.

Smiling, he turned to put his glass back on the tray, but

as he did so, Uther lifted the jug to pour out more beer. There was a clash and both jug and glass shattered onto the grass, amber liquid spilling.

'Damn,' Blythe said placidly, looking at the blood on his hand. 'Have you a handkerchief, Uther?' Kneeling to pick up the glass, Uther handed him a linen square. He dabbed at the small wound, and then discovered a splinter of glass on his sleeve. Without thinking he threw the bloodstained handkerchief and golden splinter into the fire, and then turned to follow Uther back to the house.

The alarm bell rang that evening. He was dressing for the reception when the sound jangled, raucous over the city.

'Oh no!' said Karis, looking up from her hand mirror. 'What now?'

Blythe sighed. 'I'm afraid we'll find out soon enough.' He had just finished tying an elaborate fall of lace at his throat, and was running a comb through his short, curly dark hair. 'It's Jarek's shift. I don't suppose I'll be needed.'

As he spoke there was a sharp tattoo of knocks on the front door below.

'What did you say?' She smiled at him quizzically, but her heart had started to plummet with fear, as usual. Not for the first time, she wondered if she'd ever get used to being a soldier's wife. Phin, characteristically, looked as if someone had just promised him a high treat. Nervously, she watched him put the comb down and edge towards the door.

'I'd better go and see what's up.'

Two of the Warden's Watch were waiting in the hall, heavily armed, in the familiar silver-grey uniform. They were both men from his own company, old companions.

'Caver attack, sir,' said the taller of the two, coming to greet him across the cool shady hall. Elegant spindly furniture lined the walls and feathery palms stood in brass pots on the chequered marble floor. A long, gilt mirror reflected the brightness of the men's armour and weapons.

'Sorry to disturb you, sir, but Captain Duparc said could you come right away.'

'Can't he cope?' Uther, unasked, was already collecting Blythe's battle kit and weapons from the armoury.

'There are too many of them. Over the pier. Captain Duparc said he'd be glad of assistance as soon as possible.' The guard successfully kept a straight face. What Jarek had in fact said was largely unrepeatable, and to the effect that Blythe was indulging in the idle pleasures of matrimony with little regard to his responsibilities.

Blythe grinned as he pulled on the fine mail; he was not without imagination and had known Jarek Duparc for a long time. With satisfaction, for he was also a vain man, he glanced in the long mirror and adjusted the fall of his short battle cloak. He was not tall, but broadly built, with capable square hands. Dark eyes gleamed in bronzed skin either side of a dramatically hooked nose. He picked up the heavy leather sword belt and was about to buckle it when Karis appeared at the top of the stairs.

'Must you go? Can't Jarek manage?' She came down to join them, with a whisper of scent, a rustle of silk.

'Apparently not. I'm so sorry, love. You'll still go, tonight, won't you? Lord knows what time I'll be back.' He looked down at her and noted the faint trembling of her hands. He kissed the crown of her head, and then tilted her face up towards him.

Her eyes were of a violet so deep that they were almost black, her mouth wide and generous. He thought, yet again, that he had never seen a woman more lovely, and that even this beauty paled beside the loving warmth of her nature, the quick intelligence of her mind. That she should consent to live with him struck him afresh as the most unexpected and extraordinary of miracles.

'Will you go tonight?' he asked. 'I wouldn't like you to miss the party.'

'No, I think not, Phin. It won't be the same without you.'

'No one to sing while you dance?' Briefly, he held her close, ignoring the waiting men. 'Don't leave the house, then, will you? The Caver attack is over the pier. I don't think they'll come any further this way, but you never know. Stay in, honey, just in case.'

'I wasn't actually thinking of gardening tonight.' She looked down at the pale yellow silk, and sighed. 'Ah well, there'll be other receptions.' She paused. She hated this part of it. 'Take care, Phin. Please.'

His mind was already on the coming fight. 'Don't worry,' he said. 'I won't fail you and the little one.' Gently he touched the curve of her waist, and then in a clatter of boots and swords the three men were gone. She stood alone in the elegant hallway, and began to wait.

Chapter Five
The Ferry

The pier was strangely illuminated that night as fire flared all along its length. It jutted far out into the lagoon, with boats and small ships moored alongside, and was usually a favourite place for fishermen and walkers. But tonight it stood deserted, enlivened only by flame. Blackened wrecks of boats smouldered all around, some still alight, some drifting far out on the smooth sea. Choking smoke clouded the air.

Blythe and his twenty men from the garrison arrived too late to defend the pier, for the fighting had moved on, along the quayside towards the Ferry.

In a freakish parody of its customary carnival glory, the Ferry was ablaze with light and action. Flaming bolts flared around it, smoke wreathed from scorched hangings. It glowed gold and red from innumerable small fires, and the shouts of men echoed around.

Over and above, swooping and swerving, the Arrarat flew.

Although Blythe had fought them often before, he still found himself pausing to watch. Immense, hawk-like birds, with fierce, hooked beaks and cruel talons, each one could easily bear a fully-armed man. Surging with power, vast wings cast scudding shadows, and the air whistled as they passed. Their plumage was chestnut, brown and grey, difficult to see in the night.

Only their eyes glowed, golden and amber, with a predatory, alien intelligence. Graceful and strong, they skimmed lightly over sea and land, wedded to the wind in silent mastery. Each carried a Caver crouched low on its back, cloak fluttering, almost unnoticed in the wild force of the Arrarat flight.

But the Caver riders were effective too, in their unique way. In telepathic communication with the Arrarat hawks, they attacked the Ferry with accuracy, uncannily avoiding every defence. Their extraordinary night vision was always a shock, even though everyone knew the reason for it. They were armed with lightweight bows, and arrows that flared as soon as they were released into the air. They carried swords and knives too, but no one was fighting hand to hand yet.

The Warden's Watch dodged and ran, throwing buckets of water onto the springing fires, cursing as the Arrarat wheeled overhead. They were covered by archers, crouching behind crates and packing cases, using powerful crossbows.

It was with the archers that Blythe found Jarek Duparc, his face blackened with smoke, his cloak torn and half wrenched off.

'Took your time,' he said, glancing, mouth twitching, at Blythe's splendour. 'Dear me. Are we on parade? Or are you going on to a party?'

'Sod off, Jarek,' said Blythe amicably. 'Why are you still here? Let's meet them on their own level.' He waved up at the Ferry, towering over them.

'We were just waiting for you, of course,' said his friend ironically, but Blythe wasn't listening. Edging round the corner of a packing case, he was looking at the chaos around the Ferry, frowning slightly. 'Now, why tonight?' he said softly. 'And why so many?'

Before Jarek could reply, there was a shout from the quayside and a tall stack of cases beside the Ferry suddenly burst into flame. A deep grey Arrarat flung itself high into the air, its Caver already reloading his bow. A man staggered away from the blaze, his cloak flaring around him. He stripped it off, swearing, and ran for cover.

'No time for speculation now,' said Jarek. 'They'll be in the city soon, if we don't get a move on.'

'They're concentrating on the wheelhouse,' Blythe said. 'I'll be damned if I can see why they should have it all their own way.' He unsheathed his sword and grinned at Jarek. This was something he enjoyed.

'I'll take Estan, Joss and Bellis. Can you cover?'

The question was rhetorical. They had worked together for long stretches of the Stasis, had trained and fought together so many times that a fine mutual understanding had been achieved.

After a brief consultation, the four men edged round the packing cases and then ran hard, dodging and swerving, over the gangplank to the Ferry. A hail of arrows whistled through the air all around, and the dark shapes swung high in the sky above them.

It was like an obstacle course in the dark. Coils of rope, corners of crates, the chasms of stairwells all conspired to delay and obstruct the dash to the upper decks. At first, movement upwards was unhampered, shielded by the structure of the Ferry itself, but as they approached the top they were more exposed and vulnerable to attack. The flaming bolts fell closer; they had to jump and fall back to avoid the sudden flurries of sword and dagger, the heavy swirl of vast beating wings. Eventually all four of them, breathless but unhurt, emerged on the top deck.

It was empty apart from stacks of deckchairs and the wheelhouse, a cabin on the north side of the deck. This was the focus of the Caver attack. Repeatedly the hawks dived at it, while their riders loosed arrow after flaming arrow. The wheelhouse, like the rest of the Ferry, was sturdily built, but even so one corner was beginning to smoulder.

Whistling tunelessly, Blythe ran straight for it, holding his small round leather shield over his head to protect himself from the hail of arrows. He let it drop just in time to squeeze in through the cabin door.

The other men stationed themselves around the top deck, keeping cover by the deckchairs, using their crossbows with telling accuracy. But somehow the Arrarat managed to avoid direct hits, seeming to possess some sixth sense of warning. Over and over they swerved at the last moment, fleet and agile, and the bolts went wide.

It was hot, scorching hot, inside the wheelhouse. Flames sprang, leaping in the gush of air from the opened door. Slamming it behind him, a handkerchief tied over his mouth and nose against the smoke, Blythe worked quickly. There were sandbags under the seats around the cabin walls. He pulled them out, sweat running into his eyes, breath searing in his lungs. He piled the bags up around the smouldering wood, slashing some of them with his knife so that the sand ran between the gaps, smothering the fire.

A crash, and the glass from the window shattered in around him as a sword plunged into the wheelhouse, releasing cold fresh air to fan the flames. He ran through the door, out onto the deck.

Deserted moments before, it was now a battlefield. Dark, frantic shapes whirled around him, limbs threshing, entangled and violent. The Cavers had landed, in force, and their birds were now wheeling overhead, ready to drop to the rescue if needed. Over the clash of weapons and shields he heard Bellis shout to his right, and then his sword was almost dashed from his hand as Estan crashed into him. 'Hundreds of the buggers!' he gasped. 'Fell out of the sky, while you were in there –'

'Get reinforcements. Now! Watch it!' A rising shout as two Caver riders jumped at them, swords straight and unwavering.

For a moment the fighting was ugly as the Cavers drove forward.

They were ragged, wiry and agile, and desperate. Their use of the strange, slim, serrated swords was lightning quick, lethal. But Blythe and Estan had years of professional training behind them, and their swords were of a heavier weight. In moments one of the Cavers had fallen, mortally injured, and the other, staggering back, gave the strange, warbling cry that summoned the Arrarat.

Instantly the heavy shadow swooped down, talons striking at Blythe and Estan, the hooked beak snapping and lashing out. The survivor stumbled across to it, grasping the leather strap that gave purchase against the smooth feathers, and hauled himself on. A rush of air, a swipe of talons, and the Caver was whisked off into the smoky air.

Estan ran for the stairs, and met Duparc on his way up with reinforcements. Together, they ranged against wave after wave of Cavers, still dropping out of the night onto the Ferry.

Smoke clogged in the breath, and swords shivered

through the air. There was blood slippery underfoot, and bodies blundered into each other.

For a while the Peraldonians stumbled and swore, virtually blind in the dark, while the Cavers darted here and there, unnervingly sure-footed, but as the fire in the wheelhouse flared up, they could see what they were doing.

There were too many of them.

Blythe's men were hopelessly outnumbered, and still the hawks swooped down, discharging grim, reckless Cavers. Fleetingly Blythe wondered why this attack should be so intense, why so many of them were risking so much, so soon after one of their routine raids. This was of a different order from the usual desperate grab for food and supplies.

But then a group of Cavers suddenly converged on him, surrounding him with determination, and he was too busy to think.

Now he was truly pressed, breath coming in gasps, sweat streaming into his eyes. He fought with skill and agility, with a precise eye and a strong wrist, but he was no match for so many.

In desperation, he began to use a technique of defence taught only to the most fit: a series of leaps and side steps designed to mislead and deceive the eye. It was flamboyantly successful in the short term, but too strenuous to maintain for long.

He was tired now. There was no sign of further reinforcements, and he could not for much longer ward off four Cavers at once. He could see Duparc facing similar numbers. There would be no help from him.

A shriek split the air. For a moment everyone was transfixed. A different foe was now swooping down out of the dark.

Something vile.

Curved black claws swallowed the unsteady light. As it landed the stink of decomposition began to overwhelm Cavers and Peraldonians alike. Casting leaping shadows, winged horror settled on the deck.

Not a hawk this time, but something scaled, red-eyed, with pointed teeth and swinging leathery wings. A reptilian creature, mounted by a living nightmare. The winged lizard was bad enough, sharp claws at the membrane edge of its wings, the scream that distorted the edge of hearing, the eager mouth and small bitter eyes; but its rider was more than grotesque.

Clinging like an incubus to the ridged scales, it gibbered at them. Grey-white skin trailed in rotting rags around pale lidless eyes, six long double-jointed limbs ripped through the air. No hands; pointed claws, some paired like pincers, the others sometimes retracted, now spread wide, ranging eager to tear living flesh. For all the activity of its limbs, its face remained blank, set in a frill of grey skin like the petals of an obscene flower. Its mouth hung slackly open, stinking saliva trailing over the decaying skin.

It laughed, soundlessly, and sprang from its mount. It moved with malevolence, with purpose. It hacked at the Cavers with the grasping claws, slashed with the razor-sharp hooks. One set of claws was clenched into a ball, swinging like a club, crushing. As it prowled over the deck, another dozen dark angels swooped onto the crowded deck, their riders striking out at the black-cloaked Cavers.

At once they began to fall back, calling their hawks. A defence against a surprise attack by the Fosca was simply not possible in such limited space. If ever.

The Peraldonians ran to the sides, out of the way, and watched as the Cavers retreated, the Arrarat clutching the wounded and dead in their strong talons, vanishing up into the night sky.

For a moment, Blythe was thrown. Fosca? Here? They had rarely been used in open battle before, being too wild, untrustworthy and dangerous tools, liable to cause far more trouble than they were worth as mercenaries. There had always been lengthy council debates before calling them in, for they were expensive and there were always accidents. Blythe had not heard of such a debate recently.

He stood, still breathless, against the rail and watched with appalled fascination as the Fosca angels and their riders decimated the Cavers.

The Arrarat were darting down to the deck, whisking off the defeated Cavers, lashing out at the Fosca with curved beaks, and the Peraldonians made no attempt to stop them. It was almost as if they were glad to see the Fosca thwarted, glad to see the enemy escape.

Several Cavers had fallen before their hawks could rescue them and the Fosca riders leapt at them, sharp pointed teeth reaching for the wounds.

They lived on blood, Blythe remembered. Freshly killed blood, straight from the vein.

One of the Cavers, a young boy with straight black hair, staggered to the edge of the deck. His shattered knee was giving way beneath him, and all the time he was calling his Arrarat.

Blythe was trying to help a wounded Peraldonian slumped against the rail. At the edge of his vision he saw a Fosca rider rushing straight at the Caver. The boy fell, all awry and off balance, onto the hovering bird. He was too precariously positioned to right himself, and the Arrarat was already in the air, desperate to avoid the slashing claws. But the boy was beginning to slip; sensing it, the bird immediately glided down to the quayside just beyond the Ferry.

The wounded man was not seriously injured; Blythe hung over the rail, trying to catch his breath, watching the scene below. It was illuminated by the fires still burning there, wreathed around with amber smoke.

The Caver had tumbled from the hawk's back, and was sprawled in the shadow of some crates on the quay itself. The Fosca angel and its rider had pursued them down to the ground, wild with blood-lust, chattering and shrieking.

The rider slid from the reptile's back and capered towards the Arrarat with its curious, fragmented leaps, mouth gaping in anticipation. For a moment it seemed that the bird would stand its ground over the boy, but he yelled furiously for it to save itself; it took off just in time to avoid the angel's teeth.

The boy tried to edge himself deeper into the shadow of the crates, but the Fosca rider had seen him and, screaming with triumph, was slowly edging closer, appearing to enjoy spinning it out.

Blythe watched in unwilling fascination, hoping that

somehow the boy would escape the thing. He was not at all prepared for what happened next.

A flash of light further along the quayside caught his attention away from the scene. At first he did not recognise where it was from, in the black shadows, but then his hands clenched with shock.

The light shone from his own house, as the back door opened and someone came out, dashing through the garden, flinging open the gate out onto the quay.

It was his wife Karis, running. Her yellow silken skirts billowed in the dark as she fled across the grey wasteland towards the Ferry. Blythe's breath froze in his throat.

'Karis! Get back! Get out of it!' he shouted, but his unrecognisable voice was drowned in the shrieks of the Fosca rider.

What was she doing, running to the centre of a battle? What was going on? And then he saw Karis notice the boy in the shadow of the packing cases and, without hesitation, turn towards him.

She's going to try to help the boy, he thought, helplessly, incredulously. Images sprang into his mind, Karis pulling a cat from the lagoon, freeing a bird from some netting. Getting scratched for her pains, but taking no notice. Warm with concern and compassion.

He ran, clattering, down the stairs. She's going to try to get between it and that monster, and she won't stand a chance . . .

Stairs were too slow. Quickly, along a gangway, ducking under the rail, he dropped down to the next deck. As if in slow motion, as he ran, and ducked, dropping again, and again, he saw Karis getting closer to the boy, her dark hair streaming in the wind, her arms held out, pale in the flickering firelight. And the six-armed creature taking its time, dancing across the quayside.

He slipped through the last deck rail, shouting continually, uselessly. This time the drop was further than he remembered and his ankle twisted painfully beneath him. He barely noticed it, for Karis had nearly reached the boy and the Fosca was only yards away from them both.

Oh, God, don't let it happen, he prayed, and cried out her

name over and over again in the dark. As he finally touched the quay and began to run, she was kneeling, lifting her hand to the boy's face. He saw the boy try to push her away, and she turned her head and looked at the monster almost upon them. It shrieked and leapt forward, eager claw poised. Holding out her arm to stop it, she cried out, but it made no difference, and Blythe was still far away.

For a moment she shielded the Caver with her own body, and then the creature lunged. She shuddered once, convulsively hunching forward as the claw jabbed at her, sinking deep into her breast. She fell sideways across the boy. At that moment, a lifetime too late, Blythe crushed the creature's skull with his sword.

He never even saw it drop. Trembling, he fell to his knees beside her, the sword clattering on the ground. Ashes in his mouth, shaking uncontrollably, he reached out to gather her up.

The world stood still in a timeless moment.

There was a great silence; the fire and the violence receded into a distant past and he held her fast to himself. Oblivious of the boy, he cradled her, murmuring useless words into her scented hair. His hands were held tight against the black flow of blood staining the bright silk, and there was nothing else he could do.

She stirred, once, opening her eyes against the weight of agony. 'He was so young . . .' she said, her voice threadlike. 'I couldn't leave him . . . so sorry, love . . .' And then her eyes went blank and her head fell silently, heavily against his chest.

Chapter Six
The Arrarat

Standing in the bitter drizzle, everyone looked up into the sky. They were silent. Tense. Breathless with an anxiety Eleanor could not begin to understand.

The sound of beating wings grew louder and Eleanor found that she too was holding her breath. Then the clouds were riven by hundreds of birds falling out of the night towards them, making no sound apart from the heavy beat of wings pushing against air.

She shrank back against the rock, too shocked to realise how frightened she was. The rose garden flashed through her mind, an image she thought she had forgotten. A hawk, coming for her, over fire . . .

These birds were dropping down out of the sky.

They were as large as racehorses.

Their wings reached out into the dark.

Their eyes glowed like lanterns.

The people around her were rushing forward, crying into the wind, and others were joining them, pushing past Eleanor, others who had swarmed down ropes from the caves in the Cliff face, eager, excited and fearful.

The birds, settling on the plain, were fierce like hawks, with hooked beaks and piercing eyes. They were exhausted, and many of them were injured, blood showing glossy against the feathers, arrows jutting at cruel angles.

Tumbling from their backs, in no better state, were weary men, some streaming with blood, archaic weapons dangling from fingers numb with cold.

The people from the caves were running through the birds and riders, unhesitating in the deep twilight, calling out, searching for relatives and friends. Shouts of joy mingled with the wails of those receiving bad news. Some ran to get stretchers for those too injured to walk.

After the main force had landed she watched three birds, larger than those on the sand, circle overhead. Deep grey, they were only just visible against the cloudy twilight sky. They swooped low over the Cliff, revelling in the power of flight. The people below paused in their activity, watching them. They were the focus of all eyes. When they eventually touched down, on the edge of the plain, it was as if everyone sighed with relief.

Three black-cloaked figures strode through the settling birds and wounded men, towards the Cliff. Each held a strange carved wooden staff, and looked neither to left nor right. They seemed to compel silence from those around them, a silence that only broke into a subdued murmur after they had passed.

People were tending the birds, examining feathers and flesh for wounds, bandaging and massaging. A group of men brought a cauldron to stand over a fire on the scrubby ground. Bowls of broth were set before the birds, and they began to eat, raising their heads to the sky as they swallowed.

Eleanor stood frozen with disbelief. Her mind had glanced over so much, refusing to accept it, seeking spurious explanations. A joke, a dream, a mistake, a delusion. But it was all adding up too strongly now. It was almost undeniable.

She was somewhere else, amongst strangers, with no one and nothing she knew.

None of it was possible. She looked away for relief, down at her hands. Familiar outlines, familiar shapes. Her small silver ring . . . Her hands were the same, ordinary and constant. Her dress, damp and muddy though it was, was still the one she had put on before the party. She had not changed, her heart was steadily beating in the old, unexceptional way. But everything else, everything around her was impossible.

No answer at all presented itself. It would be frighteningly easy to let the huge weight of incomprehension dissolve into hysteria.

The only other possibility was to take things at face value. She could allow a more simple curiosity to occupy her thoughts. It would be a way of surviving. The lunatic alternative did not bear consideration.

Hesitantly, she moved towards one of the birds waiting to be relieved of its burden. It stirred as she approached, shifting from foot to foot, and she nearly turned and ran. She was nervous of flying creatures, but by then she had seen that its rider was a youth, almost a child, collapsed forward across the bird's neck.

It would be something to do, something to pass the time until this stopped happening.

Blood glinted in his hair, and his right arm was twisted at an unnatural angle between the bird's neck and the shield he carried. Trying to avoid the creature's eyes and sharp beak, she edged closer. For the while she closed her mind to the problem of hawks the size of horses.

She looked round for someone to help her, but everyone was occupied. Gritting her teeth, frightened of the pain she might cause, she tried to tip the boy over towards her, to get him off the bird's back which stood higher than her shoulder.

The same desperate instinct that had kept him mounted made it difficult to persuade him to relinquish hold. Eventually he gave in, and sagged against her, bloody head lolling against the shoulder of her dress. She staggered under his weight, cursed as the sharp-edged shield jammed the boy's leg, and with a heave manoeuvred him to the ground.

She knelt beside him, pushing the hair back from her eyes, and wondered what to do next. The wound in his head had opened up again. The blood needed staunching, but she couldn't find her handkerchief, and remembered throwing it, bloodstained, onto that other fire so long ago. In the end she used the hem of her dress, damp from the constant rain, trying to clear the blood from his face and hair.

Nervously, she tried to gauge the extent of his injury.

He had received a blow above and behind his left ear and there was considerable bruising and swelling. The cut was not deep, and looked clean. He murmured indistinctly as she brushed the hair from his eyes, and then opened them, looking straight at her.

'Hello,' she said, trying to smile reassuringly. Distantly she recalled some elementary first aid. She held up two fingers in front of him.

'How many fingers do you see?'

'Two . . .' He was uninterested, his voice very faint.

Again, she tried.

'Three . . .'

'You'll be fine,' she said, with a confidence she was far from feeling. Next she would have to attend to his mangled arm. Just as she was about to pull his sleeve back, she was pushed firmly aside.

'Timon, are you all right?' An older woman, trembling with anxiety and relief, knelt beside the boy and with authority took over.

'I don't know about his arm,' Eleanor said, 'but his head's okay . . .' The woman glanced at her dismissively, finding her superfluous, and turned back to the boy. Eleanor stood up, brushing down her soiled dress, aware that there was nothing else for her to do there.

Most of the birds were now unladen, quietly feeding on the cold plain. The wounded had been taken into the caves, the discarded swords and bows gathered up. Eleanor looked back to the Cliff face, at the caves all filled with warm fires and people talking. Rocks were rolled back across many of the cave mouths, against the cold night, shutting her out. She turned away from the Cliff, looking out into the twilight dark.

There were no caves or cliffs near Oaktree House, no quagmires, beaches or areas of wasteland. No sea for many miles.

The birds – were impossible.

The people were incomprehensible, with bizarre and extraordinary preoccupations. Bleak, meaningless ritual, wounded men, antiquated weaponry, and a chaos of angry, desperate emotion.

'Not your world,' he'd said. 'Somewhere else, nothing that you know.'

And the birds were still sitting there, heavy dark outlines, breathing, preening, huge and alien.

Inescapable realisations flooded her mind. There were no other diversions. Unwilling though she was, the solid evidence of experience could be denied no longer. Her dress was bloodstained, her hands numb with cold, and the birds still sat there, ignoring her, living their own lives.

It was no longer tenable to think she was drunk, or drugged, delirious or dreaming, because this was all too strong. She closed her eyes, imagining herself back in the garden at Oaktree, furiously and passionately wanting it to be *so*. She counted slowly to ten, praying for a return to normality, praying for her old life back, and then warily opened her eyes again.

It was unchanged; dark, cold, wet, the looming Cliff, the settling birds, the lighted caves full of strangers.

A scream was the only reasonable response. But who would listen to her here? She didn't know what to do, where to go.

Blank with misery and confusion, she wandered away from the strangers in the caves, out into the dark, hoping against hope to come across fields, the rose garden, anything familiar and ordinary.

The tall man, Lukas, had said that the sea lay in that direction. But the coast was over forty miles away, she knew; why should he lie to her?

Drearily, she trudged on through rain, mud and scrubby grass. It seemed to be getting even darker as she moved further from the Cliffside, and soon she could see virtually nothing in front of her. She stumbled on, tears of loneliness washing her cheeks again.

At length she became aware of the sound of waves tumbling against a pebbly beach. In a few steps mud gave way to stone, stone to sand. She smelt salt, sharp and pungent. Spray fell on her wet face.

At last she halted, understanding this at least: the unchanging relentless waves, astringent and unforgiving, the eternal tide.

As her eyes became adjusted to this deeper dark, she began to pick out shapes in the gloom. She was in a small rocky bay, and the tide was far in, crashing in a foam of white against rounded pebbles. She looked up, hoping to catch a glimpse of the moon through the rushing clouds, but the dusk was unrelieved. She took a few steps further, and found herself bumping into a rocky outcrop. She felt around it until she found a ledge to sit on and cautiously leaned back against it, waiting.

Chapter Seven
The Stasis

Matthias, when at last he found her, was tired, irritated and worried. He had the Council to face, when recriminations would be flung at himself and the other three mages. There were the anguished families of the dead and dying to be comforted; his own sister Margat, still waiting for her son's return. The realisation that their last hope had failed . . . all these things needed facing, for they were his responsibility. And here he was, lantern spluttering in the rain, chasing after a stranger, an incredible and irrelevant nuisance.

Yet he felt a responsibility to her as well. No one else here would care what happened to her. She hadn't asked to come. Only the women would be interested in her, would want to absorb her into their dark mysteries, and then she would be lost indeed.

So he had left the Cavers with their grief and reproaches, and wearily traced the ludicrous, high-heeled footprints across the plain to the sea.

At last, with relief, he recognised a dejected silhouette against the rocks. Considerately, for he was a kind man, he kicked the pebbles as he approached, so that she should not be startled.

He sat down next to her, leaning his staff against the rock. He would wait for her to formulate her own questions. Then he would do his best to answer her in terms she might understand. She spoke their language, after all. Of course, she would not be here unless there were connections, common ground between her world and that of Chorolon.

When she did speak her light, petulant voice came as a surprise to him.

'I'm tired. I want to go home.' She sniffed, and fumbled

in her empty pocket. 'Have you got a handkerchief?'

Half-smiling, he handed her a rough square of material, and waited patiently while she blew her nose and dried her eyes.

'When can I go back?' she said, at last. 'I don't much like it here.'

He did not immediately reply, so she tried again.

'Can you send me back, please? Soon?'

'No.' There was no way of softening this. 'Not now, not ever.'

She became very still.

'We did not set out to bring you here at all. You are – the unexpected side effect of an experiment that failed.' He sighed. 'Look, are you cold? Would you like an extra layer?' He held out to her a heavy black cloak. She stared at it, unmoving.

'An experiment? What kind of experiment?'

'There was a prophecy,' he said slowly. 'A prophecy that if we conducted the Seventh Rite of Synchronicity, the Stasis would end and the Boundary break. It failed: the Stasis stands eternally still. That's what I mean by an experiment that failed.'

'The Stasis?' She frowned. 'What Stasis? What do you mean? I don't understand!'

'Not many do. It's difficult . . . You haven't been here long enough to notice, but time does not pass here, not in any ordinary sense. The same conditions prevail, without change, an eternal wet, cold, windy winter's dusk. It is unaltering, the same dreary dark, rain and cloud, ceaseless and static. It *never* changes.'

He paused, looking sideways at her disbelieving face. 'Neither do we. We neither age nor die, except through accident or injury. Our women are barren, we have no children. We live frozen in an eternity of gloom and dark. We call it the Stasis.'

'What has that to do with me? I want to go home!'

He went on as if she hadn't spoken. 'The prophecy implied that the Seventh Rite, if properly conducted, would break the Stasis. It didn't. Its only effect was to send you to us. And I don't know how to send you back. No one does.

There's nothing about it in either the Cabbala or the Scriptures.' He sighed. 'There was always a possibility that the Seventh Rite of Synchronicity, if properly applied, might form a bridge between the dimensions. Might even transfer someone from world to world, if the resonances were compatible, if there were enough cross-references. Such a person would be a side-effect of the Rite. Something we could not foresee or control. But to return someone, to find the right place amongst the infinite variety of co-existent dimensions . . . would be out of the question.

'The Rite depends on the bizarre chance that glass spinning through air, over heat, a situation of extraordinary and fleeting physical properties, should be matched exactly in another world. The very unlikeliness of the combination of events makes its duplication impossible. No one could tell where they'd finish up. It would be a suicidal chance to take.

'Somehow, unlikely though it may seem, you're going to have to learn how to cope here.'

'I don't want to! I hate it here!' She was frantic, beginning to understand what he was saying. No way back, no return to normality.

'It's not difficult, really. You just have to endure.'

'Endure? In this?' Furiously, she waved her arm at the bleak beach.

'You'll have eternity to get used to it, after all,' he went on relentlessly. 'There's no reason why you should be exempt from the immortality that afflicts us all . . . the women will look after you.'

'How could you do this to me? Wreck my life? Destroy everything I know and love?'

'Don't dramatise.' He was cool, trying to defuse her rising panic. He was aware that she had every justification for it, but he had no energy for dealing with hysteria now. 'I'm sorry for you, of course. An innocent victim of circumstance, just like the rest of us.'

'What circumstance? *What is going on*?' She was impossibly distressed, grey eyes wide with nightmare visions. In his quiet voice he carried on, calmly destroying her world.

'It's a long story,' he said. 'No one's quite sure how it all happened. Time stands still here and we don't know why. At other places it moves on, controlled by the whims of a man called Lucian Lefevre. There are an infinite number of theories and rumours about why this should be so, but I can't tell you which of them is correct.

'Lefevre has the ear of the Sun God, power even, it is said, over the Benu Bird of Time, but he's untouchable, too powerful for us to reach. We just have to keep trying anything, anything at all to end the Stasis. I'm sorry you've got dragged into it, but there's really nothing I can do. Nothing any of us can do, for you or for ourselves.'

For the first time he allowed the bitterness to show through. 'Do you understand any of what I've been saying? Does it make any sense to you?'

'No, of course I don't understand! How could I? Life just isn't like that! Things like this don't happen!' She tried to batten down the rising hysteria. 'I mean, it's all impossible. Time standing still here and there – it's nonsense. How old are you, anyway?' Fear made her belligerent.

'I was thirty when the Stasis began. We don't calculate years or months or even days; they have no meaning. But it seems to us all that years and years have been lost. Our children grew to maturity and then aged no more. The rest of us were caught, frozen at the time of our lives when the Stasis began and so some of us look old, some middle-aged and some young. But we will never change, never lose our hair or become more wrinkled. And the Stasis endures, the Boundary holds.'

'You're lying!' she shouted, but the truth was stamped deep into the dark eyes, and for an instant the strong wiry body seemed like an insubstantial illusion.

'We try – periodically – to alter things. This is a situation fraught with horrors, for a number of reasons. We are cut off from the rest of our people by the Boundary, which marks the extent of Lefevre's power and the Sun God's Empire. We are isolated in a hostile world. That is one of the worst things.

'The least of it is that all creativity has become stultified under the Stasis. There is no new music, no new poems, no plays or songs. Trivial, you might say. It is however a symptom of the essential sterility of our lives under the Stasis.

'But the unforgivable, the truly intolerable thing is this. Immortality is no blessing to barren mortals. We mourn the children we cannot have.

'We started by petitioning Lefevre peacefully, but it soon degenerated into violence. Astret, the Lady of the Moon, and Her people were a threat to the stability of the Stasis, this cursed condition of immortality. That is why the Boundary was set up, to keep the people of the Moon Goddess out. We were caught on the wrong side, at the wrong time. It's not surprising that the Lady Astret should be opposed to it.

'There was a war, the Banishment War. That is a long story. Someone will tell you, one day. The followers of Astret were defeated. How could it be otherwise? A few thousands against the entire Peraldonian Empire. Those who survived were rescued from Sarant, our island home. We live here now, the only place left to us in these regions, following the instructions of the Lady Astret Herself.

'Some of us – my brother Lukas, Stefan Pryse and the Guard – try force. But guerrilla warfare is all we can manage.

'The result is that the Cavers are outcast, pariahs, hunted and feared by the Peraldonians. We are herded into this place, patrolled by their Warden's Watch, grudged an existence. We steal our food, robbing both the islands and the mainland. We are being eliminated by slow degrees.

'It's not really much of a life you'll be taking on. The women find consolation, on the whole, in their religion. They divert time and attention from husband and family to the various rites of the Lady.' He was being too critical, he knew, but the girl seemed by now to be lost in a daze of incomprehension and fear. He was not surprised.

'Listen, Eleanor. It always rains here. The sun never comes out, the moon never rises. It is always cold, wet and windy. Always. No change, ever.'

'But – it was summer, at home. There was a storm, but it had been hot . . .' She was still clinging to her past. 'It was June,' she said, and he almost laughed at the innocence of it.

'That world is gone,' he said. 'I've told you already. Lost

amongst an infinity of dimensions. There's no going back.' Patiently he emphasised it. 'Your presence here proves only that our two worlds co-existed closely in the continuum at some stage.'

'Is this another planet, then? Was I brought here through space?' It was as unlikely as any other explanation.

'This is nothing to do with distance, or physical place. There is an infinity of moving dimensions which occasionally touch each other. Strong influences reverberate elsewhere . . . Perhaps the Sun God is eternally opposed to the Moon Goddess, and this opposition occurs in all dimensions at some time, in some form . . .

'You could not have made the crossing unless we shared many aspects, many archetypes. The bridge of Synchronicity must be supported on both sides by similar structures; religion, events, society, language . . . there are undeniable connections. We speak the same language, after all. But a thousand other worlds share this same close relationship. Finding the same bridge again, exactly the same, would be out of the question. As unlikely as breaking glass over fire following an established pattern.'

'It's all nonsense!' Tears were now openly falling. 'I don't believe you, I can't, it must all be a dream!' Her protests were weaker now.

'Does it feel like that, then? A hallucination, drink, drugs, something like that?'

'No.' Her voice was almost swallowed by the wind.

'Then, for a while, just stop thinking about what is real, and what is not. Reasoning won't help. If it makes you feel better to imagine that you might wake up, then go ahead. But while you're in the dream you may as well come to terms with it.'

He was being hard, he knew. But he had little energy to spare for her, and the Cavers would be needing him. She was the least of his responsibilities. A pathetic, bedraggled figure, she would find the austerities of Caver life hard to the point of impossibility.

Searching round for a little comfort, he said, 'You never know. The prophecy may have held good. You might be just what we need, some kind of help . . .'

'As what? A ray of sunshine?' The strength of her anger and bitterness took them both by surprise.

'Perhaps.' He looked at her thoughtfully. 'Who can tell? You don't belong here, you're not part of the Stasis at all. A wild card, something incalculable, plucked from a myriad of choices. Who knows? You might be just what we need to break the deadlock.'

'You think I could help?' She was incredulous that it should have anything to do with her.

Silently he looked at her, wide-eyed, pale, pretty and plump in her party dress, and knew her to be only an irrelevance. It was an indulgence, to toy with a fragment of hope, for nothing would change. Nothing could.

But he was a kind man, so he smiled and said again, more gently. 'Perhaps, who knows? But if we don't get you some food and rest soon, you'll be in no shape even to try.' He stood up, and slowly pulled the edges of the cloak together over the bright dress.

'Come on,' he said. 'Let's get back, you're frozen.'

Meekly, she followed him, because he was at least aware of her incomprehension, and not without sympathy, and her thoughts, echoing wildly in the void of her understanding, gave no help.

As they approached the Cliff a thin reedy singing drifted towards them with the wind. Matthias paused.

'A funeral,' he said, his voice empty of expression. 'They probably don't do it like this in your world.'

People were gathered on the edge of the marsh. It looked as if all the inhabitants of the caves were there. The thin wailing sound of chanting came from a group of women, dressed now in sodden white. Everyone else stood silent, grim-faced, drawn. A row of covered bodies lay on stretchers, groups of mourners standing or kneeling at their sides.

A forbidding tableau. Shivering, Eleanor thought with a chill that it was a fitting setting for the nightmare that was her new life.

Three black-cloaked figures stood tall at the edge of the quagmire, at some distance from the others. They each held a wooden staff similar to Matthias's. Carved spirals reached up into the night.

With one accord the three black figures raised their staffs high into the air, and a strange warbling sound echoed round the Cliff. Jagged lightning flew from the carved wood, illuminating the livid faces around them.

The chant ceased. Everyone looked up into the night. The beating sound of enormous wings filled the air, and huge hawks swooped down on the bodies on the stretchers, and plucked them up into the air, clutched in strong talons. Once they circled above the crowds; then, slowly, calmly, they flew a little way out over the quagmire, circling gradually lower, closer to the surface. Gently, smoothly, they deposited the bodies on the watery surface and, as the lightning flared wildly in the dusk, began to weave in wide arcs overhead.

The marsh stretched far out into the gloom. As the lightning forked down, it was reflected in pools of stagnant water. Suddenly, clumps of springy grass were sharply illuminated, unmoving in the cold air. Moisture clung in a haze all over the bog.

The crowd watched, silent, anguished. Slowly the mire shifted and the bodies began to sink into the mud. A sigh rippled through the mourners, but no one cried aloud.

It took almost ten minutes for the bodies to disappear completely. Every moment was wrenchingly drawn out by the movement of the inexorable mire, regarded in stillness by the watchers.

After what seemed an age to Eleanor, people began to disperse. Huddled in the drenching rain, weeping women were led back to the caves across the wet waste of sand and mud. Appalled, Eleanor turned to Matthias, but he was scanning the passing faces intently, looking for someone. Then he called out, and a tall thickset man came towards them. 'Where's Lukas?' Matthias said.

'Fabian's still not back. He's with Margat, on the tower.' The man's voice was rough, but not unfeeling. Matthias frowned, tiredness almost tangible, and murmured, half to himself. 'Arrarat have been late before. It may mean nothing.'

The other man nodded. 'There's been no message from the others,' he said obscurely. He shrugged and glanced with curiosity at Eleanor. Hurriedly, his mind elsewhere, Matthias introduced them.

'Niclaus Witten – this is Eleanor, Eleanor Knight – a visitor –' For a moment he looked silently at Witten, passing some indecipherable message. 'Can you and Letia give her shelter and something to eat?' Phrased as a question, this was nonetheless a command. 'I'm needed at the Council. I'll see you later, Eleanor. Niclaus will look after you.'

'Please don't go –' Alarmed, she tried to hold him back, but he smiled briefly, waved, and disappeared into the drab throng.

'Come on,' said the man tersely. 'You need to get warm.' Firmly and kindly, he took her arm, and guided her back through the crowds to the Cliff.

Niclaus Witten's cave was on the fourth tier. Some people were swarming up rope ladders to get to theirs but, fortunately for Eleanor, there was also a stone staircase at the back of one of the ground level caves. Puddles underfoot; no light. No one seemed to need it, moving surely through the deep black at the heart of the caves. Stumbling, Eleanor was glad that the steps were at least regular and that there was a rope handrail.

At the third landing Witten turned down a dark passageway towards a faint glow of light. His shoulders nearly filled the narrow space, but Eleanor could smell food and hear the clash of pans.

It should have been reassuring, but by now she was highstrung with misery and exhaustion. Her stomach ached with the tension of it. She couldn't bear to encounter anyone or anything new. She would have been happier on that cold seashore, she felt, waiting to wake up, than having to make sense of more incomprehensible strangers.

But she was deeply cold, and clumsy with tiredness. She took a deep breath and followed Witten through an open door set in the rock into the large firelit chamber at the end of the passage.

The strange pungent mixture of smells became

overwhelming – savoury cooking, damp clothes drying and woodsmoke, all underlaid by something rather unpleasant Eleanor failed to identify. She was too weary to take in details. She had an impression of warmth from the fire, of rough tables and chairs, a multi-coloured rag rug on the floor.

A small, thin middle-aged woman stood up as they entered. Like the other women outside, she was wearing bulky layers of cloth; petticoats, dress and shawl, brown, beige and white. Her hair was greying, curly, framing delicate features.

She darted a bright-eyed glance of enquiry to Witten, who repeated almost word for word his own instructions from Matthias.

'My name is Letia,' she was saying, guiding Eleanor over to the fire. 'You've met Matthias, have you? He's a great friend of ours . . . we used to call him and Lukas and Margat our foster children, but it seems silly after all this time –' Her voice ran on, friendly and reassuring. Deftly she took Eleanor's cloak, shaking her head over the damp flimsy dress beneath. 'What can they have been thinking of, keeping you out there dressed like this!'

They hadn't planned it, she wanted to say. I wasn't what they wanted at all. But she was too tired to talk. She said nothing.

'Are you hurt?' Letia said suddenly, sharply. Eleanor vaguely followed the direction of her glance and stared uncomprehending at the patch of drying blood on her shoulder. Then she remembered.

'No –' she said. 'I tried to help someone off one of the birds. He was injured –'

'Ah, yes,' Letia nodded, satisfied. 'So nothing ails beyond cold, hunger and tiredness? We can soon put those right. First, some dry clothes.' With one sharp, bird-like movement she plucked a coarse brown dress and petticoat from the line of clothes hanging overhead. It was warmed from the heat of the fire burning in the mouth of the cave. Eleanor allowed herself to be shepherded into a small chamber hewn out of the main wall.

'Now you put these on, and come out when you want

something to eat. I've got a stew here ready, only fish again, of course, but at least it's hot –' Chattering still, Letia lit a candle for her, and drew a curtain across the opening to the chamber.

Eleanor was alone.

Filled with a sudden loathing for emerald green silk, she struggled out of its clammy embrace and pulled on the petticoat and dress. She wished that Matthias had not abandoned her so casually to these strangers. He alone had made an effort to explain what was going on.

His words, remembered, made her shudder. With hands that trembled she touched the cloth of her full skirt. It was rough and warm, an unfamiliar loose weave which provided little comfort. She looked around.

The chamber was a bedroom, the bed a rocky ledge covered with pillows and eiderdowns. A scrap of polished metal hung as a mirror on the wall. Irresistibly, Eleanor stared at herself and automatically began to tidy her hair, to wipe away the marks of smudged make-up. So strange to think that only a few hours had passed since she'd tried out, carefully, a new kohl eye pencil in her flat.

Desolation swept over her. She sat on the bed and began quietly to cry into the damp rag that had been her new party dress. Soon exhaustion claimed her: she slipped sideways onto the pillows, and slept.

Chapter Eight
Loneliness

'Oh Lady, Lady, where are You? Our need is so great, our despair a poison in our lives. And still You don't come!

'Have You in truth abandoned us? I never thought You would. I've told them all so often, for so long, that You would come again to us, as You used to.

'What holds You back? Where did we go wrong? You were an inspiration and joy to my mother, and my mother's mother. What happened to make You desert us? I've honoured every one of Your rites, kept every word of Your Rule bright and untarnished. I have never wavered, not in the smallest detail! Why should You punish me like this?

'Heresy and insurrection grow. Your voice is mocked by false prophets and still You ignore us! It's hard following Your path, my Silver Lady, when there's no help, no warmth in it. I'm tired, so very tired, and there's no sign of an end. Will it ever end, Astret?

'Or is this our fate, a dreary eternity of sorrow and pain? Must we go on like this for ever, is this it, is this all there is?'

Violently Nerissa pushed herself up from the hard floor, breathing hard. The silver Moon set in the stone of her altar gleamed in the torchlight, and for a moment she almost hated it.

She wished she could cry, but that relief had deserted her when the Lady disappeared from their lives. She looked in the mirror on the wall and wished that her hair was white, her skin more wrinkled. The signs of ageing should be written on the face, not on the soul alone.

She should go to Oswald. He would be needing her. But Alaric was waiting in the outer cave and she could not just pass him by.

Broad and muscular, Alaric Warde had always been a commanding figure, and now he seemed to fill their austere cave. She wished that his strength extended to his character. A serrated knife jutted from his belt, and his tabard was scuffed and torn from the relentless search for food, the desperate Caver existence. His face and hands were scarred, but unlined, like hers. It was not right.

'Nerissa.' He was standing facing her, his eyes dark and unhappy beneath the heavy brows. 'I must talk to you.'

'What is it, Alaric?' Her voice sounded harsh, but she couldn't help that.

He looked down at his hands, turning over between them the heavy silver armband she had given him when they were first married. He looked weary, she noted dispassionately. Was he going to start it all again?

'I must go and see Oswald,' she said. 'I haven't much time.'

'This needn't take long.' He lifted his head and looked at her again. 'I can't go on,' he said. 'Our marriage is a mockery, a pretence. I can't see why it should continue. I've had enough.'

'It's up to us to set an example,' she said.

'Why? What possible good can it do?'

'We have no choice.' She sounded patient, but rage was flaring within her. 'Others follow our lead. We give them the courage to continue. We can never falter, or they will lose heart.'

'Do you think they haven't noticed? Was that just a little marital tiff outside by the fire? Lukas didn't think so.'

'He is destructive, that one. Wild and reckless; he would waste all our lives to break the Stasis. No one would take any notice of him if the Mage Matthias were not his brother.' She almost spat the words.

'You underrate him. He has both power and influence, and the younger men will always follow his lead. If he can see that our marriage is over, so can everyone else.'

'So we split up in order to reinforce Lukas Marling's position?' Her eyes flashed with anger. 'I think you should strive for a little loyalty, Alaric. They will soon forget that scene by the fire, if we present a united front. The only way to defuse idle gossip is to remain steadfast. And when the Lady returns –'

'She never will!' He shouted passionately, slamming his hand hard onto the table at his side. 'How long are you going to go on deluding yourself? This goes beyond mere loyalty. Astret is gone, there is no point in this senseless hanging on to the past.'

'What else do we have?' she said quietly. She stared out at the driving rain beyond the cave mouth. 'Our lives were only worth anything in the past, for the present is desperate and the future impossible. We have to accept that this is Astret's will. We have to live in the memory of Her Will, in the faith that She will return. There is nothing else. The centre of our lives was lost when Astret was banished. We're still at that point, nothing has changed . . .'

'But we have. Oh, not physically, of course not. But emotionally, we're tired out, exhausted. And all I want now is some humanity, some warmth and love.' His voice cracked slightly.

She stared at him, contemptuous, implacable. 'Fool,' was all she said, and brushed past him towards the door.

'Nerissa!' He caught her arm as she passed. 'Please! I beg you! I cannot say this again. Listen to me.'

'Quickly, then.' She was impatient. He paused, frowning, trying to find the right words.

'I have loved you. I still do. And yet the pain of being with you, of maintaining this farce, when you clearly feel nothing for me, is too great. All day, every day, you give yourself to the Lady. There is nothing left for me. No love, no relief, not even any ordinary friendliness. Nerissa, we must either have a marriage in every sense of the word, or live apart. I can bear nothing else.'

'You are weak, Alaric, to give way to such need. The Lady demands much of us all, but our only possible choice is to follow Her, accept the Rule, live our lives as She directs –'

'Acceptance is not enough! Your own priestess Richenda has shown us another way!'

And had died. Richenda, falling to the ground, speaking terrible words in a cloud of smoke. The words that led to the Seventh Rite, to the Guard's attack on the Ferry.

'Richenda lost her life in a farce! It was a false prophecy, a heresy! The Lady Astret would never have required the death of Her own priestess –'

'Unless it was desperate. Unless there was no other way. Should Richenda have died for nothing? We owe it to her to keep trying.'

'What is the use? What have we gained? More wasted lives! That useless girl!'

There was a sudden silence between them. He was looking at her, frowning. His eyes were sad.

'Nerissa. Is there really nothing for us apart from dissension? Can we not at least live together in peace, loving each other as we used to? It should be easy, we've had time enough to learn tolerance.'

'You know nothing. You understand not the smallest part of the Lady's Rule. You never will. If you can't live in faith any longer, it's just too bad. I at least will never desert Our Lady.'

Oh, Alaric, she thought, why are you so blind?

He stood aside stiffly, upright and contained.

'That's it, then,' was all he said, and she left their cave, unable to bear those sad eyes any more, slamming the door behind her.

She walked quickly along the corridor to Oswald Broune's cave, her face stony. But when she reached the door she paused, hesitating for a moment.

She took several deep breaths, willing her heart to stop racing. Deliberately she composed her face until she knew she was looking calm and serene once more. Only then did she raise her hand, and knock on the door.

'Who is it?' The voice was urgent, surprisingly loud.

'Nerissa. May I come in?'

The door swung open, and Oswald stood there, as if he had been waiting for her. She went into the cave and sat on a chair by the fire. The room was untidy, blankets rumpled on the bed, dirty cups and glasses everywhere. There was a smell of sour wine.

'How are you?' she asked gently. Oswald sat down opposite her and she could only see him through the flames. They tinged his pallid skin into health, but his eyes were swollen from crying.

He was a young man, rather plump, with mousy, curling hair framing a mild face which under other circumstances might have appeared amiable and easy-going.

'Are you still decided?' she said. 'You will speak against Marling at the Council?'

'Yes, yes, what else is there to do?' He was impatient.

'You know that they will brand you a traitor?' She had to be scrupulously fair with him. 'The Mages are powerful and will resent interference.'

'What does it matter, now that Richenda . . . now that my wife is dead?' Tears sprang again to his pale eyes. He blinked them away.

'Remember you will not always feel so strongly . . . grief loses its edge in time, impossible though it may seem now. You may not always feel so angry with those who asked Richenda to prophesy, to try to break the Stasis.'

He rejected this with force. 'Break the Stasis? Just think what it would mean!'

'Astret will never forgive us for losing faith,' she said, watching him.

'No. But it's not just that. What do they want to *die* for?' He surged to his feet and began restlessly pacing the cave. 'Do none of them realise what death does? How it hurts?' His voice rose. 'Why do they long for death? It's a curse, a horror upon humanity. It's so lonely when someone dies, how can they bear it? It's like dying yourself, trying to reconstruct a life after – after . . .' The words were lost and he choked on heaving sobs.

She gazed at him, considering. He was no ally for Astret. Unstable with grief, he might rage against those who tried to break the Stasis, but he would change. He was too anchored to earth, too warmly involved with friends and lovers to risk everything for the love of the Goddess. Like Alaric he would deny the Lady's Way of tranquil acceptance. In the end he would join the Marling brothers and Stefan Pryse in fighting back, rebelling in violence and heresy.

Sighing, she put him out of her mind. She would have to continue on her own. Alaric had lost faith, and now this frail hope had failed too.

Abstracted, she patted his back, murmuring meaningless words of comfort.

'Will you come to the Council?' she asked neutrally, when he was calmer.

'Yes,' he said, pouring himself a drink with unsteady hands. 'I'll come. They need to know, don't they, all our brave warriors, our four learned Mages, what it leads to.'

'Perhaps you should wait until you feel better,' she suggested.

'Perhaps . . .' His voice trailed off, and he returned to looking at the fire. 'You go on, Nerissa. I'll follow later . . . perhaps . . .'

There was nothing she could do for him in this state, and it was now time for the Council. She patted his shoulder once more and left the lonely cave.

Chapter Nine
Dissension

The Great Hall was beginning to fill up when she arrived. Most of them were observers only, for the Cavers' custom was that all should be able to witness the process of decision making. They stood round the edges, men on one side, women on the other.

Under the unmoving silver pendulum Nerissa swiftly crossed the floor, and took her place in front of the silent line of women. The Hall was more brightly lit than at other times, and she could see clearly the weariness and disarray of those members of the Guard who had chosen to attend. They slouched against the far wall, still in their battle clothes, talking in low voices. At least they had had the grace to leave their weapons outside.

A slight rustle in the crowd at the back entrance, and Stefan Pryse came in. Taller than most men there, he was striking, wild black hair tumbling round his shoulders, eyebrows almost meeting over bright, dark eyes. He wore the customary black cloak, but his was lined with red, and fell from his shoulders blatant as revolt.

He moved with a slow, easy authority, used to command, used to obedience. There was no one there who did not respect him.

The Cavers' lives were governed by three forces. The Guard, led by Stefan Pryse, lived with danger. Most of their life was spent flying through the wind with the Arrarat. Hunting and fishing, falling from the skies to seize prey in strong talons. Ranging far over the wild seas, searching for food and other necessities.

Robbers, thieves, bandits . . . there was no gentle term for the Guard. They raided the farms on the eastern islands and mainland, stole from barns, carts on the way to market, stores and houses. They tried to avoid the poor and downtrodden. They were not rapacious, but desperate.

Often food was left out for them, weapons and clothes. In lonely caves, deserted barns, sometimes on a raft set adrift. Old loyalties, old friends . . . hostages to fortune, offerings to the Banished Goddess, superstition . . . there were many reasons why people helped the Cavers. Astret was not forgotten everywhere.

The Guard defended the Caves from attack. Reprisals from Peraldon were rare for the simple reason that the sea between Peraldon and the Caves was treacherous and rough, prone to sudden storms and vast waves. And the Peraldonians had no Arrarat. But sometimes Lucian Lefevre, High Priest of Peraldon, instructed the Fosca to harry and punish the Cavers for their depredations.

Only occasionally did the Cavers attack Peraldon itself. The raid on the Ferry was indeed unusual, and risky.

Only a Mage could have persuaded them to take such a step. Only Matthias Marling, whose brother Lukas was Pryse's closest colleague.

Stefan Pryse was battle-stained and weary. His cloak was torn, his clothes dirty and scorched. He halted in front of the other men, looking across the stone floor to Nerissa. Bowing his head, he dropped to one knee and the men behind him followed suit.

It was a perfunctory gesture, she thought, as they stood up. They had no real respect, or they would not have gone on the raid. She decided to show only indifference to them, however, for they were not her real enemies.

She was waiting for the Four. The Mages. The second of the three forces governing the Cavers' lives. She could feel the eyes of the women behind her watching the main entrance, but she looked only ahead.

Then there was silence, a sudden ceasing of all the rustling and whispering that had accompanied her own entrance, and she knew that they were coming.

Quietly as a cloud the four men took their places at a distance from Pryse and herself, forming the triangle of power.

One of them stepped forward out of the line, and struck his staff against the floor. Immediately the torches around the walls flared up, and in the brilliant light Nerissa saw that it was Matthias Marling.

He spoke to Pryse across the floor, but his voice carried effortlessly, and she knew he intended them all to hear.

'Greetings, Commander. We are glad to see you safely returned.' He paused. 'Lukas cannot be here. Margat is still waiting for Fabian and needs him. He sends his apologies.'

'Fabian may yet return. I saw him –' Stefan Pryse's voice was deep and slow.

'Later.' One of the other Mages, a small man with piercing eyes and an arid voice spoke. 'If you please. We will ask for your report in due course, Commander. But the formalities must be observed.' He inclined his head slightly, condescendingly, in Nerissa's direction.

The third force in Caver society was recognised by them all as crucial. It was why they lived on the edge of the time-locked Boundary, in the realm of eternal twilight.

The worship of Astret, the Lady of the Moon, the Banished, but not forgotten, Goddess.

Nerissa raised her arms to the pendulum above, and began to chant the Hymn to Astret, and nearly everyone joined in. It was not enough. She saw two of the Guard whispering at the back, and abruptly dropped her arms, pointing through uneven light to them.

'Silence!' she cried. 'Is it not enough that you come to the Lady's Hall in all this dirt? Must you interrupt Her song as well?' The Hymn died to a ragged murmur and then ceased.

The two men looked at her, and one of them gave a half laugh. He stepped forward, tossing back brown, curly hair, and stood legs wide, hands on hips, daring her to go on.

It was Haddon Derray, her own sister Selene's son. Heresy and insurrection within the family now. White-faced with anger, she was about to speak when Matthias forestalled her.

'Derray. Either apologise to our Lady Priestess or leave the Council now.' His voice was quiet as ever, but the man flushed, and dropped his eyes.

Without looking at either Matthias or Nerissa he turned

on his heel and strode out of the Hall. His friend muttered an apology, fading back into the crowd.

The Hymn resumed with no further interruptions.

Matthias remained in the centre of the Hall, and spoke again. 'First I think the Guard should know what happened at the Rite –'

'It failed,' said Nerissa. 'What else is there to know?'

He went on as if she had not spoken.

'As far as we understand it, the Rite was performed in accordance with the Cabbalistic tradition. The laurel fire was built and burnt for the required time. The sequence of glass casting proceeded in due course.' He smiled wryly, looking at the small scratch on his right hand. 'The glass globes shattered as ordained.

'The storm that then broke was unforeseen. We do not know whether it was part of the Rite or some resistance from Peraldonian priests. It should not have taken place at all during the Stasis as we understand it. I think we might take some encouragement from this. The storm was violent and the fire was almost drenched in the downpour. I for one was no longer in control . . .'

He raised an eyebrow at Alaric Warde who shook his head. 'None of us was. There was lightning and thunder, and at the height of this a girl appeared beside the fire. She seems to be the only result of performing the Rite. She is young, immature and shocked by the transition. Her value to us is at best questionable.'

Pryse's anger whipped round the Hall. 'We lost eighteen, possibly nineteen men in the raid! Are you now telling us that it was for nothing?'

'It is too early to say.' Thibaud Lye, the small, dry Mage, stepped forward. 'We will have to examine her. She may have knowledge that could prove useful to us.'

'The only knowledge she could ever have would be evil, distorted!' Nerissa moved nearer to them, trembling. 'What did you expect?' She hurled the words at the four Mages. 'If you insist on using forbidden lore, and neglect the Lady's own instructions . . .'

'There's nothing anywhere to say that Astret forbids the Twelve Rites,' said Matthias quietly.

'But they are not in the Scriptures!'

'Neither is much of our knowledge. We cannot rely on the Scriptures alone.' Matthias still spoke gently, but firmly. The Cabbalistic tradition belonged only to the Mages, only to the men who were ambitious enough to pay the price demanded by magic.

'This is old ground.' Pryse's deep voice broke in. 'Men have died. The question is what to do next. How to make the best of this disaster.'

'There is only one possible course.' Nerissa again, trying hard to remain calm. 'The girl must be introduced to the religion of the Lady, and initiated into our ceremonies. We can look after her, she could be ordained. I would even allow her to live with my own family.'

'A generous offer.' The Mage Lye bowed courteously to her. 'One we may certainly call upon later. First, however, we must talk to her, and find out who she is, and where she comes from. I repeat, she may have useful knowledge.'

'Born of heresy, she will only beget heresy, unless welcomed first into the Lady's heart. I insist that she is initiated into the College of Priestesses.'

'Later.' Lye was implacable. 'We will talk to her first.' Without waiting for her reply he turned immediately to Pryse. 'Tell us now about the raid.'

Nerissa stood there, stony-faced, determination thinning her lips, and barely heard the bald account of the attack on the pier and Ferry.

'The turning point came just after Rodric's death,' said the slow voice at last. 'We must have killed some six Peraldonians, and there were more wounded. They were outnumbered, but fought well.'

He spoke with measured fairness. 'But then a score of Fosca attacked in their defence. As you know, it is not possible to prevail against such numbers of Fosca. The whole thing turned into a shambles. We retreated as soon as we could, but not before many had fallen. I saw Fabian wounded, but he was picked up by Amaris. I have no further news of him.'

He paused, frowning. 'It seemed to me,' he said slowly, 'that the Peraldonians themselves were not expecting the

Fosca attack. They were certainly taken by surprise. I would be interested to hear your opinion of this.'

'What makes you think this?' said Thibaud Lye. He spoke with sudden intensity, and the other Mages exchanged glances.

'Only the look on their faces.' Pryse paused. 'One of them was sick,' he said.

'A not unnatural reaction,' put in one of the other Mages, a thin, cavernous figure.

'No. But if they'd been expecting Fosca, they would have been prepared. They are not novices.'

'This is of interest.' Aylmer Alard, the thin Mage, held up his hand, and all eyes turned towards him. 'Watching the raid from above, I too saw that the Peraldonians were unprepared. I also observed the death of a pregnant Peraldonian woman.'

There was a rustle around the Hall. Slowly, his wispy hair glinting in the light, he surveyed them. 'She was killed by a Fosca rider,' he said.

This time there was an audible gasp.

'The implications of this are far-reaching,' he went on coolly. 'It may have been accidental, but there was occult power in the air that night, and I think that nothing was unforeseen . . .'

'If they are killing their own kind to preserve the Balance –' Lye broke in, excitedly.

'Quite.' Aylmer Alard nodded. 'The Stasis must be seriously at risk.'

'We should let Reckert know,' Lye said. 'He may be able to explain some of this.'

'It could be Lefevre's own decision,' Matthias offered. 'I think few Peraldonians realise how far Lefevre controls everything.'

'This is all nonsense!' Nerissa's voice was hard and sharp. 'What you are all forgetting is that the raid was a tragic waste of life, Caver and Peraldonian. A pregnant woman has died! While we fight, and kill, we are always outside the Lady's Rule. The Rite's only result has been to abandon this girl to us, and at best she will only be another mouth to feed.'

She walked forward and stood in the centre of the assembly. 'None of this would have taken place, none at all, without Matthias Marling's interference. He is responsible for everything, from Richenda's death through to Fabian's disappearance. I demand that he is judged, and his brother with him!'

'Nerissa, this is not helpful,' began Matthias.

'Lukas isn't here, and anyway the ultimate decision to send the Guard out was mine alone.' Stefan Pryse spoke loudly over the growing murmur of protest.

'But Richenda died because of Matthias . . .' A new, thin voice caused them all to look round.

Oswald Broune was standing by the back entrance to the Hall, blinking nervously. He moved along the wall and stood under one of the torches so that everyone could see him.

'I join Nerissa in calling the Mage Matthias Marling to judgment. All this present disaster comes from trying to end the Stasis. Why couldn't we just leave it all alone?'

Nerissa moved to stand beside him, and put out one thin hand, touching his arm, as if lending him strength.

He looked at her blankly and then back at the Mages.

The Mage who had not yet spoken now threw back the hood of his cloak. Everyone rustled aside, leaving a path for him to walk forward. Light gleamed on the bald head and empty eye-sockets, and for a moment no one spoke.

Unerringly he moved across the floor, straight to Oswald and Nerissa. He held his staff out in front of him, drawing vision from its strange spiral. There was utter silence.

'Lady Priestess, it is not yet your turn to judge,' he said, and it was as if acid were slicing through the air. There was no possibility of argument. 'And you, Broune, would do better to moderate your grief, and think clearly about the implications of your words.'

'Do you think I *haven't* thought?' Oswald was shaking with anger and fear. 'Richenda prophesied because Matthias asked her to. He suggested the laurel fire, the form of words, everything, and her death is therefore his fault!'

Matthias closed his eyes momentarily. 'I don't deny it,' he said. 'But Richenda *did* reveal the voice of Astret – did she not?' He suddenly swirled round, regarding the crowds around the walls. 'Does anyone dispute that Astret spoke then? That the Seventh Rite was performed explicitly on Astret's instruction?'

'I deny it! Astret would never sanction a Cabbalistic Rite! It was a false prophecy, and we should never have attempted such a thing!' Still Nerissa spoke out, although the blind Mage stood before her, and she was trembling.

'Enough!' He banged the staff on the floor and sparks flared from it. 'Recriminations are useless. In all honour to you and the Lady, High Priestess, we must first find out what the girl can do, whether she is in fact of such slight significance. And this in the context of a Stasis which appears to be unstable.' There was a pause.

'Then, and only then, you may attempt to introduce her to the mysteries of Astret's Rule. No one will yet give judgment on Matthias Marling, for the worth of his action has not yet been proved.

'Oswald, your understanding of the Stasis and its evil is distorted by emotion. You must remember that Richenda died because the Lady spoke through her, and she was not strong enough to bear it. Astret's priestesses should not have to suffer so. There is evil at work, and our only concern must be to end it.'

'No!' Oswald's shout was a shock to them all. 'You are wrong, all of you! If there was no Stasis, you would be dead!' He pointed furiously at the three older Mages, widening the gesture to include the other people in the Hall. 'The Stasis gives us immortality, to live together in love. Don't you remember what happened when people grew old? Don't you remember what it felt like when your parents died? The Stasis is the only good thing ever to happen to humanity!'

'But where are our children?' A soft-spoken woman moved out of the crowd towards him. 'What is the point of life, if there is no one to care for, and nurture?'

'We have each other! Isn't that enough?'

'Name me one happy marriage,' she said sadly. 'We are only torn apart by the Stasis . . .'

Nerissa could not speak. She saw Alaric, standing against the wall over the other side of the Hall and knew he was looking at her.

Torn apart by the Stasis. Astret mocked, false prophecies, death after death and no children. Nerissa shuddered, and looked away from Alaric. Driving each of them into loneliness, the Stasis ate away at the soul. The only way to endure was to accept, in faith, that this was the Goddess's will. Quiet prayer, the structure of ceremony and service, and one could lose oneself. To fight, to strive, to meddle, were all actions leading to despair.

In her bones she knew it to be true. Faith was the only way. The Mages used forbidden lore, the Guard dared to take life and destroyed what little peace there was. Astret would never return while they lived in such dissension.

They were all shouting now, Oswald crying, Matthias grim and tired. The Great Mage, Blaise, turned his sightless gaze towards her and she knew that he was ready for her to close the Council.

She raised her arms once more and began to declaim the Hymn of Conclusion. Her voice was reedy and thin to start with, but as the women behind her gradually joined in it grew in strength until it drowned the shouting and there was peace.

Together for once, united in the order of the song, for a brief while they thought only of Astret, the Moon Goddess who had once ruled their lives, and was now frozen in the grip of the Stasis.

Then they parted, the Mages to confer with Pryse, the women to their husbands and lovers. And she would return to her cave, where the lonely altar still gleamed in the firelight.

Chapter Ten
Letia

When Eleanor awoke a new candle was burning at the bedside. She had no idea how long she had slept, and at first expected to find herself out of the nightmare, back in her flat, safe, warm and comfortable. When she realised the wall of the bedroom was rough-hewn rock, that she was wearing strange coarse clothes, that it was all still going on, a curious numbness overcame her. Tears, anger, sleep – nothing had helped so far. She would have to be patient, waiting for the time when reality would reassert itself, as of course it would. Things like this didn't happen. Soon she would wake up *properly*.

Forgetting Matthias's description of perpetual twilight – there had been so much to absorb – she sat up, looking for some glimpse of daybreak through the curtains. There was none. And when she had straightened her dress, combed her hair and drawn aside the separating curtain, she was surprised to find the cave still in darkness, apart from the bright beacon of the fire near the cave's mouth.

In the uneven firelight she could see three figures; Letia tending the fire, glancing up with a quick smile of welcome, Niclaus polishing and sharpening knives on a table to the left. The third figure, lounging on a low-slung stone bench against the wall, hands in pockets, eyes in shadow, she recognised as Lukas, the tall man who had shouted at her by the fire.

He looked up as she approached.

'Feeling better?' he asked neutrally. She nodded, and held out her hands to the blaze.

'What time is it? How long was I asleep?'

'Long enough.' Niclaus's answer puzzled her.

'I mean, have I slept the clock round? Is it night again?'

'You could put it like that,' said Lukas.

'Don't tease her!' Letia hurried to her side. 'Take no notice of them,' she said confidentially. 'I expect things are different where you come from. You must tell me all about it one day. They –' she nodded over her shoulder towards the two men, 'they're just being wilful. The truth is –'

'The truth is that it is as it always is, rainy, dark and cold,' said Lukas impatiently. 'We call this part of it the afternoon, but it may as well be midday or midnight. I thought Matthias had explained all this to you. It never changes, so you may as well get used to it.'

Unwillingly she recalled the impossible conversation on the seashore. Slowly, painfully, the reality of the shadowy cave and the unnaturally pale skins of the Cavers was beginning to sink in. She didn't like it, at all.

'Now, how about something to eat?' Letia was stirring a pan. 'I expect you're ravenous, with all that junketing around outside . . .'

'Damn it, woman, we weren't out there for fun!' Niclaus's chair scraped unpleasantly against the floor as he rose to his feet. 'Must you always be so bloody domestic?' His voice was raw with anger and tension.

'No, no!' She laid a placating hand on his arm, 'I'm so sorry, my love, of course I know it's no fun. It's just I find it comforting, it takes my mind off it all . . .' He brushed her aside brusquely and crossed to the wide mouth of the cave, looking out into the dark.

Stricken, Letia stared after him for a moment, and then took a quick breath and turned back to the fire.

Lukas unfolded from the bench and briefly touched her shoulder. 'It's all right, Letty,' he said. 'This waiting does none of us any good.'

'I know, I know. I just wish I didn't always say precisely the wrong thing.' She smiled, blinking.

Lukas regarded her affectionately. 'You'd think we'd all know better by now, wouldn't you?' he said, and went to join Witten by the cave mouth.

Eleanor felt an intruder. This was nothing to do with her.

She turned back to her little bedchamber. The place still had that odd, musty smell.

'My dear!' Letia's voice called her. 'Don't go away, that's just a small domestic mishap. Now, let's find you something to eat.'

Partly to relieve the older woman's embarrassment, but mainly because she was indeed hungry, Eleanor allowed Letia to fuss round with plates, cups and implements and sat down by the fire. She was handed a bowl filled with a fragrant fishy stew with rice floating in it, and a beaker of warmed, rather acidic wine. Then there were small sugary cakes and undersized, unripe apples. There was not quite enough of anything.

Letia watched her with satisfaction, chattering about trivia Eleanor could not understand and hardly attended to. She was preoccupied by the tension in the cave.

Eventually, she put her plate down.

'What are you all waiting for?' she said. 'And where's Matthias?' Letia pursed her lips and looked uneasily at the two men. She knelt down beside Eleanor's chair and, under the pretext of tending the fire, said in a low voice, 'Matthias is with Margat. She's still waiting for Fabian, her son, to return. It doesn't look good, the raid didn't go well –'

'What was this raid?' She spoke clearly, understanding that no one was going to volunteer anything unasked. Although the subject seemed to be fraught with pain for them all, she needed to know.

'The attack on the Ferry.' Lukas had heard and turned back to the fire. He began restlessly to pace the width of the cave. He had too much energy for its small area. 'We didn't actually need to raid the Ferry, of course, but a diversion was required.'

'A diversion from what?' Unaccountably she felt nervous of his reply.

'From the Seventh Rite,' he said. 'The experiment that resulted in your presence here.'

It was as she feared. She would be caught up in it all, whether she liked it or not. Moodily, Lukas kicked at the fire.

'It's not your fault, of course, you didn't ask to come, did you? But we needed a fire for the Rite, a big one, and it's possible that it would have been noticed.'

'By whom?'

'A patrol of the Warden's Watch.' Noticing her incomprehension, he explained. 'The Warden is the secular power of Peraldon. The Priest Lefevre maintains the Stasis, and orders their religion. The Warden runs the military and polices the city and its surrounds. The Emperor Dorian, of course, lives retired and does not muddy his hands with such affairs.' He was contemptuous. 'They all live in the luxury of daily sunlight over there. They even have seasons, spring, summer and autumn. But then, they have banished the Lady.' Here, the vivid blue eyes looked across the cave to the rain outside.

'They live in sunlight, you say? Then it's not always dark?' This was crucial to her.

'It is here. We're too close to the Boundary, you see. The Stasis is not consistent. Time does pass further from the Boundary, can even be manipulated. Not here, however. And the only way for us to escape, to live in the lands where dawn follows night, would be to abandon the Lady, and instead acknowledge the sovereignty of the God Lycias.'

'We will *never* do that!' Niclaus Witten had joined them, and spoke with unwilling passion.

'This Lefevre – tell me about him.' She was trying hard to put it all together, trying to work out if there was any chance of a more comfortable existence in this dream world.

'His title is "Beloved Priest, Lord of Lycias's Will". In effect he is indeed ruler of Peraldon, and no longer even bothers to consult the Emperor, or so rumour has it. All Peraldonians are subject to his authority.'

'We are not, however,' said Witten. 'We are free to honour the Lady as we wish – providing we stay here, in rain and dark.'

'And cause as little trouble as possible,' added Lukas. He half smiled. 'So we built a fire, and sent the Guard out, and tried as hard as we could to make one hell of a disturbance.'

'And you are the only result.' Witten's voice was heavy.

'Well, what were you expecting?' Eleanor said sharply, on the defensive.

'The end of the Stasis. Armies, weapons, soldiers, magicians, the Lady Herself, who knows? The prophecy was not precise.' Glowering, Witten reached for a goblet of wine.

'Prophecies never are precise,' said Lukas dryly. 'That is their only consistent characteristic. It may even be that you can help.' He shrugged. 'And meanwhile we wait for Fabian's return, for the sun to shine, for a prophecy to come true. And for more wine. Letty, where do you keep it these days?'

Diverted, they passed the flagon round, and drank in silence for a while.

'The Lady Astret . . . why do you follow her?' said Eleanor eventually.

For a moment Lukas's face was turned away from her, out to the dark night beyond the cave. 'The Lady Astret lives with the stars, moving the tide, our breath, shaping life itself with Her song. There is no meaning without the rhythm of change. There is no grace in life, stripped of mystery under the relentless sun. Without Her, no reason to live at all . . .'

His voice was quiet. Then he turned to look at her and she watched, fascinated, the play of firelight over his eyes. 'Further from the Boundary, away from the rain clouds, people see the Moon existing as a meaningless lump of rock in the sky, with no power or influence to shape lives. A mockery, a farce is the presence of the Moon in Peraldon, for the Lady Astret no longer acts through its light. But Nerissa's the one with all the details,' he said shortly. 'I wish you joy of it.'

'Let me show you round,' said Letia, springing to her feet. 'There's just time before evening prayers. I expect you'd like to come to those.' She bustled off before Eleanor could refuse this last treat.

It was soon obvious that the cave was much larger than she had at first assumed. Another four chambers in addition to her own ran off the central area, reaching back into the cliff. Two of them were bedrooms, furnished in the same sparse, homely style as her own. There was a bathroom where water could be drawn from a pipe that ran horizontally across one wall and into the next cave. A dish of fine powdered sand lay near the basin. Letia waited, still chattering, while Eleanor washed, surprised to find how clean and refreshed she felt by the application of cold water and sand.

The fourth room was a kind of store, with small bags of grain, bunches of dried herbs, a few bottles of wine and beer and a cold compartment, open to the elements, forever cooled by the near freezing temperature. Fresh fish was stored there, a little cheese.

It was all efficient and tidy but thinly-stocked. Eleanor began to feel depressed again. What would she *eat* here? And then, without warning, Letia casually pulled aside an embroidered curtain at one end of the store room, and Eleanor froze with shock.

For there, gazing steadily with huge unblinking yellow eyes, stood one of the giant hawks. Deep chestnut-brown plumage shot with russet glowed in the candlelight; glossy breast feathers gleamed with borrowed luminescence.

It inclined its head at their entrance, and Letia caressed the side of its face. Through a daze of fear and loathing, Eleanor at last placed the strange unpleasant smell that permeated the cave; it was the pungent, musty odour of birds' droppings.

'This is Arkemis,' said Letia, smiling. 'She is our Arrarat, our very own beauty. She catches fish for us, provides us with transport, and with down for our beds' – Eleanor remembered the soft duvets and pillows – 'and in return we provide warmth and shelter. Do not mistake; she is our friend. We could not exist without her.' Letia was briefly severe, offended by Eleanor's evident mistrust.

'I'm sorry,' she muttered, 'but we have nothing like this in our world.' Even to her own ears this sounded lame.

'She understands everything you say,' Letia said. 'You must try to make friends with her. The loyalty of the Arrarat is never bought – it must be won, and cannot be valued highly enough.'

But Eleanor was afflicted by a phobia of long standing, and hated the fluttering unpredictability of flying creatures. She remembered desperate thrushes caught in rooms hurling themselves against windows, screaming seagulls plunging, the horror of a wounded sparrow tormented in a cat's claws. The eagle soaring with its prey clutched in cruel talons. The fear of falling.

And a hawk coming for her, stealing her from her old life . . .

The Arrarat she had met on the beach earlier had been weak, exhausted, and too strange to worry her in the usual way. But this, beady eyes glaring at her, had both the power and the vulnerability she hated in all flying things.

Disregarding her alarm, Letia gestured to a sack of grain. 'Give her some,' she suggested. Feeling sick, but obedient, Eleanor took a handful and approached the bird, hand outstretched, shaking.

Arkemis regarded her coldly. For a long moment the bird held her unwilling gaze, before bowing its head to accept the grain. Eleanor could barely prevent herself from shuddering. Arkemis raised her head and looked at her again, and Eleanor could not rid herself of the suspicion that the bird was laughing at her.

Compelled by an unknown force, she nerved herself to stroke the creature's neck, as Letia had done, and found that the feathers were soft and silky, warm and welcoming. Briefly, she and the bird regarded each other in silence. Then Eleanor nodded, curiously reassured, and turned to follow Letia back to the main part of the cave.

'Now,' said Letia briskly, 'we'll just pop along to Evening Prayers, and then I'll make supper.'

'There should be some news by then,' said Witten heavily, and turned away from the cave mouth. Eleanor took his place beside Lukas and found herself scanning the bleak horizon for just a brief break in the dark. She was finding the continual gloom so lowering.

How did they ever endure it? The swollen sea, black in the distance, crashed rhythmically against the rocks, and Eleanor longed for bright lights, loud music, the laughter of friends. This was all dreary beyond imagination, and she hated it.

'Come on, dear,' said Letia, 'or we'll be late.' And because Eleanor could no longer bear the sight of the everlasting night, and could think of nothing else to do anyway, she followed Letia through the door at the back of the cave down the stone steps to the vast hall within the Cliff.

Chapter Eleven
Home

Her hair lay soft against his chest. Slowly he stroked it, the fine raven hair that had clouded so gently around her face. She always used to complain about it; even now he could hear her voice, laughing at the untidiness of it. He had loved the tender drift of midnight across his pillow each morning, the curls tumbling, unruly like a child's.

For an unmeasured time Phinian Blythe remained motionless on the quayside, cradling the body of his wife. Any action, any movement, and events would inexorably begin to move on. His life would start to take place without Karis.

A sound on the quayside beside him. He raised his head and found himself regarded steadily by the Caver. Young though the boy was, pain-wracked and in fear, his eyes were compassionate.

'She was brave,' he said, haltingly.

'She – carried our child.' Blythe's voice was calm. The words were stark in the new wasteland of his life. Gently, he stroked ebony hair back from her pale skin. Silence fell.

Later, there was the sound of footsteps running across the quayside. Jarek Duparc and Ton Bryant, suddenly stopping.

A brief, appalled silence.

'Oh God –' said Jarek. 'Phin – what's happened? Is she . . . ? Oh God.'

There was no need for him to speak. Jarek would take over, start things happening. Already, he felt his friend's hand on his shoulder, the warmth of the touch.

He hardly recognised Jarek's voice. 'Phin. Let's go home now . . .'

A pause. Home? Where was that, now?

Jarek turned to Bryant. 'Take the Caver to the guard-house. I'll deal with him later.'

Blythe looked into the boy's open face. 'No,' he said. 'Leave him with me.'

'But . . .'

'I said, leave him!' Suddenly his voice was edged with unmistakable danger. 'Bring him to the house. Now.'

With rigid control he bent and lifted Karis's body. Limping, he took her back through the garden. It was still and fragrant with the flowers they had planted together. The ashes of the afternoon's bonfire clung around his feet.

To the house that had been their home.

While Duparc went to make his report, two men, on Duparc's own instruction, scooped up the Caver, following Blythe back to the house.

He had walked straight through the drawing room and hallway, hardly pausing when Uther came out of the kitchen to see what had happened. Uther looked from Blythe's face to the limp body in his arms, and stepped forward, hands outstretched in anxiety.

'She's dead,' said Blythe. 'I shall not need you tonight.'

He turned away and limped slowly through the cool hall-way up the stairs to their room. The door shut behind him.

'What happened?' Uther was suddenly pale. For a moment neither guard spoke, and it was the Caver who broke the silence.

'The Fosca attacked. I – I had fallen on the quayside, and one of them was coming at me. She came to help, to try to keep it off. It killed her –'

Uther lashed out suddenly, uncontrollably, and struck the boy's face with his fist.

'Liar!' he said furiously. 'Little bastard! No Fosca would harm a Peraldonian!' He was shaking with rage and grief, tears rolling unheeded down lined cheeks.

'This one did.' The boy spoke without rancour. Blood began to drip from his bruised mouth.

'He's telling the truth,' said the taller of the two guards. They had put the Caver down on a velvet-covered sofa which was quickly being ruined by the mess from the boy's smashed leg.

'I saw it all,' the guard went on. 'It wasn't the kid's fault.'

'He's still scum, like the rest of them!' The other guard spat with contempt.

'Maybe.' He shrugged; a straight, slow-speaking, sandy-haired man, not much younger than Uther. He nodded up towards the door. 'Married long?'

'No,' said Uther, 'not long.' And then, after a long pause, he added, 'She was pregnant.'

There was silence.

Babies were unusual in Peraldon. Women rarely conceived, and those who did often sickened and failed to produce healthy children. The priests consoled, saying that in this way was the Stasis maintained, and Lycias's purpose fulfilled. But still the Peraldonians grieved, and treated any pregnant woman as a queen. The death of one was more than a personal tragedy: it spelled another step towards sterility for them all.

Uther sighed. 'What's he doing here anyway? If he caused the Lady Karis's death, wittingly or not, he should be hanging from the nearest gibbet.'

'No.' The tall guard was emphatic. 'Captain Duparc commanded that he should be cared for. He said that the Lady Karis should not lose her life for nothing. You're to dress his wound and hold him till tomorrow. Captain Blythe may want to see him then.'

'And if he doesn't?'

'Let him go.'

'Let him go? A filthy little Caver?'

'Captain Duparc's command. He said you wouldn't like it.' The guard cast a considering look round the marbled hallway. 'I should move him from there, though. He's spoiling the upholstery.'

Wearily, Uther bent to pick up the boy, but the guard waved him away. 'I'll do it. Go and put some water on. I'll bring him down.'

A tray for Captain Blythe. Coffee, sandwiches. Whisky? When would it ever be more appropriate? He could do with a drink himself. Oh God. Karis's parents. Someone ought to tell them. Perhaps not whisky yet.

Uther stared unseeing at the tray on the table in front of him. Then he shook his head and turned to the cupboard, taking an unopened bottle from it. A glass, from the dresser. His hands were unsteady and it rattled against the bottle.

He glanced quickly across the kitchen to where the Caver boy was slumped in a chair. He was still unconscious, having fainted when they bound up his leg. It was propped now on a stool in front of him, blood beginning to fleck the bandages. He looked desperately uncomfortable. They'd tied his hands together behind the chair. There would be time enough to attend to him later.

The door at the top of the stairs was closed. He put the tray down and knocked once. Twice. No reply. Suddenly anxious, he tried the handle. It swung open easily, so he picked up the tray and went in.

Karis's body lay on the bed. He could hardly bear to look at it, and felt tears pricking in his eyes. This wouldn't do. He put the tray down.

'I told you you would not be needed tonight,' said a voice from the dark chair in the far corner of the room. Blythe was sitting motionless in the shadow, his face unreadable. 'What do you want?'

There were things to do, of course. Messages to send, arrangements to be made, people to tell. But not now. All his busy plans fell away into the silence of that room.

He forced himself to look into the shadowed face.

Unprompted the words came.

'I'm sorry, lad. So sorry . . .'

But there was no answering glimmer of warmth. Icy hard, black as night, the eyes looked back at him, and Uther dropped his gaze.

He left the room, stumbling down the stairs back to the kitchen.

It was a long night.

Chapter Twelve
Questions

At dawn Phinian Blythe rode through the silent streets to Karis's parents' house. It was hours before he returned, his face set hard.

Milner, his secretary, had arrived soon after the uneaten breakfast and took over the outstanding arrangements. Blythe was courteous to him, as usual, undemanding and kind.

Watching, Uther was chilled to the soul.

Duparc arrived next, concerned and angry. Uther showed him into the study, before returning to the kitchen.

Jarek seemed relieved to find Blythe dressed immaculately as usual in a white shirt and black breeches and riding boots. He was sitting at his desk, his back to the window, looking through some papers.

'I'm glad you've come,' Blythe said, looking up at him. 'There are things we need to discuss.'

'God, Phin, I'm so sorry –'

'I know. I know. Thanks.' Blythe was getting better at this. Would Uther ever forgive him? He stood up. 'Do you want coffee? Or something stronger?'

'Thank you, no.' Duparc sat in the chair by the fire, upright and contained. He was taller than Blythe, of a slighter, more wiry build. Light brown hair curled rakishly over his forehead; he affected a slightly foppish appearance, and drawled when speaking. But his mind was clear and sharp, and aside from their long friendship, Blythe was glad he had come. He needed his intelligence that morning.

He asked a few perfunctory questions about the raid, the condition of the wounded, how many dead, the extent of the damage to the Ferry. Because Jarek would be expecting it.

Then, picking up a paper-knife from the desk, Blythe asked the central question, the question that had been worrying him ever since the Fosca had first appeared over the Ferry.

'Why were the Fosca called in last night?' he said. This was the first time he was to ask that question.

'We needed them, remember? You were surrounded by four Cavers, I had my hands full with three others. We were all facing those kind of odds.'

'Fosca have never been brought in before except by Council decision. Who authorised it?'

'I expect it *was* the Council. Or Lefevre himself.'

'But Lefevre runs the Council and their decisions take weeks to implement. We would have been told – the Warden would have been consulted at the very least. And how did the Fosca get there so quickly? A Fosca deal is not negotiated on the spur of the moment, and then they have to travel. Who arranged it? Why?'

'The Caver attack was expected, you mean? A traitor?' For once Duparc had lost his drawl.

'Perhaps. But on whose side? It couldn't be the Cavers, because the Fosca were decimating them. And if the traitor was working for us, why weren't we warned? The whole thing was a shambles!' He paused, turning over the ivory knife in square, capable hands. 'And another thing. Why did the Cavers attack in such numbers? They don't usually risk so many at once, they can't afford it.'

'Let's ask them.' Duparc was already making for the door. 'You've got one of them prisoner in your kitchen right now, remember? If Uther hasn't decided to take the law into his own hands, that is.'

Blythe had indeed forgotten the presence of the Caver boy in his house. He followed Duparc out of the room.

The Caver was awake, still strapped to his hard kitchen chair, the shattered leg sticking out stiffly across the stool. His tousled hair was damp with sweat and his eyes flinched from the light. He was feverish and in pain.

Blythe looked at him for a moment and then poured some water from a jug, and drew the curtains part way to block out the direct glare of the sun. He untied the

Caver's hands and helped him to hold the glass to his lips.

'Sir!' Uther, standing at the window, was shocked. 'He might escape!'

'With that leg? Don't be a fool. Go and see if his Arrarat is still out there.'

'Don't hurt her!' The Caver clutched frantically at Blythe's arm.

'Of course we won't.' Duparc pulled up a chair, and sat down close to the boy. 'We just want a little talk with you, and then she can take you home.'

'I've nothing to tell you! You used Fosca!' The Caver snarled with contempt.

'Dear me. Cavers worrying about what's fair? After all this time?' Duparc smiled unpleasantly.

'Never mind that.' Blythe was calm, focused. 'What we need to know is why so many of you attacked at once. We haven't seen such a display since the War. I didn't think you had so many men left.'

'They haven't,' Duparc interposed. 'Look at him. They've taken to using children instead.'

'Shut up, Jarek. Is the Arrarat still there?' This to Uther, returning from the garden. The older man nodded. 'Good.' Blythe turned back to the boy. 'Once more. Why did you use such numbers? Why was this raid so different?' The boy averted his face, lips resolutely closed. 'Uther. Take that crossbow and shoot the hawk –'

'No!' the boy almost screamed with anguish. He tried to get out of the chair but his leg collapsed beneath him. He sprawled on the hard floor, blood staining the untidy bandages. Blythe knelt on one knee beside him and with one hand roughly turned the boy's face towards him.

'Listen,' he said softly, dangerously. 'I would not willingly destroy any Arrarat outside battle. But my wife died for your sake, and I am not feeling over patient this morning. So, you are going to give me this information, and if I have to shoot the Arrarat to get it, I will.'

He paused, his hard, dark stare locked on the boy's blue eyes, bright with unshed tears of fury and pain.

'Do you understand? Uther is a good shot, and will not miss. If your hawk is killed you will never be able to return.'

He waited; then, without shifting his gaze, said, 'Uther. Shoot the Arrarat.'

Uther moved swiftly to the door but as he reached it again the boy cried hoarsely.

'No! Don't! I'll tell you –' Tears were falling and he dashed them away impatiently with the edge of his sleeve.

Blythe held up his hand, halting Uther and turned back to the boy, his eyes compelling speech. He waited.

'There was a Saying,' he said at last. 'I'd never seen anything like it before . . . it killed Richenda –' his face was white with despair. 'Richenda was our greatest Prophetess, the Lady's chosen one, I don't know what we'll do now –'

'Tell me about the Saying.' Blythe drew closer.

'She – inhaled the laurel smoke, as usual, and then, then, there was this light.' He began to cry again. 'White light it was, so bright and beautiful it hurt, oh, it hurt –'

'Get on with it, boy.' Duparc was impatient. The boy shuddered with the visible effort of collecting his thoughts.

'I can't, I can't, I mustn't say –'

Blythe silently gestured to Uther, still standing by the door with his crossbow. Sickly, the boy opened his mouth as if straining for air. He reached again for the water and nearly retched over it. Implacably, Blythe waited until he was calmer, and then said mildly, 'What happened?'

'Richenda said, only her voice was changed, not the same – she said, build a laurel fire, a big one. And then the Seventh Rite – don't ask me about that, I don't know what it is. If we did this, the terrible voice said through her, then help was sure to come. The world would have to change, the Stasis would break . . .'

He paused. 'Richenda died! The voice left her, and she just collapsed. It drained her of life. She died.'

'What has all this to do with the raid?' put in Duparc, mystified.

'It was a diversion, wasn't it?' said Blythe.

'Yes,' said the boy simply. 'The fire had to be huge – we thought the Warden's Watch might see it, if they were on far patrol. We never know when there's going to be a patrol . . . So Matthias and Lukas Marling, they persuaded the Council to send the Guard out, all of us, even the other Mages, and Matthias built the fire. He's one of the four Mages. Alaric and Lukas had to stay behind because the Mages had gone. They knew enough to help Matthias with it.'

'What happened at the fire?' Uther had joined them.

The boy shrugged. 'I don't know yet, how could I? Nothing much seems to have changed to me, but how could I know? You kept me here.' He was gathering courage, now he had told them what he thought they wanted to know. Blythe sat back on his heels, considering.

As usual the sun glared in through the windows, mercilessly clear. Time for Peraldonians did pass, at least as far as the sun was concerned; it rose and burned and set every day, under the control of the Sun's priest Lefevre, who possessed so many extraordinary, occult skills.

Their God, Lycias, was of the nature of sunlight itself, and had never yet forsaken them, unlike the Cavers' sad Moon Lady. The Cavers' pocket of unchanging time on the fringes of the Boundary was a freak in this world, a freak constructed through the will of Lycias for a purpose none of them understood.

The people of Peraldon believed that the Cavers could leave their exhausting, depressing wasteland, if they so chose. All that was required was an acknowledgement of the sovereignty of the Sun God. It was their own choice, their own decision to stay at the Cliff. The continuing warfare was a source of bitter resentment and amazement to the Peraldonians. There was no *need* for it.

The divisions between them all were long standing, fuelled by hatred, guilt and incomprehension. It was almost forgotten that long ago they had lived peacefully together.

All they shared now was immortality. Barring accidents or injury, they would all live forever. But there were strange side effects to eternal life. It felt as if there were nothing new under the face of the Sun, no room for exploration or creativity. The famed goldsmiths of Peraldon wrought ancient designs, repeated tired ideas.

And only in Peraldon were there ever any children born, and then only as a balance to the occasional death due to warfare, accident or suicide. The population of Peraldon was completely stable, while that of the Cavers declined steadily.

'To hell with it,' said the boy bitterly. 'You used Fosca! What does it matter what we do, when you play that dirty? I was sorry that woman died, she was trying to help, but it was Fosca that killed her, not us.' And it serves you right, was the unspoken rider.

Duparc looked across at Blythe. He had gone to stand by the window, his back to them all. He spoke without turning round. 'I shall find out why the Fosca were called in,' he said calmly. 'You can go now if you want. Call your Arrarat.' He opened the wide window and stood aside.

There was a moment of stillness as the overwhelming relief registered with the boy. Then he cradled his hands to his mouth and gave the low, ornate warble that summoned the Arrarat. Immediately there was the heavy sound of wings beating, a rush of air, and the huge shadow of a great hawk fell across the window as the bird alighted on the terrace outside.

Blythe straightened the boy's bandages and carried him out to the bird. Like many Peraldonians he had always been in awe of the Arrarat, jealous of their incomprehensible bond with the Cavers. And although he had often fought Cavers hand to hand beset by the sweeping, lethal birds, he had never before been at liberty to observe at close quarters the glossy sheen of the feathers, the fierce curve of the beak. The heavy musky smell of it, tinged with the salt tang of the sea was somehow evocative – of what? Innocent days on the lagoon. Fishing, sailing with Karis.

Memory almost shattered his calm. More roughly than he intended, he placed the boy high on the bird's back. For a moment he thought it would take off right away, but the boy glanced back down at him.

'What was your wife's name?' he asked.

'Karis.' The word cost too much.

'She should have lived.' He paused. 'My name is Fabian . . .' There was a swift rush of air and the hawk leapt up into the bright morning sun and disappeared from view.

Interviews, social calls. Morning coffee, afternoon tea, powdered and scented cheeks to kiss.

'My dear Phin, I don't know what to say . . .'

'A tragedy, so beautiful . . .'

'And the baby!' Usually whispered to each other, sidelong glances not meeting his eyes.

Karis's mother took to her bed. It was a slight relief.

He put his arm round Emms, Karis's little sister, and listened to inarticulate sobs. He poured wine, offered tea and whisky. Received their condolences and listened to their memories, and reassured them that he was bearing up.

They were not to know that he was not actually listening to a word they said. None of them realised that Karis's death had been locked away in his mind. It was an immense weight, pulling constantly at the edge of his attention, but it did not divert him from the central question.

What had gone wrong?

Between these social visits, late into the night, Blythe followed a different path. Tramping the long avenues of Peraldon, over bridges and through parks, past the workshops and tradesmen's quarters, to the homes of friends and acquaintances.

'A Fosca deal? Not to my knowledge . . .'

'No, I'm sure you're wrong. Perhaps Fitzwilliam might know . . .'

'Try de Montague . . . I was away last week . . .'

'Are you feeling quite well, dear boy? Perhaps a little holiday . . .?'

The Warden himself, a calmly smiling, grey-haired man with hard eyes, received him in the plush offices overlooking the harbour. He was a distant connection of Blythe's family, some kind of cousin. Never before had Blythe traded on the relationship.

Emile Blanchard had granted this unprecedented request for an audience with only a little surprise. Blythe was one of the brightest of his captains, and there was the family connection. He was genuinely regretful to learn of his bereavement. But business was business.

'A word of warning, Blythe.' His voice was light and pleasant, his large hands quite still on the heavy mahogany desk. 'Things . . . are under a certain amount of strain at present. Our beloved High Priest of course has everything under control. But it may be wise not to question too closely . . .'

'Strain? What strain?'

The older man across the table suddenly pushed his chair back over the deep pile carpet. He stood silently for a while, turning his back on Blythe, watching the unloading of the big clipper that had just put in from the east. Coffee beans, cocoa, rubber, hemp. Cardamom and saffron, cochineal and cobalt. Bales of silk and linen. The cases were piled high on the quayside, people moving with orderly efficiency, loading the carts and coaches.

Armed soldiers stood at one end of the harbour, guarding the small, heavy boxes of gold that formed Peraldon's chief export.

'The Emperor is dead.'

He spoke so softly that for a moment Blythe thought he had misheard.

'The Emperor of the Sun has left this realm of eternal peace.' His voice was briefly severe, cynical even. He shrugged, and turned round, looking at Blythe beneath bushy eyebrows.

'It will be announced tomorrow, although in fact we have been without an Emperor now for some time . . . You do not seem unduly concerned,' he said.

Blythe met his eyes. He had other things on his mind.

'When did the Emperor last play any part in the affairs of Peraldon? There have been rumours that he was dead for as long as I can remember. I've never even seen him.'

'No . . . you are by no means alone in that.'

There was a long pause, and then Blanchard sighed. 'There will be an election, I suppose. A new Emperor will be chosen . . . but until then, nothing must be done to upset the status quo. There is change in the air . . . And if the High Priest sees fit –'

He stopped suddenly.

'Let it be, Blythe. Take my advice. Have a holiday, you're due some leave. Things will settle down, sooner or later . . .'

He turned back to his charts and maps. Ordering the patrols around the islands, maintaining the peace of the city. Policing the world within the impenetrable Boundary, between Stromsall and Peraldon, where time moved no more.

He was an important man, with many responsibilities, many worries. But after Phinian Blythe had left his office, he paused for a moment, watching the weary figure threading through the busy crowds thronging the harbour.

Blythe had not noticed, he was sure. The slip of the tongue, the unguarded phrase.

There is change in the air.

The priests of Lycias were no better. Typically obscure, they seemed to want to confuse things even further. They were preoccupied by the long-winded funeral rites of the Emperor, unwilling to turn their minds to questions of strategy. The use of the Fosca was nothing to do with them. Wreathed in strange-smelling mists inside the bright temples, they cast doubts on the validity of Blythe's questions.

'Do not meddle . . .'

'Faith is enough . . . only faith matters –'

'Are you questioning the Lord's will?'

'This is heresy, Blythe. Be careful . . .' This last from a young acolyte with worried eyes. 'Be careful. Don't interfere with matters outside your experience . . .'

He returned home on the fifth night bleak with exhaustion and frustration. He sat slumped forward at the dining table, brow propped on hands, ignoring the food.

Uther, bringing coffee, set the tray down and sat unasked opposite Blythe across the polished wood.

'Listen, lad,' he said softly. 'You can't go on like this. Give it a rest, and when the fuss has died down a bit, when the election's over, start again with a fresh mind. Someone will have an answer.'

Blythe lifted his head from his hands and almost smiled. 'Lull them into a false sense of security, you mean?' he asked. 'But who? Who are we trying to catch?'

'We can't tell yet, can we?' The prosaic common sense of the man was refreshing in itself. 'Let it quieten down a bit, conserve your strength, give it a rest. Much more chance then, to find out what's going on.'

'I can't.' The smile had vanished. 'It won't do, Uther. I couldn't sleep now even if I wanted to.'

'I can give you something for that.'

'No.' Blythe leant back in the chair and tilted it away from the table. 'It all narrows down to Lefevre, of course.'

Uther became very still. 'Why do you think that?'

'No one else has any ultimate authority with the Fosca. The Emperor is dead. No one else knows how to contact them. Lefevre must be at the centre of it.'

'You can give that up right now. He hasn't seen anyone except the Council for as long as I can remember.'

'All the more reason for seeing me now.'

'They won't let you through. They didn't let Erskine through when the Militia mutinied, or even Lord Gallatley before the last attack on Sarant . . .'

'I'll use the back door.'

'What back door? People get scorched for looking through windows. *No one* gets in.'

'I will.' Blythe stood up, and quickly drank the coffee.

'Then I'll come with you,' said Uther. He sighed, not trusting the look in Blythe's eyes.

'Not this time.' He turned and took his grey cloak from the hook by the door. Uther was standing blocking the way, feet apart, fists clenched.

'I'm coming with you!' he repeated pugnaciously. Anger flared, but only momentarily, in Blythe's face.

'Don't make me fight you, Uther. Not you too.' His voice was tired.

Uther nearly gave up, then. Nearly.

'All right then. You go alone. But promise me one thing.' Fool, Uther thought to himself. What are you risking now? But this was desperate, and he could see no other way.

'What is it?'

'My sister – has a friend, a kind of seer. It would be dangerous, illegal . . .' How was he to explain the life of a spy, a renegade, to a pillar of Peraldonian society? 'You might try asking there first, before approaching Lefevre. She sometimes knows the answers to questions no one ever asked.'

'She? A woman, a seer? God, Uther, you have some

murky friends! What is she, a Caver? Some warped little Moon-worshipper?'

'Try it!' Uther was suddenly impassioned. 'Give it a try, at least, before you commit suicide, trying to see Lefevre!'

There was silence for a moment. Blythe's gaze was withdrawn from the face of his friend and servant.

'All right,' he said. 'I'll give your Moon-seer a chance. And then I'll go to Lefevre.'

It would be sooner than he thought.

Chapter Thirteen
Underground

The brief Peraldonian night was sultry and close. It was late now, and the streets were almost deserted. Doors were pulled to, shafts of yellow light spreading across the pavement from between the slats of wooden shutters. Voices murmured, contented, at ease.

Across a dusty square a party blared from the windows of one of the larger houses. There were many parties that night in Peraldon, the eve of the Election of the new Emperor. People met, conferring with their friends, consolidating alliances and factions. There was no need to take it too seriously, for the Emperor held little power. A figure-head, he would be, someone to lead fashion, to dress in the ceremonial robes, to lend variety and glamour to the many performances of tedious plays, stale music, old, familiar entertainments. The Peraldonians were looking forward to it. Whoever it was would be an improvement on the previous Emperor, locked away with his grief.

Light, laughter and music tainted the air. They passed only a few people. Late workers hurrying home from the prestigious showrooms, craftsmen who had stayed up to complete orders for the coronation. A pair of lovers lingering on a bridge, untouchable in their private enchantment, whispering, caressing.

Other lives, varied in their joys and stresses. Not wrenched apart, ruined, destroyed. Whatever their problems, people laughed in the warm Peraldonian night, worked at their trades, chatted to each other. It was a world of comfort unimaginable to Phinian Blythe now.

As they left the main thoroughfares, they came to poorer quarters. The beggars crouching round the public fountains mumbled as the two men passed, waving bony, clutching hands at them. The Election meant nothing to them. They were always there, shaking stunted limbs, whining and sullen, but usually Blythe did not even notice them. Tonight they were appropriate, unlike the lovers on the bridge.

Blythe and Uther did not stop, following an irregular, winding path away from the lagoon, into the heart of the city. They knew enough to avoid the routine patrols of the City Police.

Soon the streets became more narrow and convoluted. The canals stank beneath the rickety bridges. Rank piles of rotting rubbish blurred the outlines of decaying buildings. Occasionally they startled half-starved cats rooting in dustbins. Rats scampered down alleyways. Shadows flickered round corners, wavered at the edge of sight.

They walked quickly, silently. Blythe, who thought he knew the city well, found that he was relying on Uther. The path they took was needlessly complicated. Uther was trying to ensure some level of secrecy for his sister's friend. Blythe was trusted, but not without reservation.

And sometimes it did feel as if they were being followed, as if shadows moved in concert with them. Sometimes they turned, swords at the ready, but the shadows turned out to be perfectly ordinary; a doorway, a dustbin, heaped rubbish. Their fears appeared foolish.

Without warning, Uther halted. Using an irregular code, he tapped on the shutters of a shabby chemist's shop deep in the run-down maze of streets.

There was no reply. He tried again, using the same pattern. The door opened a fraction. He whispered something Blythe could not catch. There was a brief discussion and then they were admitted.

They stepped down into the room, bending their heads under the low ceiling. It was an ordinary enough shop. Cramped, a little dusty, hot behind the shutters.

The rows of bottles and jars were entirely familiar, although there were few of the lotions and creams carried by more affluent shops, and none of the expensive cosmetics Blythe was used to finding in Karis's room. It was a poor shop in a poor area.

Rows of small drawers lined one wall, bearing labels. Quicksilver, arnica, ginseng, camomile, digitalis. Other names Blythe did not recognise. A pestle and mortar stood on the counter, some fine brass scales by its side.

The man who had so reluctantly admitted them was clearly the shopkeeper. Small, bald and worried-looking, he blinked at them behind thick pince-nez.

'What do you want? Why are you here?' Rubbing sweaty hands over his grubby apron, he was both hostile and frightened. His voice sounded high and insubstantial in the oppressive dark of the shop.

'Lucette is my sister,' said Uther. 'She gave me the code, if ever there was a need.'

'And is there? Or are you wantonly curious?' He looked with distaste at Blythe's fine cloak and gleaming boots. Sharply, the little man turned and took a lighted candlestick from a shelf, and held it steady two inches from Uther's face. The lined, leathery face with its knowing brown eyes stared impassively back through the candle flame.

Blythe refused a similar scrutiny. He stepped back, frowning.

'Come on, Uther. This is a waste of time,' he said. 'We're not children, we don't need secret societies and passwords.'

'Go then,' said the shopkeeper. 'We want no unwilling petitioners, here.' He moved towards the door and was about to open it when there was the sound of a door, flung back.

'No.' A compelling voice cut through the airless atmosphere.

Blythe swung round.

A silhouette, the figure of a woman. She was standing far away down a corridor leading from the back of the shop. Lit from behind, her clothes were dark, curiously draped and hooded. He could not see her face or any other feature except for one hand which pointed steadily to his head.

'It is not time for you to go yet,' she said. 'The other can leave. There is nothing for him here.'

'He's coming with me,' said Blythe, curious to see how she would handle it. A moment's silence. Then she turned, and led the way through the open doorway behind.

Blythe and Uther glanced at each other and followed. The shopkeeper bolted the shop door, and came after them, carrying the lighted candle.

There was a flight of stairs leading down from the empty dusty room at the end of the corridor. They passed through a series of dank cellars, long disused.

The woman walked quickly past the rows of empty racks and broken barrels. Spiders lurked in corners, web trailing in rags from the ceiling. The place reeked of damp, greasy dust thick on every surface.

They went through several interconnected rooms, their footsteps muffled by dust, shadows leaping in the uneven light from the shopkeeper's candle. At last there was only a blank wall ahead, a dead end in grey stone. The woman turned sharply to the right and crouched down beside one of the barrels.

The shopkeeper caught up with her here, and together they pushed at the barrel. It swung round on silent hinges. Where it had stood against the wall, a small wooden door was revealed. She tapped on it, the same pattern Uther had used outside the shop, and the door opened.

Two men stood there, serrated knives in their hands.

'Who's this, Selene?' The older of the two men glanced at Blythe and Uther. He was thin to the point of emaciation, his clothes torn and patched. But his hands were steady and the knife never wavered.

'Petitioners, Collin. They have right of entry.'

'Get rid of them, woman.' The other man, younger, with a strange fanatic light in his eyes, looked them over. Obsessively he noted and catalogued their clothes and weapons. 'There's a lot of activity above,' he said. 'Jenner reported unusual patrols, extra guards. There's something on.'

'It could just be the Election,' said the older man.

The woman turned sharply to Blythe.

'Were you followed?' she said.

'Not to my knowledge,' he replied, and then remembered the strange shadow that had flickered at the edge of sight, moving along with them through the Peraldonian streets.

'We can't afford to risk it,' the older man said.

'They know the code, they know the way now,' said the shopkeeper.

'We can soon fix that,' said the younger guard, and drew one finger across his throat in graphic illustration. At once Blythe and Uther drew their swords but the woman unhurriedly stepped between them.

'This man' – she pointed to Blythe – 'will be admitted. It is his destiny, and ours. His companion is of no account.'

'We'll regret it.' The older man was dour. 'It's too dangerous tonight.'

'Tonight is the only chance,' she said, her voice desolate. Reluctantly the guards lowered their knives.

A woman, commanding obedience from men. Serrated knives. Blythe was moving amongst Astret's followers, rebels and traitors.

If it were not for the urgency of his enquiry, he would have walked out there and then. Good Peraldonians felt only contempt and mistrust for the hidden pockets of Moon worshippers who subverted society, thieving, smuggling for the Cavers. Blythe had, after all, spent most of his life fighting them. Part of him longed for the openness of the shabby street above, away from secret passages and passwords. But he had promised Uther at least to try this, and the resources of his own society had proved useless.

The two guards stood aside. Selene swept on past them, Blythe, Uther and the shopkeeper following. They were in a tunnel, just tall enough for a man to stand upright, lit by torches stuck in brackets at intervals along its length.

The floor was free of dust, and everything here was much cleaner, as if people used the tunnel regularly. But the smell of damp was still pervasive, and in the distance Blythe could hear the faint, insistent drip of water.

Without warning the woman crouched down, and lifted a trapdoor in the floor, swinging herself onto a rope ladder hanging there. It dangled down some twenty feet into another corridor, exactly like the one they had just traversed. On they went, the passage continually sloping downwards.

And then again there were more guards at a door, a similar

argument, and Selene's authority prevailing. The door swung open, and Blythe and Uther stood stock still, rooted with shock.

Crowds of people. A long, low hall, dimly lit by torches, stinking of unwashed humanity, crammed with pale, sweaty bodies.

An entire community of people lived here. They crouched in corners, sat on rough wooden stools, slouched listlessly against walls. Tunnels branched off the central hall; the activity and noise of people echoed down the length of them. Although there were torches burning in brackets, everything was dim, swathed in curtains and hangings. It was impossible to tell the exact dimensions of the occupied area. It went on as far as they could see, crowded and noisy and malodorous.

The hangings divided the area into booths and kiosks. People sat in small family groups, old men, young women. Men with hopeless eyes.

So many. Blythe did not understand. How could so many live here, in crowded squalor?

He saw a woman, bending over an old man lying on a pallet. Her hair was fair, shining in the feeble light, soft and fine, falling over her thin face. He took a step nearer, and heard the murmur of her voice, soothing the fever-wracked man on the ground. He tossed about on the grubby sheets, his cheeks red against white. She looked up at Blythe, and he saw bitter resentment in her drawn face. She moved closer to the man, as if to protect him within the shelter of thin arms.

It was the gesture Karis had made, to shield the Caver boy.

All around, other figures sat in numb loneliness. Apathetic eyes regarded them listlessly. They were ragged, half-starving, hopeless. What was this place? What was happening here?

'Who are they?' Blythe asked the shopkeeper.

'Refugees,' he said briefly. 'Adherents to the only truth, who have no place in Peraldon. The Lady Astret is truly present in their lives. They live here to send help to the Cavers.'

He stood still suddenly, aware that perhaps he had given

away too much. He stared at Blythe. 'If you betray this, you will live to desire death as a longed-for benison.'

It was either a prophecy or a curse. A chill in the air . . .

An old woman came to stand next to the shopkeeper. He took her arm, moving his hand to brush lank grey hair back from her head. She was shivering, although the air was hot and oppressive. He led her to a stool against a wall, sitting her down. He looked back at Blythe.

'Remember,' he said. 'This is inviolate.'

They continued on through the hallway, avoiding the suspicious eyes of the men who watched them, fingering their knives. They sidestepped the bodies of the old and sick who sprawled at their feet. There were faint smells of sour cooking from one area, where a rough soup kitchen had been rigged up.

It all looked temporary, an emergency existence, but from the staleness in the air, the dullness in their eyes, Blythe thought that they had probably all been there a very long time.

The woman led them through one of the tunnels which branched off the central area, through a heavy curtain to a small empty cubicle. The thickness of the curtain blocked the sounds from outside; it was quiet and isolated.

There was no furniture apart from some stools, on which they sat, and a low, circular table. There were none of the familiar implements of magic Blythe expected to see, no bunches of herbs or silver divining rods, crystal balls or other glass shapes.

In truth, he did not really know what to expect. His knowledge of Moon lore was limited to the sensational propaganda published by the Priests' office. This on the other hand was austere and bleak, and the only gleam of vitality sprang from Selene's eyes when she flung back her hood.

She was almost beautiful, but privation had blurred the delicate bones of her face. Her shadowed eyes were sunk deep. A fine network of lines mapped her white skin. Although she gazed at them steadily, her breath came in faint gasps, and the thin hands lying in her lap were trembling.

'What is your need?' she asked softly.

For days, Blythe had asked every question under the sun, about tactics, treaties, decisions and politics. He had thought that the answers he sought would be contained there. But those issues faded away as he looked into the clear eyes of Selene. Only one question was relevant.

'Did the Cavers' use of the Seventh Rite work?' He had no idea what the Seventh Rite was, or what it would accomplish, but he knew that no other question was worth asking here.

She grew even paler, staring down at the restless hands in her lap. Then she spoke, so quietly that only Blythe could hear.

'Yes. It worked.' She shuddered.

'The Stasis will break?'

'If the conditions are met.' She looked directly at him, and pure light seemed to stream from her eyes, searing across the table.

'What are the conditions?'

'You will find out.'

'Here? Or somewhere else?' Leaning forward, she touched her finger tips gently to his temples. 'There . . .' she said, and light flooded his mind.

It was excruciating and unbearable. He sprang away from her, tumbling back against curtain and stool, hands clasped to his head, breathless with shock. Uther was immediately on his feet, running to his side, shouting at the woman.

'What have you done?'

'It's all right . . .' Blythe whispered through the daze of pain, with strange conviction.

At the same moment there was a clamour of clashing swords and screams behind the curtains. The shopkeeper ran out, knocking the table over, stumbling over Blythe slumped on the floor. Uther followed him out into the tunnel, in the direction of the noise.

Swiftly, the woman knelt beside him. Conscious, but paralysed by the pain in his head, he forced himself to look into those terrifying eyes again.

'Remember . . .' she said intently, 'when the Bird is released, the conditions will be met. Then you must kill it –'

'Kill – ?' Hazily he struggled to understand.

'You must kill it – or it will all be wasted –' and then she spun round, cringing as the curtains were torn aside and the chaos in the hall was revealed.

The community was being raided: heavily armoured men wearing the High Priest's Sun insignia were streaming in, tearing down curtains, bundling women and old men along the tunnels, brutally cutting down those who resisted or were too slow. Many ran away down the tunnels, soldiers in pursuit.

Cooking pots were overturned, cushions slit, hangings torn. Women, screaming and running for shelter, were sent flying by the violence of the fighting. Sticky blood began to smear the floor from the wounded and dying, as the remaining refugees tried to defend themselves. The serrated knives flashed and ripped, but Astret's pale followers were outnumbered, and stood no chance.

Both the shopkeeper and Uther were lost in the confusion. The woman tried to escape, but was forced back into the booth by the chaos outside. Only seconds remained before they would be discovered.

'Get out!' she hissed to Blythe. 'You must go now . . .' He stared at her blankly, unable to move or respond. Then the curtains swung wide, and one of Lefevre's guard stared in at them.

He moved quickly to the woman, and grasped her wrist. She swung round, scratching at his eyes, so he casually caught the other wrist and twisted them both up behind her back. She stamped and kicked, twisting, but he took no notice, passing a rope round the front of her neck, and round the wrists straining behind her.

Then the guard looked down at Blythe. His face seemed faintly familiar. For the moment he could not place him . . . The man laughed, an eyebrow raised. Clearly he did not share the feeling of recognition. 'What have we here?' he said, taking in the expensive clothes, the military boots. 'Out for cheap thrills, were you? Slumming? Or are you a traitor, too?'

Suddenly, the deadly paralysis was gone. He surged to his feet, butting the guard with his head, reaching for his sword. In an instant he had slashed the rope round the woman's neck and shoulders, and grasping her hand, ran out into the hall. Only briefly winded, the guard was already picking himself up.

The hall was empty. No sign of Uther, or of anyone else. From further down one of the tunnels he heard the clamour of prisoners being taken. Retreating footsteps echoed down many of the others.

'This way –' she pulled him away from the main hallway and ran off down a different tunnel. It divided and branched repeatedly as they tried to lose the guard following close behind them.

The tunnel curved and wound, always sloping downwards. The air was hot, close and dusty, and they were soon gasping for breath as they ran. The woman was agile enough, although hampered by skirts. At one stage she stumbled and Blythe had to wait for her. It seemed as if they must soon be caught by the pounding footsteps behind them.

The steps ceased.

Blythe skidded to a halt, holding the woman against his chest. 'Shhh –' he said. 'Can you hear anything?'

There was silence apart from the sound of their breathing. The woman shook her head.

'He's given up,' said Blythe. He looked at her thoughtfully. 'Now, I wonder why.'

'I know why,' she said, her face colourless. 'Quick! We must hurry!' Before he could ask what she meant, she was running down the tunnel again, black skirts fluttering in the musty air. He raced after her, gripped by the fear in her eyes. The ceiling was too low for speed; they had to crouch. Sometimes the slope fell away steeply under their feet and they began to slide, balance lost, skidding and unsteady against the clammy stone.

Eventually the angle of the slope changed, and they started to move upwards once more. At one point Selene paused for breath, and he asked her, between gasps, where they were going.

'To the Lock,' she said, 'the Lock gate by the Palace. There's an exit there. Come on!'

'What's the rush?' he asked. 'There's no one following.'

'They're going to open the flood gates . . .' she said, and at last the full significance of their headlong flight dawned on Blythe.

They were escaping through the ancient sewage system of the city of Peraldon. In centuries past, the sluice gate from the Great Canal was opened daily at high tide to flush the sewage from the city out into the surrounding Lagoon. More sophisticated methods of sewage disposal had since evolved, and the passages were now used by some as cellars, by others as stores. Most of their length was deserted, except for the areas adopted by the refugees as their home.

He caught up with her, and pulled her round to face him. 'Did they get out? Did those people realise what was happening?' He was cold with apprehension. Uther was there, too.

'You saw only a fraction of their number . . . miles of those tunnels are occupied by people, hundreds of them.' Her eyes were huge and bleak. 'They will all drown if the gate is opened. I think that guard turned back because he knew the gate would be opened. We must stop it!' She wrenched away from him and ran on through the dark. He hurtled after her, terrified now both for Uther and for those other pathetic refugees.

The tunnel rounded a corner, there was a small flight of stairs with a door at the top. The woman took a key from beneath her robe and with difficulty turned it in the rusty lock.

They found themselves in the cellar of some great house. Racks of expensive bottles lined the walls, and the dust here was not due to neglect. Swiftly they passed down the aisles, from room to room, not daring to talk.

Another flight of stairs, a long passage, the cautious opening of a second door. In daily use, oiled and dust free, it swung gently on its hinges, and they edged round it.

They were in a great kitchen, the early morning light just catching on polished pans. Soon the maids would be down to lay the fires, start the breakfasts. They were just in time.

A minute later and they were out in the familiar Peraldonian streets. Their pace did not slacken, but they took care not to cross paths with any of the Warden's city patrols. Blythe knew now where they were, in the impressive squares and terraces that surrounded the Emperor's enigmatic palace. Karis's parents lived close by, and many of his friends. Parks and gardens divided the streets; birds were singing, cats stretching, tradesmen beginning to stir.

Quiet, clear sunlight filtered across the pavements.

Morning.

Election Day.

Chapter Fourteen
The Lock

The Lock-keeper's house stood on the junction of two canals: the tidal Great Canal, dividing the city in two, and its smaller feed canal. The water sparkled in the early light; edged by palaces and gardens, thronging with boats of every description from canoes to liners, it was the focus of Peraldonian life.

The Lock was necessary to adjust the level of the tributary canal. Some of the houses on that side of the city were in danger of flooding, having slowly sunk into the soft mud of the lagoon. The control house thus had large windows looking out over both canals, so that the keeper could gauge their respective depths. In addition to the Lock itself there was the heavy sluice gate to the sewage tunnels. This was also operated from the Lock-keeper's house. It had not been used for a long time.

They approached the building cautiously, and stopped just in sight of it, down a side alley. Unusual activity was taking place. Half a dozen of the Warden's police were standing outside on guard around the door.

As they watched, pressed up against the wall of a shuttered bread shop, they saw three of Lefevre's personal guard ride up in a clatter of horses' hooves. They wore purple and gold cloaks, gaudy in the bright morning. Their faces were grim.

Blythe stepped further back into the shadow. He knew one of the men, a hard, ambitious man called Grogan. It would not be easy. They were accompanied by some eight or ten more of the Imperial guard, all heavily armed, the golden sun motif glinting on their uniforms. Force was out of the question.

Selene had fallen back beside him. She was breathing hard. He glanced at her.

'Have you a mirror?' he said.

'A mirror? No –'

'Well, it will have to do. It's only bluff, but there may be a chance if I look convincing. I know one of those men.' Blythe's standards were high too, and Grogan had commented before on his immaculate appearance. It would not be easy. His boots were scuffed, his cloak torn and crumpled. Quickly understanding, she gave him her own dark blue cloak, shaking out the dust from its folds.

There was a fountain in the square behind them; he washed face and hands, running fingers through dark curling hair. Then he tackled the boots, washing off dust, and hoping that the water would give enough temporary shine to get him at least into the Lock-keeper's house.

'Why are you doing this for us?' she said suddenly, as he returned from the fountain.

'We led Lefevre's men to you.' He paused, not looking at her. 'There was something following us, but at the time I thought it was just a shadow.'

'A scurry,' she said, nodding. 'Lefevre often uses them, they make excellent spies.' She paused. 'So you are driven by guilt?'

He could not understand her attitude, why she asked such an irrelevant question.

'I left my servant there, too,' he said. 'And those people were old, sick . . . Isn't that enough?'

'Beware guilt.' She seemed not to have heard him. 'Don't indulge. The way is too long for that.'

But he was preoccupied now, working out what to do, and hardly heard her words.

'Wait here,' he said, adjusting the fall of his borrowed cloak. 'Whatever happens, don't try to join me.'

'Remember –' she said, thin fingers suddenly clutching his arm, looking up into his dark eyes. For a moment he felt the brilliance of that light burning in his mind, and passed his hand across his brow, distracted. Then he shook her off, and stepped out into the sun.

Taking a deep breath he crossed the cobbled street to the

Lockhouse, aware that he was being watched by the soldiers. Unhesitating, he went up to the most senior of the men, a tall, battle-scarred man with weary eyes.

'Lock-keeper in?' he said. 'I need to talk to him.'

'Sorry, sir.' The sergeant recognised authority but knew his duty. 'There's an emergency. No one's allowed in.'

'Yes, I know. This is relevant to the situation. I am Phinian Blythe, Captain of the Warden's Coastal Watch. I have the necessary authority.'

The sergeant saluted, clicking heels together, but did not stand aside.

'This is urgent, man.' Blythe sounded slightly irritated. 'You will do yourself no good by obstructing state security. This is a matter of treason.'

'My orders are clear, sir. I'm sorry. You can't go in.' He was disturbed by Blythe's rank, but would not stir from the letter of his command. Some of the guards nearby were beginning to shift uneasily, worried by the conflict.

Blythe swore to himself; trust Grogan to have picked one of the few incorruptible guards for this job. He looked up at the wide windows of the Lock-keeper's house. He could see that some kind of argument was taking place inside. The High Priest's three officers were not having it all their own way. The Lock-keeper kept shaking his elderly head, refusal written in every inch of his stance. As he watched, one of Lefevre's men looked his way.

'Grogan!' Blythe yelled cheerfully, and as the sergeant swung round to see what was happening, Blythe pushed past him and ran up the short flight of stairs into the control room. The sergeant started after him, but then noticed that Grogan was waving back, and was reassured. He returned to his position, and Blythe was inside.

The room was functional, bare boards on the floor, maps of the city on the walls. Pictures of the Lock-keeper's family stood on the desk. A geranium shed brown leaves on the window sill.

The controls were operated from a panel between the two windows, overlooking the canal. It looked simple enough, dials and gauges to show water depth, and two heavy levers.

'What are you doing here, Blythe?' Grogan was not

unfriendly, but there was something in reserve at the back of his slate-blue eyes.

'Message from the Warden. For your ears alone . . .' He looked meaningfully at Grogan's two companions and the Lock-keeper. The little man stood by the levers, nervously twisting a handkerchief round in his hands.

'You there. What's your name?'

'Beavis, sir.' Anything to give them more time, Blythe thought.

'Beavis, now be a good chap and go and find something else to do for a while . . .'

The little man gasped and looked at Grogan in confusion, his mouth open. Grogan stepped towards Blythe, his eyes hooded.

'Phinian, my old friend! What is this important message from the Warden? Sit down and tell me all about it. Lecroix and Manton are close colleagues, fully in my confidence.' He waved to a chair. 'Beavis knows better than to speak out of turn, too, don't you, man?' He raised an eyebrow towards the small figure edging towards the door. 'Don't leave us, Beavis. We have work for you.'

'Sir! Not today! It can't be done like this!'

'Grogan.' Blythe spoke quietly, with authority, hardly glancing at the Lock-keeper. 'It's off. There's to be no flooding today.' He paused, trying to gauge how far he was trusted. Grogan was regarding him with a quizzical eye, and his two companions were standing together, talking in an undertone. It wasn't going to be easy.

'Go on,' said Grogan again. 'You begin to interest me exceedingly. Tell me more.'

'The sewers are not to be flooded. Until further notice.'

Grogan was undisturbed. 'I'm afraid that the system is long overdue for a clean out. The new Emperor will want to find the City in good condition. There are one or two small problems down there.'

'Not today, surely.'

'When else? The new Emperor should be honoured in every possible way. My orders are clear, Phin. You are in no position to countermand them.' His voice was still polite.

'I'm not, no. But I speak in my capacity as Captain in the Warden's Watch. This instruction comes direct from the Warden.'

'We may often work with the Warden but I am not obliged to take orders from him.'

The longer this goes on, Blythe thought, the more chance they'll have to get out of the tunnels.

'There will be serious trouble if this goes ahead,' he said, moving closer to Grogan. 'The Warden's son is still down there.' He spoke in a low voice. 'He was separated from the raiding party that went down last night. Raoul Blanchard. He's not back yet.'

It was only a slim chance, but not totally without foundation. Blythe had at last remembered who that guard was, the one who had pursued them only so far.

Grogan was unperturbed. 'He'll have found his way out by now. We are touched by this story of paternal concern, indeed we are. But we have just left the Warden's offices, dear Phin, and I must admit there was little sign of it then.' His eyes narrowed and his tone lost its courteous timbre. 'Our orders are pressing, and admit no further delay.' Without taking his eyes from Blythe, he said to Beavis, 'Open the gates.'

'Sir!' The little man was anguished. 'We can't do it, just like that! Three days warning must be given before the system is flooded; we have to, the homeless sleep there, people keep chickens there, store things. We have to give them some warning.'

'Not today. The High Priest's orders are clear. People who use the system are doing so illegally and will have to take the consequences. Stop delaying, and get on with it.'

Grogan's two companions had moved imperceptibly closer to Blythe. Their swords were drawn. He took no notice. Anything to keep the man talking.

'What's so important down there, Grogan?' he asked. 'Why should the High Priest concern himself with this?'

'It has been discovered that a number of outlaws live there,' said Grogan formally. 'They are a cancer in the life of our city, and must be destroyed.'

'What? A few beggars and thieves? Surely the great city of

Peraldon can absorb them without difficulty amidst its teeming millions.'

'You don't know what you're talking about!' said Grogan, goaded at last. 'They are heretics, Moon-worshippers, that kind of scum! They threaten the Stasis in every way! They are responsible for the traffic to the Cavers!'

Through the wide window Blythe could see the woman, thin skirt and blouse fluttering in the light breeze, staring straight at him. He remembered her urgency, and the hopeless, feeble little family groups with their gaunt, fever-ridden sick and elderly.

Grogan had turned to Beavis. 'Do you want the Stasis upset? These people do. They're evil, dangerous subversives! That's the kind of person who lives in your precious passages. We don't want to warn them, we want to get rid of them! Now, do it! Or you'll never work again.'

The little man flinched, and looked despairingly towards Blythe.

Suddenly, roughly, Blythe pushed him aside, shouting, 'Get out! Now!' and drew his sword, turning to face Lefevre's three guards. His abrupt action had not caught them unprepared; one was already summoning the officers outside, while Grogan and the other had also drawn swords and were circling round the desk to reach him.

Recklessly he lashed out, spinning so fast that he nicked the forearm of one man, and ripped Grogan's bright cloak. Neither noticed. They were competent and determined, coldly efficient, totally unlike the desperate Cavers Blythe usually fought. They lunged forward and he leapt up onto the catwalk of the control panel itself, running along it until he reached one of the windows.

He turned there, and from his high vantage point warded them off just long enough to see Selene vanish into the warren of the city.

The door swung back on its hinges; a group of guards rushed in, weapons flashing, whistles blowing. Blythe whisked a chair up from the floor and began to swing it round, catching helmeted heads and weapons alike. Someone grasped at it, catching one of its legs. Blythe hauled on it, and the man gave a shriek of surprise as the chair was wrenched from his hand and went crashing through the wide picture window in a shatter of glass into the canal outside.

It was hopeless, of course. He had delayed them for only minutes, and had no chance of holding them off for much longer. As he thrust and parried, dodging and weaving, he tried to concentrate on how the controls might work.

There were two levers placed centrally on the control panel. There were two gates, one to the feed canal, and one to the sluice. If he could open the gate to the feed canal, the weight of the water would hold the sluice shut for some time. But to pull the wrong lever would direct water from both the Great Canal and the feed canal straight into the sluice.

They would all die if he didn't take the chance. He would have to risk it.

He was sweating now. They were trying to keep him pinned into one corner, and in truth he preferred it there, for at least his back was shielded and only two at a time could come within his sword's reach. Vaguely he wondered why he had not been cut down, and then realised that Grogan wanted him alive.

He used every trick he'd ever been taught in the Guard, and some he'd learnt from Uther, unorthodox and effective. But every time an assailant fell back, he was replaced by another, fresh and eager.

Through a haze of exhaustion he was dimly aware that the Lock-keeper was edging round the room towards the control panel. He was still trembling with fear, but he was moving with purpose. He knew which lever to pull. Blythe hoped passionately that he would make it.

He began to slacken the pace of the fight, allowing them to think he was tired, and they pressed forward. Wildly he surged out into the midst of the flashing swords and, ignoring the shock and warm rush of blood on his side that told him that he'd been wounded, grabbed one of the guards and held him strongly against himself as a shield.

For a moment the attackers hesitated; it was enough for Blythe to fling his hostage away and to dart forward to the controls. He gasped to the white sweating face of Beavis,

'Which stops the sluice?' But Grogan's sword plunged through the old man's breast and his mouth, open to reply, became a gushing fountain of blood.

Two levers; one to open the lock, one to open the sluice. No time for choice, nothing to give the clue. Praying to he knew not what god, he fell forward, towards the lever on the left, his weight heavy, his hands outstretched.

The pain from the wound in his side caused him to fall short, and his hands locked round the right hand lever.

As he was overwhelmed, in pain and exhaustion, he heard Grogan laugh, lightly. 'Thank you, Phin,' he said. 'You've done our work for us.'

Gathering mists of weakness mingled in his mind with the sound of water rushing and swirling, flooding down through the sluice gate, flooding through the tunnels, rushing and tumbling and battering.

He remembered that woman, trying to protect the fever-stricken man from him, looking at him as Karis might have done.

And another memory, as the mists closed in.

If you betray this, you will live to desire death as a longed-for benison.

Chapter Fifteen
Margat

The Great Hall in the centre of the Cliff was already crowded by the time Letia and Eleanor reached it. Letia had passed Eleanor a dark blue cloak as they ran down the stairs, and as everyone there was wearing one, it was impossible to recognise individuals. There was only a scattering of men, standing round the walls.

For the first few moments everyone knelt in silence on the cold stone floor. Then a woman stood up in the centre of the mass of dark figures, and began to declaim another strange prayer.

'We abide in the stillness of Your Word, we construct and build in the void shaped by Your love, pity us!' Unmistakably, it was Nerissa again. 'We dutifully and carefully structure both night and day in accordance with Your wishes, secure in the knowledge that You will return. Pity us, and reveal Yourself to us, as You have done before. For only You hold the key to our liberation, the answer to our unknowing, the love to drive away our hate.'

A wordless chant was taken up by the women. Repetitive, insistent, mournful, it was like a drug to quieten their distress. Some of the women were swaying, some were openly crying. Was this their release, their joyless relief, wondered Eleanor?

She shifted uncomfortably as she knelt, longing to sit back on her heels. How long would this go on? She should have found out before agreeing to come. Not that there had been much agreement about any of it, as she remembered. Ever since she had first awoken near the fire people had been ordering her around, telling her what to do, where to go. Like being in Alice's Wonderland, she thought irrelevantly.

And where were the other men? Was the division between Nerissa and her husband typical of the Cavers? She remembered sharp words between Niclaus and Letia. Things weren't right there, either. Religion appeared to be mainly the province of the women.

There was a pause in the chanting and, as one, all the women looked up into the vaulting dark above. Hanging there, unmoving, glinting in the torchlight, was the heavy silver pendulum. The women's silence was reflected in its unyielding immobility. It was as if the whole world was holding its breath. Eleanor knew, for sure, that nothing would ever move that pendulum.

The silence ceased as the women stood up. They began to file out past Nerissa, who stood at the main exit. She was passing news to each of them.

Standing in the queue with Letia, Eleanor heard the words 'failed again . . . heresy . . . Fabian'. It was going to be another catalogue of misery.

The shock, when it came, resulted from the meeting of Letia and Nerissa. The priestess turned on the older woman with extraordinary virulence. They were clearly old enemies. Waiting her turn, Eleanor heard every word.

'Have you still not decided where your duty lies? Does not the dangerous farce of heresy disgust you?' Nerissa's tone was harsh and unpleasant. Letia replied with uneasy bravado.

'My first duty is to my husband and our foster children, Matthias, Lukas and Margat. I have told you so often, Nerissa. I will not desert them.'

'It is in their own best interests. You can aid them in no more effective way,' said Nerissa forcefully.

Letia stood her ground, unshakeable in her loyalty.

'That is only wishful thinking!' she said. 'Name me one success, one achievement that has resulted from prayer!'

'Fool! Look at these women! Are they not tranquil and at peace?' With thin fingers, Nerissa swung Letia round to face the assembled women.

Silent for a moment, Letia looked at her friends. Sadly, quietly, she said, 'Ah, Nerissa, can't you tell the difference between peace and despair? Are you so lost to reality?'

'I *know* what is real and of benefit! Foolish experiments and forbidden heresies will bring no relief. Is Lukas happy? Margat? They would do better to join us, as would you.'

'I can't do that. We may not be happy, but at least we have hope. We haven't given up!' Letia was shaking with emotion.

'Neither have we. Your duty is with us.' Regarding the force of that implacable will, Eleanor began to admire Letia's resistance. Nerissa's determination was welded into the unchanging stasis of this world; immovable and eternal. All too easily, it would crush the bright, bird-like frailty of its opponent.

Suddenly frightened for Letia, Eleanor stepped forward and faced Nerissa. 'Why don't you leave her alone? At least she comes to your dreary ceremonies, she does give you a chance! You don't have to be foul as well!'

Letia gasped and tried to pull Eleanor away, but she stood still, glaring at Nerissa. A faint smile curved on the Priestess's lips.

'What else could we expect? Like putrid fruit, you fall from the rotten growth of heresy. You are a contamination in this world, you should be hunted down and destroyed as the vermin you are, diseased and cancerous –'

Appalled, hand over mouth, Eleanor tried to back away, but the crowd of women was pressing in now, drawn by the conflict. The terrible words, spoken so coldly and calmly, filled her ears, and she wanted to scream to blot out their force.

'Evil and licentious, your eyes are empty of understanding. You interfere in what is good and right, bringing poison to our lives –'

'What does all this matter?' A new voice interrupted the flow. Its strange, desperate timbre turned every head. Standing in the entrance of the Great Hall, swaying, her hand outstretched to the rock for support, was a tall thin woman, tangled black hair glistening with raindrops. She was preternaturally pale, eyes enormous dark hollows. She was staring at Nerissa.

Letia immediately rushed to her side, pulling Eleanor with her, out of danger. 'Margat! Is it Fabian? Fabian's back?'

Numbly the woman shook her head. She continued looking at Nerissa. 'You are right of course,' she said. 'Fabian would still be here if we hadn't tried the Seventh Rite. There would have been no need for a raid. I came to tell you that. At least lives are not lost through prayer.'

She paused, gathering strength. 'But there's no need to gloat, to bludgeon. You have it all your own way quite thoroughly enough as it is. We have no choice other than to suffer, and suffer, and suffer, for ever, in order to follow the Lady. We are marooned here in dark and cold in Her service. We don't complain. Astret is worth all of our lives. Be content with that, and leave Letia and the girl alone.'

Her voice failed on these final words, and her knees buckled.

There was a bustle of helping hands, and no one noticed Eleanor walking out of the cavern into the dark. She walked away, blind in the unremitting gloom, deeply shocked by the scene. The rain was streaming down, bitter and drenching as ever. It was very cold. This was getting worse and worse, a nightmare rather than a dream. She could not bear those anguished women, the hostility and desperation. She longed for solitude, an escape. Even that was denied her.

A breathless figure came rushing out of the dark and crashed into her.

'Eleanor, good! Where's Margat?' Matthias's voice was buoyant with joy and relief.

She pointed silently to the cavern and began to question, but he paused only long enough to catch up both her hands, saying, 'The Arrarat have heard! Amaris is on the way back, and she's got Fabian with her! I must let Margat know right away. Go and tell Lukas – he's up on the tower –' He waved vaguely up at the Cliff face and then ran headlong into the cavern to find his sister.

It was something to do. With relief, Eleanor put away the memory of that frightful tirade and ran through one of the caves towards the steps at the back of the Cliff. She pounded up them, pulling her ungainly skirts out of the way with impatience. Up past Letia's cave, on up another four flights and round the last corner out onto the top of the Cavers' Cliff.

A gust of wind-driven rain struck her like a blow. She staggered under the shock of it, and tried to make some sense of the rain-sodden night. The Cliff dropped away to her left, and to her right a dark shadow reared up narrow and forbidding. Steps were hacked out of it in a spiral round the outside. A brace of torches spluttered at the top of it.

Pulling her cloak closer around herself, she began to stumble up the stairs, heart thudding with the unusual exertion, towards the lights.

Two men stood at the top, Niclaus Witten and Lukas Marling, their dark cloaks flapping like birds' wings in the buffeting wind.

'Fabian's coming!' she shouted above the noise. They bent nearer to hear her words. 'Matthias said to tell you. He's heard that Amaris is on her way, with Fabian.' In the torchlight she could see relief suddenly illuminate Lukas's face.

For a moment she thought he was going to hug her, but he only nodded, acknowledging her information, and returned to scanning the bleak skies as if he could see in that deepening dark, trying to hear the beat of the Arrarat's wings over the howl of the wind.

'How do the hawks know – ?' she began. Lukas turned back to her but the wind was too strong, blowing away her words. She tried again, shouting this time.

'How can the Arrarat tell Matthias what's happening?' Lukas handed his torch to Niclaus and bent his head closer to her. 'The Arrarat are telepathic,' he said, raising his voice, 'if the circumstances permit. Most of us can communicate with them – I'll explain later.' It was too difficult to speak over the constant din, and they both turned back to the night sky.

The two men were undisturbed by the rain and bitter wind. They were used to it, she supposed. Lukas was methodically scanning the distant horizon, black hair plastered unruly to his forehead, eyes narrowed against the rain. He was always thoroughly involved in whatever he was doing or saying, she thought resentfully. Never in any doubt about what was dream, what was reality.

A shout from him broke into her thoughts. From far

away, faint between gusts of wind, came the sound of giant wings. And then the great hawk was there, its rider slumped unconscious on its back, swooping down to join them on top of the tower.

The bird was drooping, staggering with exhaustion. Carefully, they pulled the boy over into their arms, gently lowering him to the ground. Eleanor saw that he was little more than a child, skin unlined, bleached and smooth. Straight dark hair showed black with moisture.

There were bloody, rough bandages round his knee, which sprawled sideways at an unnatural angle. Without thinking, she took off her cloak and spread it round the boy's thin shoulders. Then, with Eleanor holding the two torches to light the way, the men swiftly carried Fabian back down the narrow stairs to Margat's cave, next to Letia's.

Margat was waiting there, frantic with anticipation. There was a man with her, tall, dark-haired, quiet. Margat ran forward, and immediately took Fabian from them, staggering slightly under his weight, and laid him on a rocky ledge lined with cushions, near the fire.

There was then an appalling time, the examination of the wound, hurried, muttered consultations, the grinding edge of dread affecting them all. The dark quiet man with the short neat hair was some kind of a healer, and under his hands the boy stopped tossing and threshing. Eleanor heard them call him Comyn but no one introduced him to her.

It seemed that the mangled flesh and bone were infected. Eleanor heard Matthias and Lukas discussing amputation with the healer. Letia's arms were round Margat, and soft, small groans came from the semi-conscious boy.

Dumbly Eleanor helped to heat water, tended the fire and gazed out into the rain. What else could she do? There was a distressing interruption, when a woman's voice at the door shrilly demanded that 'the stranger' should be taken to Nerissa.

Bleak with rage, Niclaus Witten slammed the door in the woman's face and bolted it. He briefly laid his hand on Eleanor's shoulder in reassurance. He was too distracted to notice her pallor.

She was lost in an abyss of horrors.

What was she doing here? She had no place in the misery of these people's lives, no purpose or function to fulfil. Of course, she had never worried about being useful before. It had all been reasonably simple, the pursuit of happiness in her previous life. She had never questioned her right to pursue her own desires, to gratify such whims as might occur to her.

Her parents' separation had been a relief after years of antagonism. She had been a bargaining counter in a dreary sequence of fights and reconciliations, of hectic affairs and hidden secrets. As a child, they had fought for her devotion with presents and treats, but sent her away to an expensive school at an early age.

She had learnt to distance herself, to observe the manoeuvres without involvement. She had broken away as quickly as possible, leaving home as soon as she finished school, glad to be free of commitments.

They had given her the flat for her eighteenth birthday. The Porsche she bought for herself, and everything else. She had worked hard, guarding her independence, free to please herself, free from emotional tangles. She met her mother for lunch once a month, her father more rarely. It was more than enough, she thought.

She deliberately cut herself out of their messy and traumatic lives.

What was she doing here? Sitting by a fire in a gloomy cave, surrounded by preoccupied, distraught strangers. Staring at chipped nail varnish, she shuddered, and yearned for home.

What would happen now? Would they give her a cave, teach her to cook fish stew, initiate her into the Lady's religion? But she was forgetting the violence of Nerissa's attack, and the woman at the door demanding her presence had been both hostile and angry. There was nothing for her here, and would never be.

Suddenly she stood up, looking at the pale, wracked boy and his grieving mother. Then she realised that Lukas was grimly approaching the fire, a heavy long knife in his hands, to sterilise it in the flame.

She backed away from the fire and the man, looking

wildly for an escape. Witten had bolted the door, and she couldn't bear to encounter any of the other Cavers. That left only one way out: the rope ladder that swung lightly down from the cave mouth. No one was paying any attention to her. Swiftly, quietly, she placed one foot and then another on the rope rungs and gently let herself out of the warm, ominous firelight.

Chapter Sixteen
Moonlight

The usual bitter shock of wind and rain. She was getting used to it. She found the ladder difficult to negotiate, and was at first confused by memories of childhood adventure stories which advised climbing sideways, feet on either side of the vertical ropes. But that way she kept banging painfully against the rock face, losing the next rung as the ladder swung diagonally away from her feet.

Facing inwards was only slightly better, because her shoes and fingers kept grazing against the rock. But at least progress could be made that way and soon she had edged down the frightening drop, passing unnoticed the other inhabited caves.

Her feet touched damp mud. There was no one about. News of Fabian's return had spread, and even the lookouts had retired to the safety of their caves.

The relief of being alone was overwhelming; the combination of anguish, hostility and despair had terrified her. She needed time and space, to try to make some sense of this extraordinary nightmare.

She was sickened and wearied by the eternal rain and dark, but where could she go? Ahead there was the sea, to the left and right only marshland. She wandered away from the Cliff. Although cold and wet, the night itself was at least neutral, demanding nothing from her.

She found herself passing the ruins of the bonfire, returning to the little rocky bay where Matthias had tried to explain what had happened. The sea was curiously attractive, pulling her ever closer by the rhythm of its motion.

She settled herself as comfortably as possible on a small rounded rock and watched the waves crashing against the shore. Part of her hoped that sitting here, close to where she had first appeared in this alien world, she would perhaps slip back again to her own time. Gradually her mind became blank with exhausted incomprehension. She watched the waves automatically, and thought of nothing.

Slowly the night wore on, becoming yet more grim.

At first Eleanor was too depressed to notice. The wind subsided, and the black clouds hung unrelieved overhead. The waves no longer crashed on the shore, but stilled to a sluggish wash, as if the oppressive sky were draining the sea of energy. Gradually, she came to her senses, and realised that her palms were sticky, that the feeling of wet and cold had ceased. She was sweating, breathless, enervated.

What was it? She stood up, deciding that perhaps she would be better off at least within sight of the Caves. Her heart was racing with an inexplicable tension, and she began to feel nervous. Better return, she thought, better the devil you know than this distortion of the night.

Labouring, she took one step towards the Caves, but her feet were heavy, so heavy. The sand dragged at her shoes. She tried to struggle on but her body was leaden and she could hardly move. Breathing in jagged gasps, now seriously frightened, she tried to force herself onwards, but her limbs refused to obey.

She stood still, trembling in the black night.

There was something else too, nagging for her attention.

A muted hum, the faintest murmur of music, drew her round to face the sea again. The sound drifted on the heavy air, light as a dream.

The night was as impenetrable as ever, but suddenly a shining path of moonlight shot along the beach from the far band of rocks directly to her feet. It was dazzlingly bright, silvery and clear. Rain danced like diamonds above it.

And yet there was no moon visible in the sky.

She was terrified.

Unable to escape.

She found that she could move again, that her feet were now drawing her down this shining path along the waters' edge to the rocks at the bay's margin. The music became stronger and clearer; a wordless voice, throbbing with the rhythm of the quietened waves, cool, unbearable, entirely alien.

Slowly she approached the black rock, fear only just kept under control by the sweetness of the sound and by the clear path of light. It was not coming from the rock itself, but from a point some distance beyond. The light path curved softly round the contour of the rock. Unable to resist, dreading what she might find, Eleanor followed.

Nothing met her gaze but more rock. The path turned and snaked between huge boulders, doubling back on itself many times. She could not refuse its claim; although she was almost whimpering with terror, her mind skittering round like a panicked rabbit, she was also wholly enthralled.

She walked on.

Black rocks reared high around her, creating fantastic anthropomorphic shapes; gargoyle giants, pouncing cats, clutching hands. They cast bizarre shadows against each other, but not on the path, the twisting silver path.

Clear and enticing, it offered her no choice but to follow. At first she flinched at the under-lit, monstrous rocks, but then realised that they disappeared if she concentrated only on the line of light.

She was soon hopelessly lost in the black and silver labyrinth. Listening for the song, she forgot the sound of the waves. She was no longer sure where the sea was.

Once she glanced behind her and was shocked to discover that the gleaming path vanished as soon as her steps had passed. She would not be able to follow it out again.

The path rounded one more crag – and there, knuckles pressed hard against teeth, Eleanor stopped. The rocks gave way to an endless expanse of open ground, reaching far out beyond the horizon. So vast it was, so featureless, that all sense of perspective was lost. It cleared the imagination of limits, freed the mind of boundaries. Space, clear and light, unfolding forever, away into infinity . . .

Flooding cold white dazzling light everywhere. It was the only context; air, sky and ground only existed in light. All around, within her blood, within her soul. Nothing but light.

There was no understanding this, no possible way to comprehend the light.

Because nothing could happen, could exist in the light, a change took place. The song of light breathed a different metre and the nature of light altered. It seemed to gather in a vortex of burning intensity. There, the sound, the power and the moonlight all were contained, enhanced, in the severe and brilliant figure of a woman.

She was singing the song.

At every beat of this ceaseless threnody the distant waves crashed on the shore. The sound and movement lived in the very air Eleanor breathed. Relentlessly and rhythmically, it conjured up both the tide and her breath.

The woman was tall, and invincible. Without reasoning, Eleanor knew Her to be the power of the Moon itself, the essence of its cold light given human form. Her back was turned, but Eleanor knew she was required to draw nearer.

Unwillingly, she found herself crossing the enormous space, her heart frozen not with fear but with awe. She moved in light, not air. She was being drawn in, deeper and further, by the Moon's will.

She did not even know if she wanted to escape.

When she was within twenty paces of the woman her knees buckled, and she collapsed into a heap on the carpet of light, soundless tears streaking her cheeks.

The song ceased. The waves stopped their monotonous crashing. Silence held time eternally still. Eleanor's face was buried in her hands. She could not bear to watch as the woman turned round.

'Look at me.' The voice was cool, passionless, neutral. 'Eleanor. Look up.' She was infinitely patient.

Sobbing, Eleanor raised her face and shuddered at the power in the other's eyes. Implacable, flawless, inhuman. Power held crystal clear in endlessly black eyes. Her skin gleamed, Her hair rippled in light like water.

'You are here for a reason . . .' Her voice was slow, the words burning like ice into Eleanor's soul. 'Don't forget that. This is no accident. Listen, and remember. Not of this world, summoned randomly, the responsibility is nonetheless yours. You can break the deadlock: you alone, stranger, are separate enough to act.' There was a pause.

'You must find the Bird of Time, and release it. Be brave, and the balance will be restored, the Boundary broken. I will help where I can, but the Sun is strong, defending His obsession. So be careful, Eleanor, for it will not be easy. And you must not fail.

'All the harmony in the world, the rhythmic dance of life and death, depends on this. If you fail, all human love will die, like a fly caught in amber. Already people are suffering. There is not much time left. You must not fail.'

Calmly, deliberately, She laid Her hands on Eleanor's temples, and allowed icy power to blast through her mind and heart.

'You will not forget, now, where the Bird of Time lies.'

She turned away then, back to Her song, and as She sang the waves resumed their usual motion.

The brightness of the sand, the air, and the figure grew more intense, more dazzling, until Eleanor shut her eyes, cradling her aching head in her hands. The sound and light filled her, crushed and stunned even through closed eyes. The pain in her head began to shatter thought; and, as she slowly lost consciousness, the imprint of light was welded into her soul.

'Eleanor.'

Another voice: human, warm, rough. 'Eleanor, wake up.' Her shoulder was gently shaken. Reluctantly, she opened her eyes. The light had gone. It was over. The ordinary damp, gloomy, night had been restored.

Matthias was kneeling at her side. Lukas, standing over them, holding a smoking torch.

'Are you all right? What happened?'

She could not frame words. Thought and speech had deserted her. She pushed herself up, concentrating on the movement, and gradually memory returned.

Had it been a dream, or reality? A dream within a dream? She didn't know what to say. Clumsily, she pushed the hair out of her eyes. Her hands were still shaking.

Matthias was frowning with anxiety. 'For Lady's sake, Eleanor, what's happened? Are you all right? Why did you run away?'

She had to speak. What had he said? Why did she run away? She tried to remember.

'I – had to. I thought you were going to . . . Is Fabian – ?'

'He'll be all right.' Matthias sat back on his heels, sharp lines between his brows. He was staring at her in a way she did not understand.

And then she realised that at the back of her mind, beyond the edge of vision, a beacon glowed and beckoned. She did not know what it was, except that it changed everything. She did not know enough to feel fear then.

Instead, a strange surge of confidence swept over her. It belonged to the light, as she did now. She pushed aside Matthias's helping hand, and stood up.

'I'm fine . . . I must have fallen, or something. There was no need to worry.' Informed by light, she noticed with shame the anxiety and weariness in their faces. 'I'm sorry you came out, I wouldn't have added to your difficulties for anything . . .'

'I brought you here, understand?' Matthias was bleak. 'I'm responsible for you.'

'Never mind about that now,' Lukas interrupted. 'We're needed back at the Cliff. Let's get going. Come on.'

As he turned, the inaccurate light from the torch caught a glint from a small silver scar on Eleanor's temple.

'Where did you get that?' He had pushed back her hair and was staring straight at the crescent shaped scar. Eleanor put up her hand and felt the shiny patch at her brow. She stepped away from him, suddenly cross.

This was nothing to do with him. With her new-found strength she resisted him.

'I've always had it,' she said, jerking her head away. 'Ever since I can remember.' And it was not entirely a lie, either. In one way her life had only just begun, in that moment when the Moon printed her soul with light.

'I've seen it before,' he said slowly. 'The Lady's sign –'

'Really.' She was sarcastic, but he still looked at her. She turned away. Nothing to do with him.

'Later.' Matthias's voice was tired. 'There is much to think about, much to discuss. We should be getting back.'

He had lit his torch from Lukas's and started to lead the way back to the Caves, leaning on the wooden staff.

The light at the back of her mind flared brightly.

'I'm not coming,' she found herself saying from nowhere.

'What do you mean "not coming"?' Matthias swung round.

'Just that.' Why was she saying this? The words continued. 'I've got something else to do.'

'What *do* you mean?' Matthias peered through the gloom at her with irritation. 'Did you knock your head just now?'

'No, I just stumbled. It's quite different. I've something else to do,' she repeated. It was forming in her mind, growing strong and overwhelming.

An unalterable obsession, pushing aside all her doubts, suppressing all her reasonable and natural instincts.

'What, exactly?' Lukas was mocking. 'Are you going to fight the Peraldonians single-handed? Build a boat and sail the seven seas? Find a mermaid and win a wish?' He laughed, not ungenerously. 'Come on, dear, it's getting late, and Letia will be worrying.'

She could have stamped with frustration. 'Well, go on then. I'm not stopping you. Go and get warm in your nice comfortable cave. I'm going somewhere else.'

Faced with their incomprehension she wondered irritably if there was any use in trying to explain at all. She did not understand it herself. She glared at them.

Lukas was shrugging, the long mouth twisting with amusement. 'There, Matt, what did I tell you? Trouble all the way. She'll be wanting an armed escort next. I'd let her go, if I were you. It'll make Nerissa's day for a start.'

'She'd not last five minutes.' Matthias sighed. 'She doesn't know what it's like here. She didn't ask to come. It's my fault she's here at all. I owe her something.'

'Good of you.' Eleanor strongly resented being discussed like a parcel. 'However, I need neither you nor your objectionable brother. I'm going that way.' She found herself pointing along the seashore, following the undeniable light shining in her mind.

'What will you do?' Lukas was derisory. 'Swim? This is

an island, you know.' For a moment she was nonplussed.

'There must be boats then. Could I hire one?' She pulled a silver ring from her finger. 'Would this pay for it?'

'This is ridiculous!' Matthias had reached the limit of his temper. 'There are no boats for hire, no way to travel without the Arrarat, apart from on foot. And that shoreline leads to marshes, and if you get across them there are only rocks, and more sea. There's no way through!'

'I shall find one.' She spoke with bravado, although doubt was beginning to undermine this extraordinary confidence. An *island*? But perhaps she would not have to go far. Nothing had been said about distance. Perhaps she could find the Bird of Time, whatever it was, here.

Ignoring the two men, she flung her cloak more securely over one shoulder, and set off along the shore.

'Hell and damnation!' Matthias was angry now, and exasperated. He tried to moderate his voice. 'Look. Come back to the caves, have something to eat. Nerissa won't worry you, if that's what has upset you. Come and get warm, and we'll discuss how to get you on your way.'

You'll change your mind, he meant, out of the wind and cold. He wanted to get her comfortable again, so that she wouldn't want to run off. It wouldn't work, Eleanor knew, but she wasn't even going to try to resist temptation. She turned and sat down on a rock.

'I'd be grateful if you could bring me some food, and a map so I can get going. I think you owe me that much.' There are always strings available to pull, she thought. *What am I doing*? Assailed yet again by doubt she refused to meet their eyes, and missed Lukas's quick smile.

'She's mad, brother mine, and there's no dissuading the insane. Besides, it rids us of a problem. I don't know how you imagine she's going to get round Nerissa. I, for one, wouldn't like to try.'

Lukas turned to her. 'Well, my lady, you shall have your way. You shall have your provisions and maps, such as they are, and you shall undertake your great quest. We'll keep the home fires burning for when you come back. Just don't keep us hanging around out here any longer.'

Laughing, he walked away into the dark.

Matthias remained for a moment. 'Something has happened, hasn't it? Why won't you tell us?'

'You'd never believe it anyway.'

'Try me.'

'No.' Her encounter with Astret, Lady of the Moon, was strictly private. She was not going to share it with anyone. She lifted her chin and stared at him.

'You don't know what you're doing,' he persisted. 'This is not an easy country. There's danger everywhere. You're totally unequipped to handle any of it. Do you want to die?'

'I won't die.' Unreasonably, she was sure of this. Light like that could not be extinguished. It would not die, and neither would she. It was how she kept the fear at bay, understanding so little. She tried again. 'Look, I know you feel responsible. You're one of those people who always does, who worries, who feels that everything is their fault. But I'm not willing to be on your conscience. Okay, you brought me here, but what I do, what I make of it, is all up to me.' That was a lesson she had learnt long ago in her old life. She had made her own career, run her own life, relationships, friends and home. It was the only tolerable way.

She paused, wondering how to make him understand. 'I release you from responsibility. You've done your best, but now it's my turn. Let me go.'

'Just think, Eleanor! Existence is difficult enough even within the shelter of the caves . . .'

'I'll take my chance. All I want is some food, and an idea of how to travel. Let me have those, and I'll not bother you again.' She stood up and faced him squarely. 'I know what I'm doing. I won't be stopped by you.'

He regarded her, frowning with indecision.

'The only alternative seems to be the use of force,' he said at last. 'I'd rather believe you. The Lady knows why, but I accept what you say. Have it your own way. I'll get your supplies. Wait here. I won't be long.' He followed his brother, disappearing into the bleak night.

She smiled, hugging her secret to herself.

Chapter Seventeen
Ash

Alone again on the cold seashore, Eleanor sighed with relief. Since awakening in this strange land, she had been lost in a maze of anxiety, incomprehension and discomfort. The Moon Lady was anything but familiar, but She was at least something definite, something clear and urgent in the distressing nightmare that was Caver life. And, incredibly, She seemed to think that Eleanor was important, too.

That was what was so irresistible. That was why she had gone against all advice, all common sense. She had a role here, something crucial to accomplish. At this stage, it meant much more to her than any fear. She had received more than an explanation for her presence in this alien world, she had been given a reason for existing. She had never experienced this before, here or anywhere else.

Then it occurred to Eleanor that perhaps the Moon was only a dream too. For a moment she floundered in miserable self-doubt, worrying that it was all a hallucination. But undeniable light still shone at the back of her mind, both a reassurance and an inspiration.

She waited a long time before anyone returned; her feet were cold and wet, her hair damp and straggly, rumpled by the unceasing wind. Yet she did not doubt that someone would come, or that what she was doing was the only reasonable course.

It was Lukas who came back to her, not Matthias. He was carrying one rucksack on his back, another in his hands. He looked grim and tired.

'Why two? I can only carry one,' she said, almost embracing him in the wild hope that perhaps she would not have to be alone, after all.

'I'm coming with you.' He sat down on a rock near to her and gazed out to sea. She had only seen him look like this once before, when he was sterilising that knife in the fire. She was about to ask him why, when he spoke again.

'It's certainly mad, if not suicidal.' He paused, idly kicking the damp sand into a mound. His voice was quiet. 'It's no use at the Caves, you see. Nothing is ever going to work here. It's taken me a long time to realise. It's not a view shared by anyone else, though. We're not going to have company on this great quest.' He smiled briefly, but then the irony vanished.

'Nerissa is too strong. Faith, acceptance, endurance. The Lady's Way. I can't believe that this is all Astret requires. Surely we have to act too. That's what that prophecy was all about. That's why I persuaded Stefan to send the Guard out, why I helped Matthias with the Seventh Rite.' He almost laughed. 'But so much for prophecies.'

He was still looking at the sea. The bleakness of his expression frightened her. 'It can only get worse now. They'll go on being torn apart by religion and privation. Margat will care for Fabian, but he'll never walk again. Oswald will drink himself stupid. Matthias will have to spend forever defending last night's work, and they still won't trust him. Nerissa will give Alaric hell, Letia and Niclaus will scrap, and the dissension will in the end sour them all, if it hasn't already. They'll plan further raids, more ceremonies, more sacrifices. And for what?'

Furiously he turned to face her as if it were all her fault.

'I thought we might achieve something, the last outpost of Astret's people this side of the Boundary. The chosen people, Nerissa calls us sometimes, chosen to keep the Rule of Astret pure in the south. It was a fool's hope. There's nothing to be done here but suffer. It's got to be altered from outside. Accepting it, working within the terms of the Stasis, won't change anything. It's far too passive.'

There had never been anything in the least passive about Lukas, she thought, almost amused. He went on. 'So . . . a hazard for the future. I'll take a chance on a discredited prophecy. I'm coming with you, Eleanor Knight, not because I know where you're going or why, but because at least you're going to be *doing* something, something different and extraordinary.'

'Does Matthias know?' This mattered to her. She had not said goodbye to him.

'Yes, he does.' Lukas kicked the rough pile of sand at his feet.

'Does he mind you leaving?'

'Far from it.' He smiled, cynical now. 'That's the other reason why I'm here. It's not just running out. He said you would need help. That he could manage without me. He sent his regards. So, you see, there's nothing to hold me back.' He appeared to hold her completely responsible for this.

She sighed; and considered that, on the whole, she would be glad of company, even if Lukas was going to be in a filthy mood.

'Are you ready?' he asked shortly. 'Shall we go?'

She nodded. He stood up, and cupped his hands together over his mouth. He gave the low, ornate cry which carried so far against the wind, and immediately there was the now familiar sound of beating wings. Within seconds an Arrarat hawk had alighted on the sand some feet away.

Lukas went to it, reaching out his hand to caress the downy neck. It was a soft dove grey in colour, with huge liquid black eyes. 'This is Astrella,' he said. 'She will take us to Arrarat Isle, where we'll see if one of them will consent to fly with you.'

It would be unlikely, he implied.

Eleanor didn't move. 'I'd rather walk,' she said.

Lukas looked at her for a long moment, his mouth unsmiling. She saw contempt in his eyes, but when he spoke it was with patience.

'Don't despise what you don't understand here, Eleanor. It is an honour to be granted a visit to Arrarat Isle, a great honour. Without the help of the Arrarat we would be unable to travel at all. There is nowhere to walk to . . . only marshes and the sea. Your great quest would die, here and now, in this damned drizzle. Is that what you want?'

She stood dumb, paralysed. One part of her recognised that he was right; but sickening vertigo assailed her at the thought of flying high, swooping on the soft back of the Arrarat.

The giant hawk regarded her steadily. It seemed almost to read her mind and was not without compassion. She forced herself to meet its calm dark gaze, and remembered the dignity and humour of Letia's Arkemis. She stepped up to the Arrarat and gently touched its face.

'Sorry,' she murmured. It blinked once, and inclined its head as if in invitation.

Wordlessly Lukas offered a hand to help her up. She clambered on, gracelessly, without taking it. The feathers felt strange, smooth and hard rather than soft and downy as she had imagined. There was a leather strap around the bird's shoulders and another behind the wing joints, so that there was something to hang on to. She had to sit like a jockey, her knees tightly bent beneath her so that the wings could move freely. Lukas arranged the two rucksacks as panniers on either side and then swung up behind her.

At once the hawk soared up into the chill air. It was dreadful, the sudden loss of stability and balance. Her breath was snatched from her in the speed of it: she clutched wildly at the neck feathers in panic.

'Relax,' said Lukas in her ear. 'Don't clutch, she doesn't like it. You won't fall.'

She didn't believe him, although his arms were round her waist. Black night spun dizzily around her. She was gasping with shock, trying to unclench her fingers, unclench her teeth, failing.

The hawk was already high above the damp beach, swerving and swooping, on a bizarre, unrecognisable course, following chaotic wind patterns and thermals. They were hundreds of feet above the ground. She shut her eyes, but that was even worse. She thought she was going to be sick.

'There are the Caves,' he said, pointing down, ahead and to their right. His voice was quite steady. She could not think how he did it. She didn't want to look down, but the hawk wheeled round, tilting as it rose higher, and she saw the huge cliffside with the small winking fires in the cave mouths.

Why had she ever left it?

The air was rushing past them, whipping through her clothes and hair.

Catching the thermals, buffeted by gusts, dancing over the wind, the hawk soared and dipped. Sometimes it lost height at enormous speed before climbing up again. She knew she was going to fall off. It was far, far worse than any big dipper, totally unpredictable, totally terrifying.

In one of the wild troughs she saw, far below them, another island. A tumble of buildings covered it, but there were no lights, no sign of life. She wanted to ask what it was but it was impossible to frame words and sentences. The Arrarat swerved round and rose higher.

She was shivering with wind-chill, the rain soaking through every layer of clothing. Cold, however, was the least of her worries.

Suddenly they were above the cloud.

Stars here, shining clear and unfamiliar. The moon only a drab, pale disc. High over cloud, the cold penetrated even her bones. Cloud formed a carpet of uneven white beneath them, stretching far out through the black night.

The dreadful dipping swoops stopped. They flew straight and unswerving for endless miles, with nothing to guide them but the instinct of the bird. There was silence, peaceful, quiet and lonely under the stars, broken only by the steady pulse of beating wings, the wind blowing through her hair. She was beginning to breathe more easily, learning how to turn her head sideways so the wind was not full in her face.

'Not far now,' said Lukas in her ear. His teeth were chattering, too.

With a swoop the Arrarat lost height once more, plunging through the icy layer of cloud down into the driving rain. Her eyes adjusted to the different light, dusk once more, unleavened by stars or moon. Looming ahead of them was a shape more solid than cloud. At reckless speed Astrella hurtled towards it. It was a massive, blank wall of rock, and Eleanor knew there would be no shelter there.

At the last moment, unmindful of her cringing passenger, Astrella swerved sharply to one side and they skirted round the edge of the mountain.

Through the gloom it appeared like an armoured fortress, thrusting out of the sea almost as high as the clouds. There was no possible place for a boat to put in, and Eleanor could see nowhere for a bird to alight either.

Unfaltering, Astrella flew on through the chilling air and rain, always close to the sheer face of the rock, occasionally swooping under wild arches, wing tips almost touching the rock face.

The speed lashed rain into Eleanor's face. Suddenly Astrella swerved again and without hesitation flew straight at the rock. It seemed again that they were about to smash into it when a deeper blackness revealed itself in the wall. The hawk flew straight and fast into a natural gateway, a small, almost unnoticed hole in the cliff.

Abruptly the rain ceased.

Bright golden light dazzled them, and warmth flooded all around. The air was musty, fetid, a sharp reminder of Letia's cave.

Too amazed to remember vertigo, Eleanor looked down, and saw, hundreds of feet below, a huge fire vigorously burning on the rock-scattered floor. Its heat was shocking, unexpected and fierce.

The flickering light illumined the sides of an enormous arena, vaulting high above them, plunging far below. Lit by the raging fire, the plain below them stretched for miles, stained white with bird droppings.

Hot yellow light sent leaping shadows over the walls. At every level the rock face was broken up by serried ranks of caves, just like the Cavers' Cliff. From these, caught in the flickering firelight, thousands of Arrarat hawks gazed unblinkingly as Astrella and her two passengers soared through the arching space to Astrella's own cave.

Lightly, the bird settled on a ledge some two thirds of the way up one side. Lukas slid from her back and turned to help Eleanor. Her knees were shaking. She subsided onto a ledge in the rock.

Stunned by the flight, she could hardly take in the scene around her. It was too much, too big, too hot, too bright. Trying to steady herself she turned away from the fiery space, watching as Lukas unloaded the panniers, distributing their things around the cave.

Another change, another dream. Where would this end?

Lukas was looking at her.

He was deeply happy, she realised resentfully. All his previous cynicism had vanished in the exhilaration of the flight. He loved it here, loved flying on Astrella. He was watching her, and laughing.

'How was that, then?' he asked. 'Quite something, isn't it, one's first flight on an Arrarat?'

She could only nod. He fetched her a drink of water from a pool at the back of the cave, and grinned at her. 'Don't worry, everyone feels like that at first. It'll be better next time.'

He began to whistle through his teeth as he constructed a small cooking fire in the hearth. He had been here before. He was completely at home.

'Do you come here often?' she asked, trying not to sound sour. The trite phrase brought back other worlds, other people. Sudden tears blinded her; she turned her head away, but Lukas wasn't even looking, and answered her cheerfully enough.

'Many times. First when I was twelve, to be chosen by Astrella. Now, that really *was* exciting!' He sat back on his heels, regarding the small fire with satisfaction. 'My parents – they're dead now – brought me here, before the Stasis began. We went to Josquin's Cave –' he pointed across the vast space and up to the right where an opening bigger than the others yawned, empty, 'and held a feast. There was conjuring, songs, and all my friends were there, Matthias and Margat too, of course.' He barely checked.

'Then, Father took me to the edge and called the Arrarat.' He smiled. 'Waiting for a reply was the most intense event of my childhood. It seemed to go on for ever. And then my beautiful Astrella came to me, fluffy and warm she was, not quite full grown.' He stood up, and looked at her. 'Astrella says there's a hawk here for you, too. You're in luck.'

'For me? How does she know? How does she *say* things, anyway?' Eleanor was stirred from depression by curiosity.

'Pictures are what I usually get from her. You'll find out.

Pictures and feelings . . . if we're not too far apart. It grows gradually between rider and bird. Not words, nothing ordinary like that . . . the Arrarat are far beyond the constraints of language. Sometimes there are resonances of feelings, concepts, experiences quite outside human understanding. Emotions . . . intuitions. We have nothing to compare with the mind of an Arrarat. It's worth waiting for. Most of us can communicate with our Arrarat quite efficiently, but it's not precise, because we are always limited by words. And of course, the Arrarat all understand each other.'

He turned to the rucksack, and drew out some dried fish and bread. 'Hungry?' As he set about assembling the usual Caver fish stew, she watched the birds soaring through the space below. Which of them would come to her? She hardly dared to think what it would mean to have her own Arrarat.

There were so many questions to ask, so much she didn't understand. Still, she had to begin somewhere.

'What was that island we passed? There was a city on it, but it looked deserted.'

'Sarant,' he said briefly. 'I was born there. It was devastated during the War.'

She wanted to ask him more, but he abruptly turned his back on her, attending to the cooking. As an attempt at eliciting information it had not been a great success.

Astrella was standing on the outer edge of the cave, preening herself. After a while she launched off into the warm air and Eleanor moved closer to the edge of the cave, watching the flight patterns of the birds below. As the stew cooked, Lukas joined her at the cave mouth.

'The Arrarat saved us from Sarant,' he said quietly. 'Towards the end of the Banishment War there was a siege, a hopeless situation. We were starving. And then Lefevre sent the Fosca at us. Flying creatures they are, monsters sometimes known as dark angels, ridden by what can only be described as sentient fighting machines. Deadly dangerous, they have an unpleasant line in claws and fire-arrows. But the Arrarat came and lifted us out, every one of us.' He paused.

'It was an extraordinary thing for them to do. Up to that point they had refused to be involved in the war at all. No one could ride them into battle, or even use them to carry supplies. They helped to move the wounded, but that was all.'

'So why did they change?'

'Because we were losing, I think. They would not allow all of us to be wiped out. We are their chosen riders, of course.' It was said quite without arrogance. He went on without a break. 'They're wonderful fishers too. Not only for themselves, of course. The Warden's Watch destroyed most of our boats. We'd probably starve without the Arrarat. And then there's the down.' He fingered the light, thin material of his voluminous black cloak. Eleanor touched it, and was astonished at the warmth of the fragile-seeming cloth.

Later, as they ate, Eleanor felt herself relaxing. It was something to do with the warmth, with Lukas's own happiness. She leant back against the cave wall, listening to him describe what had happened in the Banishment War.

It was an extraordinary saga, by any standards. Lukas started far back, in his grandfather's time, well before the Stasis.

A golden age, he called it. A time of peace and co-operation, of delight unthinkable in their present existence.

'We lived close together, you see,' he said, 'although by and large Astret's followers stayed in the north and west on Stromsal, and Lycias's people kept to the south and east. The city of Peraldon was a half-way house between two cultures. My family was part of a community based on Sarant, the island we passed on the way here. We often travelled to Peraldon, on our Arrarat hawks. Our cleverest children were educated there. Matthias went to a Peraldonian college . . . It was a meeting place for the best and brightest of our people.

'There was even a temple to Astret within the old city of Peraldon. In the colleges of learning both Mages and scientists pooled their knowledge, working together.'

'Who was in charge?'

'That, indirectly, was the start of all our present difficulties. Our ancestors were ruled by a Sun Emperor and Moon Empress, both elected representatives of their own religion. The Moon Empress came from the north, the Sun Emperor from the south, more often than not. A marriage of convenience, which rarely remained a dry, political bond. They ruled as equal partners, with equal power, and the Empire stretched throughout both the north and south continents. When one died, the other abdicated and a new couple were elected.'

'What about their children?' It sounded entirely unworkable.

'Adults made their own lives, their own marriages and careers. Often, girl children returned to the care of the Moon's Priestesses, boys entered the College of Priests. There was never any question of inherited power.'

In the time of Lukas's grandfather, however, there was a change. The Sun Emperor, Dorian Toussaint, was granted a special dispensation when his Empress died tragically young, in childbirth. He was also young, a man of great charisma. Popular with everyone, intelligent, courteous, courageous . . . It seemed a waste that someone with his experience and knowledge should have to step down, while still strong in mind and body.

'He was asked to retain the throne. He was reluctant, unwilling to go against such a long established tradition. In the end he agreed, provided he could marry the woman of his choice.

'Everyone agreed, with relief. He could be trusted to do the right thing. But he turned to his own cousin, Therese, a woman dedicated to Lycias. He said he would forego the Imperial throne rather than give her up. Therese was popular and well known. Everyone liked her, including the followers of Astret. But still, a Sun Empress. Such was Dorian's personal charm, his integrity, that this unusual situation was countenanced. Just this once, they thought. During the next reign, everyone agreed, there would be a Moon Empress once more.'

Lukas paused. 'One can hardly credit it, now. The trusting naivety of it, the innocence! But perhaps they were right, perhaps it would have happened as they anticipated. But at this stage Lucian Lefevre, the High Priest of the Sun, grew to prominence. And somehow, because of a situation set up by Lefevre, the thing that no one understands, the Stasis fell into place. Immortality for everyone, no death, no ageing.'

'It *sounds* all right . . .' She spoke doubtfully.

'That's what everyone thought, at first, before they realised that the Boundary could not be passed. And then it became clear that there would never be another Moon Empress anyway, because Dorian and Therese would never die. At one stroke, Astret's followers had lost all political weight.'

Long shadows from the dying fire were playing over the rock walls of the cave. She could hardly see his face, dark shaded. His voice continued, light and pleasant. Very quiet.

'Against all advice from our College of Priestesses, a group of Astret's followers took the matter into their own hands. My father was one of them. They broke into Solkest, the palace of Peraldon, and attempted to murder the Sun Emperor and his Empress.

'They succeeded only in killing Therese, an act of desperate and horrific violence. It triggered the War, not surprisingly. A furious campaign of revenge and aggression. It partly explains Nerissa's opposition to warfare, of course. There was fighting in the streets, chaos in the government. Astret's people were banished from Peraldon, the temple torn down. Some people went underground, hiding in Peraldon, rather than leave. Lefevre held the government together, while Dorian retreated into grief and despair.

'Back on Sarant, we licked our wounds, rebuilding the religion of the Lady on new terms. But something was missing, something wrong. And gradually, slowly, we began to realise just how evil the Stasis is. We were cut off from the rest of our people in the north. If time seems not to move at the Caves, a few miles north of them lies the Boundary. It is the central distortion of the Stasis, dividing us from the rest of our people by a realm where there is no time. Literally. The same instant, over and over. Anyone blundering into it becomes trapped, frozen there in that moment.

'That is bad enough, the loneliness of our existence. We do not know what has become of the lands further north, Eldin, Shelt, Hoel . . . the countries of Stromsal, that were dedicated to Astret. There is no way of crossing the

Boundary. But the worst of it, the thing that afflicts Peraldon as well, is the sterility of life under the Stasis.

'No children. No one to care for, to nurture. No life for the imagination, for creativity. Not one new idea.

'Astret Herself seems to have left us, no longer appearing in visions and dreams to Her trusted Priestesses. The women felt it worst, and threw themselves into the rites of the Lady. It drove divisions between the sexes. There is not one single marriage I can think of amongst our people that could rate as even halfway happy.

'As the Stasis ground on, the War gained momentum. We built ships and boats, and sailed on Peraldon. There were sea battles, sieges, ceaseless attacks, ceaseless violence and aggression.'

'How stupid.' She spoke clearly. Why could they not have accepted it, and enjoyed their immortality?

'We were not the only aggressors.' He spoke severely, ignoring her. 'Lefevre decided to wipe out the colony on Sarant. Because of our adherence to the Lady, we are perceived as a deep threat to the Stasis. It was at this stage that the Fosca angels entered the game.

'There was nothing we could do about them at that time, because the Arrarat would take no part in any kind of battle against them. They lifted us out at the last minute, while Sarant burnt, and brought us to the Cliff, which is where we have lived ever since. And that is where you found us, still quarrelling over whether it was worth trying to change anything.'

A long silence.

A grim saga, indeed, full of unanswered questions.

'Why ever did Dorian choose Therese?'

'The key to it all, you might say.' He frowned. 'Love can be such a powerful distorting factor. There must surely be a place for judgment too. The world well lost does not seem to me to be a reasonable excuse.'

There was a pause and then he stood up, moving forward into the light. 'Enough of the past. Are you ready, Eleanor? Shall we see who the Arrarat have got lined up for you?'

She drew in her breath, her palms suddenly clammy.

This was why they were here.

He went to the edge of the cave and stood still for a moment, gazing out into the appalling space before him. He gave a strange low cry, similar to the summoning call he had used on the beach. Gradually the chatter of the numberless birds became softer.

'Hear me, Arrarat!' His voice rang clear, magnified in mysterious echoes. 'We are, as ever, indebted to you, and now there comes a stranger needing help –' He beckoned Eleanor forward.

She approached the cave mouth, and then the background chatter of birds ceased as she stood in the light from the great fire.

She felt she should say something into this enormous silence, but words were superfluous. She could only think of excuses anyway. As if weighted, her arms slowly rose and stretched out into the space where the birds lived. For a moment, silence hung heavy around them all.

Then there was a sudden clatter of falling rocks and beating wings as a huge black shape hurled itself into the space below them.

A hawk, its plumage darker than night. It wheeled round the central fire three times before swinging, arrogant in strength, in a lazy spiral up towards them. There was no sound beyond its wing-beat. Its golden eyes glinted in the firelight, its black strength transformed light and colour into power.

Lukas moved once, uncontrollably, as the wide sweeping circles began to centre in towards them. With a rush, bright eyes implacable, it gathered speed, and raced straight for them.

She did not move: her arms held wide, she waited. The midnight hawk fell out of the fiery air to join her in the cave mouth. In breathless silence, it laid its glossy head against hers. As if nothing could be more natural, she wrapped her arms round the strong black neck, and felt the alien heart beating next to her own. Then she stood back, and let her arms drop. They regarded each other in silence, bird and girl, and discovered that a bond now existed, undeniable and enduring.

She stood still, allowing a vast power to flow into her

mind. Pushing back the boundaries of experience, illuminating and expanding. There was no limit to this feeling of breadth, of wide stretches opened up for her. She caught at the edge of an endless sky, wild wind, the lift and lilt of flight. She felt that she was on the brink of extraordinary knowledge, extraordinary understanding. She was faint with the wonder of it.

She knew why Lukas had said that words were inadequate.

Most strongly of all, underlying it all, was the sense that she was no longer alone. The light that shone in her mind was now a shared burden, a shared enchantment. There was no explanation for it. All that mattered was that there was someone with her, someone with a deep and powerful understanding, strong, loving and passionate. She was no longer abandoned to the whims of this strange world. She sighed, as if released, and lightly ran wondering fingers over the smooth ebony feathers.

An image flowed through her mind, a gentle fall of dust, soft and light.

'Your name is Ash,' she said quietly, in recognition.

The Arrarat inclined his head, once. His beauty was breathtaking, the way the light glossed over the deep dark feathers, in darting shades of emerald and turquoise and violet.

For a moment he allowed her to run her hands over the dry, warm feathers. Then he turned silently away and, without a backward glance, plunged back into the dizzying void.

She stared after him, already missing his presence, obsessively following the wide stretch of black wings, until he was lost amongst the other Arrarat far away beyond the firelight.

'Well,' said Lukas softly, coming up behind her. 'I never thought to see a midnight Arrarat, and here you are naming one as your own. I feel I understand not the smallest part of this.'

She was still trying to see where Ash had gone and hardly heard him. What could she say, anyway?

'You know, you're going to have to tell me what happened

on the beach before we left,' he said eventually. 'There's too much unexplained now.'

He lifted one hand, and brushed the hair back from her face, exposing the small scar once more.

She sighed. 'Is there any more of that fish stuff left?' she said, stepping away from him. 'I'm still hungry.'

'Oh yes,' he replied. 'Yes, let's have some more to eat. It may of course all become clearer on a full stomach.' He turned away from her, beginning to cut bread.

In the event she could eat nothing more. For a while, she sat at the edge of the cave, watching the desultory circling of birds beneath and beyond. Everything had changed once more, another shift of perspective, because Ash had entered her life.

Perhaps her old life was beginning to lose its grip. There had been nothing like the Arrarat there, after all, among the round of work and parties, lovers and family. What would her mother have thought, confronted with the flight of an Arrarat hawk? She would have reached for a strong gin, probably finding a way to blame Eleanor's father for it.

Eleanor smiled. It no longer seemed quite so threatening, so worrying. Looking back over her past, she remembered a dazzling array of trivialities. New cars, what film to see, whether the hem was too long, who Rob was moaning to, what Lewis thought, her father's latest girlfriend . . . a series of bizarre and ludicrous preoccupations. Nothing there could match Ash.

She was still stunned by the experience: Ash's strength, the unswerving courage, the way he had stepped into her thoughts with such loving compassion and released the limits of her imagination.

She wondered why she did not resent this intrusion into her mind. It was not constant, of course, fading as soon as Ash had flown away. And there was also the element of choice; she had welcomed him into her mind, and knew that she could have held back.

They would have to be physically close, and deliberately wanting to make contact, before it would happen again. It was still enough to make her feel like singing.

Lukas was preoccupied, washing the dishes and pans,

building up the fire, laying out soft sleeping bags at either side of the cave. When at last she stood up, stretching, and went to wash at the pool at the back of the cave, he looked up, and said to her, seriously:

'Tired, Eleanor? Never mind, there's no rush now, is there? You've found your hawk, started on the journey. And tomorrow you shall meet Reckert, whom you may find useful.' He paused, azure eyes examining her face. 'And I wish to hell I knew what to make of you, and what you're doing.'

'So do I,' she said softly.

He gave a small laugh. 'Sweet dreams, and don't worry if you wake in the night and I'm not here. I may go to prepare Reckert for his distinguished visitor.'

The smile in his eyes defused the sarcasm.

She settled into the bag, and pulled it up around her. She drifted into sleep, but later awoke to find the cave empty. Lukas had gone; but she was too tired to worry. She turned over and soon fell asleep again.

Chapter Eighteen
Reckert

She awoke to the smell of frying fish. Lukas was sitting by the fire, turning fresh silver fish in a pan. She rolled over and sat up, pushing her hair back. Still here, not back in her flat, still in the dream. But instead of being depressed she felt a curious joy, for the Moon had found in her something considerable, and Ash had chosen her.

'Do you never do anything but eat?' she said.

He smiled. 'It's just that I feel warm sustenance is required before encountering Reckert.'

'Who is he?'

'Reckert? He lives here with the Arrarat, has studied them for years. He trained under Lefevre, but was outlawed during the Banishment War. A very useful man, is Reckert, but not easy.' He slid fish onto a plate.

'Breakfast in bed, lady? We'll call on Reckert before we set off.' He paused. 'Where are we going, by the way?'

Unhesitating, she pointed south.

'That's Peraldonian territory, that way,' he said. 'Not a restful place for Cavers.'

'I'm not a Caver. And I didn't ask you to come,' she said ungraciously.

'True.' Ruefully he stood up and looked down at her. 'Unbend a little, my dear. Why must we go south?'

'Because that's where the light is.'

'Which light?'

The one I see in my mind the whole time, she wanted to answer, the one welded into my soul by the Moon, but it would sound too silly.

'I can't explain,' she said flatly. For a long disturbing moment his eyes held hers, as they had done once before, when she had first arrived here. Again, she shivered, with that odd feather touch of fear.

She did her best to tidy up at the rainwater pool and then ate some of the cooling fish. Lukas had finished already and was sitting with his long legs dangling over the edge of the cave, watching the flight of birds. She didn't know him well enough to assess his mood. She didn't know him at all.

When she had finished breakfast, Lukas showed her how to call the Arrarat. It was less difficult than she had expected, a simple, low-pitched arpeggio. No longer was she panicked by the prospect of a solo journey, either. Eleanor could hardly wait. To fly, alone, with her extraordinary companion.

Leaving the ordinary world behind, a flight with Ash, unknown and enthralling.

The two great hawks blocked the light from the centre of the cave as they alighted on the ledge. Ash, huge, black and powerful, Astrella, the softest of greys, every line informed with grace. A wild surge of exhilaration as she looked at them.

Lukas greeted his Arrarat with easy affection.

Eleanor took a deep breath and stretched out a hand towards Ash. A slight inclination of his head, a generous feeling of welcome, and she tried to climb up unaided. She was still ungainly, but Lukas pointed out the two shoulder bones which gave some purchase. When she was at last in place, he fitted Ash with leather straps he produced from one of the rucksacks, so that he could be ridden in safety.

Then there was a sickening drop as the birds swooped from the ledge into the void below. This flight was brief; for one dreadful instant, Eleanor wondered if she was going to tumble off into the great central fire, but at the last moment Ash's wings fluttered and they put down on the warm dusty floor some yards from the blaze.

It was all she needed, a flight over fire, and she knew that only death would come between them.

From ground level she could see that it was not a bonfire, as she had assumed. The roaring flames sprang direct from a crevasse in the rock floor beneath them. Gas, she thought, or the vapour from oil . . . It was almost too hot to bear, even there, so they quickly moved back towards the rock, and the hawks took off again.

'Reckert! Where are you?' called Lukas, looking round the rows of cave entrances. 'It's not that I can't remember where he lives,' he explained to Eleanor, 'but he will keep moving round. What we need is a scurry.'

He looked round, peering closely at what appeared to be perfectly ordinary rocks and boulders. Abruptly, he nudged one of the rocks with his foot, and it came to life, detaching itself from the others.

It was one of the most bizarre figures Eleanor had ever seen. No more than two feet tall, its outline was almost impossible to distinguish. Coloured grey like the rock around them, it also reflected the glow of the fire and the sandy floor. It consisted of loose moving folds of skin which mimicked the shapes of the objects it passed, becoming first rock, then fire, then the folds of Lukas's cloak.

It was, she realised, fascinated, the perfect chameleon, changing both colour and form to blend with its background. It was difficult to see anything resembling eyes or ears in the featureless folds of skin.

Eleanor found it repulsive and worrying in the way it insinuated itself into its surroundings. Even as she watched, knowing where it was, her eyes kept stubbornly glancing over it. It slid and wavered its way towards them.

'Minis-scurry,' it said in a high, wheedling voice, diverse folds of skin vibrating. 'Follow.' It turned around and headed off over the dusty plain to the caves on their right.

'What is it?' she whispered to Lukas.

'Just a scurry. That one's called Minis. They always announce their names before speaking because you can never tell one from the other – or from its surroundings.'

'They're revolting!' He glanced at her, surprised by the strength of her reaction.

'Not really,' he said. 'They're quite useful in a way. Reckert has them as servants – he smuggled the originals out from Peraldon when he left. Lefevre created them, in his workshops. They're unusual in Peraldon, though. Lefevre likes to reserve them as spies for his own personal use.'

'Does it understand what we say?' she said with distaste.

'Every word. And in whatever language you use, too. That's their other function, as translators. Reckert says he uses them to communicate with the Arrarat. For some reason, he can't understand them any other way.'

'Even though he lives here with them?'

'He was never chosen, you see. It goes a long way to explain why he's – rather difficult. It must be a disappointment to him. If you are chosen, you understand the Arrarat. It's as simple as that.' He paused, looking at her. 'You know what I'm talking about now, don't you?'

She nodded.

'It's not all bad, is it?'

No, she thought, not with the Moon's light, not with Ash sharing her thoughts and life. It was not constant, this feeling of companionship. More as if occasionally she hit the right wavelength, and found Ash there, waiting for her, a source of strength and love.

The scurry led them uncomfortably close to the fire, round to a cave in the far wall. There it stopped, blending into the rock surface, and a man emerged from the black cave mouth.

He was thin, elderly, and almost bald, with a greasy lock of grey hair that kept flopping over his eyes. He was shabby, dressed in an unlikely, grubby version of white tie and tails. He wore a long cloak, lined with bird feathers, slung over one hunched shoulder. His wrinkled neck, almost lost above the grey wing collar and the high shoulders, was in need of a good wash.

'Well now,' he said slowly. 'Let's see who has taken my beautiful black hawk.' He smiled suddenly, warmly, at Eleanor and clasped her by the hand. His small grey eyes were shining, softening the effect of the rigid beaked nose.

'And what brings such a very strange stranger to my little island? Did Lukas promise you an Arrarat for your convenience?'

'Yes, as it happens.' She snatched her hand back and stared down her nose at him. She didn't like him, with his shiny bald head and patronising words.

He was unworried, exchanging glances with Lukas.

'And just why has my most glorious Arrarat chosen you,

little lady? It seems, shall we say, a little unlikely?'

'Need we listen to this?' she flared to Lukas. He said nothing, lounging back against the rock face, watching, considering. But as she turned to look at him, the light from the fire caught the small silver scar on her forehead, and Reckert exclaimed, and caught her again by the arm.

'Who are you, then, you with the Lady's mark?' He spat the words at her. She shrank away, dismayed.

'What's it got to do with you? Lukas, I've had enough of this. Let's go.'

'No, no, not yet.' Reckert let go of her arm, but stayed close, thrusting his face close to hers.

'From another world, no doubt? Entranced by a silver lady?' His breath smelt foul, and she wanted to get away. But now Lukas's attention was caught.

'What are you talking about, Reckert? What silver lady?'

'Ah, my old friend Lukas, noble champion of our Lady Moon, don't you recognise an ally when you see one?' And then the cynical laughter vanished from his tone and he said, staring her full in the eyes, 'Your pretty little friend has met more than Cavers here, Lukas. Ask her how she got that scar.'

Lukas shook his head. 'I have. She won't tell.'

'Oh yes she will.' She tried to pull herself free but his grip on her wrist was painfully strong. With one hand he reached into a pocket, extracting some grains of powder, which he flung into the small cooking fire within the cave entrance.

She was trying to twist away from him, hardly noticing the clouds of smoke drifting from the fire. He was laughing at her again, at her fury and dislike. She kicked and pushed, but he wouldn't let go. She couldn't see Lukas now in the grey smoke.

A heavy cloying scent arose, of cloves and musk and dying flowers, befuddling the senses, masking clear thought. The floor began to waver beneath her feet. Her head was throbbing. She swayed, struggling to keep a grip on understanding, trying to remember why she didn't like him, why she wasn't going to tell him anything.

'But you have no choice,' the light thin voice replied to her thoughts, 'And Lukas needs an answer, too . . .'

It seemed that the smoke was pulling her memory from her, giving it solid shape around her. The firelight was no longer warm but cold and bright, and the dusty floor became sodden sand. Most terrifying of all, the elderly, mocking figure of Reckert dissolved and instead the figure of the Moon was there, singing . . .

But the clarity was almost lost in the smoke, the truth and the power. Only the terror, and the words, echoing, dragged from her mind, resounding in the air.

She found herself awestricken, kneeling in the dust, knuckles pressed against teeth, tears soundlessly streaming. And it was her own voice that repeated the Moon's words, reciting, reliving it, terror, beauty, bewilderment and all.

And so Lukas, shocked and fascinated, knew why she was here.

She slumped sideways onto the ground. Again, rough warm voices woke her. But this time, Lukas was gentle, worried, somehow apologetic. He helped her up and sat her on a ledge, brought her water, wiped away tears.

She was in a daze, unable to think straight or to act. All she understood was that something evil had happened, and that her precious secret was now revealed. She was unwilling to consider the implications of this.

Listlessly she watched and listened to Lukas and Reckert discuss what to do next.

They were in agreement; a meeting was to be called, Nerissa, Stefan Pryse and the Mages informed, an embassy sent to Jeren, to Selene Derray on Peraldon. Her encounter with the Moon would become public property; they would base political acts on it, would continue their useless battles fired by the inspiration of it.

She loathed them all; she was shaken beyond words by the rape of her memory and furious that she had not protected the Moon's secret better. The Moon had spoken to her alone, had made no mention of anyone else. She had a clear path to follow, a lodestar beckoning her onwards, and it had nothing to do with councils, embassies, strategies and battle-plans.

She felt that she had betrayed a trust. She didn't know how to make amends.

Lukas returned to her. His eyes were bright with excitement, his walk loose-limbed and confident.

'Eleanor!' he said, smiling down at her. 'Wonderful girl! Don't you see, this makes all the difference? We have something we can use now, some real knowledge! All due to you!'

Unable to bear it, she scrambled to her feet, pale and furious.

'Damn you!' she shouted to him. 'I hate you and your horrible friend! I wouldn't help your precious cause if it was the last thing on earth, I loathe you and your pathetic Cavers and your stinking fish!'

He raised an eyebrow in mild surprise, but was too euphoric to take her seriously. 'Look,' he said placatingly, 'I'm sorry Reckert had to use that drug on you, but it's vital that we know just what the Lady wants. You should have told us to begin with, then there would have been no need to make you go through all that again. But now we can really get going –'

He had not noticed Ash silently alight just to one side of Reckert's cave, neither was he prepared for Eleanor's sudden action as she picked up the full beaker of water and flung it straight in his face.

Then she ran to Ash, leapt up onto his back. Black wings stretched wide and high. Together they sprang up into the fiery air towards the dark opening which led out over the sea. She was too furious to care if she was followed, too angry to notice that she'd left everything behind.

'Which way?' She said it aloud, but the reply in her mind made no sound.

Ash knew what to do, where to go. No sooner did they strike the bitter cold of the sodden air than he wheeled about and flew straight over the top of the hollow mountain that was Arrarat Isle.

She laughed with incredulous triumph. Ash was following the light that burned so clearly in the back of her mind. He was following the Moon's light. He understood all her thoughts, all her longing, swept away all her fear.

She crouched low on his back, clenching her fingers

round the leather strap, trying to duck below the worst of the wind. Within seconds her dress was drenched, her hair whipping wet and stinging across her face. The wild euphoria abruptly deserted her. She began to shiver. She understood waves of confidence and reassurance from Ash, and leant forward against his neck, trying to warm her hands in the deep feathers.

No stars or moon were visible in the cloud of rain. She could hear nothing beyond the howling wind all around, the flapping of her sodden dress.

The Arrarat flew swiftly on, never hesitating, only changing direction to take advantage of slight shifts in the wind. She lost all sense of time as they dashed through the air; fingers numb, she could only rely on Ash's intuitive knowledge to take her to safety, somewhere, soon.

Then, shock. His anger suddenly flared through her mind. Ash abruptly banked to one side and she almost lost her grip at the sharpness of the movement. Then there was a whistling gust of freezing air as some other huge bird blundered into their path. A high scream vanished into the night. Grasping Ash firmly with her knees, Eleanor swung round to see what had so nearly collided with them.

In the dusk she could just make out a spiky outline, crazily darting away.

Was it a bird at all? She felt deep unease as she began to realise that no bird ever flew so jerkily, or so fast . . .

Ash swooped again, ducking sharply to the right. This time she caught a rank smell of rotting flesh, saw the grey-white frills around the face, the blank lidless eyes of an inhuman rider, the gaping mouth shrieking at them. It was on the back of something that was not a bird at all, but a reptilian, scaled creature.

Nausea rose in her throat; the petal-framed face contained such alien intelligence, such vivid malevolence that she knew the near-collisions were not accidental.

Again it sprang out of the night at them, and she saw that the rider was reaching out with long, strangely jointed limbs, and claws were ripping through the air.

Gasping, she swung herself down round Ash's neck and the tip of a curved talon lightly raked at her shoulder. Pure anger supplanted fear; she sat upright on the broad back, and looked after it, weighing their chances. Her eyes were well adjusted to the dark by now; in the streaming rain she could see the predatory shadow poised above and behind them. Daring, high on adrenalin, she clutched at the leather strap, waited until it began another assault, waited as it darted towards them, waited until it was nearly on them.

Then, 'Drop!' she hissed into the air, and Ash instantaneously stilled his wings and plummeted like a stone for a brief, heart-stopping second.

'Up – to the left!' she breathed and almost laughed as the reptile creature overshot them, screaming with fury. It recovered immediately, and swung round to try again.

A rush of air behind them, a grasp of claws slashing through air, a vicious burning pain just below her ear, and another flying thing spun past them wailing into the night. Ash dropped and surged. She found she no longer had to speak – the thought had only to cross her mind and Ash swerved and soared, adding his own wild flourishes and embellishments to the crazy flight.

There were two; no, three, four of the lizard things now, wheeling round them. It was beyond excitement now; their only hope was that their attackers were not actually trying to kill them: it was more as if they were trying to push them in one direction, back towards Ararat Isle.

Powerful and graceful though Ash was, moving with wit and elegance, he was no match for the mind-wrenching agility of these scaled creatures. The curved claws flying out on multiple limbs ripped and tore. She could not see much of the riders, for they crouched low behind the lizard heads, grasping like parasitic incubi, screaming on the narrow edge of audibility.

Ash was beginning to tire. Although they had so far evaded serious injury, both were covered with small cuts and scratches that bled and stung in the rain. Panic had taken over from anger. What if they could not get away?

If only she could see. They were too quick, leaping out of the dark at them. She did not have enough in the way of warning to prepare Ash. She started to pray that the Moon might come out, just so that she could see more clearly where to go, where they were coming from, and then drew a ragged breath as power flooded her mind.

She remembered the Moon, and the vast white light that echoed in her soul.

She remembered the wide sweep of Ash's imagination.

'Come, come now,' she whispered out into the rain, half a prayer, half an incantation.

For a moment it seemed that the wheeling dance of bird and dark angel was held still, locked in position. Then the clouds parted, rolling swiftly aside, and the enormous shining face of the empowered Moon gleamed down onto the wilderness beneath. Brilliant, stunning light flooded the heavens.

Eleanor reached forward to shield Ash's eyes with her hands. She was laughing with wild ecstasy. She saw the reptiles, stunned and maddened by the cold bright glare, turn tail and flee. Inaudible, lunatic screams shredded the air above the level of consciousness. Then there was peace.

Ash flew steadily on, gradually losing height, eyes almost closed against the unaccustomed streaming light. Eleanor gazed up into the austere, overwhelming face of the Moon and was engulfed by fierce joy. She was no cipher here. The Moon would lend her power, would give her a role, would make her life meaningful. She need worry no more; the decisions would be taken for her.

In the distance, in the unnatural white moonlight, she could see a tree-filled island jutting out of the sea. As they approached it, the clouds began to roll back over the Moon's face. Darkness once more dominated the landscape; she was alone with Ash.

As they drew nearer the island, and her eyes became used to the dark again, she realised that the trees were so tall that their tops were hidden in cloud. They towered, huge and black, over the small sandy beach that ran along the shoreline.

Ash put down a little heavily on the wet sand, and Eleanor slid wearily from his back. Her knees buckled beneath her. She staggered unsteadily to a rock and sat down. She ought to see to Ash, she thought tiredly, although she didn't know what to do to help him. Sighing, she got up and began to examine the hawk.

Ash gazed calmly back at her, and began to preen himself, ruffling and shaking out the blood-stained feathers so that the rain could wash them clean. His wounds were not serious. He could find his own food. He would be all right.

She subsided once more onto the rock, and looked around her. The trees lining the narrow beach were far taller than any she had ever seen before, reaching up out of sight into dark rain-clouds. The shadows around the massive trunks were black and unknown.

She sighed as her scratches began to sting again, now the excitement was over. She was bitterly cold, too, unable to stop her teeth chattering. The worst slash was to her neck, just behind the ear; another inch or two and it would have caught the vein, she thought dispassionately. She bent down and with some difficulty managed to tear a small patch from the hem of her dress. She rolled it up and held it to the wound, wondering what to do next.

She was not surprised when she heard the heavy sound of beating wings and saw Astrella and Lukas swoop down onto the beach. She watched with some amusement as he slid off and unloaded the panniers before coming towards her. He looked both tired and angry.

'That was some display,' he said coolly. 'How did you pull it off? Wave a magic wand or something?' He was extremely cross. She decided to ignore it.

'I'm cold,' she said mildly, as if nothing had happened. 'Did you bring my cloak?'

He bent down, tore open a rucksack and flung the cloak at her. She was too grateful for its warmth to mind his anger.

'How did you get here?' she asked, politely. 'Did the Arrarat communicate with each other?'

'They may have done.' He was curt. 'We followed you. What the hell do you mean by running out like that?'

'I don't like your friend, or his tricks. I don't have to put up with treatment like that.' The arrogance in her voice was acid and unpleasant even to her own ears. She decided to moderate her tone. 'What happened then?'

'We were quite a way behind and lost you in the cloud. Next thing I know, the sky's all awash with light, and there are you and Ash making for Jeren.'

'Is that all you saw?'

'Oh yes, there were three or four Fosca, dazzled and running. An everyday occurrence.'

There was silence. Eleanor felt unequal to this. She just wanted him to settle down, find her some shelter and start frying fish again. She'd had quite enough confrontation for one day.

She stood up and went over to the rucksacks, rummaging through for something to eat. Impatiently he took the bag from her, saying, 'We need to find shelter first. Don't unpack here.'

'Why are you so angry?' she asked. For the first time since his arrival he looked directly at her.

Bedraggled darkened hair, rain running like tears constantly over the pale skin, eyes wide and considering in the dreary half-light. Also, with irritation, he noticed the scratches, the cut on her neck. But she was confident now, sure of herself for the first time since appearing so suddenly on the damp sand by the fire, and he did not know, really, how to handle it.

'You could have been killed, running out like that!' You're far too valuable to us for that to happen, he implied. 'What have you got against Mortimer Reckert then? He only tried to find out the truth in order to help.'

'He's evil! There's something really vile about him, loathsome. He's no friend to the Moon!' She was impassioned, trusting strongly to instinct.

'Don't be ridiculous. He's eccentric, that's all. It may have offended your precious sensibilities to be drugged, and I must admit it's not the way I would choose myself, but we have to know where we stand. You just don't understand.'

He took some lint from the bag and began to cut a strip for the cut on her neck.

'I'm not offended!' She stepped away from him. 'Those – those flying things, what are they called?'

'Fosca. I told you before. Dark angels. Flying monsters invented by Lefevre during the Banishment War. They're mercenaries.'

'They, the Fosca, were trying to push us back towards Arrarat Isle. They weren't out to kill us – they could certainly have done that without even trying. They were just trying to herd us back to Reckert. They were probably working for him.'

'Rubbish. The Fosca only ever work for Peraldonians. We can't afford their prices. And Reckert is certainly with us, on our side. He has been as long as I can remember. Besides, the Arrarat trust him.'

'They don't communicate with him. He's never been chosen. They're probably just keeping an eye on him!'

'You don't know what you're talking about. You've been here hardly any time at all. You have no idea what Reckert has done for us in the past. He is almost a Mage, works closely with Blaise and the others. He has a great deal of influence with them. We – and the Arrarat – owe him an enormous debt.'

This was unanswerable. They both looked at the two great birds, still preening on the sand.

Then, as they watched, with one accord the Arrarat took off, flying straight up into the cloud, and disappeared.

'Where are they going?' she asked him, feeling bereft once more.

'Fishing, I expect.' He paused. 'They'll be back when we need them.' The anger had gone from his voice; it was as if the flight of Astrella and Ash, so infinitely graceful and powerful, had swept away all the irritation.

He grinned suddenly at her. 'Come on, Eleanor. Give it a break. We'll finish this some other time. Let's see to that scratch first, and then we'll go and find my old friend Thurstan and get a bed for the night.'

Not ungently, he washed and covered the wound, and then, as if she were a good child, gave her a small oatcake to eat. They gathered up the panniers and set off along the beach.

He explained as they walked that they were on Jeren, an island much larger than Arrarat Isle, inhabited by the Cavers' allies, the Jerenites.

'They're not followers of Astret, though,' he said. 'They left Sarant at the start of the Stasis, disliking the Rule of Astret. Instead of priests or Mages they're ruled by the Lady Martitia Merauld. Thurstan is her son. I've known him as long as I can remember. I come here quite often, although Nerissa doesn't approve. She has never liked the Jerenites, but the alliance has endured, even after they left Sarant, to our mutual advantage.'

'What holds you together if it's not religion?' she asked.

'A common past and a shared hatred for Peraldon,' he said grimly. 'The Jerenites are natural rebels, really, and didn't like being told what to do. It goes back a long way. We have the same ancestors. But divisions developed within the community on Sarant.'

'Why?'

'Not everyone is religious. A bit wild, they are.' He smiled. 'Artists, actors, musicians . . . they were responsible for most of the entertainments in those days, the theatres, galleries, concerts . . . It was fine in peace time; they were appreciated by everyone. But they were never chosen by the Arrarat, you see. And when the Stasis began, and we realised that the religion of the Lady was under serious threat, they decided to leave.

'Not their problem, they maintained. They wanted nothing to do with what they saw as a fanatical adherence to the Lady. Or with sectarian violence. They put their trust in a fleet of old boats and rafts, and set out to seek their fortunes. Dreamers and dissidents, they are, underneath it all. Most of them survived, made it as far as Jeren. That's when they began to call themselves Jerenites. Lefevre kept them penned in here north of the mainland, and no one got any further. The policy of non-involvement got them nowhere. They were almost wiped out in the Banishment War, in a series of unprovoked attacks. Not because they were anything to do with Astret, but because they were essentially subversive, unwilling to accept the official line. They haven't forgotten, those who are left.'

They were tramping along the wet beach next to the sea, and she was still cold, not quite recovered from the shock of the Fosca attack. She wanted diversion, something else to think about.

Lukas had fallen silent.

'What about Reckert? Where does he fit in?'

'A native Peraldonian who fell in love with the Arrarat

long ago, before the Stasis. He couldn't bear to give them up, you see, when we were banished from Peraldon.'

'So he left too?'

'That's it.' He stopped and looked at her. Rain was streaking through his dark hair and he looked sombre and certain. 'You'll have to get used to him,' he said. 'He's too powerful in all our lives to be offended.'

'Are you afraid of him, then?' She was contemptuous.

'No.' He answered her without heat. 'He has proved himself time and again our friend. I could tell you stories long into the night, of the help Reckert has given us, tireless and unstinting. I would not have him offended because I like the man.'

'Does he like you?' She couldn't leave it alone.

Lukas sighed, and wearily reached out, tucking the cloak more securely around her. 'Don't be a pain, girl. He's all right. Trust me.' And, as she followed him along the shore, she was surprised to find that she did, indeed, trust him.

Chapter Nineteen
Doubts

'Is the Stasis breaking up? Was the prophecy true?'

'Did you ever doubt?'

Matthias Marling, eyes unfathomable, looked at the Mage Lye. 'Oh, yes,' he breathed. 'I have doubted. I still do. Do you really think it's working, just because a girl appeared on the sand?'

Thibaud Lye shrugged and poked the fire at their feet.

They were in the Mages' private quarters, set far back in the Caver Cliff, through an unmarked maze of passages.

Mortimer Reckert was with them, his tatty feathery cloak giving off unsavoury clouds of steam as it dried by the fire. He stood quietly, near the door, saying little. He was no stranger to the four Mages, having worked with them since the start of the Stasis, although he had never been able to accept the Lady's Rule. Instead, Reckert had decided to stay with the Arrarat.

The Mages and Mortimer Reckert only ever met on Arrarat Isle, because the Arrarat refused to fly with him. But things were changing. That evening, an Arrarat hawk had brought him across the stormy seas to the Caves, he said. He knew that some crisis must be at hand.

Books lined three sides of the walls. Strange glass shapes stood on velvet-lined shelves on the fourth side, not bottles, but triangles, spirals, globes and hexagons. Coloured green, blue, gold and brown, they reflected the spluttering light from the torches in brackets round the walls. Only the central fire lit all their faces into rosy warmth.

'It may be nothing to do with her at all,' said Aylmer Alard, stooping his thin body, round-shouldered, over the fire. 'She could still be just a side effect. The Stasis may be at risk now, but it won't end until the Benu Bird is released. You know that as well as I do.'

Educated in Peraldonian colleges, trained in magic and disguise, introduced to the abstruse, Cabbalistic theories of Synchronicity, they all knew what held their world together. Beyond their studies, beyond all the mysteries of both Astret and Lycias, leaping beyond the limits of imagination, or human understanding . . . the Benu Bird, whose flight governed the passing of time, the context of all life.

'It is still not free.' Thibaud Lye was emphatic. 'We would have had a dawn by now. The Benu must still be imprisoned, but . . .'

'Lefevre's control is not what it was?' Matthias looked at his companions, raising one eyebrow. 'Can he – just possibly – have lost the Benu? Has he no longer absolute power over the Bird of Time?'

'I find that an extremely unlikely proposition.' Alard's voice was arid and high in the sultry cave.

'It is the only possible explanation.' The sightless face of the Great Mage Blaise was turned reflectively towards the fire.

'We will need another Saying to make sure,' Reckert spoke at last. He was still in shadow, his eyes flickering from face to face.

'Another death, you mean?' Matthias sounded bitter. The picture of Oswald's distress still hung in his mind.

'How else are we to find out?' Reckert looked at him with impatience. 'We cannot afford to remain in ignorance now!'

'Let us review what we do know,' said Blaise quietly. 'One. At the last Saying, Astret spoke. Richenda died, I know, and that is sad for us, a tragedy for Oswald. But the only thing that ultimately matters is that Astret spoke through her. Our Lady has not been able to speak to us directly since the Stasis began.

'Two. We followed Her instructions exactly. Again, the obvious result, the girl Eleanor, may not appear to be what we wanted, but what matters is that there has been a change. Something new has happened here, the Seventh Rite of Synchronicity has altered something. Someone from outside the Stasis has appeared, and who knows what she may yet do?'

'Precious little, I'll wager,' said Thibaud sourly.

'It's beyond our control now anyway,' said Matthias. He had been dreading this moment. 'She's gone.'

'Gone? Where?' The Mages swung round to face him, and anger crackled in the air. As he explained he watched their distrust and disbelief grow.

'You let her go? With your fool of a brother?' Aylmer's voice was shaking.

'Short of force, there was nothing I could do to stop her –'

'You didn't even consult us!' Thibaud said excitedly.

'Lukas will at least keep her alive –'

'We'll have get her back.' Thibaud, again.

'I did try,' said Reckert mildly. 'They stopped on Arrarat Isle overnight. She was chosen by a midnight Arrarat. I tried to delay them, but there was a misunderstanding. I imagine they're on Jeren by now.'

'There's nothing we can do. She appeared to feel that she had some instructions to go south . . . something happened on the seashore . . .' Matthias looked suddenly at the elderly, shabby little man. 'Did you find out anything else about her?' he asked.

There was an infinitesimal pause before he answered. 'Not enough to go on,' he said. 'There is something there, some mystery, but to make any sense of it I think you should indeed hold another Saying.'

'Nerissa won't allow it,' said Aylmer.

'She shouldn't be asked to!' Matthias sprang to his feet. 'She has just lost her dearest Priestess! You must be mad to think she would countenance such a thing! The last Saying was held against her will.'

'It's all right, Matthias, no one will ask you to take responsibility again,' said Thibaud kindly. His pale grey eyes met Reckert's thoughtfully. 'We could put it to the vote. Nerissa's authority is not what it was.'

'There's a good chance we'd carry it.' Aylmer was confident. He stood up, a tall, gaunt figure, dwarfing the others. 'What do you say, Blaise? Another Saying?'

The Great Mage, who had remained seated throughout, blind face turned to the fire, said quietly, 'It is unnecessary. Matthias is right. Nerissa should not be asked to permit another Saying. One of her priestesses would almost certainly lose her life again, if it worked, and if it didn't the whole exercise would be futile. Things are happening. The girl has been chosen by an Ararat. And have you forgotten the death of the Peraldonian woman?'

He seemed to stare at each of them in turn, and there was no reply. 'There is a possibility – a slight possibility – that the Stasis is under threat now. We must wait and see. There is no need for us to do anything else for the time being. We should risk nothing further.'

His words were always respected, and his advice was always both sane and constructive. For the moment they let it rest.

Risk nothing further. Stefan Pryse, tramping down the corridor to Margat's cave, felt it engraved on his heart. For that one desperate attempt, eighteen men had died. The Mages asked too much, Lukas Marling asked too much. And where was Lukas now? On some wild, irrelevant adventure, leaving his sister Margat to cope with the crippling of her son.

He knocked on the door, and Letia opened it. At another time he might have smiled, for he liked her warmth, her bright courage.

'Stefan! Fabian will be so glad to see you, he's awake now . . .' She stepped back and let him into the overheated cave.

He looked round for somewhere to put his cloak, squinting in the sudden light, and found it taken from his hands. Margat was standing in front of him, looking at him quizzically.

'Come in, Stefan. Fabian has been waiting for you.'

Her wild black hair had been caught back in a silver clasp and the bones of her face showed clear and elegant. There were dark rings beneath her eyes, and new lines of stress showed in the fine ivory skin.

She started to move towards the curtained alcove

across the cave, but he caught her hand for a moment.

'Are you sleeping, Margat? You don't have to do all the nursing alone?'

'What, with Letia and Niclaus forever here?' She smiled towards the older woman, standing at the fire.

'If you need more help, you will let me know, won't you? I hope, now that Lukas has left, you will come to me, if you need anything . . .' He was not an articulate man, but knew what he wanted to say.

'This is kind of you, Stefan, but truly we are managing, and Caspar is always here, of course.' He was always disconcerted by the faint suggestion of amusement in her voice. Even now, with one of her sons lying desperately ill, one brother missing, and the other under general disapproval, he wondered whether she was laughing at him.

Fabian was lying propped on pillows, playing cards with his twin, Caspar. Although they shared the same dark hair and blue eyes, Fabian was white as the sheet rumpled around him, and his eyes were hazy with pain. The blankets were held in a cage away from the remains of his right leg, and every now and then he shifted, trying to ease it. He looked desperately tired, flushed with fever.

Caspar stood up as Stefan came in, bowing formally. Stefan took his chair, and looked at the injured boy.

'I'm sorry . . . about the leg,' he said, and because he was sincere no one minded the inadequacy of the words.

'We lost eighteen men,' said Fabian simply. 'What does it matter, except that I shall be even less use now?'

'Stefan, you will stay for supper tonight?' Letia called through the curtain. 'We've got plenty.'

'We're waiting for Matthias.' Fabian looked up at him. 'He's caught up in some conference with the other Mages.'

'Poor Matt,' said Margat, sitting on the edge of Fabian's bed. 'They'll be putting him through it.'

'I've survived to tell the tale.' A quiet voice from the doorway, and Matthias came in.

Letia set out wine then, and began to serve the supper.

Although Fabian was in pain and Matthias abstracted,

the meal was shot through with a kind of gentle warmth. Later, thinking about it, Matthias remembered it as the calm before the great storm, as if they all knew that change would soon seize and shatter them all. This was their last chance to seal their companionship.

Blaise, alone in his cave set deep into the cliff, was waiting for his murderer to arrive.

He knew it would be soon. He was not afraid, for he had looked forward to death for a long time now, but he regretted that he would not see whether the hazard had worked.

Staring sightless at the golden spiral hanging over the fire, he tried once more to see the shape of the future, but as usual it stopped with his own death. That had always been the limit of his manipulation of time, and he wondered if men would ever discover a way to see further.

He cast his mind once more over all his arrangements and dispositions, and knew that he had left everything in order. For his murderer, using clairvoyant sight, he had prepared volumes of diaries and notebooks containing events, knowledge and theory, all slightly awry and misleading. He hoped it would take his murderer some time to discover their inaccuracy.

He had another hiding place, under the floor of his cave, where true and secret information was kept safe for Matthias to find. Secrets that no other man, except possibly Lefevre, possessed. Knowledge won through pain and suffering. His eyes had been lost in its pursuit, and then the will to use that knowledge had deserted him. He had been old when the Stasis began, old and cynical, lacking in daring. He hoped that Matthias Marling would have the courage and vision to take the risk. There was always a price, of course . . .

The murderer would not know the spell to unlock the secret chamber beneath Blaise's feet; only Matthias knew that.

There was a knock on the door.

'Come in,' he said.

* * *

Later that night, after supper, Stefan left the Cliff. Standing on the seashore, looking out towards Peraldon, he wondered how many more men he would have to lose to death or injury before the Stasis ended. If it ever did.

There was an air of hope, of expectation almost, amongst his men. The Mages' words had stirred them from the weary aftermath of battle into a precarious state of uncertainty. He could not share their frail hope.

He would have to watch Haddon Derray and Brendan Leafe. They were wild, unstable and violent. Only Lukas had ever been able to control them, with his particular brand of ruthless mockery.

Sighing, he almost missed the light footfall on the sand behind him. But he was not surprised when Margat spoke softly at his shoulder, for he was always especially sensitive to her presence.

'I miss him too.' She looked sideways at him. 'It is Lukas you're thinking of?'

'Yes. He should not have gone.'

'Matthias said it was necessary, that someone had to look after the girl . . .'

'Perhaps. But what about you, Margat? Who looks after you? Matthias lives for philosophy and magic, and the twins are both young –'

'None of us is young, not in any real sense. And what makes you think I need "looking after"?' She tossed her head, and a lock of black hair escaped the silver clasp. 'It has been a long time since Dacien died, and Lukas has always been tied up with the Guard. Nothing has changed.'

'I suppose not. But nothing gets easier, does it?'

'We could try . . .'

He almost missed the words. He knew what she meant. False hope, lying dreams. He shook his head.

'It would be no good, Margat.' He watched the strength in her steady eyes, the curving smile of her full mouth. Before the Stasis he might have loved this woman, with her gallant courage and laughing eyes.

But not now. Marriages under the Stasis ended either in death or bitterness. With no children, no easy warmth or security, there was no future for the companionship of marriage. Keeping the religion of the Lady alive demanded so much from them all that there was no energy left for anything else.

He would not have it otherwise. He would not deny Astret. He would fight, again and again if necessary, to restore Her. If they achieved the end of the Stasis, then, only then, he might allow himself to love Margat. But only if the Stasis ended and the Boundary was broken. Only if they could live together in peace and calm.

There was no other choice.

Chapter Twenty
Quake

First there was a scream, harsh and strangled, far back in the caves, and then a rumbling sound.

Matthias leapt from his bed, all senses wrenched into awareness, his hand braced against the shivering rock as it started to tremble.

He snatched up his staff and cloak, and began to run.

The corridors were full of people screaming and jostling, pushing towards the outer caves. The ground slid and crumbled under their steps. Shoving, terrified and distraught . . . it was a stampede through a disintegrating multi-storey maze. He saw his friends collide and fall, tumbling, crying out.

He saw Merrick, a young soldier of the Guard, disappear suddenly down a crack that yawned wide, briefly, at his feet. Matthias fell to his knees at its edge and tried to reach the clutching hands yards below with his staff, but the chasm was too deep and, even as he tried to assemble the power to hold it open, it closed with relentless speed. Just in time, he snatched the staff back and the scream below was abruptly cut off.

Shaking, he stood aside from the panicked crowds hurtling through the unstable corridors, and tried to concentrate.

Clearing his mind of shock and terror, he gazed at the spiral carved in the top of his staff and tried to find a way through to the other three Mages.

Aylmer, Thibaud - yes, they were there, reaching out to each other in the chaos around them. But where he was used to finding the peaceful clarity of Blaise's mind, there was nothing.

'Blaise is dead!' The three minds echoed to each other, grief and misgiving clouded with dread.

'We'll mourn later. Now –' Matthias, strongly to the others – *'What is happening, who does this?'*

Putting aside dismay in their various corners of the crumbling caves, the three Mages felt cautiously out into their surroundings, ignoring the agonised cries of distress around them.

It was Matthias again who found it first, an electrical charge of great strength. Where did it come from, shuddering away at the ground beneath the Caves, shooting through the rock, destroying stability?

A rumbling immediately above recalled him abruptly to his surroundings.

The roof was collapsing around his head, rocks and stones scattering, showering over him. Cursing, he held one arm over his head, and turned and ran back to the Mages' quarters.

Blaise was dead. Matthias could help him no more. But his cave held a legacy of knowledge Matthias could not afford to abandon. As the ground continued to tilt away beneath his feet, he leapt and slid, bruised and battered, down the shifting tunnels deeper into the Cliff.

The Arrarat were soaring outside, people clinging to their feathery backs, lifting from the shuddering Cliff face to safety. The thundering roar of falling rocks distorted hearing, and the grim twilight was bitter with dust.

Stefan seized Margat's hand and ran with her back along the beach towards the Caves, breathless with dread. As they stumbled over the pebbles, he thought he saw shadows, flying past them at the edge of understanding, speeding towards the sea. Scurries, he thought blankly. What are scurries doing here? Then the shouting from the Cliff, the running figures and swooping hawks, took all his attention and he forgot the fugitive shadows.

The sight which met his eyes bereft him of thought.

The Cliff was crumbling. An impossible chasm yawned on its north side. Ruined rooms were cruelly exposed, tumbling into the vast ravine. It stretched deep into the

Cliff, under the lookout tower, which hung, just balanced, on the edge of the gulf.

As he watched there was a further deep rumble and the Cliff face shivered again. Rocks began to drop from the top of the tower, bouncing as they fell, and then the whole thing seemed to groan, a tremor running through it, and it started to collapse down into the chasm. Clouds of dust obscured everything as the tower disappeared.

The screams of his people filled his ears, and his only thought was how to save those who were trapped.

'I must go –' he said to Margat. 'I'll find Fabian –'

She made no attempt to hold him back, but with tears in her eyes began to search through the crowds gathering on the sand.

Twice Matthias's path was blocked by piles of rubble and once by a gaping hole at his feet. Doggedly, ignoring aching, bruised muscles, he pressed on, turning aside as necessary, retreating from the obstacles, retracing his tracks, taking other crumbling passageways.

The Cliff was a warren of tunnels, winding through the soft rock. There were few chambers of any size; the Great Hall was by far the largest. The others were small, often cramped, connected by uneven stairs and branching passages. Few people had bothered to explore them all, the empty miles of dripping, dank burrows.

He passed friends running the other way, friends too much distressed to take any notice of his dash to the heart of the caves. But Haddon Derray stopped, an injured woman in his arms, and blocked his way.

'Matt! Don't be mad! There's nothing you can do down there!' Broad as a young oak he stood squarely in the passageway and Matthias couldn't get past.

'Blaise is there –'

'He's dead. Aylmer told me and you know it too. There's no point in going that way. You'll be needed –'

The wounded woman in his arms, a frail pale-skinned girl with blood on her forehead, moaned and stirred.

'Haddon – get her out of this and stop meddling. And –' Matthias paused. Haddon, one of Lukas's protégés, was strong, almost foolhardy with courage, and reckless. But could he be trusted? The ground beneath them shuddered and he put out an arm to steady himself.

'Listen, Haddon, if I don't get back, tell Aylmer – tell Aylmer that scurries started this. I haven't time to reach him now. He'll know what it means. Tell him the scurries set off the earthquake!'

Puzzlement creased Haddon's handsome, sweating face. 'Scurries . . . how could they?'

'Just do as I say. Remember!' Pushing past, Matthias ran on through the dark maze.

He seized a torch from a wall bracket and it spluttered and spat as he ran.

He used his staff once to relight the torch after he had dropped it in one of the rockfalls, but he regretted it. He could not afford to use the spiral often. He knew he would need all the staff's power to unlock Blaise's secrets.

The entrance to Blaise's cave was blocked by a fall of small rocks and boulders. With the staff he could have cleared it in moments, but he knelt and started to scrabble with his hands, conserving its power.

Suddenly he paused, listening. The faintest of moans reached him from deep inside the cave. Could it be Blaise? Had they mistaken unconsciousness for death in the silence of the telepathic communication?

He did not think so, but could afford to take no chances. Picking up the staff, he stared at the spiral and emptied his mind.

Immediately light and power began to course through him, inspiring and liberating. In the mystic trance of magic, caught between times, he moved one stone from the heap of rubble to the far side of the passage. Instantaneously, the entire heap had shifted, existing now where that first stone had been placed.

Blaise's cave was before him. The door had been wrenched from its hinges and was slanted sideways across the entrance. Crumpled cloth stained the floor and a pool of red glinted in the torchlight. The fire was still burning.

Hardly breathing, Matthias fell to his knees and pushed the splintered door aside.

Blaise lay there, empty eye sockets staring up at him, the back of his head crushed in like eggshell. He was quite cold. There was no possibility of life.

'He is indeed dead, Matthias.' A cool, arid voice brought him spinning round in shock.

Sitting at the unharmed desk deep in the cave, Mortimer Reckert, his feathery cloak clogged with dust, was looking through Blaise's diaries.

'I'm glad my artistic little moan induced you to use the staff, it'll save me some effort,' he said, smiling. He put down the diary and stood up. 'I've been waiting for you.'

'Reckert. What is this? Why the earthquake?' Matthias was standing too now, clutching his staff, white with anger.

'Oh, many reasons.' A flicker on the wall and a scurry drifted towards him, wreathing around the room, becoming rock then wood, then an extension to the folds of his cloak. Matthias resisted the temptation to kick it. He knew he would only receive an electric shock if he touched it in violence. It coiled itself around his ankles, others joining it from hidden places round the room, trapping him, tightening round his limbs.

He began to struggle then, lashing out, and Reckert laughed.

'Don't waste energy, Matt. I need your help.'

Furious anger swept through Matthias. Reckert had betrayed them all, had destroyed the Cavers' home, killed Merrick and the Lady knew how many others. With sudden force he spun round, lashing out with his staff, sending the scurries flying, ignoring the shocks. For a moment their howls split the air and flashes of sizzling heat zigzagged as they collided with the wall.

Reckert raised his arm, shouting, '*Loaliyin a'naiil! Venta a'naiil!*'

A cloud of immobility flooded through the air and held Matthias frozen in appalled vulnerability.

Reckert was holding Blaise's staff, using it. He knew the words of power, was controlling the scurries through mind transference, knew the spell of Immobility. These were all skills known only to qualified Mages. There was treachery here on a scale Matthias had not envisaged, and he did not know how to combat it.

He could just see Blaise's body and the rock stained with blood that had crushed his skull.

'No,' said Reckert in confirmation. 'It was not the rockfall that killed Blaise. And now I need you to show me where his real secrets are.' Contemptuously he threw the book he had been reading onto the fire. 'You were ever a favourite pupil, Matt, weren't you? The long confidential sessions while the women prayed and the Guard fought. What did he tell you, little magician? Where are the diaries?'

'What diaries? I don't know what you're talking about.' In shock, his bluff was feeble.

'Don't be foolish, Matthias. You cannot resist me now.' He looked down at Blaise's staff, cradling it in gnarled hands, smiling. 'I've wanted one of these for a long time,' he said. 'I'd like to have a chance to try it out.'

He looked at Matthias, a crooked smile distorting thin lips, and then threw a thought, amplified by the staff, at his prisoner.

Pain swirled round him. He gasped, clenching his fists on his staff, and resisted as agony tore through his nerves. It was difficult to assemble the correct defences under the assault of such pain, difficult to push aside the fog of immobility that held him impotent.

Blaise's staff would not, could not, fatally injure another human being, he tried to remember, his face wrenched into a rictus by agony. It was as if red hot needles were flaring down each nerve, transforming his whole body into a blazing inferno. Surely the flesh would melt, the bones become ash?

Concentrate. Resist. This was not real, it was only illusion. He thought fiercely of the spiral, the unfurling power of time, and held his agony up before it, offering it to the centre of that power. He saw the pain being absorbed, drawn down the narrowing spiral away and beyond him.

Head held steady, he walked free of the cloud and looked once more at his spiral staff. Its tip was glowing with red fire, which as he watched became white and brilliant, flaring into eternity. It faded; wood once more.

Matthias stared into Reckert's eyes.

He was standing back against the cave wall, mouth hanging slackly open. He tried to raise Blaise's staff once more but it had suddenly become heavy, unwieldy, and he found his unwilling fingers loosening their grip. The staff fell to the ground, and Reckert grasped at more familiar weapons.

With a surge, the scurries fell on Matthias, dropping from the ceiling, leaping from the walls and ground. Moulding themselves around him, shivers of electricity sparked and pricked.

Matthias refused to believe in them, refused them his assent and denied their existence. He was moving now in different realms, working within other, arcane parameters, and they were nothing to him. All around him they crumpled like rags to the floor, and the force of Matthias's will stood free and unhampered.

Matthias took one step, and then paused as shattering weakness overwhelmed him. He had used so much power to defeat Reckert and the scurries that he was drained, empty of strength. He swayed once, putting his hand out to the wall to steady himself. He did not see Reckert draw a long knife from the folds of his cloak, edging round the fire towards him.

Matthias's staff shivered in his hands and, alerted by the warning, he tried to recover control, but it was too late. The long knife flashed towards him as he half fell, half threw himself sideways. It sliced deep into his thigh.

Reckert came forward, drawing the knife back once more, and Matthias rolled, struggling, his limbs like jelly in his weakness.

There was another vile pain as the knife plunged into his belly and he bent double, hands spread wide like starfish over the wound.

'You'll never find out now, will you?' he gasped, and then black waves of unknowing swamped him.

Chapter Twenty-one
Jeren

Leaves like fingers slid across her face. Twigs caught in her hair, brambles pulled at her skirt. The tree trunks stood far apart, wide, dark avenues dripping with moss and rain. Eleanor and Lukas kept going, following paths that only Lukas knew, deep into the heart of the Island of Jeren.

The trees were more like beeches than anything else, wide squat trunks and arching roots reaching high above the mud. But they were tall, so tall. Sometimes Eleanor and Lukas had to duck beneath the roots, sometimes they had to clamber over the writhing tendons anchoring each tree to the ground. The tree tops were lost in cloud, and silence hung around their trunks.

Eleanor's Moon-inspired confidence evaporated in the mud. Ash was no longer near. She felt as miserable as she could ever remember. Her cuts stung, she was bone weary and felt flat, let down after excitement.

Lukas took no notice. One look at her face, and he started to talk. Thurstan Merauld, Martitia, Powel Hewlin . . . the names littered his account of the Jerenites. Sourly, she wondered why he bothered.

'Parties,' he said. 'They're what it's all about on Jeren now. You should feel at home. Not for the Jerenites the solemn rites of the Lady.'

Looking at the dripping trees, the mire of mud beneath her feet, she sighed.

'What have they got to celebrate, here?'

He stopped, looking straight at her. The long mouth smiled, but his eyes were severe.

'Not much. But what else is there to do? Think. In a society where there are no children, few deaths, no change of any real sort, people have to occupy themselves somehow. The arts fell by the wayside during the Stasis. No new lines for the poet, no new songs for the musician. The Stasis halts new life in more ways than one. It's worse for the women. After all, we can hunt, fish, fight . . .'

'Does it help? Fighting, I mean?'

'We have to eat. Nothing grows near the Boundary, in the dark and rain. There are other reasons for the raids, of course,' he said, cynically. 'I suppose they make us feel we're achieving something; making some kind of statement. An outlet for anger, frustration. Not least of all, the raids make damn sure the Peraldonians don't forget us. That's important. But ultimately it's all the same. People just get killed.'

She was too tired, too weary to comment. 'How much further?' she said.

'Not far now. Look, have you noticed?' He pointed to one of the massive tree trunks. A thick ribbon of moss hung down, loose, concealing, and beneath it a small arrow was cut into the bark, pointing the way. 'Ever helpful to strangers, are the Jerenites –' He paused.

'In fact,' he said slowly, 'I thought we might have heard something by now . . . we must be close to the Guildern.'

He stopped suddenly, lifting his head as if sensing something in the air.

She could smell it too, the acrid scent of ash and wood smoke.

'Stay here.' There was no question of disobeying. He dropped his rucksack at her feet and she saw the glint of steel in his hand.

He vanished into the gloom beneath the trees before she could begin to argue.

Dispirited, she heaped her own sack on top of Lukas's and sat down on the pile, wrapping her cloak tightly around her.

There were whispers and rustles in the leaves everywhere. She looked up into the dripping canopy above. Giant trees. Monstrous reptiles. The Arrarat, her beautiful Ash . . . What if other creatures were also larger than normal? Woodland creatures, hedgehogs, mice . . . rats. Snakes.

A twig cracked behind her. She jumped to her feet,

staring wildly into the shadows. A slither of clammy leaves brushed her cheek.

She turned and ran, down the avenue where Lukas had gone, stumbling, panicky and uncontrolled. She almost crashed into him, standing still in the dark in a vast, blank clearing.

He stood there, not looking at her, not turning around, although he must have heard her blundering through the undergrowth.

He was staring at the smoking ruins littering the forest floor. The remains of many fires still smouldered. Broken planks, shattered doors and window frames, huge logs tumbled into untidy piles, all were charred and covered with a fine layer of wood ash. Even the leaves from the neighbouring trees were scorched, hanging in shreds.

'What's happened? What is this place?' Her voice was high and unsteady in the deep silence.

He didn't answer her immediately. Bending, he picked something up from the rubbish at his feet.

The remains of a stringed instrument, the neck broken. For a moment he stared at it, and then let it fall, twisted, to the ground.

'Parties,' he said. 'They used to hold parties . . .'

'They still do.'

A man stood on the other side of the clearing, watching them. Tall, broad, dressed in a shabby green jerkin and what looked disconcertingly like denim jeans, he held a bow and arrow poised and pointed directly at them. His gaze was steady, his hands unwavering.

'Powel.' She hardly recognised Lukas's voice. 'What the hell's been happening here?'

The tall stranger lowered his bow, and spat into the mud, crossing the clearing towards them.

'Fosca. Last night.'

'Deaths?'

'Some. No one you know.' There was a strange edge to the big man's voice. Close to, he was enormous, broad shouldered, thick limbed. She could just see the curl in the brown hair but it was cropped close to the head, making him look rough and thuggish. This impression was intensified by the tattoos on his forearms, the studded leather bands round his wrists, the ragged tears in the green jerkin and jeans.

'What are you doing here, Marling? And who is this?'

'A friend . . .' She was standing close to Lukas. It was all she could do not to take his hand. The hostility in the air was almost tangible.

Were these Lukas's friendly Jerenites?

'We're in the old camp.' The stranger nodded over into the shadows. 'You'd better follow us. You'll never find it on your own.'

As he spoke, other men stepped out of the shadows around them, all carrying bows and arrows, all wearing torn and patched jeans. Heavy dark cloaks hung loosely over exotically coloured shirts. Some had close-cropped heads, like Powel; others wore their hair long, plaited with ribbons, or dyed, or caught in pig-tails. As she looked at them, Eleanor recognised a thread of self-dramatisation, of recklessness, in the Jerenites.

A young man, long hair roughly clasped back in a scarlet ribbon, was carrying their rucksacks. His shirt was a patched rainbow of scraps and embroidery, and the cloak slung over his shoulder was deep black, very like Lukas's own.

'Come on, Powel! It's Lukas! Why all the heavy suspicion?' He took Lukas's hand with warmth.

Lukas smiled at him, but his eyes were still on Powel. 'Jocasta?' he said. 'Thurstan? Martitia?'

'They're all right. I told you, no one you know.'

'Come *on*!' The younger man again. 'They'll be wanting to see you. There's a long way to go. This way!'

He turned and set off through the trees.

At least he was still carrying the rucksacks.

The girl with chestnut hair was singing. Accompanying herself on a small bowed instrument, held upright like a cello on her lap. The two lines of melody, from voice and instrument, wove around each other like seaweed, drifting in the tide. Sometimes the intervals were strange and uneasy, sometimes the lines moved in pleasant thirds.

Her voice was pure and clear, very fluent in the upper register, husky and warm lower down. Lukas was leaning against one of the wide trunks, watching her, faintly frowning.

Eleanor sat at a small table, amongst strangers, listening to the performance. The table was in an alcove, beneath a high-arching root draped with midnight blue cloth. Other men and women sat nearby, but they were paying little attention, talking in low voices.

Eleanor put her drink down, entranced. She was no musician but it seemed to her a wonderful performance, eloquent and varied in its range. A delightful expression of lyrical and instrumental skill.

When the singer finished, Eleanor sat still, waiting for the applause.

There was none. No one even looked up.

Eleanor came across them during the course of a party. At least, that was what she had been told it was, people drinking, dancing, smoking, talking in small groups.

After some initial suspicion, the Jerenites had welcomed her. They had asked few questions and she assumed that during the long tramp through the forest, Lukas had told them something of her story. She had been trailing too far behind them to take part in the conversation, and had not heard what explanation Lukas had given. Back at the old camp, there was some curiosity in the women's faces, a kind of suppressed impatience in the men's.

She liked them, the ones who spoke to her. They were relaxed and calm, lacking the driven intensity of the Cavers.

The older women, smoking cigarettes and long pipes, were dressed in flamboyant rags. Such was their confidence that Eleanor could not decide if the rags were due to poverty or fashion.

The younger women wore tight denim, like the men, with bizarre make-up and glittery, rather ugly beaten metal jewellery. There was an air of audacity about them, an atmosphere of licence and freedom. Eleanor began to think that she might enjoy herself here.

Someone lent her jeans, someone else donated an

embroidered shirt, a palette of make-up. They were comfortable clothes, a familiar style in which she could relax. She was cheered by the traditional feminine rites, reassured by their lack of curiosity. After washing and changing, she tried out the make-up in a small ill-lit room, watched appraisingly by a young woman who introduced herself as Idony.

'You look fine,' she said, laughing as Eleanor considered herself in the inadequate light. The shiny metal disc that served as a mirror reflected the usual face, wide grey eyes, pale skin. And a small scar, shaped like the moon, almost hidden among the waves of bright hair at her temple.

It was echoed in her mind, nagging at the edge of consciousness, in a shining light. She shook her head with irritation. For a while she wanted to forget it all; responsibilities, urgencies, conflicts, the lot. She had had enough of quests for the moment. She wondered instead whether Idony had any mascara.

Her companion was slight, with bubbly blonde hair threaded through with vivid emerald and violet ribbons. Eleanor was taller, her make-up less striking, but she had never lacked confidence in her appearance. She thought she looked fine too, if not as flamboyant as her companion.

'A celebration, tonight,' Idony said. 'To mark our return to the old camp.' Although she still smiled, Eleanor sensed something grim in her tone.

'What happened last night?' Fosca, that man Powel had said, those flying lizard creatures with their unthinkable riders. Deaths . . .

'A Fosca raid. No one knows why. Complete with fire arrows. The Guildern was burnt to the ground . . . but of course you know that, don't you?' Idony darted a sharp glance at Eleanor. They had been standing in the ruins of the Guildern when Powel had found them, Eleanor realised.

Idony was still looking at her. 'New here, I understand. One of Matthias Marling's contacts. When did you arrive?'

Eleanor was about to answer when the girl rushed on. 'Not that it matters . . . We weren't expecting a raid, we've not had one now for a very long time. To say we were unprepared would be putting it mildly. We lost over forty men and women, and many more were wounded.' She paused, looking down at her long, pointed fingernails, hair and face shadowed. 'Thurstan says we can't afford losses like that, so we moved on. No one objected. The cover is better here.'

The room they were in was underground. On arriving at the camp they had traipsed down a narrow stairwell hidden in the roots of one of the great trees. The air was musty, unused. But already Eleanor could sense that the Jerenites were making an impression on the place. Someone had daubed paint on one of the blank walls, a caricature of someone she didn't recognise wearing a crown shaped like the Sun.

There was a brightly lined cloak flung over one of the chairs, a half-empty jug of wine on the table, a rag rug on the floor, ashtrays on the table. Idony was smoking, shrugging when Eleanor refused.

At last, confident and not a little vain, Eleanor allowed Idony to guide her through dark shadowed passages, lit by flickering torches, to a larger central area, above the ground.

It was one of the most extraordinary places she had ever seen. The roof was supported by the high arches of roots around one of the massive tree trunks. Strung between these irregular arches, reinforced with beams, were heavy woven draperies of purple, black, blue, scarlet, emerald, blocking out the wind.

The roof was constructed from interwoven branches and leaves, from which coloured paper and foil, streamers and bells dangled. This garish, flimsy-looking mixture formed a series of tight platforms wedged between the arches. Rough rope knotted them into place; even that was dyed in rainbow shades. The ceiling was thus divided into sections, waterproof, strong and light. Clearly it was so constructed in order to be quickly dismantled.

The hanging draperies, dividing the space into sitting and living areas, were similarly insubstantial. Everything had an air of impermanence, tawdry and casual, like a fairground.

Torches burned in brackets fastened to the tree trunks, slanting away from the wood. It was full of people, of all different ages, all dressed in the easy, comfortable style that Eleanor found so reassuring. The atmosphere was heavy with smoke, from the torches and from cigarettes. Nearly everyone was smoking, but it smelt nothing like tobacco.

She found Lukas and Powel Hewlin sitting round a table with some other men. They were deep in discussion, involved and serious. They broke off as Eleanor and Idony approached, and Lukas sprang to his feet with an unlikely courtesy. No one else moved.

'Allow me to introduce – Eleanor, Eleanor Knight,' he said. There was a suggestion of laughter in his voice. She had never seen him like this before. Was he showing off to her or to Idony? 'A visitor, she is,' he said, 'a friend to us all . . . we hope.' The quicksilver laughter was there again, and she frowned at him. He took no notice, suddenly glimpsing someone across the room.

A woman stood there, looking at him.

A message passed between them, something Eleanor had no difficulty understanding. She was not surprised when, after the briefest of acknowledgements, Lukas left the table, crossing the floor to the woman with chestnut hair.

Eleanor turned back to the men round the table, sighing. Some of them nodded to her, but most were clearly uninterested. Charitably, she tried to remember that they were hard-pressed, frightened.

She turned away from the table to Idony, still at her shoulder. 'Do you know Lukas well?' she said.

'Oh yes . . . Sometimes we wonder why he doesn't just pack up and come and live here, he comes so often.'

'I suppose there's his family back at the Caves . . .' said Eleanor.

'There's Jocasta here.' She shrugged. 'I don't know that the claims of brother and sister can quite match that. His parents were killed long ago, at the start of the War.'

'He seems fond of Letia . . .'

'Yes, I know. But, if it's difficult here, it's nothing like as bad as the conditions at the Caves . . . Or at least, it wasn't until last night.'

'There's the Moon, of course . . .' Eleanor spoke slowly, trying to piece it all together.

'Ah yes, the Lady Astret . . .' Idony's voice held only the faintest hint of irony. 'Well, each to their own. Come on, let's go and get a drink, shall we?' She nodded across the floor to where a few, undistinguished bottles stood behind a counter.

They had to push through crowds of people, talking together, often laughing. As they jogged elbows, inching sideways, cautiously avoiding feet shod in heavy boots or light slippers, Eleanor caught sudden flarings of anger, as if violence was only just below the surface. Perhaps it was the Fosca, she thought, perhaps they were worried about another attack.

Idony met a friend along the way, and started talking to him about someone else who had been hurt in the raid. The conversation was full of medical details. Eleanor tried not to listen, but it still made her stomach turn. It was with gratitude that she accepted the offer of a drink from a young man standing close by her shoulder.

'See you,' she said casually to Idony, and followed him to the bar.

He spoke to her amicably enough, a slim, pale youth, his dark hair plaited with silver ribbon. There was a long scar down one side of his face, dragging the skin at the side of his mouth and eye, giving the face a not unpleasant, lopsided look. He was called Albin Rede, he said, and he liked her red hair.

She smiled, and let him choose her a drink before finding somewhere to sit. The bar, despite its strange surroundings, was in some ways like others she had visited. Shadowy groups of people crowded round small tables. Drinks and discarded glasses littering every flat surface. The air, heavy and dense with smoke from cigarettes and the torches stuck into brackets round the tree trunks.

Without preamble Albin started to flirt, clumsily putting his hand on hers, paying lavish compliments, moving his stool close. She was not displeased but he was too obvious, too uncouth to be interesting. It was a familiar situation. Without rancour, politely, she stood up and wandered off, looking for Idony.

* * *

In the alcove, where the girl with chestnut hair sat near Lukas, there was no applause. Eleanor was not one to show appreciation where others sneered, so she sat back, watching curiously.

She saw Lukas go towards the musician, speak a few words, his hand on her shoulder. He looked up, directly at Eleanor for the first time. She saw a complicated series of expressions flicker through the eloquent eyes, and then he smiled at her.

'Our visitor . . . let's have an outsider's opinion. Eleanor, this is a friend of mine, Jocasta Garraint. Jocasta, this is Eleanor Knight.'

The woman nodded, unsmiling. She was slim and elegant, with dark eyes, a wide generous mouth. The deep chestnut hair with bronze glints framed smooth creamy skin. This went some way to explaining the attraction of Jeren.

'Did you enjoy the performance?' Her voice was clear and cool.

Eleanor found herself in a quandary. She had enjoyed it, very much. But she was puzzled by the lack of reaction around her. Would she make a fool of herself expressing naive enthusiasm?

Before she could answer, a man to her right spoke.

'It was fine, Jocasta. Really nice . . .' He turned back to his companions, hugely unexcited.

'Yes, a good performance. I particularly liked your use of Bence's progression towards the end.' The woman across the table leant forward, lighting another cigarette.

'Did you like it, Eleanor?' Lukas was still watching her. She didn't understand their bored comments, the strange timbre of his voice. She decided to chance it.

'I thought it was wonderful!' she said recklessly. 'It made me want to cry, I've never heard anything like it!'

For a moment there was an incredulous silence. A ripple of laughter.

'Unfortunately everyone else here has.' Jocasta's voice was tight with stress. 'It was hopeless. As usual.' She stood up abruptly, leaving the instrument on the floor by the side of her chair.

'A drink, Lukas?' She was staring at him with a kind of desperation. His arms were round her waist, his face against her hair. He was gentle with her. Eleanor could only just hear his voice, warm and passionate.

'We'll change it, Jocasta, you'll see. The Stasis is going to break, and there will be new songs to sing, new pieces to play. Believe me.'

'You and the shining bright Moon and this stranger from who knows where?' The words were cynical but she was no longer frowning and Eleanor thought, she hasn't given up. She keeps trying, that's why she still plays, why Lukas loves her.

It was unusual for Eleanor to spend much time considering the emotions of others. She decided to leave them to it. She picked up her drink and went looking for Idony.

She couldn't see her at first, so Eleanor found another small alcove out of the light and sat down there in the shadows. There was only one other person at the table, a pale-skinned youth, collapsed face down. His lank fair hair was flung indiscriminately into the ashtrays and puddles of alcohol. She sat back, holding her drink, and regarded the people of Jeren.

To some extent, her capacity for questioning her situation had been exhausted. Caro's party was so very far away, so irrelevant to this existence, that it was hardly worth considering. Her family, friends, work, flat – all these were now only dreams to her. They *had* to be dreams if she were to remain sane. Without consciously making that decision, she knew it to be true. This world had to be experienced at face value. It was, after all, difficult enough to remain alive here without worrying about the philosophical implications of her presence.

At some other time, she supposed, she would be able to ask how and why. For the moment it was enough just to cope with the problems of existence. And there was always the Moon's light, beckoning and demanding.

Across the floor, to the left of the bar, a band had started up. More strange instruments, more bored musicians. An unenthusiastic splatter of applause from the people around. Some of the instruments were blown, some plucked; Eleanor thought they might benefit from amplification, but no one seemed to have heard of electricity.

She found the music complicated and difficult to follow. There were cross rhythms tinkling around in improvised-sounding percussion. People hitting tin cans might sound more lively, she thought. A duet of two reedy, wind-blown instruments sounded shrill over a pounding bass. There was nothing resembling a melody. She didn't understand, could find nothing to relate to. She soon lost interest in it.

People began to get up to dance to the uneasy rhythms and then her attention was caught, for Eleanor liked dancing. She saw Lukas's tall, rangy figure moving around amidst the mass of people. He was dancing with Jocasta, his hands on her hips. She was laughing at him, reaching up to his shoulders, her dark eyes gleaming.

Crossly Eleanor picked up the glass from the table in front of her and drank deeply. Not unlike beer, the liquid was bitter-sweet – and went straight to her head. It was ages since she'd last eaten.

'Have a sandwich,' said a light voice companionably. A slim, neat man, fair-haired like her derelict friend, but decidedly in control, held out to her a plate of curled, dry-looking bread.

Wordlessly she shook her head.

'Can't say I blame you.' He balanced the plate carefully on the uncaring head of the youth next to her. 'May I join you?' Quietly, smoothly, he sat down opposite her. For a moment they regarded each other in silence, and then Eleanor took another drink, looking away.

She didn't like this man, with his confidence and poise, his immaculate jacket and jeans, his clean white shirt. His hair was short and tidy, his eyes a hard blue. She thought he would probably feel at home in a three-piece suit. She was on the verge of getting up and drifting off again, when he spoke, leaning forward.

'Why are you here? Who are you? What are you?'

'What's it to you?' Perhaps the alcohol had made her brave, or rude, she couldn't decide which. He held her eyes steady; held her fascinated like a doomed rabbit. There was a pause, a dangerous dislocation of frightening potential. She became very still.

'Who are you, anyway?' she said, suddenly breathless.

'Ah, I asked first.' He smiled, and leant back. The danger appeared to lessen. 'I know your name, of course, Eleanor Knight, and I know that Fosca attacked you and your Arrarat. Lukas seems to think you're a good thing, he even says he trusts you. But tell me this, Eleanor Knight, what reason has he for this? Why should I accept it?'

'Ask him yourself. He's the one with all the answers. You all seem to know him well enough here.' Sourly, she watched Lukas enfold himself around the beautiful Jocasta with tender familiarity. Following her gaze, the fair man's face changed and became unreadable, eyes hooded. For some reason, she knew he was angry; and then again, that here was a dangerous man.

'Lukas is – an old friend,' he said. 'But his judgments are not always immaculate. I prefer to make up my own mind.' He took out a cigarette and lit it in a leisurely way. He appeared to feel totally at liberty to interrogate her at his ease. She become irritated.

'You shouldn't smoke, it's bad for you,' she said severely.

Laughing, he held it out to her. 'Try it,' he recommended. 'You may even like it.' With revulsion she struck his hand, knocking the cigarette onto the mud floor where it hissed and fizzled in a spilt puddle of beer. He continued to smile, but his thin face was now tinged with contempt.

'Why so angry?' he said. 'If you're a spy, I'm sure you'll have a good story prepared. And if you're not, well then, there's no need to be frightened.'

'I'm not frightened!' she shouted, surging to her feet. 'I'm just sick of all this petty nonsense, spies, raids, little battles – it's all irrelevant, don't you see? A diversion from what really matters –'

'And what is that? What does really matter?' He was on his feet too, intense, concentrating on her, willing her to give an answer.

How could she say it? How could she explain the Moon's anguish? She stared at him blankly and said, slowly, 'This – bloody – gloom. This dark, foul weather. How can you bear it, why do you put up with it? It's depressing and horrible. No one should have to live like this. Why don't you all just – move somewhere else?'

There was a stunned silence, and then, again, he began to laugh, with a mixture of surprise and hopeless cynicism. He sat down again, and not ungently pulled her down beside him.

'Oh dear, oh dear,' he said, pouring half his drink into her empty glass. 'All right, you're no spy. I'm Thurstan Merauld, by the way. My mother, Martitia, is in charge here, for what it's worth.' He had relaxed, she realised, no doubt reassured by her incompetence. Resentfully, she went on.

'Well, why don't you? Move somewhere else, I mean. Lukas says you're not bound to the Moon, after all.'

'It's not that simple, of course. In the north is the Boundary, to the south Peraldonian territory. To live there we would have to acknowledge Lycias. There's no room for agnostics in Peraldon. You can't be expected to understand if you really are new here. There are other factors not immediately obvious. If we move, well, then we're acknowledging that there's no hope, that it's not ever open to change. That there will never be a new song, or a different story. Some of us choose not to believe that.'

This was true, she thought. It made a kind of desperate sense. Then he looked at her and she couldn't tell if he was laughing at her or not.

'And also – perhaps we like the hidden secrets of the dark,' he said.

'You can't,' she said flatly. 'No one could.'

'But the dark conceals much, hides and heals . . .'

He was still being honest with her, she thought, looking round the dim dance floor, with its seething entangled mass of people. Others were sprawled intertwined on cushions, lounging back against the roots. The glittering hangings from the ceiling were almost invisible in the smoky atmosphere: the air was thick and heavy.

It *was* like some dissolute party, she thought. The cigarettes were not made of tobacco and smelt stronger than pot. The scene was only just within the bounds of decorum: if she stayed longer, who knew what might happen? She remembered the Cavers, with their solemn, simple, grief-stricken lives, and wondered which was the better method of coping with the unvarying gloom and rain.

'Do you ever visit the Cavers?' she asked, curiously.

'Rarely,' he said. 'We have no Arrarat, you see, and have to trust to our boats. They serve us well enough on raids to Peraldon, but it's a dangerous voyage to the north – the currents are unpredictable and the seas heavy. The Peraldonian patrols are particularly active towards the Cliff, too. We don't do it unless it's essential. And although we are allies, the Cavers do not entirely approve of us.' This was an understatement, she was sure. 'And on our side, well, we have no liking for – ritual.' There was the faintest undercurrent of contempt in his tone.

'No liking for ritual?' a mocking voice broke in. Lukas, one arm casually draped round Jocasta's shoulders, was leaning against a tree root. They had not noticed his approach.

'Thurstan, my old comrade in arms, *what* nonsense! What about the Guildern ceremonies? Or the Birthday observances? And there's always the Salutation dance –' He pushed himself away from the root and Jocasta twirled under his arm. They began to cavort in a wicked parody of some courtly dance, the girl bubbling with laughter, Lukas's eyes shining down at her appreciatively.

The noise brought others closer to watch, and the musicians altered their rhythms to fit in. It no longer sounded like an improvised jumble. Soon it seemed that everyone was laughing, stumbling in complicated patterns. Accidents were frequent, tumbled bodies wriggling to get out of the way.

Watching, Eleanor had a strong but inexplicable sense that there was a degree of tension amongst the dancers, and that this tension was focused on her elegant, cool companion. The dancers deliberately avoided his glance, weaving away as soon as they neared their table. He was still smiling, however. Relaxed and calm, he stood up and held out a hand to her. Unable to resist the rhythm, she smiled, and joined the dance.

Chapter Twenty-two
Fosca

For a while she almost forgot where she was. Rhythmic, funky music, a warm darkened room, the jostle of other bodies. So familiar, so comfortable that it was almost reassuring.

Thurstan danced with restraint. She could see Lukas out of the corner of her eye, flinging long limbs about with graceful disdain. Jocasta was exercising both agility and skill to avoid injury, still laughing at him.

Eleanor stopped watching them and began to concentrate on her own dancing, of which she was proud. She had invested both time and energy in acquiring a reasonable technique and decided, quietly, to show it off. She began to enjoy herself, for her style was unlike that of anyone else there, and soon people began to drop back, watching with curiosity Eleanor's best efforts at jazz dance.

People began to mimic her movements. She spun round, hands outstretched, relying on the heavy beat of music to release the gesture into something else. People began to applaud. Flushed with pleasure and exertion, she laughed aloud, still spinning, still delighted.

Not for long.

A scream ripped through her laughter. With a crash, part of the ceiling fell in and a rush of chill air broke through.

A Fosca angel, with its rider, spitting and snarling, was suddenly among them, cutting swathes through the unprepared crowds. Blood was running over them both from a hundred small wounds. The hooked claws lashed out in all directions, and the music died, and the shouting started.

Instantly it swooped back through the broken roof panels

to the tree branches above, leaving trails of bright blood everywhere. But before the Jerenites could begin to arm themselves or clear the injured from the floor, a further company of dark angels plummeted through the shattered panels, falling with spite and ferocity on the scattering crowd, screaming with a high-pitched wail.

Suddenly appearing through the chaos, Lukas pushed Eleanor under a table to one side and joined the dash for weapons. She heard him give the familiar Arrarat call, but it was lost amidst the Fosca screams.

Even though she was breathless with shock, she was amazed by the speed of the Jerenites' defence. There was no panic or disorder; it was almost as if everyone had been waiting for just such an event, waiting to release tension in violence.

A hail of arrows met the next wave of attackers, and two Fosca riders fell injured to the ground. The winged creatures, bleeding and unable to fly, writhed, snapped and snarled about them, rank and stinking. Other riders sprang to the ground in a whirl of razor-sharp claws . . .

Something was wrong about them, thought Eleanor, something quite obscene about the way they moved.

Then, as if in slow-motion, she saw that each wiry rider had six long double-jointed limbs, each tipped by retractable claws, some paired like scissors, some splayed wide like rakes. They writhed across the floor, not quickly, but with a crazed jerky gait, like puppets on elasticated string, like clockwork toys on the verge of running down. They were hacked to pieces by the more agile Jerenites, but the cost in torn limbs and ripped muscles was appalling.

Another wave of lizard-angels, fell onto the dance floor, lacerated by the sharp edges to the roof panels. All the Jerenites now had weapons, men and women, and were stationed around the edges of the dance floor, taking what shelter they could from the roots and woven hangings before darting out to attack the Fosca.

Apart from bows and arrows, they held knives, swords, sticks, clubs, even catapults – but no firearms. From her place of comparative safety Eleanor watched Jerenite and Fosca clash, heard the appalling Fosca scream, watched the blood flow, too fascinated and revolted to be scared.

She would be all right. No one would touch her, nothing would happen to her, because the Moon would always help her . . .

She saw Thurstan, still neat and cool, issue commands, telling people to remove the injured and warn the hospital. He ordered the replacement of the damaged ceiling panels with spares which were stacked up around the main trunk. The replacements were without ornamental streamers and draperies, and Eleanor saw that they were pierced by razor sharp twigs sticking both up and down out of the plaited panels.

It was why each Fosca crashing through arrived in a shower of blood. She had never seen so much of it, red and shining, spraying over everything, the sickly sweet smell of it all-pervading.

Powel and Lukas were struggling to slot one of these vicious barriers in place when the third wave attacked. Screaming like stuck pigs, two Fosca managed to slide through the gap, heavy leathery wings beating, teeth and claws flashing in a chaos of slimy scales and sharp talons.

Immediately Lukas fell on one, knocking the rider off, slashing at its wriggling, jerking limbs. Blood was spurting and the lizard, clumsy on the ground, lurched round, mouth slavering, razor sharp thumbs at the top of its wings, reaching for Lukas's face. She looked round wildly for someone to help, but everyone else was busy, trying to help the injured, putting up further barriers.

Powel Hewlin saw what was happening, the bleak, bull-necked man who had been so hostile. In moments he had reached the creature, had ducked down, dodging under the tough, supple wings, and then, amazingly, straightened his legs, his back beneath its breast.

The noise was appalling. On the narrow edge of audibility, like chalk on a blackboard, it lacerated the nerves. Sweat was pouring from Hewlin's crimson face as the reptile rose from the ground. His head was just beneath its chin, stretching its neck backwards, warding off the avid teeth. Even in such extremity, Eleanor could almost taste his nausea at the stench of the thing. And then she saw what he was doing, as the Fosca's back touched the downward pointing, dagger-sharp twigs.

The screaming intensified as it was pinioned on several spikes at once. Hewlin's legs were almost straight; with a last reserve of strength she saw him take a deep breath and then jump right off the ground, massive thigh muscles bunching with strain.

The scream degenerated into a rattle; then there was silence as its mouth fell open, and blood gushed wetly over Hewlin's head. Choking, he staggered away, leaving it pinioned there, and Eleanor began to retch.

She did not notice then, until it was almost too late, what had happened to the second Fosca.

A shrill screech brought her spinning round, out of her shelter, to see the dark angel spitting and snarling, claws scraping only a few feet away. One wing was almost torn off, and its rider, horribly injured, was sliding from its lacerated back. It had lost one arm, and only one eye was visible behind a shining curtain of brown-black blood. With astonishing and gruesome vitality, it slithered across the slippery floor, straight for Eleanor's table.

It was smaller than she, its body no bigger than a child's, its arms and legs long and flexible like a rubber doll's. Pale flesh hung in rotting rags from its jowls and limbs. Its wide mouth was drawn back in a parody of a grin. It caught and held her eyes. For a moment she was petrified, unable to move.

'Fosca!' Lukas's furious shout diverted it only for a moment. He was charging straight at it, over the blood-spattered bodies and chairs on the floor, a long sword in his right hand, a double-edged knife in his left. The rider took no notice, defending its back with one waving tentacle, still concentrating, staring at Eleanor.

Coolly, unhesitating, Lukas sheathed his knife, dodged the creature's flailing talon and crashed his own sword, double-gripped, down onto its head. It crumpled, inches from her feet, and at the same instant its mount collapsed, Thurstan's knife jutting from its throat. Lukas kicked the body out of the way, and reached over, dragging Eleanor away from the table.

'Okay?'

She nodded, beyond words.

'Come on,' he said, pulling her towards the edge of the dance floor, where a cavern of arching roots offered sanctuary.

They never made it. A sheet of flame sprang up ahead of them, violent heat beating them back. One of the broken platforms had fallen on a torch. Stained with alcohol, it had flared up into an impenetrable barrier.

Through the choking smoke, Eleanor saw more Fosca approaching. Lukas thrust his dagger into her unwilling hand.

Skidding on the slippery floor, they ran towards the only group of Jerenites still fighting. The neat pale figure of Thurstan was at its edge, moving rapidly and accurately. A handful of men and women, including Jocasta, stood with him. Together they held back an attack from three riders on one side, while more Fosca dashed onto the floor, falling from the skies, through the shattered roof.

Lukas hurled himself into their midst. She had never before seen anyone move so fast.

Thurstan spoke coldly. 'Get her out of here NOW!'

It was too late. He pulled her into the group, behind himself, as more riders slid up to them on the far side.

Chaos erupted. Thurstan and one of the Fosca circled each other in a catherine wheel of clashing blades and claws. Only his eyes remained steady, considering. Lukas was similarly engaged to her right; Hewlin had long since disappeared into the forest in pursuit of an escaping rider.

The dance floor was now almost deserted, treacherous with blood, glinting in the firelight from still burning hangings.

Sickly, she saw Albin, the boy who had first welcomed her, staggering slowly to one side of the floor, dragging one foot painfully behind. A grinning Fosca rider was suddenly there, talons eager. It began to dance around him, playing and jeering as the claws twirled closer. It was grotesque, stinking, hideous in its action, an offence against the senses.

She could no longer remain passive. It was as if the violence were reaching out to her, drawing her in. Without thinking she ran out, behind the creature, locking one forearm round its slippery neck and with the other hand driving up and in, again and again, with Lukas's long dagger. For a moment it seemed that the flailing arms would not stop; and then it sagged against her, limbs still twitching, sinking to the sodden floor.

She tried to repossess her knife but its blank eyes grinned at her, and in a slithery mass its entrails spilled out onto the floor. She put her hand to her mouth, stepping back.

Wordlessly, Albin stooped over it, freed the dagger, wiping it before handing it back to her. He gave her a sort of smile and murmured, 'Thanks,' as he moved back quickly to rejoin the fighting.

It was still chaos all around her, screaming violence and blood everywhere. So much blood.

I cannot bear this, she thought. This is too much.

The fight went on. More Fosca riders had joined those surrounding the remaining Jerenites. Roughly Albin pushed her behind the men.

'Get down!' yelled Thurstan, no longer calm. She crouched on the floor, drowning in fear, and watched the steady, confident gains of the Fosca.

They liked to tease, as cats torment their prey. Back to back, the Jerenite defence was successful within limits, just managing to keep them far enough away to avoid serious injury.

But the Fosca worked as a team, prepared to lose individual members, and one of them darted forward, impaling itself on Lukas's sword. Before dying it managed to flash beneath Albin's guard, thrusting a long talon deep into his shoulder. His sword fell from his useless hand, and he began to keel over, muttering inaudibly.

Another Fosca leapt at him; shrieking, it flicked one of the long flexible limbs, whipping with the sharp pincers held open, and Albin's head was sent spinning in a dazzling spiral of gore across the floor.

Open mouthed, paralysed with horror, Eleanor watched the swords come closer. Two of the men had fallen, and the other woman. Lukas's upper arm was laid open in a long gash, white bone glinting beneath the blood. They were all exhausted, desperate for reinforcements. No one came.

They could endure no longer, she knew, and neither

could she. She saw Thurstan stagger with weariness, his sword missing its aim, and the Fosca yelled victory. The scream that had been gripping her heart since the first Fosca had swooped down began to well up, choking her throat, blanketing out thought.

Sound and flooding white light were one, and the world stood still, a breath gasped and held.

The implacable face of the extraordinary Moon shone, devastatingly, down through the ruined ceiling.

The light swamped all feeling, drowned all perception, battening down consciousness, conjuring madness. The Fosca, stunned into sudden silence, ran wildly to escape, falling onto each other's claws, dying in an excess of brilliance. Shielding their eyes, senses distorted, wonder and fear mixed, the remaining men and women shrank back into the darkness, trying to evade the pitiless clarity.

Only Eleanor stood free, in ecstatic communion with light, laughing aloud with the joy of such beauty, creating and recreating in her own being the Moon's radiance. In a trance of delight, she raised her arms in welcome and homage. She was light and strength. Power and glory were hers.

Jocasta ran forwards to join her, arms held wide, head thrown back.

I have done this, thought Eleanor. I have done this, I am brilliant with the Moon, unassailably powerful. Light swirled around her in a dangerous ecstasy, and she laughed, careless with triumph, arrogant in pride.

I have such power, she sang. The Moon is one with beauty and so am I, for She comes whenever I need Her . . .

In reply, a ruthless coruscation of energy startled the air like electricity.

With a sigh, Jocasta was shrivelled to ash where she stood.

A voice sounded, dreamlike, in Eleanor's heart – 'I will help you, Eleanor Knight, whenever the need is great. But do not think you can direct Me . . .' and then the light vanished, abruptly and completely.

Abandoned, Eleanor staggered. And then whirled round to look for Jocasta. From the shadows figures surged forwards, Lukas reaching her first.

'What was that? What was that? Where is she? What did

you do?' He was shouting, frantic and furious, grasping her shoulders. 'What have you done!'

Blankly she stared at him, no longer understanding or knowing anything.

'I didn't mean . . .' she began, and crumpled, falling to the floor.

Chapter Twenty-three
Solkest

'Move on!'

A painful kick in the ribs, icy water on his face, and a wrench on the chain round his wrists. Unwillingly, Blythe swayed to his feet and stumbled after Grogan's horse across the bridge which spanned the first of the rings of the Imperial palace. The early morning sun burned hard and bright. His head ached as he looked around.

Solkest was not so much a building as a city within a city, protected by seven concentric walls of heavy grey stone. There was a walkway around the top of each wall, patrolled by guards. Only one bridge linked each ring; this too was heavily guarded. The walls ascended towards the centre, where the Emperor's quarters had an overview of the entire palace. Blythe had been here before, of course, on the rare occasions when the Warden's Watch was required to attend the Rites of Lycias. Usually at such times the ordinary life of Solkest was suspended, the shutters drawn, the gates closed. Honouring the God required total devotion from everyone.

Never before had he been able to observe the daily life of Solkest. It offered no reassurance.

The outer ring was the widest, and contained hundreds of dwelling places for the servants, untidy stacks of flats, barracks for the soldiers, stables for their horses. It was crowded with people, working; scrubbing, cooking, washing, training with weapons and horses. But as Blythe staggered over the bridge, hauled on the chain running from Grogan's pommel, the unnatural silence of the place struck him.

No one spoke, except to issue orders. No one chattered, sang or shouted. A deathly stillness held all those teeming crowds in a discipline as rigid as the grave. Discipline,

Blythe thought, or despair? Perhaps no one ever came here without a legacy of despair.

The second ring was also quiet, but at first sight not so disquieting. It contained fields and trees, kitchen gardens and orchards, cultivated to sustain the thousands in the other rings. All appeared pleasant, sunny and ordered, until Blythe noticed a shadow within a grove of fruit trees.

A creature some fifteen feet tall, with long thin rubbery arms, was harvesting apples. Blindly it grabbed and plucked, hairless, eyeless, sniffing like a hound at the fruit. Its mouth hung slackly open, emitting a thin wail. It had a chain round its neck, and a man seated on a horse was controlling the creature with a pointed goad.

'Hell! What's that?' Blythe pulled back for a moment, and Grogan, glancing round, smiled at him.

'A useful servant. No more, no less. One of Lefevre's more successful experiments.'

The creature moaned and gibbered at the sound of his voice. Its grey, greasy skin was lacerated by cuts and bruises, its bones jutting out at painful angles. It was tormented, in hell, picking apples in a rich lord's garden.

The chain jerked. Blythe stumbled and had to run a few steps to avoid being dragged. Through a haze of exhaustion he saw other monsters: a flying thing, half bat, half bird, spinning in blind circles through the air, uselessly circling a flower garden, a herd of dairy cattle with udders so grotesquely swollen that they could barely walk, a small toad-like animal flinching in the sun.

The third ring contained more buildings. Workshops, said Grogan, happy to show off knowledge. He pointed to a long low shed to one side. Through the windows, Blythe could just make out rows of giant birds in cages, not hawks like the Arrarat, but gulls and crows, vultures and owls.

'They don't fly,' said Grogan. 'The Fosca were the only success in that respect. The Arrarat, of course, have a different origin. But Lord Lefevre keeps trying, and will succeed again soon, I'm sure.'

'Why are there no Fosca here now?'

'They were rewarded with their own territory after their loyal service during the Banishment War, a rather special place, far to the south east of here . . . They are genuinely free, you know. They obey no man except by agreement.' Grogan smiled with complacency. Maliciously, he spurred his horse into a trot, and Blythe had to struggle to remain on his feet.

The fourth ring was a moat, filled high with water. It was fed by the tide itself, running through a wide channel from the lagoon. Deep shadows lurked under its surface; Lefevre's curiosity was not confined to birds and animals. Silvery shoals scudded through turquoise water, pale jellyfish drifted idly, and then there was a flurry, a blunt snout snapping, teeth pointed and vicious. A turmoil of splashes, writhing scales and fins, and a red stain spread across the surface. Grogan looked round at him. 'The Lord Lefevre has great power, you see. Never doubt that, Phin. You'll find out soon enough.'

The next ring, bleak and narrow, was heavily guarded and contained the prisons and dungeons. Grogan hailed one of the guards cheerfully, and then kicked his horse once more. As it cantered over the bridge Blythe fell, rolling in the dust, bruised and battered. He was unconscious when they passed him over to the prison officer.

He awoke some time later in a cold, stone-built cell to find himself slumped, half-standing against a damp wall, his weight painfully hanging from the chains still fastened round his lacerated wrists. They were attached to a ring set high in the stone wall. Wincing, he stood upright.

He didn't know where he was, whether this was part of the prison ring or a separate chamber within Lefevre's own quarters.

There was a window, small, high up in the stone. He tried to see out of it. A strange, greenish light came from it. At first he thought the glass was distorted, and then realised that it was heavy, reinforced, in order to keep back the weight of water. His cell was beneath the water level of the moat. There was no possible way out through the window.

He leant back against the clammy wall, head aching, limbs feeble and weak. He was desperately thirsty from loss of blood. There was a jug across the floor, but beyond his reach. He wanted to sit down, for his legs were unsteady, but the chain was too short to allow that. He could only stand or kneel.

He stood. How long would it be before he was brought before Lycias's High Priest? Soon, he hoped.

He remembered Selene, passionate and mysterious. He remembered the shopkeeper, those sick and desperate men, and that old, frightened woman, trembling, feeble. Those other feverish, emaciated remnants of Astret's people, running in panic down the long tunnels. Uther, lost there. Beavis, dying in a fountain of blood. His own act, pulling a lever.

And Karis. Overwhelming everything, Karis, Karis, casually murdered.

Wondering how much it was possible to endure, he closed his eyes, leaning against the cold stone. The light planted in his mind by Selene was still there, beckoning and insistent. There was nothing he could do about it. He shifted against the wall, waiting.

It seemed a long time before the door swung open. A guard, wearing Lefevre's personal uniform, the purple with yellow diagonal stripe, unloosed the chain from the wall. A brief, impassive glance at Blythe, a jerk on the chain.

'Follow,' he said.

There was no other choice. As they went out of the door, two other guards fell into place behind Blythe.

He had watched men in this position before. He had marched manacled prisoners through to the Justices in Peraldon. He had seen them stumble with exhaustion and pain, seen them sometimes march head held high with spurious bravado. He had not thought that one day he too would be led before authority in chains.

He would be no passive victim. He watched every detail of the short journey to Lefevre's quarters on the lower levels of the seventh ring, noting the disposition of guards, their readiness, weapons and uniforms. He watched doors open, tried to hear passwords, observed his captors, charted his surroundings. He ignored the pain in his side, the pain in his wrists and bruised body, and concentrated instead on the details, from the way the guard ahead of him carried his weapons, to the length of the grey corridors they were traversing.

Also, almost with abstraction, he noted the burgeoning of hatred.

They had to pass three separate sets of guards; the first admitted them without question. The second set demanded papers and authorisation. The third set, at the end of a red-carpeted corridor, tight lipped and grim, waited for a whispered password before letting them through.

Blythe did not hear the password, did not know which games to play here. Bleakly, he took in the scale of the final hall, its heavy, wide-spaced pillars and arched ceiling. There were soldiers on guard, round the pillars, along the aisle, standing at the doorways. Viewed as a problem of odds, the situation was hopeless.

Lights shone from torches set in the wall, casting vivid pools of yellow which glinted against helmet and sword. There were no windows. The silence, apart from the tread of their feet, was absolute.

In the centre of the hall, under the highest arch of the ceiling, stood a wide dais of bare, polished boards. On it stood a wide desk of heavy and functional design. It dominated the hall. A tall stand, set with three brackets for torches, shone onto a wide bowl of roses, their colour shocking in the dark hall, their scent heavy and cloying in the still air.

Seated at the desk was a man Blythe had never seen before. He sprawled in the chair, fingering a silver goblet. A golden cloak tumbled opulently around him. At ease, he regarded the approach of the guards and Blythe with what could only be amusement, for his thin lips were curved. Long-limbed, broad shouldered, he was constructed on the same massive scale as the pillars around. He gave the impression of power, unadulterated and dangerous beneath the confident sprawl and gaudy cloak. Dark curling hair, deepset eyes, firm chin, aquiline nose; all was conventionally handsome until one looked closer at his face.

His eyes were empty.

No flicker of life, warmth or awareness betrayed itself there. It was not that he was blind, for his face followed their progress up the hall, glancing from the almost spilling wine to their movements. It was not that the eyes were too deepset to display feeling, for Blythe could see the surface of the iris. It shone black as night; intelligence and emotion had no possibility of reflection there.

The question Blythe found himself wanting to ask was not, who are you? It was instead, what are you? Unreasoning panic gripped him; this was not something he had encountered before, even in nightmares. He shivered; the musty air of the hall seemed tainted with a feathering touch of dread.

The man at the desk nodded once and the guards fell back, leaving Blythe alone, facing him. The voice, when it eventually came, was soft and even, cultured and elegant. It was so devoid of any humanity that it had a quality that bore more relation to screaming than to conversation.

'Why are you interfering, Phinian Blythe? What is your purpose?'

Blythe remained silent, trying to work out what was going on.

'You will tell me,' he said. 'You will tell me clearly and precisely everything I need to know. There is no other option.'

The voice was neutral, empty of emotion or pressure, and Blythe wanted to crawl, to shrink away from the obscenity of it. Breathing hard, he forced himself to look directly into the eyes; and then the breath froze in his throat.

The blackness reached out and engulfed him, a tide of pervasive darkness. It was as if every acquired protection and defence in his mind was stripped from him. Every layer of warmth, of personality, of thought, was trampled on and destroyed. His soul itself was excoriated, laid waste, left flinching, exposed to the assault of evil. The creature's brutal mind rummaged around within his most secret thoughts, wrenching them about, discarding them as futile. He thought he would faint, that he simply couldn't bear it, the vile feel of it, but the empty eyes held his own still in a rigid communion. And then the creature blinked once, and leaned back in his chair, laughing softly to himself.

Released, Blythe fell to the ground. He lay there,

shuddering, barely conscious, only half listening to the stream of commands being issued over his head.

The Lagoon was to be dredged, the bodies to be examined to see if Selene was among them. Uther was to be watched and arrested if he tried to move. Jarek Duparc was also to be watched, and questioned later after the coronation of the new Emperor. A sample of Blythe's handwriting was to be obtained, so that a suicide note could be prepared.

Ashes in his mouth, Blythe rolled to his knees, shaking his head, trying to reassemble the ruins of memory and thought. Amidst the devastation, one question formed.

'Where's Lefevre?' he said, thickly. He felt as if he had never spoken before, and that there would never be anything worth saying ever again.

'Where is he? Where's Lefevre?' More strongly, he began to shout. 'Where is the bastard?'

'Calm yourself, my friend.' Another voice, light and pleasant from a side doorway. 'There's no need to make such a fuss. I've been here all the time.'

He stepped out from behind a wide pillar, a small, elderly, insignificant figure, dressed in the loose bleached linen robes of High Priest. He was carrying a rose, which he raised to his nose, fastidiously, as he approached Blythe.

'Dear me, you have been getting into unsavoury company, haven't you, Phinian? Still, none of it is irretrievable, thanks to Idas here.' The light from the lamp on the desk shone on his balding head, fringed with soft white hair. Kindly eyes regarded Blythe with affection and regret.

'I'm so sorry, my dear boy, that you felt obliged to meddle. There was really no need, and now it's too late, for you, at least.' He sighed, elaborately, and nodded to the man behind the desk. Idas had snapped briskly to his feet when Lefevre first spoke, and was standing to attention.

Strange intuitions flaring in the wreckage of his mind, Blythe knew that the creature with the empty eyes was more completely terrified of that small elderly man than he could comprehend. And Blythe himself now knew the meaning of terror to a degree hitherto unimagined.

'Why?' His voice rasped strangely.

'Why?' Lefevre repeated, almost surprised. 'You know

the answer to that, don't you, Phinian Blythe?' He smiled calmly. 'The Stasis must be maintained, of course. Our cardinal concern, our only priority. Why, you've sworn an oath of allegiance to that effect yourself, haven't you?'

Impatiently Blythe remembered the brief ceremony of initiation into the Warden's Watch so long ago. He had been more interested in the uniform, he remembered, than the form of the oath. But throughout his adult life it had been the same. Unthinking acceptance of the eternal Stasis.

'No one was threatening it! Nothing was happening!' He was frantic.

'Ah, there you are in error.' He walked slowly across the stone floor to where Blythe was still kneeling, and put out a bony hand to stroke his hair. 'Poor boy,' he said. 'It doesn't matter now, your knowing.'

He looked down into Blythe's face. 'The Stasis is at risk from a number of factors – not least from the Cavers' paltry magic making. And the death of the Emperor –' For a moment the pale eyes were strangely hooded. 'We couldn't allow one of our own people to behave in an irregular fashion, it might have made things worse. Nothing can be risked now. And you, Blythe, fathered a child on your lovely young wife, didn't you? We couldn't have that, upsetting the balance, without control. New life, outside the calculations, would threaten all our immortality, don't you understand? Lord Lycias would not have been happy, no, not at all.

'But now we have a new Emperor, and things will, I trust, settle down once more . . .' His kind eyes were turned away, and Blythe, struggling to understand, missed the flash of desperate panic.

He heard the words, accepted them, stored them. But he could not now, in this extremity, afford to absorb and react to them as they deserved. It was too much. Only one thing was clear.

'You had Karis killed!' The conclusion was inescapable. 'Was that why the Fosca were called in?' His eyes were wide with the memory, his voice raw with hate.

'I'm afraid so. A false message, that you needed her . . . She was a good wife to you, poor Karis. She ran out without any hesitation at all. And the Fosca are loyal servants.'

'To you? Your servants?' He was being stupid with shock.

Lefevre shook his head. 'No. The God ordains; I only obey.'

'The God – He does not ordain. He does nothing!' Furious with refusal, he lurched to his feet.

'Lycias wishes the Stasis to be maintained. I merely execute His wishes.'

'*Why*?' Explosively, it rang out, echoing from the stone pillars.

'Why should we live for ever? Or why do as He ordains? The first is a mystery not for your ears, and the second, because I have no choice. The Lord has created His own willing servants, just as I do, by His grace.' He waved his hand to the tall eyeless creature at the desk. 'I have no option, just as Idas here has no option.'

Lefevre paused, still smiling. He was unruffled, even enjoying the encounter. For all his gnarled hands and balding head his face was smooth and unlined, a little plump. Generously he spread his hands wide, eyes laughing.

'Would you like to see for yourself?'

'What do you mean?'

'An encounter with Lord Lycias. It is possible, you know. Then you can ask Him yourself.'

Blythe stared. 'You're mad. This is nonsense!'

'How do you know? You, Phinian Blythe, who have never done more than pay lip service to the Lord. Have you ever attended a Laurat Rite? Heard the Forbidden Teaching? Taken the sanctified fruit of the Sun? Can you recite even one chapter of the Scriptures?' For once his voice was raised. 'Of course not. Like the rest of your kind, you reserve not the smallest part of your attention for the Lord. You know nothing of your own religion. You understand not the first thing about the Law which governs your life and that of all Peraldon.' He paused, breathing a little harder.

'I'm doing you a signal honour, Blythe. It should be some recompense for losing your life. You may meet the God.'

For a moment, Blythe glanced round; but the waiting guards had stepped closer. He was surrounded by fully armed men. Idas towered over them all at the dais, hand negligently on the hilt of his sword. It would be useless to resist.

Anyway, what would he be struggling to preserve? A dead

love, a plundered mind, an overwhelming guilt? It would satisfy some curiosity to discover Lefevre's meaning, but would that be enough? On the whole, he thought not.

There was always hate.

He spun quickly, pivoting on his heel, using his manacled hands as a club, winding the guard on his right. Then, ducking, he ran straight at Lefevre, his fists reaching for the old man's throat.

He never made it, of course. There was a brief scuffle, some shouting, a clash of steel, and someone screamed. He lost consciousness before discovering whether the scream came from one of the guards or himself.

Chapter Twenty-four
The Cauldron

Dry as ashes, burnt and discarded, Blythe winced back to awareness. Something, perhaps the pain in his head, warned him not to open his eyes, but he disobeyed, and fire shattered his sight.

Coruscating brilliance inflamed and exalted the agony in his head, and he wondered if his eyes had been burnt out. There was absolute silence.

His wrists were still chained together; his clothes largely intact, though bloody and torn. His boots had been removed; he didn't understand why. He was lying on his back on some smooth unyielding surface. He could not think, through the pain, where he was.

A scorching sensation began to penetrate the soiled linen of his shirt; he shifted a little, and the burning transferred to his shoulder where it touched the surface. His feet were beginning to smart away from the heat of it, too.

He had to know where he was. Reluctantly he raised his hands and clasped them together over his wounded eyes. Then, dreading, he opened them very slightly.

It was not quite so bad, because he knew enough to expect the glare of white light. Blinking, tormented, he tried to make sense of what he had seen.

He was lying in the centre of a vast bowl lined with faceted mirrors. He knew immediately what it was; he had stood on the high platforms at its side often enough. Bored, hot and sweating, he had watched the Sun Priests sway and chant the Midsummer Ceremony, dropping cold water onto the burning mirrors where it fizzed and hissed in the midday sun, instantly evaporating. Everyone had worn shaded glass visors to protect their eyes, and even so it had been an uncomfortable, tedious duty. He had even once speculated on the temperature at the centre, when the sun was at its height.

The bowl was acres wide, gradually curving up into an overhang, designed to contain the swirling heat safely.

The sun was well through its path to its zenith; there would be an hour or so left, he estimated, before it reached that high point. The heat was already scorching. Sweat ran down his face, and he was gasping with thirst. He did not think he would still be alive to face it in half an hour, let alone one or two.

His shirt was beginning to smoulder in the rising heat; grimly, he rolled over, hands still protecting his eyes, and lurched to his feet.

He understood then why his boots had been removed; the soles of his feet began to tingle immediately against the burning mirrors.

'Dance then,' said a thin, light voice. 'As the City dances for the new Emperor, so must you dance for the God. The Lord welcomes the dance, and approves your sacrifice.'

Above the curved rim of the bowl, a platform rose high in the still air. It was a relief to look up, away from the mirrors. Two figures stood there, Lefevre and Idas, unmistakable against the hot blue sky. He could hear their voices clearly in the windless silence. He sat down again, cursing.

'The Lord desires your prayers, not your curses,' said Lefevre reprovingly.

'Where is He then?' Blythe yelled, bitter anger flaring, his voice cracking harshly.

'All around you.' Lefevre spread his hands wide at the bowl. 'Lycias's face stares at you now, from a million mirrors. Ever beautiful, ever powerful, He will unite with you in fire and love, the ultimate gift of ecstasy. Consider, and give praise.'

Shifting, aching, sweating, Blythe considered Lycias, the Sun God. The regulator of all their days, the source of warmth and light. Peraldonians basked in the unthinking benison of the victorious Sun. Daily, they sang praises and hymns, gave offerings and danced at the festivals of Lycias the Beautiful, Lycias the Eternal, Lycias the Lord of Love.

That He was dangerous they had known, but usually forgot. That He wished immortality for His subjects, eternal youth and vigour, was understood by some and enjoyed by most. Lycias ordained that the balance, the Stasis be maintained; and so Peraldonians lived forever, and seldom bore children . . .

Ah, Karis, he thought. Did Lycias order your death because of our child? Could He not have taken my life instead? Or is He wantonly cruel, enjoying the refinement of extended suffering?

'No,' said Lefevre, answering Blythe's unspoken thought. 'No, the Lord is not wanton. He is not even – interested.' He leant forward a little, peering down into the mirrored cauldron. He was wearing darkened glasses, but the reflected glare gleamed on the high, wide forehead.

'Before you die, Blythe, I'll tell you a secret. Idas knows it already, he learnt it the hard way. Listen.

'Lycias has abandoned Peraldon. He has never heard even one of our ceremonies or prayers. The sun you see reflected all around you is His only presence in our world. Your impending apotheosis, dear boy, will mean nothing to our Lord, for He will know nothing of it. He lives entirely with Love, and has forsaken our puny affairs.' His voice dropped to the merest whisper, and Blythe could hardly hear the words. 'And the prayer I make, daily, is that He should never return. So would you, Phinian, if you only knew . . .' He stopped, laughing a little breathlessly. 'But it's too late for that now. Nothing can be risked, the Stasis must be maintained, and so you must die.'

The countless suns burnt back at Blythe, unwinking, unforgiving. He gathered his fragmenting thoughts.

'If you kill me, the balance will be upset again . . .'

'Death is easily balanced by birth. Some fortunate Peraldonian lady will find herself conceiving and will bear a child. That can be your epitaph, and your consolation.

'There is one thing further. Before leaving us to the Stasis, our Lord gave me certain prophecies, detailed instructions. You cannot escape, however it may appear. You are a necessary part of the pattern. Farewell, dear boy.'

He waved negligently, and began to walk down the stairs from the platform.

Idas remained for a moment after, looking down at Blythe.

'Just over an hour you will have. Does not the Sun eclipse the Moon's feeble light?' He laughed, the elegant voice potent with malice, and turned to follow his master.

Desperately, Blythe shifted against the burning mirrors. To some extent his eyes were becoming accustomed to the glare, but the pain in his head was now producing disturbed vision. Waves of heat distorted the shape of the bowl; he found it difficult to gauge the exact slope of the curve. As far as he remembered, the rim would overhang at such an angle as to make it impossible to scale the sides. Because his sight was so untrustworthy, however, he knew he would have to try.

Sweat was pouring from him, evaporating on the hot bowl. The wound in his side had opened up again, and was beginning to throb. He felt sick with the pain in his head, in his bruised and wounded body. His tongue was swollen with a thirst which could only worsen. He was in no shape at all for a strenuous run across a burning wasteland. Light-headed, he gritted his teeth, silently promising himself that one day Lefevre and his precious Lycias should pay for this.

Then, wincing in anticipation, he took a deep breath, surged to his feet, and began to run. It didn't matter which direction he took, for the bowl was circular. From the centre, he had a hundred yards to cover before the curve became acute. Heart pumping, gasping, he sprinted so fast that his feet barely touched the burning surface.

Just as he was feeling that he could not possible keep up the speed, the surface began to rise sharply in front of him. The momentum kept him going until he was almost horizontal. Then, desperately, he jumped upwards and inwards, stretching his fingers as wide as the chains would allow, clutching for the rim. For a second it seemed that he was touching the outer surface of the bowl, but there was nowhere for him to grip and his fingers were slippery with sweat. Inexorably, he began to fall, to tumble back, rolling down the slope.

He lay still, trembling, gasping. Threads of his shirt were tearing and smouldering. Soon it would be his skin burning. There could not be long to go, he thought, forearm over his eyes. He could not survive much longer on this gridiron.

He could try once more, he supposed. It was no longer possible to avoid burning if he remained still. His only choice, his only chance would be to run, and keep running.

In a daze of pain and weakness he hurled himself onwards. He fell back, again, and then tried a different tactic, trying to edge upwards inside the curve, back and legs braced against the awkward concave. But there was no possible purchase for his fingers, handicapped by chains, no possible way out of the sun-scarred cauldron.

He moved, and moved again, exposing back, thighs, feet, knees in turn to the burning mirrors. There was no way out, no relief.

In the end, he half crawled, half staggered, back to the centre, where the heat was fiercest, the light brightest. It would be over the sooner, there.

His mind was blank, numb with exhaustion and pain. And his heart contained only hate, refined and purified in the furnace, overwhelming hate for the Sun God and His priest.

He collapsed onto the mirrors and lay there, shifting imperceptibly.

He had thus, in pain, given up. In the torment of his senses, he failed to hear the heavy beating of wings in the shrill electric air. Discarded in the hollow of the bowl, no longer caring that he was burning and dying, he missed the deliberate, darting approach of the great hawk.

It swooped into the bowl beside him, fastidiously lifting its feet to ease the scorching. It bent its huge, alien head, and nudged the man's inert body. It nudged again, more urgently, for the sun was almost directly overhead now. This time, groaning, Blythe rolled over. Hardly realising what was happening, impelled by a foreign, unknown consciousness, he crept to his feet, reaching blindly for the ebony feathers. The midnight hawk ducked, bending its backward-jointed knees, lowering itself; with a last effort

Blythe flung himself onto its back, clutching with blistered, still bound hands at the feathers.

The Arrarat took off on a rush of charged air, as if buffeted by the wild and enormous heat, banking high, up into the blue. In an ecstasy of freedom, it surged further upwards, and the air began to cool, to lose its urgent violence.

Barely conscious, Blythe's grip was not secure. The hawk just managed to clear the rings and towers of Solkest before realising that its passenger was slipping. Finely judging the angle of descent, it dipped and swerved, trying to stay beneath him, and gently, gradually brought him down to land, on the quay outside his home.

He tumbled off into the shade of a high wall. Instantly, the bird took off once more, and before Blythe even realised where he was, had disappeared far into the bright midday sky.

His feet were too burnt to bear him; he crawled, head low, along the wall to the open gate, and into the shady garden. In its centre was a lily pond, Karis's pride. He collapsed at its edge, manacled hands falling into the cool water. Lying full length he drank great gulping handfuls, splashing the water over himself.

Chapter Twenty-five
Quayside

He became gradually aware of activity to the front of the house; doors opening, horses' hooves clattering on cobbles, subdued speech.

Panic gripped him: what if Idas and Lefevre had decided to examine his home already? He hoped and trusted that they would think him dead in the solar furnace. But then, who were these people? As quietly as he could in his weakened state, he retreated into the shrubbery.

The voices became clearer as he concentrated. His family, mother and sisters. Other relations, friends.

And Grogan. Grogan was there, all elegant platitudes.

He listened uncomprehending, to his sister receiving condolences, to his mother sobbing. What was the problem, what had happened?

Such grief, such shock in their voices.

Then he remembered. The day of the Emperor's Election. Karis's funeral. He had forgotten the day of the funeral in the obsession to question Lefevre.

He had forgotten Karis's funeral.

Idas's empty eyes had destroyed more than he knew. And now he heard puzzlement, anger, distress and anxiety as his relations speculated on what had happened. Why he was not there.

He could hardly stand up and announce himself, not with Grogan there. He tried to hear what they were saying and shifted minutely behind the fig trees and jasmine.

His mother, controlling her voice with some effort. 'But Phin wouldn't have just gone off without telling anyone. He isn't like that . . .'

'Grief can distort character and judgment, my lady.' Grogan, smoothly respectful.

Another voice, which Blythe recognised with overwhelming relief as Uther. 'Will you come in, my lady? There are refreshments.'

'No, I thank you, Uther.' The quick warmth in his mother's voice caught him by the throat. 'Poor Uther. What will you do now?'

'I'm sure Uther will be able to help us find your son, my lady,' said Grogan. 'In fact I'd be glad if he'd come with us right now. Something has cropped up.'

'What, exactly?' Jarek, sharp and quick.

There was a pause. Then, as if with reluctance, Grogan spoke again.

'A note has been found. I felt we could hardly discuss it before the Lady Karis had been duly honoured . . .'

'What note? Let me see!' His mother, urgent, suspicious.

'It's down at the Justice's court. It's probably not even genuine. A tragic event of this nature often stirs up such things. It will be the work of a moment to authenticate. There's no need to distress yourself, my lady. You will be informed immediately there is any definite news. Pray remain calm.'

'He is not the man to do anything foolish, Lady Valeria.' Jarek, with reassuring good sense. Totally misplaced, Blythe thought. Wildly inaccurate . . .

'But where is he?' Her voice was openly shaking now. It was all he could do to stop himself going to her.

'Mother . . . please don't start imagining things.' His sister Victoria, prosaic as usual. 'There's probably been some accident. Phin will turn up.'

'Of course he will, Lady Valeria. May I escort you home?'

His mother paused before replying. She would be playing with her handkerchief, turning it over in narrow, delicate hands. Control would not slip for long. She sighed. 'I suppose so. Jarek, this is kind of you. Grogan, we shall be at home. Please send as soon as you have any news at all.'

'Of course, my lady.'

There was a sound of carriages and horses, a clatter of wheels over cobbles, and only Grogan and Uther were left.

'Don't go far, will you, Uther?' This was an order, not a request. 'We shall be needing you. You will notice guards around the house; they are to discourage any effort you may make to evade us.'

'Why don't you just arrest me?'

There was a slight pause.

'What for?' said Grogan. 'What have you done? We would prefer not to stir up more trouble than we need. We would not wish to alarm the Lady Valeria and her family more than necessary. And there are many calls on our attention at the moment. Nothing must disturb the election. Just don't go far, Uther. We may need you.' He laughed, unpleasantly, and then Uther was left alone.

Blythe was wondering if he'd be able to stand unaided, when Uther's voice came strongly above him.

'They've gone. Do you need a hand?'

'Uther . . .' His voice, unused and dry, was barely more than a whisper. There was a stifled exclamation, and then the shrubs were pushed aside and brown competent hands hauled him gently to his burnt feet, and helped him inside the house.

Some time later, in the gathering dusk, washed, bandaged and a little refreshed, Blythe was sitting at the kitchen table, elbows propping the heels of his hands against his aching eyes. The house around them was quiet and deserted. Uther prepared food. He had sent the other servants home.

'Captain Duparc will be back,' he said.

'Why?' It was an effort to speak.

'I've never seen him so angry. He didn't want to be left out, that evening we went to see Selene. He said I should never have left you in that warren . . .'

'Uther, I never even asked! How did you get out?'

'More by luck than judgment. I can swim, you see, and was near one of the exits . . . it wasn't too difficult.'

'What about the others?'

'A few escaped, I suppose.' Uther was grim. 'They're still dredging for bodies.'

Blythe remained slumped for a while, and then sat up suddenly. 'Uther, my wits must be wandering. We're got to get out of here, and soon. They know all about you, and they'll soon discover I've escaped.'

'I'm packing right now, don't worry,' said Uther. He was thrusting food and blankets into a rucksack. Briefly Blythe explained about Idas and the inexplicable intervention of the Arrarat hawk.

He did not then associate the hawk with the light that burnt in his mind. He understood so few of the implications.

Eventually Uther left the kitchen to get clothes for them both.

He was alone again. Silence. Blythe leant back in the chair, winced and tilted forward again, away from the hard wood. Wearily, he laid his forearms on the table and dropped his forehead down onto them.

Karis was dead, and their child. That was the worst. He wanted to weep for loneliness.

But there were other tragedies to consider.

He had personally initiated the deaths of hundreds of pale refugees. The old, the fever-ridden. The hopeless, vulnerable, pathetic underground colony. They had drowned.

Logic told him that it was not his fault, that he had tried to save them. But in these circumstances, to what extent was he free to act? Lefevre had said that there were prophecies. Had they known all along what he would do? Was he part of an ordained pattern of destruction? Had they even known that he would escape? How far were all actions circumscribed in a world where the existence of an unborn child could threaten all stability? Where the deaths of hundreds of rebels were considered incidental?

They were Moon Worshippers, he thought. For that reason only were they insignificant. Killing the Moon's people, refugees or Cavers, never upset anything because they were all outside the balance anyway, living this side of the Boundary more by accident than anything else.

He lifted his head, staring blankly at the deepening twilight.

He would leave Peraldon. He would seek out the Cavers and try to join them. There was nothing here for him, now. His family would prefer to think him dead than disgraced.

And he owed the Moon a considerable debt now. There had been so many deaths.

Uther returned, and began tying up the bags, weighing them in his hands, wondering how much they could carry. Looking at Blythe, still collapsed across the table, he wondered if he would have to carry him as well.

There was a light knock at the front door. Smoothly, competently, Uther bundled his master into the larder, flinging the bags in afterwards.

Grogan perhaps. Or Idas. Inside the larder, Blythe looked at the rows of jars and bottles, and knew that he would not be able to stand another encounter with Idas. Perhaps he only wanted to join the Cavers as an escape from that empty-eyed monster.

It was not a comfortable thought. He waited, aching, cramped in the dark, for Uther's return.

Voices approached. Jarek was saying, 'What's so interesting in the kitchen, for heaven's sake? More Cavers hidden away, or something?' The words were light, but his tone was unusually severe.

Blythe waited until they were in the kitchen, waited until he was quite sure that there was no one else there, and then pushed himself away from the wall and left the larder.

Jarek halted suddenly, and fell silent as the light revealed his friend. Under his clothes, the edges of bandages showed; any exposed skin was flushed red and sore with burns and bruises. His eyes were black, abstracted; his mouth grim. He moved slowly, like an old man.

There was an indrawn breath, and then Jarek said, 'You always did like to make an entrance, didn't you?' He started forward as Blythe swayed, but was halted by the look in his eyes.

'I didn't plan this one,' he said. He made the chair without falling. Jarek sat opposite.

'What in hell happened to you?' His customary flippancy had deserted him. 'Grogan is busy implying that you're dead. Your mother's frantic.'

Blythe did not answer immediately. After a difficult pause, he lifted his head. 'I might as well be. I'm leaving, Jarek. I'm getting out of here. Uther will have to come, too. You're also at risk through knowing me. You'd better think what to do.'

'You're not well. Has the sun turned your head?'

'You could say that.' He flexed his fingers, wondering if he'd be able to hold a sword again yet. Then he raised his eyes and looked directly at Jarek. 'Lefevre thinks I'm a traitor. Whether I am or not is largely irrelevant at this stage. I need to get out of here, and you should consider doing the same. He knows I've talked to you. You'll be under suspicion.'

'How does he know?'

Idas violated my mind, he thought. He took all the information he needed, and I could make no defence at all.

'I told him.' What else could he say?

Jarek pushed his chair back, scraping it on the tiled floor. 'The hell you did! Why?' He was white with anger.

'Listen.' His voice was compelling. 'Karis was deliberately murdered, because she was pregnant. Lefevre told me this himself. The Fosca were called in to kill Cavers, who don't matter, and to kill my wife. Because if she'd borne a child, the damn, bloody, Stasis would be under threat.

'Think, Jarek, just think about that. We are kept here, like rats in a trap, undying, childless, to preserve some balance that none of us understands! This is a sterile limbo, meaningless, hopeless!'

'Do you want to grow old then? Do you want to die? Do you know what it means, death? Have you seriously thought about it, ceasing?' Jarek was using conventional arguments, but his eyes were withdrawn, considering. 'I like the sun, I like the way we live here, look around you. This is a good life, easy and comfortable. Do you want to struggle with rain and snow, to grub an existence like the Cavers?'

'Their life is indeed hard, and desperate. I'm not denying it. Even their weather has stopped changing. So close to the Boundary are they that they almost share that frozen time. But at least the Cavers know it's wrong, they recognise that life shouldn't be static. That's why they're so much trouble.'

The other reason is the Moon Herself, he thought, and realised again that Her pale light still shone at the back of his sight. He was not in any way let off the hook yet; nor did he want to be.

'But the alternative is death.' Jarek stared at Blythe. He spoke as if to a child. 'That's what happens when there's no Stasis. That's why we live here like this. You know that. Do you want to die?' he asked, and then fell silent, appalled by the bitterness in Blythe's eyes.

'Not until I have killed Lefevre,' he said. 'That will, I think, break the Stasis. He is responsible, and he will have to pay.'

'I think you're probably mad.' Jarek's voice was also quiet, but not unsympathetic. 'Where will you go?'

'To the Cavers. There is nowhere else. They may find me useful.' He sighed. 'You should come too. They think you're involved too.'

'Just what *did* you tell Lefevre?'

'Everything. Nothing. I said nothing, but they took it all. Idas . . .' He stopped. What was the use?

'I know that name . . .' Jarek looked as if he might say something more, but then he stopped. 'Never mind that now. What did you do to get yourself into Idas's clutches? What did you find out?'

Jarek would not make any decision without due consideration. Astute and clever, he would have to weigh all factors first.

'I tried to prevent them flooding the sewers.' I failed, he thought, quite terribly, I failed. But I did try, and that is what they won't forget.

'Why?' Jarek persisted. 'Why did you try to stop that? The sewers were full of thieves and traitors.'

'They were full of women, old and young, and sick old men. It was wanton destruction, like Karis's death, for no reason other than to secure the Stasis.' Believe me, Jarek, he willed. Believe me, because Peraldon is rotten to the core, a home for maggots, not humanity, and we're better off out of it.

Uther, who had been watching at the window all this time, suddenly shot out an arm and knocked the table lamp to the floor. 'Visitors –' he whispered.

Before they could move the window shattered.

A shriek, almost too high to hear. Six-limbed horror leapt into the room. It was not alone; glinting eyes, teeth and claws betrayed more Fosca riders crowding in at the window.

They could only run. The violence in the air was exigent. Fosca never listened to argument. Jarek hauled him out of the chair and somehow they got to the door. Chairs fell behind them, china broke.

Out into the cool hall, Uther slamming the door hard. He bolted it. Immediately a razor-like claw splintered through the wood, and began hacking up and down. Impossible strength drove the vicious edge of it through the wood. It would not take long.

Jarek was making for the front door. Blythe grabbed his sleeve. 'Not that way. There'll be more waiting there.'

As he spoke the door began to rattle and another tentacle smashed through it. A spiky shadow at the window beside the front door, the glass shattering.

'Up here –' Together they ran for the staircase, stumbling over the steps.

Jarek was not with them. He stood at the bottom, his sword drawn, gleaming in the dark.

'You fool!' Blythe shouted. 'Come on!'

'I'm not going to run from any bloody Fosca!' he yelled, white faced. 'The Cavers aren't for me, either . . . Take this as a farewell for Karis, Phin. Good luck!'

The kitchen door was down; Fosca streamed through just as the hall window fragmented, and there were even more of them.

'It's your only chance,' Uther, at his shoulder. 'Take it!'

Anguished, Blythe looked down at the beleaguered figure at the bottom of the stairs – and accepted the gift. He ran on up, to the second landing window, and without thought crashed through it, reckless, down into the soft earth below. Uther tumbled after him in a rush, and together they ran through the dark garden out onto the quayside.

All was quiet on that flat expanse. Edged by swaying masts and bobbing boats it was calm and peaceful, even though it was still shadowed by the wreck of the Ferry at the south end. Blythe's own boat was moored some way from the house. It had been damaged in the attack on the Ferry and was still in the boatyard.

Although, miraculously, nothing was following them yet, Blythe and Uther dodged and wove, keeping as far as possible to the shadows, leaping from deck to deck across the boats to cut corners.

He was unsteady with exhaustion and Uther grasped his arm, taking some of the weight.

They were making for the moorings at the far end of the quayside. There were small, easily handled boats there. They could take one, and leave Peraldon . . .

Light, sudden and vivid, flooded the quayside.

Golden, bright, harsh brilliance. A familiar brilliance.

The cauldron again, all around them. Burning and tormenting.

Dazzled by glare, they stumbled on, but somehow their sense of direction had gone. Stunned and bewildered by the violent power of it, they could not tell where the light was coming from. Instinctively, they had their swords out, but there was no noisy rush of Fosca approaching, nothing tangible to fight.

The silence was absolute, heavy around them. They turned slowly, breathing hard, aware of indescribable danger. The deadly, dazzling light drained their will, left them powerless under Lycias' sun. It glared and beat down on them, and forced their swords down, too heavy against the heat. Cloying with pressure, the air was almost too dense to breathe. As if suffocating, drowning in light, they fell to their knees. The swords dropped on the silent quayside.

The heavy air shuddered, parted and closed again round the distant, clear voice of Lefevre.

'Blythe. You will indeed wish that you had died this morning. A more difficult path is now before you. The sum of your guilt is not yet complete. There is now a long way to travel through the wasteland before you accomplish my purpose. And you will accomplish it, exactly as foreseen. If you had died this morning I would have known you to be insignificant. But the Moon has chosen you, misguided as ever. You even bear Her mark. But remember this: you have been nominated, Phinian Blythe, as the instrument of Lycias's will. You will pray for death before it is over.'

Uther and Blythe could see nothing against the stunning

brightness, could not see where the voice came from. It was all around them, part of the light, part of the brilliance. A voice made of brilliance, burning words into Blythe's soul . . .

'And as for your cipher – I will retain him as a hostage to your goodwill.'

Through the fingers shielding his eyes he looked for Uther. He was only a few feet away, still there, stocky against the light, but the brightness blurred round him. His form began to waver, to lose solidity against the radiance. He shimmered and flickered, and the glow began to take over. Blythe tried to reach him, to hold him back, clasp him to the neutral earth. His hands touched nothing. Absorbed into light, Uther was no longer there.

With immense effort, Blythe dragged his eyes upwards. 'Let him go!' he whispered, hoarsely, rackingly. Almost destroyed by the effort, he surged to his feet, fists raised to the source of the soft voice. 'Let him go! It's nothing to do with him!'

'True.' Impossibly, Lefevre was laughing. 'It will, however, lend piquancy to your situation. Remember, Blythe. Your actions are all foreseen, all ordained. My deepest purpose, and that of my Lord, will come to blessed fruition through your agency, so never fear. You will not fail.'

'Never! I will never do your will, for I am going to kill you, Lefevre.' His voice was stronger now, clearer, emphatic and dedicated. 'I swear it. By the One God and His Eternal Love, I swear that I will kill you.'

'You have no choice. My will is all.' He was almost kind. 'Till we meet again, then.' The voice suddenly seemed closer to him, whispering confidingly in the wasteland. 'May the God go with you.' And then there was laughter, cruel and mocking, diminishing as the light grew brighter.

Overwhelmed, unable to breathe, he fought against impending unconsciousness, but was unable to resist. In the end, in both fear and relief, he surrendered to the light.

Chapter Twenty-six
The Saying

'A Saying! There is no choice. We must know the meaning of what is happening!'

Deep in the Cliff, Thibaud Lye's voice rang with passion. He was standing amidst the ruins of the Great Hall, looking at the survivors of the earthquake crouched against the broken rock. The cold wind from the gaping void in the Cliff flung itself around them.

'It was not a natural occurrence,' said Aylmer, more calmly, 'and although I hesitate to disregard the advice of Blaise and Matthias, now they are dead we must make our own decisions.'

'It will stretch your resources,' said Reckert, leaning tiredly against the wall. He was covered in grime and blood, as were they all. He had come crawling from the Mages' ruined quarters, with a terrible story of Matthias's suicidally courageous attempt to save Blaise. Leaderless and confused, the two remaining Mages had welcomed him with relief.

'Will your Priestess agree?' Reckert continued. If the two Mages had not been so preoccupied by the exigencies of their situation, they might have noticed the edge to his voice. They might even have probed to see if his story was true. But they were beset by worry and doubt, and did not realise how far Reckert was trying to push them.

'Where is Nerissa? Is she all right?' he asked.

'Alaric died. She's outside.' Aylmer sighed. 'So many deaths. And now what do we do?'

'The Saying will make things clear,' said Thibaud confidently. 'We'll have to ask her.'

'In my experience, Sayings only confuse things.' This was Haddon Derray, joining their group, with a brief, puzzled glance at Reckert. He was filthy with dust, his clothes hanging in rags. 'Aylmer, I must talk to you,' he continued. 'There's something I must tell you –'

'Not now, Derray. Can't you see we're busy?'

'This is important. Matthias –'

'Shut up, boy. This is an emergency, we don't have time for you now.' Thibaud swung back towards the others. 'I'll get Nerissa.' He disappeared into the shadows outside.

'Aylmer! Listen to me!' Haddon pushed Reckert aside and planted himself firmly in front of the senior Mage. 'Matthias said –'

'Not now!' Aylmer was shouting, and people turned to stare at them. 'Why must you always obstruct and interfere? Isn't it enough to fight us every inch of the way, to womanise and drink like a Jerenite, without diverting us now, in our greatest crisis?' He was perspiring, although it was cold, and his hands shook.

For a moment Haddon stared at him mutinously, and then turned on his heel and vanished into the ruined passageways, jostling Reckert's shoulder as he passed.

She could not cry. Not now, when it was too late. She had not given him one word of companionship, of simple affection even. Alaric had died a lonely man. It was her fault. Nerissa saw Thibaud Lye approaching her across the sand, and waited, uncaring.

He would want her to be strong as usual. The two remaining Mages would rely on her not to give way, even if they didn't always agree with her. She was the guide to Astret's will, and they all knew it. It was why they depended on her so much. But now she was tired, and had nothing left to give them.

'Lady Nerissa, we ask your help,' he began formally. She looked at him with lightless eyes. Alaric, my dearest and only love, Alaric, where are you now?

'We must hold another Saying.' He wasn't even trying to be tactful about it. 'May we approach your priestesses?'

'You must not,' she said automatically and then fell silent once more, staring out across the waves. Alaric had gone back into the Cliff, looking for her, when the earthquake was at its worst. She had been safe all the time, praying with her women, but someone had told him she was still inside. She had tried to stop him but he was too far away. He had run towards the Great Hall, just as the tower was collapsing. She had watched it topple, knowing he was there. She had screamed, once, but then so had many others.

'Nerissa! Listen to me!' Thibaud was pulling at her sleeve.

'What?' Vaguely she looked at him, but her eyes saw only a cloud of dust, her ears heard only the thunder of falling rock.

'We must hold another Saying! Will you allow a priestess to officiate?'

'It is not right to ask the Lady Nerissa that now, Mage Thibaud.' Margat had joined them, severe and reproving. 'She has suffered grievous loss. You should respect that.'

'We do respect it, of course we do.' Thibaud was impatient. 'We have all suffered loss. It is because of this that I must importune the Lady Priestess's help. This is important! Urgent!'

Nerissa was standing motionless there, her eyes still withdrawn; only her hands moved, restlessly wreathing around each other like small animals in the damp folds of her cloak.

'You must ask someone else!' Margat's eyes were blazing at him and he felt like taking a step back. But he was a Mage, he had the authority of Cabbalic knowledge, and a Staff of Power. He would not be forestalled by a passionate and undisciplined woman.

'It is for the High Priestess to release one of her women for a Saying.'

'How can I?' Nerissa's flat tired voice surprised them both. 'Anyone attempting a Saying will die. You know that. It is too dangerous now.'

'It is too dangerous not to!'

'Go away, leave her! Can't you see this is no time to ask her anything?' Margat flung the words at him and then put her arm round the older woman's thin shoulders, murmuring, 'Come, Nerissa, come and rest. Letia is making soup, some of the caves are still all right. Come and lie down. You can do nothing here . . .'

Together they drifted back across the sand, Nerissa unresisting, leaving Thibaud Lye staring after them, frustration and anger compressing his mouth.

The sand was damp beneath Nerissa's feet, and she could hear Margat crying at her side. Margat, who had lost her beloved brother. They had all lost friends, relations, lovers. Others knew this numbing pain too, but each was alone in grief. There was no comfort, no companionship in sorrow. There never would be. It was true isolation.

Alaric, my only friend, my only love. Why did you not wait for me? I shall learn loneliness now. I shall I learn your part, I shall endure in silence. Grief for grief, I am your equal now.

The Great Hall had been cleared of the worst of the debris. Teams of men still dug deep into the passages, trying to find survivors, for there were many missing. But the cave itself was quiet, dark, as peaceful as the unremitting wind would allow. The silver pendulum still hung unmoving over the ruins.

In silence the survivors stood around the walls. Even the wounded, those who could walk, had come. Although they were exhausted, and feared another death, they would not stay away. They would honour the Lady, for, as far as they knew, they were the last remnants of Her people.

They had found a woman, Jennet, who would act as Sayer for them. Intense and fanatical, she had lost a child in the earthquake, and her husband in the attack on the Ferry. She was desperate and eager for death. She was an appropriate mouthpiece for Astret, the banished, the abandoned, desolate goddess.

Silently, shrouded in black, the priestesses and the Mages circled the laurel fire. Further away, lost in the shadows, stood the rest of the Cavers, watching with dread. Smoke began to fill the cave.

It began with a love song, an expression of humanity's age-old affair with the changing, silvery mistress of the tides. Plain and honest, the voice of Jennet lilted in ancient patterns, and many felt tears on their cheeks. It opened hearts to longing, brought life to the gentle promptings of the mind. It was dangerous because it made them all vulnerable. No one could resist the beauty, that exquisite sensitivity.

Stripped now of artifice, the song became more rhythmic. Eleanor, had she been there, would have recognised it as part of the song Astret Herself had sung on the beach, conjuring the motion of the waves.

In the regular pacings of the song, the two Mages began casting into the air over the fire round globes of pale glass, recreating the orbits of stars, suns and moons. The watchers held their breath, and Jennet's song faltered, and died. There could be no going back.

It seemed that the wind had ceased, that the rain had stopped.

'Oh Lady, come now!' Jennet's voice cut through the silence. 'Now!'

A moment of absolute concentration, of absolute quiet.

Then –

Two globes of glass clashed and spun glittering shards into the fire.

Silence again, utter stillness.

And a laugh.

It crawled on the skin and sickened in the ears. Derisive, confident and cruel, it gloried in power.

'Fools!' said a voice, and the cave was flooded with sunlight.

Golden and glowing, the Sun God had answered their summons.

A collective moan, and many fell to their knees. Jennet He blasted to ash with the briefest flicker of attention. The Mages stood stricken into immobility.

He laughed, again. A slim golden youth standing naked in the air above them.

'Your Lady is defeated, give up! Call Her again and I will come, I promise you that! I, Lycias, am victorious and all your sterile games, your poor rites are as nothing. Continue with these ceremonies, daring to interrupt the path of Desire, and you will be destroyed. Nothing may disturb the sweetness of My Love!'

The voice filled the air around them, leaving no room for independent thought. They could only watch and listen, captives all, while the God played His games.

There appeared beside Him a beautiful woman, raven haired and unmistakably human. Dressed in ivory silk wreathed with golden chains, she was flawlessly desirable. His hand was raised to her face. She smiled at Lycias and allowed Him to unclasp the fastening of her dress. It fell, exposing the perfect creamy breasts, the curving hollows of sensuality. He drew her close.

She moulded herself to Him, floating there, bathed in golden sunlight, and began to sigh. In full view of them all, blatant and disdainful, He began to make love to the woman, moving with slow, luxurious grace. His eyes, intent and serious, looked down at her, as if He were tasting the flavour of her soul. He smiled as the pale skin became flushed, smiled as she moaned and trembled, smiled as He cradled her in His arms, washed over with joy.

A dry, passionless voice cut through the warmth.

'For this, we are imprisoned in the Stasis. This is why time stands still. This is why we live in dark and rain. Do not accept!'

Leaning against a rock, half supported by Haddon, half by the glowing staff, Matthias Marling spoke to the Cavers, softly, musingly. There were rough blood-stained bandages around his body and thigh, and he was grey-white with effort. And yet his voice carried clearly and his will was indomitable.

'Understand now, my friends, just why we exist in this dreary immortality. To allow a God the licence to love a human, eternally. That is our role. We should refuse!'

'And what do you propose, little Mage? How can you refuse?' The God had broken away from the woman, and she sank to her knees at His side, His hand to her lips. He still looked into her eyes, the same faint smile curving the fine mouth.

'I propose to release the Benu.'

The smile deepened, and the God laughed once more. 'Too late, little Mage. The Bird of Time is beyond your power . . .'

'And Yours.' Matthias thrust himself away from the rock, and pushed Haddon away. He was using the staff's power to its fullest extent in the effort to remain upright. In the strangely heightened hinterland of weakness before Haddon found him, he had remembered the secret instructions of the Great Mage. Although he was faint with pain and loss of blood, he risked it all, using every power he possessed, every last fibre of strength to unlock the hidden place.

Blaise had not failed him. By the time Haddon reached the ruined cave, Matthias had already found extraordinary knowledge. Blaise's diaries had given him pointers, possibilities, and he was trusting to unfamiliar intuitions.

'The Benu is outside your control. The Stasis will not endure.'

'It will, you know,' said Lycias, raising the woman till she was standing, His hand on her breast, stroking, teasing, while her head rested against His shoulder. 'It will endure forever, for it is built on eternal love.'

'But love is not enough.' Coldly Nerissa stepped out of the shadows into the sunlight and looked at the God and His consort. 'Love does not endure, only sorrow lasts. You are lying to that woman if You make her believe otherwise.'

'Not while the Stasis exists.' Lycias took His lover's hands and kissed both palms in salutation. She began to fade, to vanish back into the realm of Delight, and the God turned His attention to the Cavers.

He leant forward, drifting down through the air until He was standing beside Nerissa. She had covered her eyes with her hands against the brightness of His gaze and the appalled Cavers could see that she was shuddering, a violent tremor running up and down her body.

Matthias, watching, suddenly knew that she mattered to Lycias. This was why He had come instead of Astret. Nerissa had to be defeated, her will nullified, because the Stasis was at risk. And Nerissa, suffering, obsessive and loyal, was too strong, might even upset the balance.

There was no way he could prevent what was going to happen.

Lycias raised His hands, gently cradling the priestess's head, and her own hands fell away, slack to her side.

'Poor Lady, lose your grief in Me. I can give you peace, and joy. You can live in delight too, if you let go mistaken loyalties . . .'

Her face was rigid with resistance. 'What of the Boundary, the deadly separation of our people? The Moon, the Lady Astret, Mistress of the changing tide of life? What of the children we never had? What of the children?'

The cruel smile deepened. 'Barren, sad lady, what has the Moon ever given you? What have you now apart from a life of ashes?'

For a moment He stared into her pale, passionate eyes. Then He bent His head and began to kiss her frozen mouth, becoming ever more brilliant, bright with burning power. The watching Cavers put their hands over their eyes or turned away, their backs to the fiery glow. But Nerissa could not turn away, could not escape, for he held her still, His eyes locked on hers, with scorching, white hot power.

No one else saw her eyes shrivel and burn, her skin smoulder and char. No one else saw the tremor of soundless agony. He laughed, once more, and let go. She crumpled, falling discarded at His feet.

At once the Cavers surged forwards, weapons flashing, and the God grew vast in their sight, His perfect face filling all vision. With a breath He extinguished their opposition, and their swords dropped useless to the ground.

'Enough of this!' Danger crackled in the air, and Lycias looked scornfully down at the Cavers.

'Little Mage, with your petty dreams, do not think you can alter anything. The power is not in your hands, and never will be.' He gazed impartially round at them all, and His voice became ice hard, implacable, adamantine.

'Meddle once more, and I will destroy you all, as I am destroying your foolish Lady Astret and Her pathetic priestess. We have no need of arid purity, no need of chaste sterility, no need of death and ageing. Do not try to thwart Me, for I am eternally powerful, and you are only dust.

'I am more generous than you deserve to give you this warning.'

A flash of scorching sunlight, and He was gone. Only the scent of laurel leaves burning hung on the air.

The search for the traitor Reckert diverted their attention from what had happened. Pryse deliberately gave them all so much to do, clearing the caves, rebuilding, nursing the sick, guard duty, that at first none of them realised that their centre had been lost.

Matthias, lying weak and ill, wondered when the shock would seize them all, and prayed that he would be well enough to help. He knew for sure now that the Benu was outside Lycias's control and that a crisis was approaching. But nothing else was clear. He felt as Blaise must have done, blindly trusting to instinct and an unreliable collection of myths and dreams.

He hoped that they would take Reckert alive, that he might be persuaded to talk.

He was not there when a group of the Guard, under Haddon, saw the small, elderly figure running along the top of the Cliff, trailing feathers behind.

They rushed after him, swords drawn, arrows poised, up onto the barren rock above the Caves. Over the wind and rain Haddon heard a cry, high-pitched and shrill, and saw a vast shadowy creature scud over their heads, wings whistling. It alighted near Reckert; he clambered on, and the creature flashed a triumphant grin at the running Guard, the distinctive Fosca eyes gleaming red in the night.

It was the first of many. Not content with crushing their priestess, Lycias had sent His servants of the light to discourage the Cavers further.

The alarm sounded. The Cavers braced themselves for a last assault.

Chapter Twenty-seven
Martitia

It was no relief to wake. Dislocation and bewilderment were succeeded by fear and a dawning horror. Eleanor sat up abruptly, alone in a strange room, with nothing and no one she recognised.

The bed was narrow, the walls rough-plastered, the floor dirty and dusty. There were no pictures, no windows, no colours, coverings or carpet. She thought the room might be underground. Drab grey surrounded her, mud on the floor, shadows on the ceiling. A low candle spluttered on a small rickety table. She stared at it, trying to gather her thoughts.

This was an unknown limbo and she was not sure if it belonged to her everyday life or to the bizarre fantasy world of her dream. Then she realised that a light still beckoned, just beyond sight, and that a familiar voice, Lukas's, was shouting outside the room.

In someone else's jeans she sat on the bed, trying to remember why the sound of his shouting made her so frightened. And then it came flooding back. Jocasta was dead, and Lukas had loved her.

Since she had awoken on the wet sand three days ago, Lukas alone had become convinced that she was not an irrelevance, or worse. He had laughed, teased, instructed and organised her life here, and she didn't want to be left to justify her existence amongst strangers yet again.

But now the Moon had destroyed Jocasta, and Lukas would never forgive her. She had trusted the light in her mind, trusted the words of the Lady, and now Jocasta was dead.

Was it her fault? Had she been too proud, too heedless? Perhaps, perhaps she had gone too far.

At the same time, she knew this was not the case. There was far more at stake here than Eleanor's pride. There were other issues involved in this, issues she could not begin to understand.

She sat numbly, hands slack in her lap, dreading what she might overhear. A woman of courage, she thought, would either shut the door or open it wide and announce herself. She had not the strength for either.

There were two voices she recognised, Lukas and that difficult man Thurstan Merauld. Also a third voice, that of an elderly, authoritative woman. She remembered Martitia, Thurstan's mother, the one Lukas had described as being 'in charge' here. She was saying, clearly, with an edge of extreme anger in her voice.

'Let us understand this then, Lukas. The Cavers performed the Seventh Rite, under cover of a diversionary attack by the Guard on the Peraldonian Ferry. This – female – appeared at the Rite and has been in your company ever since –'

'Mother!' Thurstan's voice was quiet, but charged with violence. 'The point is that they sent the Guard out without our knowledge or consent. Powel warned us this would happen one day! They made not the slightest effort to consult us, or to warn us of the reprisals that would certainly follow. They deliberately provoked the Fosca attacks, and gave us no chance to defend ourselves!'

'Shit!' Lukas was shouting again, 'There was no time to inform the Jerenites, the Rite had to take place immediately, the Saying was clear. We had no choice, there was no other way. And without a diversion someone could have noticed what was going on. You know that!'

'We lost over forty people two days ago, and another fifteen last night. We cannot afford losses like that. Our hospital is full, our home destroyed, all for this! Some bloody girl creating chaos and destruction –'

'You forget.' Martitia was acid. 'There was real power there.'

'Without control, power like that could kill us all. I don't think we need it, or her.'

'What exactly are you suggesting, Thurstan? Murder?

A convenient accident?' Martitia was dismissive, contemptuous.

'If we can tame it, there'll be no need. But we've got to learn how to use it, first. Then it might be of some value to us.'

'You think you can control it?' Lukas almost laughed. 'What have you in mind, Thurstan? Using it and her as some political pawn? Reckert thought so too. But last night's little display just goes to show how wrong you all are. You'd be out of your mind to think of trying to harness the power of the Moon Herself.'

'What choice do we have?' Thurstan, shouting now.

Eleanor could hardly bear to listen further. She covered her face with her hands, shaking. The voices continued, rising in anger, and she longed for an escape.

A chair scraped on the floor outside; two footsteps, and the door to her room was kicked wide. Lukas stood there for a moment, glaring at her, breathing hard and furious.

There was silence. She stared bleakly at him, taking in the blood-stained bandage on his arm, the hectic glint in his eyes, the unusual pallor. She was unable to speak, and he also seemed suddenly stricken dumb. Abruptly he turned, flung himself back into a chair and took a long drink from a glass on the table. Through the open door she could see Thurstan and his mother regarding her, seated at a circular table in a large, formal room.

'Ah, the little lady is with us once more,' Thurstan said nastily. 'Tell me, have you found our conversation edifying?'

She took no notice of him, looking only at Lukas's shadowed face.

'I didn't know Jocasta would die,' she said, standing up, moving towards him. 'I had no idea it would happen. I don't understand it at all.'

'It's not your fault?' he prompted sourly. 'That's the next line, isn't it?'

'Do be quiet, Lukas. This is not helpful.' Martitia was severe. 'Thurstan, where are your manners? Introduce us.'

'This is no bloody social occasion, Mother. She's called Eleanor Knight, as you know perfectly well.' He looked directly at her. 'This is my mother, the Lady Martitia Merauld. She would like to know just what you think you're doing here, and so would I.'

There was no way out of this; reluctantly Eleanor joined them at the table. Without looking at her, Lukas pushed a filled glass across the table towards her. She drained it gratefully, absurdly reassured by this small consideration.

They were all looking at her, waiting. Her hands were shaking. A long pause. Perhaps silence would entomb her forever, because she didn't know how or where to begin.

Martitia leant forward, pouring her more wine. Fine-boned, thin, with sunken violet eyes, she was an elegant woman. Her grey hair was caught up in a high bun and there were heavy golden rings weighting her bony hands. She wore a simple dark blue robe, not unlike the Caver women, but embroidered with gold. Her eyes were kind, if distant; her mouth had understood laughter, a long time ago.

'You could, of course, begin with your life before you came here,' she said courteously. 'And indeed, I shall be interested to learn about that one day. But it is urgent, now, for us to understand exactly what your relationship with this – power – involves.'

Eleanor drank more wine, playing for time. She lacked the energy to prevaricate, but simply could not talk about the Moon. It would be another betrayal.

'Come on, girl,' said Lukas impatiently. 'It's no great secret now. Do we have to organise smoke and smells again?'

Eleanor flinched at the memory of Reckert on the Isle of Arrarat. 'Now that was evil,' she said passionately, leaning across the table towards him, glad of a diversion.

'What was this?' said Martitia.

'Reckert – is no friend of yours,' she said plainly. 'He used trickery to find out what the Moon said, he used Fosca to divert us back to Arrarat, he probably spies for the Peraldonians, I don't know what else –'

'Never mind all that,' Lukas said. 'Why? Why should he do these things?'

'To stop me following . . .' she stopped.

'Following what?' Martitia seemed almost to be holding her breath, waiting.

'The Moon, the Lady Astret, told me to find – something,' she said with difficulty. 'A key, something to break the balance, to end the Stasis. That's what you all want, isn't it?'

'Oh yes,' Martitia replied. 'Yes, that's what we want.'

'Well, Reckert doesn't. He'll do anything to stop it.'

'Damn it, this is all nonsense!' Thurstan said. 'She's just trying to divert us herself.'

'Not true!' She swung round at him. 'You're all so set in your ways, so used to everything always being the same, you don't see the treachery under your noses!'

'What about the treachery under yours?' said Lukas slowly. 'What about Jocasta?' He seemed suddenly weary, even whiter, ill and in pain.

'What are you saying? That the Moon is treacherous?'

'There is another alternative. What control do you have, Eleanor Knight?' Thurstan's voice was icy. 'How far did you direct what happened to Jocasta?'

'Not at all! I don't understand it any more than you do!'

This was the terrible thing about it all. Again, was it her fault? 'For what it's worth, She, the Lady, said that I would be helped, if the need was great. And it was, wasn't it? The Fosca were winning! And then She said that I – I would not be able to direct Her –'

'But were you trying to? When Jocasta got in the way?' Lukas held her eyes for a long moment. 'Jocasta died for that?'

No, not for that. The implications of that death were hidden from Eleanor, and she wasn't at all sure she wanted to find them out. She was beginning to realise the scale of this conflict. It brought no comfort.

'I don't think much of your Lady,' said Thurstan. 'But then I never did.'

'Foolish,' said Martitia. She went on, thoughtfully. 'There have been records of this phenomenon before, of flooding light. Moon and Sun. Before we left Sarant –' She turned to Eleanor in brief explanation. 'Far back we too worshipped the Moon with the other inhabitants of Sarant. But there was a break, early in the Stasis, when they chose the severe path, and we came here to pursue other dreams, other ways. A futile hope.

'But I remember, from my mother and grandmother, stories of such light being called up, and used against enemies or for good. There were always drawbacks; the light of the Sun was too fierce, burning, while Moonlight brought madness to the weak-willed and misguided.

'It is dangerous, fatally dangerous, used without knowledge and discipline. And since the Stasis no one has experienced it at all.'

'Until now.' Thurstan sat back, his eyes cool and calculating. 'The problem is, whether this – ability – of yours is ever going to benefit anyone. Or are the innocent always going to be devastated by it? All right, the Fosca were repelled. I'll give you that. But the cost was extreme, and in a way power like that, uncontrolled, is too dangerous to use.'

'But I don't have any choice about it!' she cried. It's too vast for me, she meant. I don't want to know any more about it at all. Jocasta died, and I don't know why. 'It just arrives! I don't want it, I don't understand it, I'm not a Moon worshipper or Caver or Jerenite, I don't belong here at all! It's nothing to do with me!'

'That position is just not tenable,' Thurstan said. 'You are central in all this. Think. The Cavers were willing, however unwisely, to risk our alliance and friendship. You appeared from nowhere on the sand; you have been chosen by an Arrarat. Yes, even Reckert is interested, for whatever reason. You are of significance, Eleanor Knight. You can't deny it, or escape it. You can't avoid responsibility.'

'But I am not responsible! In all this I have no will! Things just happen to me, I don't act!' She knew this to be a lie as she said it. She had wanted to follow the Moon's beacon, had wilfully called up the light during her flight on Ash, and again on that bloodstained dance floor. She had even, an ultimate horror this, killed a Fosca rider herself. She shuddered.

'Then you must learn how to act, how to direct this power.' Thurstan was giving her a warning, she realised. It was, perhaps, the most she could expect.

Martitia stood up, looking tired. 'Enough for now,' she said. 'There are the wounded to tend, funerals to conduct. Thurstan, you will accompany me to the Deadenhall. Eleanor –' she looked at her, not unkindly. 'You need rest, I think, and time to consider. Lukas will show you round, when he's had his arm seen to. He knows where everything is. We shall talk again, later.'

Chapter Twenty-eight
Limbo

Then began a strange period of waiting. Under Thurstan's command, the Jerenites moved all their remaining surface dwellings to the myriad underground passages and caves that honeycombed the island. Some of them were natural, formed beneath the arching roots of the great trees, others had been hewn out of soft rock and earth long ago.

Defensive barricades were positioned over the entrances to the passages. Guards on lookout duty climbed to the tops of the trees, watching in the rainy twilight for further attacks. Weapons were sharpened, tempers flared and were suppressed.

This is what war is like, thought Eleanor. Wild horrific excitement followed by aching suspense and tedium.

Lukas, as instructed, had shown her around. The recreation areas, halls, armouries, kitchens, hospital quarters, were all crowded by the hundreds of Jerenites now inhabiting them. Imperceptibly the rooms lost their dusty, unused feel, and became busy, thronging with anxious, irritable people.

Lukas was barely polite to her, depressed, ill and angry. The wound on his arm had become infected, and refused to heal. He was thinking of Jocasta, and finding it difficult to adjust to a new position amongst the Jerenites.

Word had spread that the Cavers had provoked the Fosca attacks, disregarding the alliance, and Lukas was held responsible. Powel Hewlin was instrumental in augmenting the anger. He had an ambivalent attitude towards Lukas Marling; an unwilling admiration for his military skill, mistrust of his reliance on Astret. He had wanted Lukas to leave the Cliff and join them on Jeren long ago. He had not forgiven him for refusing to do so.

Anger and resentment towards both Lukas and Eleanor were barely concealed; only the iron will of Martitia kept the uneasy peace.

As for Eleanor, everyone kept well clear. Her little room was cleaned, blankets put there, the floor swept. People seemed to treat her as if she didn't exist, as if they didn't know how to react, and so refused to act at all. She hated it.

Only Thurstan sought her out, nagging her to make some decision, some exercise of will. He wanted her to become one of them, to join their fight, to use the Moon's power to defend the Jerenites. He met her in the corridors, sat next to her at meals, followed her to her room.

'Haven't you got anything better to do?' she snapped at him.

'Haven't you?' he countered immediately. 'It's enough is it, to live here, eating our food, wasting our time? You could be helping, you know. You could at least be giving us some hope.'

'I can give you nothing. I'm nothing to do with you.'

'No?' He kicked the door of her room shut behind him, and walked up to her. She could smell the faint scent of woodsmoke about him, and his fair hair was still slightly damp from the rain outside, curling at his open white collar. The hard blue eyes ran over her, and she knew what he was going to do.

She smiled. This was a familiar game.

He took her smile for acquiescence, and gathered her into his arms. Lightly, she responded, soft and pliant. She had always found it a useful strategy in her old life, had always enjoyed the semi-serious battles for power between men and women. She remembered watching her father flattering one of his girlfriends, while her mother had sat across the room, laughing at his efforts.

It had been no joke at the time.

But now that didn't matter. Thurstan Merauld was nothing to her, and there was no one to see. For a moment she slipped back into old habits, old responses. She felt his breathing quicken, and the arms tightened about her. He was practised and skilled, and she quite enjoyed the experience. He broke away at last and looked into her eyes.

'You're not a cold woman, Eleanor. There is much to be gained from commitment. Don't hold back for too long.'

'One kiss is supposed to change my mind? The Sleeping Beauty awakes?' The bitterness in her voice jarred unpleasantly.

He stepped back, dislike in his face.

'What are you trying to do? Win some cheap ascendancy?'

'Exactly the same as you.' She was really angry now. 'You're willing to use anything to get your own way. It's an old trick. I know all about it. Try something else, Thurstan dear. I've seen that one before.'

'Bitch,' he said calmly, and turned on his heel, slamming the door behind him.

She wanted to get out, to get away, to leave them all. She wanted to follow the urgent light in her mind which still nagged with such potency, and forget about all their petty wars.

This she was unable to do for the heartbreaking and simple reason that Ash would not come to her. Periodically she climbed the stairs to the surface, and echoed Lukas's warbling cry out into the rain. Ash never came; forlorn and frustrated, Eleanor returned to her drab room, and waited.

After days of lonely apathy, enlivened only by contentious encounters with Thurstan, she sought out Martitia.

She was in the hospital quarters as usual, overseeing the medical care, giving encouragement and support to the wounded.

Eleanor hated the place; the low ceilings, the dreary rows of beds, the stink of infected wounds and the fever-dulled eyes of the sick. She had no experience of illness and no patience with other people's pain; it made her feel both uncomfortable and guilty.

The doctor in charge, Siward Smisson, a small, balding man with worried eyes, looked exhausted, talking to Martitia. They were discussing the fever.

They could not contain it, he said. The Fosca's claws were poisoned, and he had not yet been able to analyse it, to find an antidote. People who appeared cured sickened after some days, became feverish and dangerously ill. They had already lost four men that way. Sighing, Martitia turned away and caught sight of Eleanor, hovering in the doorway.

'Yes,' she said slowly, as if continuing a conversation. 'Yes, I think it is time to talk now.' She took leave of the doctor and indicated that Eleanor should follow her.

Her own quarters were just across the corridor from the sickbay, close at hand. Eleanor realised that she probably spent most of her time there, helping Smisson. She was not involved in the defences, leaving them to Thurstan.

Her living room was not luxurious, but it was more comfortable than anywhere else on the island. There was a green cord carpet on the floor, a shabby, comfortable sofa, a pretty, circular table. There were no pictures on the walls, but the candlelight was soft and kind.

Martitia settled Eleanor on the sofa and pulled a rope that hung beside it. A young girl, blonde hair caught into extravagant plaits, embroidered shirt tucked into jeans, was sent to bring the hot herbal drink they called tea. Martitia sat on a slim, high backed chair near the fire, and regarded her guest.

'How can I help you?' she asked, just as a doctor might.

'Thurstan thinks it's more a case of what I can do for you.'

'He would of course. He is aware of failure here, and it seemed as if you might perhaps offer hope. Perhaps you still can.'

'I don't see how, when Ash won't even come when I call,' she said sulkily. She knew she was behaving like a spoilt child. Martitia sighed, and then smiled as the girl returned with the tea.

'What you need, young lady,' she said with irony, 'is something to do. Too much brooding never helps.' She poured tea into china cups with saucers that didn't match.

'But I don't know what to do!' Eleanor said explosively. 'I want to follow this light, and I don't have the means. I don't even know if I *should* follow it! I mean, what is it? I don't see how the Moon can be a person, how a person can be a God, how a God can be the Moon!'

Martitia put down her cup, stood up and wandered over to the fire. For the first time since Eleanor had met her, she was uncluttered by the exigencies of their situation, clear and thoughtful.

'I cannot of course speak for your world. I wish I could,' she said. 'But here, religion – is a complicated thing.'

She paused. 'It depends on faith – and what is faith but a leap of the creative imagination? That leap, the very act of trusting in something other, that momentary forgetting of self – is the nature of God itself. In this way, the Cavers, trusting that the Moon is God, create Astret through their trust. In the same way, the Peraldonians worship the Sun and so create Lycias as God.'

The candles spun long shadows on the ceiling. Eleanor stared at the old woman whose words encapsulated a universe. She was arrested by ideas.

'The important thing is the faith, the creative trust,' Martitia continued. 'But that's not all of it. It wouldn't exist, wouldn't even be possible, if God did not also create from the other side.' She placed her fingertips together as a high arch, momentarily framing philosophies. 'Worship – the sects, rites, priests, customs, legends and ceremonies – all evolved to protect that point where our imagination and that of the God meet. That meeting point is too dangerous for humanity to handle without the safeguards of ritual and ceremony.

'In this way, people create the aspect of God they deserve. Interpretations vary; fatally they vary. It is there, in that area, that our God has become divided by our conflicting interpretations. From that conflict, the Stasis has developed.

'The Moon and Sun should not be at odds. They are not opponents, but two sides of the same coin, sister and brother, wife and husband. It is a great wrong, a terrible distortion that they do not act in harmony. The reflection of that wrong is this dreary, violent world. If you can do anything, anything at all to change this, you must do it. You can't ignore the wrong that afflicts us all!'

Oh yes I can, she thought. Conflict on a divine scale? The responsibility of it was unthinkable, impossible. Jocasta died. In a moment of pure panic, pure terror, she retreated.

'It's not my fight,' she said emphatically. 'It's nothing to do with me that you live beastly lives and never grow old. You sort it out, it's your problem!'

'Bravo!' came a laconic voice from the doorway. Thurstan was standing there, leaning negligently against the wall. 'Still running true to form, aren't you? That was a splendid exercise in self-interest, almost worthy of a Peraldonian. My mother, by the way, has unorthodox views even for a Jerenite, and would be judged a heretic by both Cavers and Peraldonians. You follow her theories at your peril.'

He bestowed an intimate, indecipherable glance on Martitia, who took no notice.

'You really should knock,' she said mildly, 'before insinuating yourself into a private conversation. What do you want?'

He pushed himself away from the wall, and sat down on the sofa next to Eleanor. She shifted uneasily.

'With your magnificent dismissal of our world and all its problems, it will presumably be of no concern to you that a half-dead Peraldonian has just been washed up.'

'No. No concern at all.' Eleanor said defiantly. She turned away, stupid tears pricking her eyes.

'Who is it?' Martitia was interested. Her son shrugged.

'I don't know. He's way beyond conversation. Powel's all for hastening the natural processes and dispatching him. What do you say, Mamma?'

'It all depends on who he is, doesn't it?' she replied acidly and swept from the room without even glancing at Eleanor. Thurstan held the door for her, and then followed after, not looking back.

Sod it, thought Eleanor bitterly. Deliberately she poured herself another cup of tea. She would not get involved in all this, these fights and feuds. She would not be judged by them. How could they know anything at all about her? They were nothing to do with each other.

But treacherously a light still shone at the back of her mind, and would not disappear.

The tea was cold. She sighed and stood up, wondering what to do next. She could not face her solitary little room, and she had already tried to call Ash twice that day. And then she remembered Lukas, and wondered why she had not seem him around recently.

He was under general disapproval too. Perhaps they should stick together. She could do with a friend.

She couldn't find him at first. People were preoccupied by news of the Peraldonian, stimulated by a kind of blood-lust, and were simply uninterested in Eleanor and her enquiries. Misled by their casual clothes and attitudes, Eleanor was taken aback by the intensity of their hatred for the Peraldonians. While Martitia was able to view their lives as a reflection of conflict on a wider scale, in the main, the people of Jeren were motivated by bitter resentment. The unfortunate Peraldonian, if he survived at all, would not be gently treated.

Eventually one harassed nurse paused on her way to the main wards. 'Lukas Marling? Oh, he's ill again. Those poisoned claws . . . he's in one of the side wards.'

Eleanor found him sitting up, propped on pillows, eyes glittering, flushed and hectic. He was toying distastefully with a bowl of muddy-looking soup.

'Ah!' he said, looking up at her. 'What have we here? Soft words and sweet comfort for the sick?' She took the untouched bowl from him and put it on the table near the bed. He subsided back on the pillows, studying her.

'Not quite the holiday you hoped for? I'm no conquering hero either. Perhaps we should mourn in unison the loss of reputation . . .' In a way it was an apology.

She said, 'How do you feel? I would have come earlier, if I'd known you were here.'

'I thought you'd gone, that you'd call Ash and just leave.' He was too tired for pretence.

'I tried to. He won't come.' Her eyes filled. He moved his hand on the sheet and said with a kind of impatience. 'Well, don't just stand there like a lost sheep. Sit down.' Then, as she sank wearily onto the edge of the hard bed, he became more gentle.

'Crying again? Poor little Eleanor, so far from home. What are we to do with you?' Thoughtfully he stroked the bright hair from her face with icy fingers.

At last she sat up and blew her nose. This was no good. He was still looking at her, an expression on his face that she could not identify.

'You're going to be having company here,' she said. 'If they decide to let him live, that is.'

'Who?'

'A Peraldonian, Thurstan said. Washed up here this morning. He's ill. I don't suppose they'll put him in the public wards either.'

They hadn't. A babble of voices, and the sound of dragging feet heralded the arrival of the injured man. Two of Powel Hewlin's rougher, more enthusiastic, guards were supporting the derelict, broken body of the Peraldonian. Thurstan and Powel were just behind.

Eleanor watched with curiosity as they unloaded him onto the bed in the far corner and handcuffed the raw, suppurating wrists to the bedhead. Martitia, who had followed them in, objected to that.

'There's no need for chains. He's not going anywhere.'

'He's Peraldonian, Lady.' Powel was contemptuous. 'He should be executed. He's either a spy or a renegade, and we can do without either.'

'Use your eyes. He's no spy. Even Peraldonians are not so stupid as to use wrecks.' She pointed to the emaciated figure, the filthy infected burns and wounds, the matted hair and drawn face. Reluctantly, Hewlin released the man's hands.

Thurstan gently lifted an eyelid and then felt for a pulse. 'It'll be academic soon, if he doesn't get treatment. Where's Smisson?'

Lukas answered without opening his eyes. 'On his rounds. Some fool tripped over his sword in the armoury. He'll be back soon.' He stopped, exhausted.

'What about the nurses? Why isn't there anyone here to see to you anyway?' Thurstan glanced round the empty room. 'Where *is* everyone?'

'They don't like it here,' said Lukas. 'Perhaps you haven't noticed: Cavers aren't very popular just now.'

'Still, there's no excuse for neglecting duty,' said Martitia wearily. 'I'll go and talk to them.'

'No need for that,' said Eleanor, getting up. 'I'll look after him.'

Thurstan looked at her as if he had never seen her before. 'Goodness,' he said placidly. 'Are you going to allow yourself a little involvement in all this?'

'Leave it, Thurstan,' said Lukas sharply. 'It's not easy for her either.'

'Have you any nursing experience?' Thurstan asked coldly.

She shook her head. She could not rationalise why she had offered to help; she only knew that here was another stranger, an outsider, and that she felt sorry for him.

Martitia studied her for a moment and then nodded.

'I'll take over here, until Smisson returns. Eleanor can help, if she wants.' She turned to one of the guards. 'Go and find the charge nurse. Tell her that I wish to speak to the next shift when it comes on.'

'I'll leave a guard here, my Lady,' said Hewlin firmly.

'There's no need at all for that. I'm sure there are many more important things for your guards to do, Powel.'

For a moment it looked as if he would argue, but then Thurstan caught his eye and he nodded, gracelessly. He turned brusquely, and left the room with the other guard.

'If you change your mind, you will let me know, won't you, Mamma?' Thurstan bowed courteously to Martitia, ironically to Eleanor, and left the room.

Martitia sighed, and turned back to the Peraldonian.

'We'll need swabs, lint, bandages, hot water –' she said, inspecting the meagre supplies in the cupboard. Eleanor took a deep breath and set to work.

It was a grim and forbidding task. Only the barest glimmer of life persisted, but Martitia cosseted and coaxed it to strength as if the stranger were one of her own people. None of the wounds was in itself dangerous, with the exception of an ugly gash in the man's side. She cleaned and stitched it with ruthless competence.

The combination of loss of blood, infection, numerous small cuts and burns, hunger and exposure had seriously weakened him. His heart rate was feeble, uneven, the breath faint and gasping. It was likely that he would not live, despite their efforts.

Eleanor fought not only against inexperience but also against nausea and disgust. Suppressing her unease with difficulty, she washed, swabbed and bound as directed by Martitia, who worked with a cool and practised skill.

In the next bed, Lukas was sleeping, so Eleanor whispered questions to Martitia.

'Will he live?'

'Possibly. If he had been a weak man, he would have died days ago. There is some will to survive at work here.'

'How do you know he's a Peraldonian?'

'Sunburn,' she answered shortly. 'Look at his hands, his face, his arms. There's been no sunlight here or at the Caves for longer than I care to remember.'

It was obvious, really. And beneath the grime, it was plain that this man's hands were without the callouses shared by both Cavers and Jerenites.

'Yes, an easy life they have,' said Martitia, following Eleanor's gaze.

'Will they let him live?' It seemed important, somehow.

'He will be healed until he is strong enough to stand trial. Then he will be killed.' Her voice was carefully neutral.

'But – why?'

'You are so simple!' Martitia flung the inert brown hand back onto the bedclothes. 'Because of this – and this!' She pointed to the brown skin, the smooth palms.

Eleanor thought for a moment. 'But he is as much a victim as you are. Do Peraldonians grow old and have children? Do they compose symphonies or write poems? Do they benefit at all from this aberration in time?'

'Oh yes. Oh, indeed they benefit, living in luxury and ease. Enough to eat, leisure to enjoy the music and art created by previous generations. They even regard battles with us as a kind of sport!' She was enraged by the thought.

'What does that matter if behind it all you are both childless?'

Her angry attention was suddenly caught by a small movement on the sheet between them. The smooth pampered hand with its suppurating and inflamed wrist had clenched, violently. Her eyes sped to his face, but no flicker of awareness was reflected there.

Martitia had missed it. Looking at Eleanor she said, 'Do something about it, then. You are not unmoved and you have a path to follow. Take it. Don't delay.'

'I would if I could!' she cried, and then wondered at herself.

It seemed to her that alternatives were dropping away. She had realised that she would have to play a part when the Moon spoke to her. But perhaps the necessity for action had been implicit in the ceremony that had brought her here. Perhaps the only real choice had been made without any reference to her at all. She had been in a significant place, at a significant time. Glass shattering over fire had followed a pattern. That was all.

Every step she had taken since then had been predestined, springing from the pressure of events she could in no way control. She was a pawn, without volition or power.

She would leave if her Arrarat came; she would stay if he did not. There was no point in people asking her for her support, her commitment. She had no choice, no alternative. And she was determined never, never again to call up the Moon's light. That responsibility was too great to bear.

The hospital bay on Jeren was an uneasy place over the days that followed. The fever gripped with increasing virulence, flaring and burning until, wasted husks, many died.

Smisson had never completed his medical training on Peraldon. He retained only shreds of knowledge and half-learned lore. Shreds were not enough now to enable him to do his work efficiently. He snapped at the nurses, frowned at Eleanor and shouted at Powel Hewlin.

Hewlin called in every day, checking on the condition of the Peraldonian. His motives were not charitable; he was simply waiting for the stranger to recover enough to stand trial. There were questions he needed to ask about Peraldon – the numbers of permanent guards, their weapons and defences, the use of Fosca – and he would not be diverted.

Smisson eyed him with misgiving, disliking the

ambivalent position of healing a man who would almost certainly be executed after his usefulness was expended.

Martitia was Smisson's constant aide, a more experienced nurse than anyone else. She, alone with Eleanor, was prepared to nurse Lukas, whose fever continued to flare.

Wiping his sweating face and hands, she told Eleanor that he had been a frequent visitor, particularly in the early days of the Stasis, and that it had been understood that one day he might settle with them, with Jocasta. But just as the Stasis had excluded both death and new life, it had also sapped will and energy. Lukas had felt obliged to stay with his family.

She said that she had always liked his warmth, his impulsiveness, and then stopped suddenly, as if aware of the comparisons Eleanor might be making.

Thurstan was often in the hospital bay, his cool blue gaze bringing confidence to the sick. He was tireless, never appearing irritable or anxious. Eleanor he largely ignored, which was also a relief.

She began to appreciate just how beleaguered the Jerenites were. After breaking with the religion of the Moon, so long ago, they had clung to a precarious and exacting existence, creating reckless and wild pleasures to brighten the cold grip of the Stasis. But their creativity had failed them. No one wrote, or sang. The plays they performed seemed drab and irrelevant.

No one had the energy to be daring. To invent, to shock, to create. And when the Fosca started attacking, they had been drawn from their twilight island lost in cloud and trees, into the battle against Peraldon. To them the Stasis was more than a threat to new life; it meant sterility for every creative endeavour. They were brave and loyal, skilful within the terms of their society; but there was an inevitable toll from the guerrilla warfare, accidents and disease.

Even with no ageing process, the population was steadily decreasing, and stood, before the current Fosca attacks, at less than four hundred.

Each death was a tragedy on a scale far greater than Eleanor could comprehend, because there were no children, no way of replacing and rebuilding. The heavy drinking, the use of drugs, the promiscuity, all these were an inevitable accompaniment to a society which would soon die away, lacking even the ambivalent consolations of religion.

Thurstan's determination and impenetrable self-control were, she thought, a defence against despair. Martitia's withdrawal from authority into philosophy and the practical skills of nursing was part of the same pattern. No one wanted to lead the Jerenites because there was nowhere for them to go.

It was somehow assumed that Eleanor would continue nursing the Peraldonian; the Jerenites were busy enough caring for their own. There was little to do after the first ruthless session; the cuts and burns healed swiftly, including the wound in his side. He was free from the devastation of fever.

Eleanor wondered how he had managed to burn the soles of his feet, his back and sides, and why his hands had been so tightly tied. Against her will she found herself speculating to Powel one day.

'Perhaps they didn't like him either,' he said heavily.

'Couldn't it mean that perhaps he was an enemy to them, a traitor or rebel or – ?'

'Or a criminal, a thief, a rapist – who knows?' Powel shrugged massive shoulders. 'We'll find out when he wakes up. It shouldn't be long now.'

But the coma was deep and unaltering. Smisson said it was due to acute exhaustion.

'He must have been adrift for several days before we found him, without food or water. And perhaps he'd received some shock. It is almost as if he doesn't want to wake up.'

'Neither would I, if I knew Powel's reception committee was waiting for me.' Eleanor looked down at the smooth brown face, the fine mouth, the thick curling black hair and hook nose. An interesting face, she thought, strong and determined. There were laughter lines round the eyes.

Smisson took his pulse. 'Normal,' he said. 'Any day now, he'll be with us.'

The Peraldonian emerged from his torpor that evening, while Eleanor was stacking sheets by Lukas's bed. She was suddenly aware of being watched and then heard the bed shift as the man attempted to sit up. She ran to his side.

'Hush! Do be quiet!' She did not want Hewlin to hear.

'Why?' His voice was deep but cracked with disuse. He slumped back on the pillows. 'Where am I?'

'In a Jerenite hospital ward. They think you're a spy.'

This was too much for him to comprehend immediately. There was a pause, while she brought him some water, tilting his head from the pillow. After he had drunk they looked at each other in silence.

It was a shock, the force of despair in his eyes. And at the back of them, beyond that, she saw something else. The Moon's light shone for him, too. She could see it reflected in his eyes. Then she saw it, his hair disturbed by the movement as he looked at her.

There was a small scar on his left temple. Recent. Moon shaped.

He stared at her and she knew that he recognised her own light, calling and enticing.

'Who are you?' she whispered, bewildered by the depths in his eyes.

'My name is Blythe,' he said, and then Powel Hewlin came striding in.

Chapter Twenty-nine
The Wave

The battle against the Fosca involved all of the Caver Guard, and those of the women who rode Arrarat hawks. Over the Cliff top they wheeled and soared, strength against macabre agility, grace against distortion, and arrows flew, and claws ripped.

The Cavers had little hope, but there was no alternative. This was their last defence. If the Fosca overran them now, here, it would be the end of them all. Astret's loyal followers obliterated, the religion of the Moon a forgotten dream. They fought with desperate courage, with reckless grief, and knew they could not possibly prevail.

In the few remaining caves, women huddled together, trying to care for the wounded in impossible conditions. No heat, no light, no water. They dared not get the fires going again, for the Fosca were always attracted by heat. They could hear the cries and shouts as the vast wings hurtled past the Cliff, and cried out as they saw their friends fall.

Their only comfort was that the Cliff was at least stable. The scurries had disappeared, Reckert had escaped. Their only enemy now flew outside the caves, screaming in the night, and would soon be amongst them.

A hurried, emergency meeting, in a brief lull. Caspar was to be sent to warn the Jerenites. Before he left, Matthias Marling, leaning weakly on one elbow, gave him messages for his brother Lukas.

Caspar had not wanted to go; he looked on it as desertion. Matthias had persuaded him. The leave-taking with Fabian and Margat was not easy. He was thin-lipped with tension as he called his Arrarat.

Now the wounded Mage Matthias leant back on the

thin mattress, and reached for Blaise's diaries, again.

They would all die. All. There must be something, some way out.

He started to turn the pages.

'Come now, my ghost grey lady! To the right, up, sharp!' Aldred hardly needed to speak aloud, for Alis always knew what he wanted.

The air whistled cold against his cheek as they whirled round to face the dark angel swooping in from above.

He fitted an arrow to his bow, and loosed it immediately. To his satisfaction the beast slightly lost height, swerving a little, the barbed arrow jutting from its shoulder.

There was another rushing at them from the side.

Alis had seen it first. She sent an urgent warning to Aldred's mind, and then hurtled straight ahead, narrowly avoiding both Fosca, a reckless manoeuvre which only delayed the reckoning.

There was a conflagration of fire and heat just above, where the bolt of leaping fire from Aylmer's staff had struck one of the Fosca. Aldred ducked low on Alis's back, and a shower of charred flesh and bone fell past them.

Sudden in the brightness, an evil face grinned and pain shot through his shoulder.

Hating them, loathing the malice, the wanton destructiveness of the thing, the hate far stronger than fear, Aldred struck out at it.

It wrenched the sword from his hand, screaming with laughter. Furious, he tried to drag his knife from his waistband, but his right arm wouldn't work, hanging loose at his side . . .

And the thing was on him, the lizard clutching at his grey hawk with claws and teeth, its rider reaching out to him with talons spread wide.

Alis wrenched round, the curved beak tearing and slashing at the reptile, but its grip was immovable. Her flight became wildly erratic, trying to shake them off, but she was constrained by ensuring Aldred's safety.

They spun and wheeled through the cold, rainy night, while fire exploded around them in irregular patterns of flares. His friends were shouting in the dark, and the strong muscles in Alis's back rippled beneath him.

The Fosca rider reached over, and dug its claws into his shoulder, its fanged mouth eager for the wound.

Its reeking breath robbed the air from his lungs, its clammy touch the parasitical embrace of death. Crooning in his ear, it began to suck blood from his shoulder, while one of its claws slid deep between his ribs.

He almost welcomed it.

'Go now, my beauty, get away and save yourself . . .'

The Arrarat, knowing the instant he died, suddenly folded her wings in, plummeting like a stone towards the sea.

The Fosca rider guessed what would happen: it had fought Arrarat before. Wriggling, it leapt back to the angel, blood dripping from its grey mouth, and searched for new prey.

'How many Arrarat left? How many survivors? Are either of the boats seaworthy?'

Three hours later, Matthias was leaning on his staff, upright only through an effort of will, talking to Stefan Pryse in one of the hospital caves. The commander's head was being bound up by Margat.

Stefan was white with fatigue and pain, guilty about even this brief break from the battle still raging outside. But the blood kept getting in his eyes, and he couldn't fight like that.

He found Matthias's questions irrelevant and distracting.

'Look, what are you getting at?'

'Evacuation. If both boats are seaworthy we've got a chance . . .'

'We'd be sitting ducks! At least the Fosca can't get into the caves yet. If we sent anyone out in the boats, they'd be completely exposed! It would be suicide!'

'We have no chance here.' Wearily, Matthias pushed aside Margat's helping hand, and hitched his hip on the table at their side. He was feeling light headed, thirsty through loss of blood, draggingly tired, but his mind was working clearly. 'With luck we could get half of us away on the Arrarat, they'll easily bear two. We'll undertake to cause a diversion, so that the others can get off in the boats.'

'What kind of diversion, for God's sake? What are you thinking of?'

'Call the Guard in, Stefan. Open up the cave entrances, but get everyone down to the harbour first. Do it! Now!' He was too tired for long explanations. Waves of weakness washed over him.

Pryse frowned at him. 'Damn it Matt, you'd better know what you're doing!' He stood up, buckling on his sword belt, and looked seriously at Margat. It seemed as if he was about to say something, but he merely lifted one hand, touching her cheek, gently. Then he turned and left them.

'What are you up to, Matt?' She was rolling bandages, not looking at him.

'Saving our lives, I hope.' He smiled crookedly. 'Blaise has left a few ideas . . .'

'Do the other Mages know?' At last she looked at him, but he was too preoccupied to notice the strain in her voice.

'They've got other things to worry about.'

Aylmer Alard and Thibaud Lye stood on the highest point of the Cliff, staffs ablaze, directing whirling spirals of fire out into the centre of the fighting. Devastating, irresistible; the Fosca fled before the potency of their attacks. But they were only two against hundreds. Fosca fell, but were replaced by others. For a while, the Mages managed to keep them away from the Cliff itself. Their powers were limited. When Pryse's messenger met them, they were almost exhausted. They were in no position to argue.

The harbour lay along the north-east edge of the Cliff. The massive wall of rock jutted out into the sea, and the small inlet that lay sheltered behind it was hidden from view. Narrow steps led down to it from the main body of the caves, but they were rarely used. The Peraldonian Warden had found the boats easy targets. There were only two boats there now, simple sailing vessels, conscientiously maintained in a seaworthy condition through long tradition.

Stefan watched as the injured were carried aboard. There were one or two fights, people wanting to take extra clothes, food, other belongings. He had shouted that it was possessions or lives; the choice was theirs. Grim faced, they had dumped bundles and bags, hating him. The boats sank lower in the water as they filled.

He began to count heads. He knew how the sum would work out, but hoped he was mistaken. There were some three hundred Arrarat, counting those released by the death or injury of their riders. A further fifty still soared around the caves, diverting the Fosca. Each bird could carry two people. Each boat would hold at most fifty.

There were over a thousand Cavers. Say an extra ten in each boat. One hundred and eighty people would have to be left. What was Matthias planning?

'They must all leave,' he said, categorically, propped against the side of the stairway. 'Somehow, Stefan, we have to get everyone away as soon as possible.'

Stefan considered. 'What about the rafts?' He turned to Dunstan Willes, the head Boatswain.

But before Dunstan, leathery-faced, dour, could answer, Matthias had shaken his head. 'They won't do,' he said. 'There's going to be a sea the like of which we've never encountered before. I'm not at all sure that even the boats themselves will stand up to it. Rafts would have no chance at all.'

'Matthias!' Stefan took him by the shoulders, forcing the other to meet his eyes. 'You must tell me! What are you planning?'

The Mage's eyes were clouded with pain and exhaustion. Blood was beginning to seep through the bandages around his waist; his cloak was torn and filthy. Grey dust masked his pallor, except where the sweat had drawn tracks from his forehead.

And yet he smiled, and there was no suggestion of fear in his gaze, no suggestion of defeat in his stance. 'I'm going to flood the caves,' he said. 'With the Fosca inside.'

'You're out of your mind!'

'No.' Aylmer Alard stepped away from the file of walking wounded crossing the gangplanks to the boats. 'He has the right of it, Stefan. The twelve Rites, as listed in the Cabbala, cover many contingencies; and now that we have access to Blaise's knowledge many new paths are open to us. There is one final pledge that Astret has sworn to honour. Eternal Mistress of the Tides, She will send us the Great Wave, if the Twelfth Rite is performed.'

'But Astret is defeated! She can honour nothing!'

Matthias pushed himself away from the rock, and took the large man's hand. 'Don't despair,' he said. 'Never despair. Only despair will cause us to fail. The waves still wash our shores, don't they? This at least our Lady can achieve.'

Dark in the shadow of the rock they watched the boats put out to sea. Hundreds of doubly laden Arrarat wheeled overhead, the air thronging with beating wings. The boats moved heavily, sluggish against the slow tide. They were filled to capacity and beyond by refugees; only a small group, less than two hundred, still waited on the harbour side.

Those staying behind were volunteers. They knew they would die. An hour, Matthias reckoned. It was cutting it fine, but it should give the boats a chance to get just far enough to the north, out of the way.

Both Aylmer and Thibaud stood at the Cliff top, helping the remaining Arrarat hold back the Fosca, diverting attention from what was happening at the back of the Cliff. Thibaud's own hawk, Aphra, stood ready, waiting to whisk them away when the moment came.

It was all a question of timing. And the daring gamble that the Fosca would follow them into the Cliff, harrying the Cavers to extinction.

On the harbour's edge, Matthias checked it over and over in his mind. Fosca, flying in from the south-east, would be drawn to attack the two Mages on the Cliff top. With luck, they would not get past them, would not fly round the Cliff to the harbour, where the boats were already passing the northern point, close to the Boundary. They would assume that the rest of the Cavers were hiding deep in the warren of caves in the Cliff. If, as he thought, their object was to annihilate them all, they would sooner or later start searching through the Cliff.

Matthias had to time it right. It all depended on that, and on luck and theory. He needed Blaise. He had not the wisdom, the experience to carry this through on his own.

And Lukas, where was he now, the brother who at his elbow had glowed with confidence and strength?

Haddon was watching him, uncharacteristically grave. 'Now?' he suggested.

Matthias looked at the small pile of firewood at his feet, ready to be kindled. Three glass crescents lay on a silken cloth at its side.

Oswald Broune was standing at the water's edge, gazing out at the retreating ships, the doubly laden Arrarat disappearing far away into the cloud.

'They've gone,' he said. 'Now?'

'Yes. Light the fire.'

On the Cliff top, knowing Matthias's decision, Aylmer and Thibaud touched their staffs together.

A fire ball of immense power shot out into the centre of the whirling battle; the Arrarat, forewarned, leapt high into the air, banking up above the ruined Cliff, and the Fosca screamed with dismay.

Without waiting to watch the result, Aylmer and Thibaud threw themselves onto Aphra's broad back. Instantly they were high up in the cold air, rushing to catch up with the retreating Cavers, their especial care.

The dazzled, enraged Fosca gibbered and squealed, darting around searching for their prey, their enemies and rivals, the Arrarat.

They had gone. High above the cloud, they skimmed the night air over towards Jeren, leaving the Caver Cliff forever.

A hundred men stepped into the cave openings, looking out at the Fosca. They carried swords and knives.

'Fosca!' yelled Brendan, at their centre. 'Over here!'

Dark angels wheeled around, eyes flashing, and closed in on the Cliff. For long enough to entice them off their mounts, the Cavers stood their ground. Then, sure that they were being followed, they turned, and ran through the winding, derelict passages, down into the depths of the Cliff.

The fire sparkled and hissed. Intent, the three men standing round it heard neither screams nor the sound of swords clash.

The words of power floated in the air around them, Matthias softly chanting over the flames.

The scent of dreams, drugging the senses, blotted out reality, and only the sea moved in the harbour, and only the flames glittered in their minds.

It was difficult to concentrate, hard to remember what to do.

A brief prayer to Astret and then, emptying his mind of all thought, Matthias held the crescent moon in his hands; an instant of quiet and he hurled it, through the flames, up above the leaping fire.

At the same moment, Haddon and Oswald threw the other glass moons high over the flames.

They clashed; as planned, brilliant shards were tossed spinning into the fire.

A breathless moment of silence, the world held still, and then wind rushed into the harbour, howling and potent. The fire was extinguished by the sudden force of it; the rubbish, boxes, nets, bags of possessions littering the harbour were picked up in an insane whirlwind dance.

The three men were hurled to the ground, all breath ripped away, their world shattering about them.

The sea heaved and began to groan.

Within the Cliff, Brendan turned to face the foul thing screaming after him.

Laughing breathlessly, he stood in the narrow tunnel, feet wide, both hands clutching the serrated sword in front of him.

'Come on then,' he said. 'Where's all this skill now?'

And the thing sprang at him, one tentacle swiping at his head, too fast to see, another ripping through his jerkin, a talon plunging for his heart.

He ducked, spinning, avoiding the lashing tentacle, and leapt forward, under the creature's guard, knocking the clawed limb out of the way.

The stink of it hit him like a blow, but he thought for a moment he might have a chance. He drew back his right arm, ready to thrust the sword forward, but the creature's fourth arm came swinging double-jointed over his back, and a burning, crippling pain shot into him, whipping all strength from his legs.

He felt himself falling, arching backwards against the agony in his back, his sword dropping from his hands.

The Fosca raised the wide-spread hand of claws, hissing as it brought it down, raking through his face, finding its hooked home in the vein of his neck.

He died in a flare of agony, and never heard the gathering wind outside, the coming victory of the sea.

The wave began to gain strength and speed about a mile east of the Cliff. The two heavily laden boats rocked violently in the gathering swell, just managing to surmount the drag as it raced towards the Caves.

In the leading of the two boats, Stefan paused in the midst of baling out, stood up and put his arm round Margat.

'He's done it.'

'But the cost!' She turned to him, and in the storm-filled light he could just see tears glinting in her eyes.

'There was no other choice . . .'

'There never is.' Then the control broke, and in a storm of weeping she fell into his arms, and he held her fast, all the time watching over her head as the wave grew.

Dragging Matthias out of the flying debris, Haddon shouted to Oswald, struggling to make his voice heard over the wind.

'Are the rafts still secure?'

Oswald cupped his hands together around his mouth to reply. 'I'll go and see –'

Crawling along the harbour edge, one arm raised over his head against the hurtling debris, he made his way to the mooring.

It was almost impossible to see through the mixture of dust and spray. He felt cautiously with his hands, and found the mooring post, embedded in rock.

There was no rope round it. The rafts had gone.

He tried again, running his hands around the smooth post. No rope. He sat back for a moment, numb with despair, and then the spray turned into a wave, and drenched him out of shock.

Choking he stumbled back along the frothing waters' edge to where Haddon crouched, trying to adjust the bandaging round Matthias.

He didn't need to say anything. Haddon glanced at him briefly, and nodded. 'They probably wouldn't have been any good anyway. It was a slim chance at best.'

'What do we do now?'

'Wait for the others. Sing. Pray. Whatever you like. Give me a hand here, will you?'

Together they struggled to pull the stained linen tighter, and Matthias stirred under their touch before subsiding once more into unconsciousness.

Shouting and clattering from the caves above.

They left the Mage lying in the shelter at the far edge of the landing stage. Drawing their swords, they went to stand at the bottom of the stairs, and waited.

The wave swept up light before it, gathering all the life of the sea into a black wall of furious strength.

Fish darted away from it, down to untroubled depths, or leapt out of the water only to fall back into the seething turmoil.

It altered the horizon, blotting out wasted stretches of water, casting shadows as dense, as unforgiving as iron. It changed everything, everywhere, and nothing would ever be the same.

The sound of it alone was enough to grind the soul, a low thundering roar that caused the centre of existence to fail, feeble and powerless as a wisp of spray in the wind.

It raced along partnered by storm in a headstrong rush towards the Cavers' Cliff, taller, stronger by far than mere rock. The land quivered in the face of it, and seemed to shrink back, wincing.

But nothing would stop it. Nothing could.

Three men crashed down the stairs to the harbour.

'The rafts!' shouted the first, a tall, red-haired man. 'Where are the rafts?' He was breathless, sweating from the run through the passages, and blood fell from a slash over his right eye.

'Gone,' said Haddon laconically. 'The storm was too strong for the moorings . . .'

'Fuck!' What now?' He spun round to watch for the others following. Already a Fosca rider stood at the top of the stairs, spitting down at them.

'Let's give them a run for their money!' said Haddon.

The wave roared as it swept towards the Cliff, hurling wind before it, a dead vacuum in its wake. It obliterated the cloud, a blue-black wall of water, irresistible and immense.

Oswald, cradling Matthias's head in his lap, heard it before he saw it.

'Oh Lady, oh hell, oh God . . .'

The fighting on the harbour was too intense for anyone else to notice at first. Exhausted, desperate, suicidally violent, the remaining Cavers fought only with the intent of murdering Fosca. They had forgotten, in the chaos, what they were waiting for.

Then a Fosca suddenly drew back from the mêlée, its scream taking on a new intensity. It started to run away back up the stairs, pushing past the struggling figures, wild with panic.

In shock, the other Fosca turned, looking out to sea. The dark was blotting out the horizon, they could see the white froth bubbling high at the top of it. The wind matched their howl of terror and they began to run.

Turning tail, they did not notice the fleet shadows skimming under the crest of the wave, did not see a flock of unknown Ararat hawks swoop onto the harbour.

Stumbling, sobbing with relief, the Cavers threw themselves onto the birds' backs. Almost laughing, Haddon pushed Matthias up in front of Oswald onto a huge, chestnut male, before leaping up himself.

A surge of wings and an effortful vault into the stressed air. The hawks whisked out of the path of the wave as it curved, crashing down onto the Caver Cliff, crashing onto the only sanctuary the Cavers had ever known.

It hit the harbour first, drowning it in an ocean's weight of foaming, tumbling water.

White, boiling power surged around the Fosca. Some

were caught in the first immense fall of water, pulverised by the pressure of it. The backwash, sending spray high into the air as it clashed against the following sea, sucked them out of any shelter, flinging them onto rock.

Dark angels swooping down, too late to rescue their riders, were caught in the tumbling swirl of malevolent salt, drowned, crushed, torn, beaten.

Rock began to collapse, already weakened by the earthquake. Boulders became dislodged, tossing through the water like toys, mixing with the debris and bodies.

But the Cavers had escaped, splattered with spray, trembling with adrenalin, soaring high into the cold air above the Cliff.

In the ruins of the Great Hall, for the first time in long ages, the silver pendulum stirred in the wash of the water. It began to sway as the wave crashed against rock, and rebounded, and crashed again, until the rock crumbled, throwing the silver disc down into the shadowy depths.

The Cavers surged up towards the stars, and cool water obliterated their enemy. They were free, saved by the Arrarat, and their home lay bathed in seawater. Their Lady had more than honoured Her eternal obligation.

The wave swept on, beyond the Cliff.

Towards the Boundary.

Chapter Thirty
Inquisition

Three hours after the Peraldonian awoke, Martitia, Thurstan, Hewlin and several other members of the council were assembled around the circular table in the formal room next to Eleanor's little cell.

The Peraldonian was strapped to a chair across the table from Eleanor. Fresh bruises disfigured his eyes and jawline. He had resisted Hewlin's coercion with a savage and skilled violence, and it had taken three men to drag him through the subterranean passages to the conference room. Eleanor had noticed Powel Hewlin's interest, weighing up the Peraldonian's expertise. He was pleased, she thought, because this man was trained, a professional soldier. He would have intelligence worth hearing.

She had not wanted to be there, knowing that it would be brutal. But Martitia had touched her arm, saying, 'I think you should come. I think this is significant,' and led the way. And besides, she didn't want to abandon him.

Blythe's eyes were closed. For a moment she wondered if the coma had reclaimed him, but then she saw that his hands were strongly clenched on the arms of the chair, knuckles white with tension.

There was a subdued buzz of conversation to which Eleanor paid no attention. She watched Blythe with dread; he would not be able to escape this, and she might be compelled to help him. Her palms were sticky, and she felt sick.

Martitia was sitting back in her chair, frowning, watchful. Her son was talking intently, leaning across the table towards Hewlin. His shirt was immaculately white, his fair hair shining in the candlelight, angel-like.

Abruptly he sat back, and such was his magnetism that

the table immediately fell silent. Taking his time, he gazed around them all, face impassive. But when he looked at the Peraldonian, Eleanor saw the thin lips curl faintly in contempt. He nodded once, to Hewlin, and the inquisition began.

Without preamble, shocking in the silence, Hewlin smashed the back of his hand across Blythe's face. His head jerked back with the force of it, but his eyes opened.

'There's no need –' he began.

'Shut it!' Hewlin snapped. 'You only answer questions here!'

The Peraldonian sat unmoving, black eyes watchful and wary.

'Who are you?'

'Phinian Blythe, Peraldonian.'

'Rank?'

'Captain – ex-captain in the Warden's Watch.'

The quiet voice with its slow drawl brought a taste of other worlds, sunlight and warmth, to the underground chamber. To Eleanor he seemed like fresh air – to the Jerenites he must have appeared a living reminder of oppression. Martitia had flinched at the sound.

'Why "ex"?'

'I have been banished.'

'Dear me.' Thurstan was softly ironic. 'What did *you* do?'

'Disobeyed Lefevre. Tried to help some rebels. Questioned the Stasis.'

'Why?' Hewlin, disbelieving.

'The Stasis does no one any good. I think it should be ended. I intend to bring this about.' His voice sounded dry, almost detached.

'Splendid!' Thurstan again, mocking. 'Kindly give us one reason why we should believe you.'

'I can only give you a negative. I will be killed if I return to Peraldon. What I want is to join your forces. I think I could help you –'

Thurstan stood up and walked round to his chair. 'Tell me then, Phinian Blythe, how many divisions are stationed on Peraldon. How the men are equipped and trained. What weapons are used, how the Fosca deals are negotiated . . .'

'No.' The refusal was absolute.

'How can you expect to be trusted with no assurances of good faith?' Thurstan was still calm and reasonable.

'Your trust is irrelevant.' The slow voice was bleak and expressionless. 'Knowledge of such matters – men and arms, tactics and strategy – would be useless to you here. You cannot possibly hope to match Peraldon in open warfare. You know that. Also, I will not betray my family and friends. The help I can give you is in ending the Stasis . . .'

'What had you in mind? A personal pact with Lycias?' Thurstan was cynical, and a murmur of derision ran round the table.

'I know where to go. Where the key to the Stasis is –'

'Ye gods, another one!' Thurstan sat down again, frustration and dislike in his voice. But Eleanor was on her feet, staring at Blythe.

'Where? Which direction?'

He smiled gently and looked beyond her, following the shining clear light that glowed, insistent in her mind.

'There,' he said.

'Oh, yes!' she whispered softly, 'Yes, that's right . . .' She had not been mistaken.

Hewlin's fist slammed down on the table.

'Enough! This is all nonsense. You are a spy, nothing else. You made some mistakes, got yourself caught, that's all. You'll take our food and medicine and then you'll just go back to your bloody family and friends and tell them all about us. Think again, Captain Blythe.'

'Listen, can't you? I'll be killed if I go back.' He looked pointedly down at his scarred wrists. 'How do you think I got these?'

'Peraldonians have used criminals before for suicide missions. What did you do? Rape? Murder?' Thurstan looked no more than curious.

'Nothing like that. I am not a criminal, I am a dissident, a rebel.' His mouth curled with distaste. He appeared to dislike labels.

'Prove it then. How many guards on duty at Solkest at any one time?'

'I don't know. I was in the Warden's company. Solkest is policed by Lefevre's personal guard.'

Eleanor saw him shudder, but no one else noticed.

'How many guards are on duty at the harbour at any one time?'

'It would not help you to know, and I can't tell you anyway.'

'You give us no guarantee.' Thurstan's voice was hard and unforgiving. 'How can you expect anything from us? We have suffered two Fosca attacks in the last seven days, as you are no doubt aware. We are in no mood to be generous to potential or actual spies.'

'I give you my word, I will not harm you or your people.'

But as Phinian Blythe spoke, he remembered the pathetic colony of Moon Worshippers in the disused sewers, and felt cold panic grip his heart. He could make no promises or assurances, and knew of no way to convince them without betraying his whole past.

'This has gone on long enough!' A thin elderly man to Hewlin's right was standing, leaning over the table. 'I demand he pays the penalty for spying. What question can there be? He's a Peraldonian, has even admitted to it. An enemy, a traitor, talking the same rubbish as that girl – we've had enough of vague and woolly theories. And who cares if he is a traitor to his own side or to ours? We don't need traitors of any kind!'

He paused, shaking with emotion. 'His people sent out the Fosca! They have reduced us to living like rats. They are responsible! *He* is responsible!'

'Quiet!' Martitia's voice cut through the rising excitement. 'He has a Moon scar like the girl.' There was a sudden silence.

Eleanor glanced quickly at the older woman. So she had seen it too.

'What's that to do with anything? Spies have used tricks like that before,' Thurstan said.

'We cannot discount it.' She turned to the Peraldonian, keeping her voice calm and level.

'If you can give us any information about the Fosca, how they are paid, where they live, what bribes they need, then we will take that as a token of good faith. You need not betray family or friends, then.'

'Mother!' Thurstan glared at her. 'I insist you leave this to me!'

'No. I am still ruler here, Thurstan, in name at least. This bargain I will make, and see that it is honoured.' He was white with fury, but she ignored him.

'Now,' she said to Blythe. 'You may trust me that you will not be harmed if you give us this information. Tell us about the Fosca.'

'I lost my position in Peraldon for making enquiries about that myself,' he said, with honesty. 'During the battle on the Ferry they were used without the Peraldonian council's authority. They were in Lefevre's personal pay. I can tell you nothing else.'

He would not allow them to pick over Karis's death, he thought grimly, he would not turn her and their child into bargaining counters.

It was clear that he was holding back. The atmosphere in that close stuffy room was charged with impatience and emotion.

'He is a spy!' repeated the elderly man. 'I demand he be punished!'

'And I!'

'Aye!' The angry voices round the table added to the clamour. The strain of waiting for another attack was leading to rising violence. They needed a scapegoat.

Eleanor began to feel frightened. 'What is the penalty for spying?' she asked the middle-aged woman sitting next to her.

The woman laughed harshly, stubbing out her cigarette in an saucer. 'Spies are blinded,' she said, 'So that they may see nothing else. We do not like to take life,' she added with cynical self-righteousness.

'Barbaric!' Eleanor was appalled.

'Barbaric, is it?' said Thurstan, overhearing. He was still furious at his mother's intervention, his lips thin and compressed.

'More barbaric than refusing to help where the need is desperate? More barbaric than turning aside from responsibility, from doing the one thing that might help? You –' he pointed viciously at her. 'You wallow in self-pity and pride, when you could *act*. What kind of civilised behaviour is that?'

She was unprepared for this attack, wanting only to retreat into inviolate loneliness.

'All right,' he said softly. The anger had turned into a cold smile. She watched with unwilling fascination the torch-light glinting on the fine hair, the golden stubble on his chin. 'All right, Eleanor. We'll do you a deal. See, Mother?' He glanced coldly to the old woman sitting so upright across the table. 'It runs in the family. I can strike bargains, too.

'Eleanor, think on this. You help us, call up your Moon light at our demand, allow us to explore it, and ways of using it, and Phinian Blythe here keeps his sight. Stay unhelpful – and he gets this in his eyes!' And he wrenched a torch from the wall bracket. A tightly bound bunch of slow-burning, sharp, red-hot twigs, it smoked and spat.

She blanched. 'Don't be ridiculous!'

'Don't tempt me, sweetheart!' he said savagely, moving over to the Peraldonian's chair. He held the torch there, burning brightly in front of Blythe's face for a moment, and then looked straight at her, holding her eyes. She thought she would have to scream, that the white light would wreak havoc again, because this was beyond bearing. He drew back his arm as if in preparation for the thrust.

Instinctively Blythe pressed himself back in the chair, turning his head aside, opening wounds again at his wrists in a sharp, convulsive movement. But there was no fear in the dark gaze; the flesh might shrink, but he seemed at some deep level not to care what happened to him.

Her breath almost choked in her throat. This was not tolerable, the sour smoke, the sharp twigs, and a man's sight, turned away.

'Don't . . .' she half-whispered. 'Please don't . . .'

A clamour outside, voices shouting and a rush of feet. The door burst open, and a filthy, exhausted young man stumbled across the threshold, half supported by Jerenite guards. From his austere, dark and patched clothes, Eleanor saw that he was a Caver. His face was thin with desperation.

'Where's Lukas?' he gasped, anxiously scanning the faces round the table. 'I must tell him, there's news . . .' His knees buckled, and someone pushed him into a chair. He was so young, drawn, frantic. Eleanor did not recognise him, but his need was clear to them all.

Martitia poured him wine; he gulped it down, shuddered, and began again.

'Is Lukas here?' His voice was stronger. 'There's news from the Caves – I must tell him –'

'He's ill,' said Thurstan. 'What's happened?'

'Ill? Dying?' The Caver's voice rose in panic.

'No, no,' said Thurstan reassuringly. 'He'll be all right. But he's not up to bad news, yet. I take it it *is* bad news?'

'Oh Lady, yes. There's been an earthquake, an attack –'

'Fosca?'

He nodded. 'Hundreds of them. They were still fighting when I left. Matthias sent me to give this message to Lukas, I must see him –'

'What about reinforcements? Shall we get the boats out?' Thurstan's mind was racing ahead, planning strategies, envisaging contingencies.

'No.' The Caver was definite. 'Matthias said, he particularly said, that no one else should risk their life, especially not in the boats. You're not to send anyone at all. It will be too late, anyway. But Lukas must be told. And you warned, for they might come on here after –'

'Don't worry,' said Thurstan meaninglessly, resting his hand on the boy's shoulder. His eyes were abstracted, his face unreadable. He nodded once, to Hewlin, who left the room. Immediately alarm bells began to sound outside.

'What is your name?' he said to the Caver.

'Caspar,' he said, 'brother to Fabian. Lukas and Matthias are my uncles . . .'

'I'll tell Lukas,' Thurstan said. 'Get some rest. We'll prepare the defences. Will there be other refugees?'

The boy shook his head. 'They decided to stay, all of them. Matthias tried to get the women to leave, at least, but they refused to go. We drew lots for someone to come here.'

His face was clouded with a curious shame. Martitia looked at him with sympathy. 'It was not an easier path to leave them. You mustn't feel guilty . . .'

'No . . . If you don't mind,' he said to Thurstan, 'I'd like to talk to Lukas alone. I have a private message for him from Matthias.'

'Very well. I'll send someone to show you the way.' Thurstan began to detail preparations that the various council members should undertake. Within minutes, the council had gathered up their papers and had left the room. Thurstan left a guard in charge of the Peraldonian, saying that he would be back soon, and then swept out.

Only four people beside the guard were now left in the council chamber; Martitia, Eleanor, the Caver Caspar, and Blythe.

'Did you say Fabian was your brother?' The deep weary voice surprised everyone. 'Did he reach home safely?' It was the Peraldonian.

The Caver looked at him, seeing the shackles and the bloodstained wrists for the first time.

'Who are you? A *Peraldonian*?' He looked disbelieving.

'Your brother, Fabian, spent a night at my house before returning to the Caves.'

'So you – are you Karis's husband?' He pronounced the name hesitantly, as if he might have remembered it wrongly. 'What are you doing here? Why did you leave Peraldon?'

Where Hewlin and Thurstan had encountered silence, Caspar elicited a response.

'My wife died,' he said, 'and our unborn child. And the explanations offered by the authorities were not good enough.'

'The authorities?' Martitia had missed none of the significance of this. At last she was receiving useful information. Blythe looked at her briefly but replied to Caspar.

'By our priest, Lefevre. He seems to have taken too much on himself, in trying to maintain the Stasis. It is, for some reason, too difficult to do this without constant use of the Fosca. And you are all suffering from this too, aren't you?' He referred to Martitia.

'Yes,' she confirmed. 'Things are . . . unstable.' She

stood up. 'If your arms are released, will you promise not to try to escape?'

He looked faintly amused by her simplicity, but merely shrugged, answering, 'Where should I go?'

Martitia nodded to the guard by the wall, a heavy looking man with silver earrings, long lank hair and a knife poised, ready. He hesitated. 'Go to it, man!' she said briskly. Muttering, he released the Peraldonian.

Awkwardly Blythe tied a handkerchief round his bleeding wrist. Then he looked at Eleanor.

'I still don't know who *you* are,' he said.

Nothing; no one here, she nearly replied, but in the end simply gave her name. Slowly he stood up, stretching. He was not tall, but powerfully built, strength implied, although illness had weakened him.

'A stranger, too,' he said thoughtfully, leaning on the table. 'Now why, I wonder?' But the question was not directed at her, and she wouldn't have known what to answer anyway.

There was an uneasy silence. Then Thurstan burst in. Quickly his bright eyes surveyed their faces, and then he spoke, single-mindedly, to his mother.

'I've asked for volunteers. Thirty of us are ready to go to the Caves. Can you hold things here?'

'No – you mustn't!' Caspar was frantic. 'You'll be too late – it's too much of a risk!'

'You will be needed here, if there's another attack,' said Martitia firmly. 'I think you should stay. Too many lives have already been lost.' He stared at her, implacable.

'Lukas is not up to any kind of decision,' he said. 'I can't neglect his family when I know he would want to go himself. He was injured fighting for us. I can do no less for him.'

'It will do him and us no good at all if you lose your life and those of thirty others!'

'Juvenile heroics are out of place in a serious attack. You should stay here –' The Peraldonian's voice sounded strange and out of place again.

'You! The last thing I need now is advice from a damned traitor! Look your last, little man, for you're going to lose those fine dark eyes tomorrow –'

'Never mind that.' Incredibly, he seemed not the slightest bit worried. 'I have some experience of warfare. I could be of use to you against Fosca –'

'Athus! Take him back to the sick bay, and this time the chains stay on!'

'Wait! Believe me!' Blythe was compelling.

With a blow Thurstan knocked him back into the chair. 'Enough!' he said, his voice ugly with anger. Martitia moved suddenly, to stand between Blythe and her son. She was very pale.

'Thurstan. I forbid you to go.'

'Mother.' He took a deep breath, trying to curb the ragged edge of temper. 'Understand this. I'm not asking for your permission. I'm telling you. You only have to hold things here till I get back. Powel will be here to help.'

The unspoken implication was that Powel Hewlin would be in charge as Thurstan's regent. Ungently, Martitia was being deposed.

For a while she argued, but Eleanor sensed that this was only for show. She was resigned to letting him have his way. Perhaps there was something she wanted to disguise.

At length, tense and angry, Thurstan kissed Martitia's averted cheek and left. He did not look back.

The guard had shackled Blythe once more, and led him off to the sick bay. Caspar stood up and followed them, in search of Lukas.

Martitia sat at the round table, and looked at Eleanor. Her hands were shaking. She pulled from her pocket a keyring, and passed it to Eleanor.

'That one will undo any locked ward,' she said, pointing. 'And this small one will release the handcuffs. You'll have to leave tonight, if you want to stop the blinding.' She sounded infinitely weary.

Eleanor took the keys and with them the legacy of action. Trembling she went to the older woman and, leaning over, gently kissed the lined forehead.

'I'll try not to let you down,' she said. 'Goodbye.'

'May you achieve all you desire,' said Martitia quietly, and watched the door close, leaving her alone in the deserted conference room.

Chapter Thirty-one
Flight

Eleanor stared down at the keys. She would have to leave now, with or without Ash, and take Blythe with her. She could barely contemplate how they would travel – by boat, perhaps. They'd have to steal one. But at least she would no longer be forced to make terrible choices.

Thoughtfully, she set off through the dreary corridors, stepping aside to avoid the hurrying soldiers. They were all preoccupied, running to defences, flamboyant jewellery flashing, urgent and sweaty in the stuffy underground.

She went straight to the sickbay. She could see Lukas through the window in Smisson's office, talking to Caspar. He was paper white, frowning with concentration, and as she watched he put his arm round the young Caver's shoulders. She had wanted to say goodbye to him, but could not intrude there. She passed the office into the darkened empty side ward with its shadowed bed at one end. Unbelievably, there was no guard or nurse. Martitia, she thought gratefully. Martitia was still helping them.

The Peraldonian was lying on the bed, wrists chained to the bed head. His face was expressionless as she released his hands. She was talking all the time in a nervous undertone.

'Everyone's getting ready for a Fosca attack; there are no guards that I can see anywhere, but we'll have to be quick. They'll go ahead with the blinding tomorrow, if we're not out of here –'

'Why are you doing this?' His eyes never left her face.

'I don't like barbarians,' she said. 'Never mind, it's not just that. Come on, let's go . . .'

He moved quietly, smoothly in the dim light, pressing against the wall, keeping to the shadows. She was not so skilful. As they passed the open door to Smisson's office the keys jangled in her unsteady hands, and Lukas, looking up, saw them both.

Frozen for a moment they stared at each other. Then, inexplicably, he smiled at her in understanding before turning back to the sobbing boy.

The corridors were deserted now; everyone had gone to their posts. Scarcely believing their good fortune, and safe back in her room at last, she leant heavily against the door.

Blythe sat on the bed, regarding her with misgiving. She was so young, so naive.

'What exactly have you in mind, Eleanor?' he said. 'Where are we going?'

She was thrusting clothes and blankets into a rucksack.

'We're going south. You know . . . you understand, where the light is.'

'Do you have access to an Arrarat? Or are there other means of transport from here?'

'There are boats I think, if we can get down to the shore. We'll have to take a chance.'

'Can I come too?' A familiar voice behind her. She whirled round to see Lukas, leaning against the doorpost.

'What are you doing here? What about Caspar, doesn't he need you?'

'He'll be all right. Matthias has sent a message directing me to stay with you, Eleanor Knight, whatever you may do.' He turned to Blythe. 'The shipwrecked Peraldonian, I see. One can only admire your good sense in getting out of here as soon as possible.'

'A boat then.' Blythe nodded, and then stood up quickly, helping Lukas to the bed. He was swaying with catastrophic weakness, but his eyes were clear and free from fever.

'No. Why not Arrarat?' he said.

'Lukas! I told you!' Eleanor cried. 'Ash won't come when I call.'

'He will tonight,' he said wearily. 'The Arrarat were just waiting for him.' He nodded towards Blythe. 'Didn't you try calling Ash today? You'd have found out then.'

With leaping hope she suddenly realised that they could indeed leave and follow the light.

'Shall we go then?' said Blythe, hauling Lukas to his feet.

Lukas led the way, familiar with the unfrequented passages of Jeren. They avoided the living quarters, the defences and armouries, and seemed to cover miles underground through shadowy stairways, unlit corridors and lonely halls.

Eleanor still had Martitia's keys, and was able to unlock all the doors. Occasionally the key was stiff to turn, the lock rusty and disused, and Blythe had to force it, while Lukas sagged against the wall, breathing hard and sweating.

At last they began travelling upwards. Without ever coming to the open surface they found themselves tramping up a spiral staircase. Wood surrounded them, coarse-grained and dusty. Their footsteps echoed on the hollow stairs. Eleanor put out a hand and touched the concave wall all around them. It was rough, neither varnished nor stained. Splinters everywhere. No one used this route regularly. The treads of the steps were hardly worn at all.

Wood, all around. The stair had been hacked out of the inside of one of the trees. Occasional openings for ventilation were cut in the walls and the cold night air blew chill on their faces.

Lukas's knees were buckling at every step. He trudged on, his head bent, face in shadow. Blythe and Eleanor each took an arm, but the staircase was narrowing and it became increasingly difficult to support him. They were all breathing in gasps, hearts thudding, leg muscles on fire with the ceaseless climbing.

After what seemed like hours of ascent, the stair swung through an arch to continue on up the outside of the trunk. If they had found the journey difficult before, it now became almost impossible.

There was no outer rail, the wooden steps were slippery in the everlasting rain, and the wind whipped around the great tree. There was no way in the dark of judging the drop on the outside. On the whole, this was a relief.

The wind level increased as they went on up, slicing through leaves and branches, distorting vision and breath with its violence. The whole tree was swaying and creaking in the gale, like a ship at sea, and the stairway sloped alarmingly and unpredictably beneath them. A rough rope twined round the central trunk was their only handhold. Ancient and frayed, it looked thoroughly unreliable.

Blythe was in front, one arm round Lukas's waist, the other clutching the rope. He was aware of weakness, but knew it to be surmountable. Lukas was virtually unconscious, moving in an automatic daze. Eleanor, trailing below, was seriously lagging behind.

She hated heights, hated this swaying, treacherous nightmare of a tree, and the violent wind seemed to shiver through her nerves. Would Ash come anyway? What if Lukas was hallucinating, as so often in the past days? He wouldn't survive any kind of journey anyway, and Blythe was completely unknown. Her legs were on fire, her breath impossible to catch, and she was soaked through.

In exhaustion she found herself repeating like a mantra, 'Astret, Astret', trying to remember what she was doing and why. But she was too tired, and the stair was endless.

'Please stop!' she called out at last. 'I can't go any further –' It took three breaths to say. Looking back, Blythe just caught the querulous sound. He nodded, and leant back against the tree. Lukas slumped onto the stair, eyes closed. Moments passed; eventually he stirred.

'Fifty feet higher – there's a platform. We can call the Arrarat there.' His voice was just a thread in the wind. Unsteadily he pushed himself upright, and smiled crookedly at Eleanor, still gasping with exhaustion.

She felt a sudden rush of affection for him, that he should still try to reassure her. She could just see the outline of his smile, reflected in – what light? For there was no Moon, stars or sunlight, no torches, fires or lanterns . . . and yet his eyes were gleaming down at her. She stared down at her hands. She caught her breath; her own skin was shining with a faint luminosity.

The Peraldonian stood in shadow against the trunk, his face unreadable 'The light of righteousness, would you say?' His voice was strangely without irony.

Calmly, Lukas took her offered, shining hand and said neutrally, 'Yes. She's full of surprises. Come on.'

Silently, wearily, they clambered up the rickety steps to

the platform. It was only about ten feet square, wedged between the swaying branches, lashed into place by the fraying rope. The noise was immense as the wind tore through the tree tops. Lukas and Blythe stood together at the side of the platform, watching while Eleanor, unsteadily balanced at its centre, trying to ignore the noise, called the Arrarat.

Her voice was true and accurate, although faint. Within seconds the heavy flapping of wings broke into the howl of wind. Two huge dark shapes alighted on the buckling edge of the platform; with an irrepressible surge of joy, Eleanor ran to Ash. Golden eyes glowed in the dark, and she felt his warm greeting, his delight in her, the suddenly altering perspective of her mind. Wide spaces, freedom . . . All her tiredness vanished, all her doubt and weariness. Murmuring softly, she stroked the dense black feathers of the bird's breast.

Lukas was poised beside Astrella. Remembering, they turned simultaneously to Blythe, frowning in the shadow.

'Come on!' she cried happily.

'Go with Eleanor,' said Lukas. 'She's lighter, and not without defences. But give me a leg up first.'

Blythe did so, and then climbed up behind Eleanor, clasping her round the waist.

With a rush of cool air, a splatter of rain, and a dizzying distortion of perspective, the hawks spread their wings and leapt into the dark.

Chapter Thirty-two
Journey

So they left the island of Jeren, its extraordinary trees lashed by the everlasting wind and rain. Exhausted and cold on their fleet birds they hurtled ever southwards, over stormy seas and lonely islands. Black cloud and deep twilight dragged at the spirit, and even words deserted them. On the ground they huddled together for warmth in silence.

The first few days were the worst, for land and sea were almost indistinguishable, observed only as changing shadows in the bleak world beneath them.

Neither Eleanor nor Blythe were capable of building fires with sodden wood, and Lukas had no resources left after a long flight on Astrella. On empty beaches they crouched together against the Arrarat, shivering and anxious, sharing out the meagre supplies.

At first Eleanor was terrified that Lukas would become feverish again, that they would have to nurse him on some rocky ledge or deserted island. He was distant, unusually quiet and very tired, but his hands were steady, his eyes clear. He smiled encouragement at her.

Blythe had reserves of strength she could not comprehend; he was driven by some force that took no account of weakness, and permitted no familiarity. She found it strange that he had so recently lain helpless in Smisson's side ward.

He refused to answer her occasional questions, as he measured out food, or rigged a shelter for the night. Unfailingly courteous, he treated her with a remote kindness, and very soon she stopped questioning him at all.

They used Lukas's enveloping floor-length cloak as a rough tent, slung between rocks or trees. It was waterproof and surprisingly large, specifically designed, said Lukas, for just such a contingency. Wedged between the two Arrarat, pressed close together, they managed to sleep most nights, more or less dry, not quite chilled to the bone.

If she had had the energy, she would have laughed at the irony of it. She had shared her nights with men before, but never before had intimacy seemed so out of place. But there was companionship, and a common purpose, and she began to feel oddly content.

The grip of the dream was as potent as ever. It was no nightmare, for the remembered irrrelevancies of her previous life astounded and bored her. This was vivid and strong beyond imagination, and for long periods she forgot what her life had been, where she used to live, what she was.

As they left Jeren far behind, her spirits lightened. She was exhilarated by the flight of the Arrarat, enchanted by their heavy musky scent and the wide reach of their wings.

And understanding grew. During the long flights she found Ash's thoughts mingling with her own, not in clear words but as feelings and moods. The ecstasy of air beneath them, steady air, rippling through the feathers, the smooth sweep of the wings soaring on a thermal . . . She began to understand another mode of existence, to think of life as something free, soaring high beyond the heavy pull of gravity, the earth and rock under her feet.

But more than this, she felt like singing. At last, at last, she was following the light printed in her mind by Astret, the Lady of the Moon. She was significant in this world. She had a role to play, an important task to achieve, given her by a Goddess. Never before had she enjoyed such prestige.

She had forgotten her fear at Martitia's words. And those words themselves, that this was conflict on a divine scale. The implication that humans are only puppets acting out an eternal drama.

Jocasta's death was only a brief aberration, she decided, a small cloud that did not at this distance seriously disturb her self-confidence. She did not want to look for wider significances. She would find the Benu, break the Stasis, a heroine for all the world to admire. She was content to live in superficial dreams.

When pressed, Blythe admitted that he too was glad to be

going south, for the light beckoned him as well. But he shared none of her joy, driven by a weight of anguish she did not want to understand.

Lukas was not much easier, depressed and irritable. At first she thought that he was still recovering from illness, but then it became plain that he was both suspicious of the Peraldonian and disturbed by the southward journey.

The sky was getting lighter. Imperceptibly, the unrelieved dusk began to give way, to reveal the shapes of mountains and islands against the sea. It was still cloudy, with few glimpses of moon or sun, but sometimes, for hours on end, the wind dropped and the rain ceased, and Eleanor could make out the darting silhouettes of birds against the paling sky.

Lukas hated it. Most of his life had been endured in the cold, wet, twilight Caver world. He had dedicated himself to an ending of that condition. And yet, here, faced with the prospect of light and warmth, all his innate loathing of the sunworshipping Peraldonians came flooding back. The past could not be glossed over. That dreary saga of aggression, fear, betrayal and guilt soured every contact between the two men. Lukas could hardly bear to look at Blythe with his fading sunburn and smooth hands.

Instead, as his strength returned, he devoted himself to hunting and fishing, disappearing on Astrella for hours at a time. He was a skilled hunter, rarely failing to return with a rabbit, pheasant or fish, a bunch of herbs thrust into his belt.

On a lonely shore off the Octal peninsula south-west of Peraldon, early in their journey, he made bows for them all, using strong shoots from a tree Eleanor did not recognise. Threads stitched into one of the seams of the black cloak provided him with cords strong enough to use as bow-strings, and there were plenty of feathers for flights.

Blythe had taken no part in the construction of the bows, preferring to lay traps around each camp, an activity that kept him well away from Eleanor's curiosity and Lukas's mistrust.

When the bows were completed, sturdy, neat weapons, each with half a dozen arrows, Lukas offered him one, a little grudgingly.

'I suppose you know how to use this?' he asked.

'Yes.' Blythe was neutral. 'Thanks.'

'Goodness. A famed Peraldonian archer, all to ourselves.' Lukas squinted in the unaccustomed light, pointing to a tree some distance away. 'A demonstration! The arrow flies as does the heart to its home . . . Can you hit that?'

Blythe barely looked at it. 'Yes.' His lack of interest was obvious.

'Well, go on then. Honour us with a small exhibition of Peraldonian skill.'

Finally goaded, Blythe fixed the arrow to the string and took aim towards the tree. Suddenly he spun round, firing the arrow diagonally up into the air, directly at a small bird flying there. Soundlessly the arrow sank into its breast. It plunged into the woodland behind them.

With an exclamation, Eleanor ran to retrieve the arrow, and then halted, dismayed, looking down at the tangled mess of feathers and blood. It was a soft, dove grey, hawk-like bird, a small relation to Astrella.

Her first thought was to hide it before Lukas saw it, but she was too late. He pushed past her, staring down at the bird, and then back to Blythe, standing at their camp.

'You have had plenty of practice, haven't you?' he said, his voice very quiet in the still air. 'Just how many Arrarat have you shot down? How many Cavers killed? Was it fun, that kind of target practice?' All the weight of the past conflict echoed in his words.

'There's no point in this.' Irritably, Blythe walked past him and bent down to retrieve his arrow. He was angry with himself for giving way to provocation.

'No.' Lukas still held the bird in long fingers. His voice was quiet. Eleanor tensed at the sound. 'No. Perhaps not. But we need to know. This can't go on. What brings you here, a sharp-shooting marksman from the Warden's Watch? What went wrong at Peraldon? What lies on your conscience, Phinian Blythe?'

'More than you can possibly imagine.' His voice was almost inaudible.

'For God's sake!' Eleanor felt the cold touch of fear, looking at the expression in Blythe's eyes. 'There's no need for this! What good can it do? He wants to break the Stasis, just as you do!'

Lukas ignored her.

'Well? An explanation is overdue, I think.'

'It won't help.' Blythe spoke wearily. He had seen it coming for days. If they were to continue together, he would have to tell them. Lukas was still watching him, unmoving.

'It's a long story. You don't need to know it.' May the God preserve me, Blythe thought. I don't want to admit to this one. But there was no way out now. Lukas would not be easily diverted. He would never let it rest.

'Explain.' Lukas spoke harshly. 'You can't stop there.'

Blythe looked at the calm wooded island where they stood. The Arrarat, the most accomplished of travellers, usually found fertile, sheltered havens to rest in long before exhaustion struck.

This was no exception, a peaceful world of trees and rustling grasses. Gentle hills spanned the horizon; the sea was only yards away, just beyond a narrow band of sand dunes on the edge of the wood. The sky arched high and clear above them. There was no movement beyond the light wind in the leaves and grasses, no sound above the distant murmur of the sea.

It could not be more different from the Peraldonian sewers, where so many of Astret's followers had died. His debt to them was overwhelming; at the very least, he owed Lukas the truth. Aridly he began to recount it all, from the Caver attack on the Ferry and Karis's death, through the encounter with Selene, to the fight at the Lock-keeper's lodge, and the flooding of the sewers through his agency.

Eleanor tried to break in here, passionately wanting to exonerate him from an unreasonable guilt. But ignoring her, driven, he continued coldly describing Idas, Lefevre, the burning cauldron and the Arrarat rescue. Unable to meet his eyes, Lukas was whittling at a stick, sharpening it to a vicious point.

'I am thus, as you see, a perceived enemy of Lefevre. A friend of mine gave his life to allow my escape –' Jarek, beleaguered by Fosca at the bottom of the stairs in his house. He paused briefly before continuing. 'My servant and friend, Uther, is held hostage. I have sworn to kill Lefevre and break the Stasis that enslaves us all. Lefevre maintains its stability; there is a good chance that if he dies, so will the Stasis.' The cold voice stopped.

Eleanor took a small step towards him, hand outstretched. But his silence was forbidding, and he looked only at Lukas.

'One cannot fault your motives,' he said at last. 'How many more Cavers will die before you attain that laudable goal?'

Blythe brushed it aside. 'There is one other thing I think you should know,' he said, looking straight ahead, out into the pale sky beyond them. 'Lefevre sent me here. He said that I had no choice but to do his will. He implied knowledge of the future. He allowed me to leave Péraldon, allowed me to take the boat that was washed up on Jeren.

'I do not understand how it will happen, but Lefevre thinks I am working for him, that my destiny is to be his tool.' He looked at them both. 'You must take this warning seriously.'

There was a long silence as they considered it. Eventually Lukas turned the sharpened stick in his hands and walked up to Blythe. He pointed the impromptu spear directly at the other man's heart.

'What should we do, do you think? In our shoes, what would you do?' His voice was almost dreamy. 'On your own admittance hundreds of my people have died through your actions. And now you say that for all your hatred of Lefevre, you are his agent, even if it's not by choice. Shouldn't we destroy you, here, now, rather than take that risk?'

'You must decide,' he said evenly. 'But I intend to kill Lefevre, whatever your decision, and although I agree that my life is forfeit, I will defend it in order to accomplish that one act. I would rather not hurt you, Lukas; there is quite enough Caver blood on my hands already. But I will not allow you to stop me.' Calmly he turned the spear aside and, turning his back on them, walked away towards the sand dunes.

Eleanor started after him, but Lukas caught her arm. 'No,' he said. 'You and I need to talk.'

There was, in the end, little disagreement between them,

for Blythe was clearly not lying. Indeed, thought Eleanor, one could only wish that he had softened it all a little.

'Do we take the chance, Eleanor? What do you say?'

'What else can we do? He follows the Moon's light, has been scarred by it. The Arrarat trust him. We can't discount that.'

'No. But what good can come of it, if he's part of a plan he doesn't understand?'

Eleanor sighed. 'There's nothing we can do about that.'

'We could leave him behind – or kill him,' he offered, grimly.

'Would you do either of those?' She looked at him curiously. Tall and slim, sheet white in the soft light, he was both bleak and powerful.

'No, my dear,' he said, suddenly smiling, breaking the mood. 'No, we'll not desert him, shall we? Let's take the chance.'

Chapter Thirty-three
Traitor

He was standing with his back to them, a lonely figure looking out to sea.

'Phinian –' Eleanor started forward but he held out his hand as if in warning.

'Where are the Arrarat?' said Lukas.

Blythe turned to look at them.

'They took off, moments ago. Very quickly, very suddenly. But that's not all.' His voice was very soft. 'A boat rounded the headland just now.'

They stared at him. There had been no sign of human habitation since they left Jeren. This was a deserted, palely lit world of quiet waters and rustling trees. There was no one else there, no one to disturb the peace.

'It was manned by Peraldonians. Grey uniforms.'

'Friends of yours?' Lukas's eyes were abstracted. 'How many?'

Blythe shrugged. 'Too far away to see clearly. Three or four, I suppose. The boat passed round there –' He pointed to the edge of the beach where a hill sloped down into the water.

'Astrella would let me know if there was anything to worry about,' said Lukas, but his hand rested on his knife.

'Are you getting anything from her? Now?' Blythe asked.

Lukas paused before answering. 'No,' he said slowly, uneasily. 'She's either out of range or not willing to communicate. I can't get through at all. I think . . . we should get the bows.'

He took Eleanor's hand, pulling her back towards the shadowy trees.

'Lukas!' She clutched his arm. 'What's that?'

She was pointing to a clump of grass on the sand dune behind them. 'I thought – I saw it move, just then. I'm sure it moved.'

He was very still for a moment. Then, quickly, 'If it's Mages, Eleanor, Phin . . . distraction sometimes works . . .'

A roar in the air as it crashed into febrile life and electric power snapped overhead. The shape of the sand dune they had been looking at began to waver and bulge, and bolts of force shot through the air from it.

'Separate!' Lukas was dashing for the trees behind the dunes, Eleanor and Phin beginning to scatter over the beach when a voice called out from the dunes.

'Marling!' Lukas abruptly skidded to a halt, and the shifting shape of the dune held steady, the power subsiding.

'Reckert?' His voice was incredulous. 'Is that you?'

Eleanor knew the voice too, from memories and nightmares.

Lukas's tone changed. 'Why are you here?'

'Looking for your little lady friend, of course.' The dune dissolved, dispersing into the rippling forms of scurries, and then it was too late. Scurries scattered over the sand, breaking like a tide all around them.

A small elderly shabby figure was standing there, dressed in a moth-eaten, feathery cloak, leaning negligently against a tree, his hands crossed in front of him.

'I've spoken to Caspar.' Lukas was grim.

'Then I need pretend no longer.' Reckert's voice was dry, almost amused. He flicked a word at the scurries and the sand surged forward in leaping shapes. They found their wrists and ankles imprisoned in a cold and clammy grip.

Eleanor shuddered at the touch, loathing the tenacious stickiness of it. The scurries held her quite still. She was unable to move. And although she was frightened, and hated the way they distorted shape and form, she found herself saying, ridiculously, 'Lukas, what did I tell you?'

'My apologies, Eleanor –' His attention was elsewhere. He called out, loud and clear, the Arrarat summoning.

There was no response.

Reckert smiled. 'They won't come while I'm here. I didn't spend all that time in a smelly cave for nothing.'

'Why are you doing this? Who are you working for?' Phin's voice was cool, his face impassive.

Reckert laughed. 'Lefevre, of course. Who did you think? I work for Lefevre and our new Emperor, Xanthon. And the Lord Lycias.' He bowed his head in a gesture of respect. Then he looked up, smiling at Lukas. 'I always have done. It's been an amusing pretence, befriending the Cavers, keeping an eye on those difficult Mages, but it's past a joke now. The Stasis is in danger and your little lady is at least in part responsible.'

At her side she heard Lukas say something to Phin. He knew Reckert well, she remembered. And was acquainted with the skills of Mages . . .

Reckert moved towards his prisoners. The smile still lifted the corners of his narrow lips. He raised his hand and gently stroked the hair from Eleanor's face, exposing once more the Moon-scar.

'Salutations, lady. But it is no easy thing, to be chosen by the gods,' he said softly. She stared back at him, and recognised something unexpected glinting at the back of his eyes.

He was both envious and lustful. She had seen the combination before in men's eyes. She had always been able to handle it. Confidence made her foolhardy.

'You were never even chosen by the Arrarat, were you?'

Sudden anger flared. For a moment his concentration wavered, and Eleanor found the grip on her limbs weaken.

A rapid whisper from Lukas, at her side, 'Hang on, we'll be back . . .' and then felt, rather than saw, Lukas and Phin break free, running for the trees. Running for weapons, she thought. She hoped they would not be long.

Reckert was getting far too close. His eyes were intent on her. She flung herself to one side, away from the pull of the scurries, but lost her balance, falling down into the soft, slithery mass. She saw her limbs mimicked and elongated, her hair spreading like water over the sand, her dress growing new folds, new flounces and layers. Their texture was vile, chill and slimy.

She staggered to her feet in revulsion, trying to brush them off. They were clinging like leeches, and she was frantic with disgust.

'No, little lady, I was never chosen. There was no need.' Reckert smiled once more, and holding her eye, gave the summoning call himself.

The familiar sound of beating wings, the disturbance of the air, the familiar lift in her heart. Ash and Astrella settled on the sand behind Reckert and gazed at her impassively.

Urgently, she tried to reach Ash along the usual wavelengths in her mind, but the channel was closed, blocked off by some external force.

'You see,' said Reckert. 'They are all mine, anyway. The Arrarat are my creatures, just as these scurries are, just as you will be . . .'

Watching his eyes running over her body, she began to realise what he meant.

In panic she looked back at the woods, wondering where Phin and Lukas were. In the darkening shade, pale grey shapes moved. Men in uniform were threading through the trees, fanning out. She was on her own.

Ash was still watching her, waiting . . .

'Ash!' She could not prevent herself crying his name. A sharp blow flung her face to one side. She looked up to find Reckert still smiling at her.

'You're coming with me, Eleanor Knight. There's much in store for you.'

'What do you mean?' she spoke with difficulty, her mouth bruised by the blow.

Ash would not desert her. Would not leave her here with this horrible man. Surely.

He leant forward and kissed her, softly, on the lips. His tongue tasted her blood. She felt sick.

'This, to begin with . . .' he said.

Scurries were like weights on all her limbs. She spat in his face, as hard as she could. In the dangerous flare of his anger she once more felt the clammy grip on her ankles loosen. She darted forward across the sand.

She had to get to Ash. She couldn't believe that he would fail her. She would leap onto the wide back and they would be off, soaring into the clear sky, far away from this repulsive man and his disgusting scurries.

But as she ran towards the great hawk, she heard Reckert's

voice directing the scurries. They moved so quickly. They were clogging round her ankles, swarming up all over her body, dragging her to the ground. She tried to scream but one of them had reached her face, and she couldn't bear it. She wanted to shut her eyes, fold herself away, retreat to some other place. Shivering, she tried to keep still. Perhaps they would fall away if she stayed completely motionless.

Reckert was still focused on her, careless of what had happened to the others, obviously confident that his men would deal with them.

He was concentrating on Eleanor. Abruptly the scurries dropped away. In that brief moment she surged up from the sand, but his arms were already round her, his foul breath in her face, his lips against hers.

She lashed out at him, kicking, hitting, scratching, but he was much stronger than she, and his hand was tearing at the front of her dress. She was screaming now, screaming for Ash, for Lukas, for Phin.

Thrown to the ground again. She wriggled back, away from him, but his hand was bunched into a fist. She put her arm up to ward it off but it crashed through, slamming into her jaw and her head jolted back against a stone. A sunburst of pain was succeeded by the rush of black.

She did not hear the harsh shriek in the air.

Wings flew at him. He was jerked from her in the clutch of wild claws. Vast black feathers beat the air round him, lifting him from the ground. A bizarre kaleidoscope of colour, sky, sand, sea and ebony feathers, a dizzying collapse of stability and perspective.

At last, Mortimer Reckert was chosen to fly with the Arrarat.

He had claimed them for his own, in arrogance and pride. And to see what he would do, waiting their moment, they had allowed him to live with them. But now that claim was turned about, and the Midnight Hawk flew high over the sea with his prey.

Soaring on a powerful thermal, the iron grip shifted, stabbing through greasy skin. The hooked beak plunged deep into his body, raking through quivering flesh. Claws ripped skin and muscle apart, and blood showered. In the blaze of agony he screamed, a high, inhuman scream spread wide on the smooth air, but it ceased when the side of his neck was torn open. The dry voice died forever in a gush of blood.

Under the trees, the shadows wavered. Lukas caught Blythe's arm. 'We're not alone –' he said.

'Where?' He could not see as well as Lukas in the deepening shade.

'All around, I think. Here.' One of the home-made bows was thrust into his hands. 'You'll need this.'

'What about Eleanor?'

'There's nothing we can do surrounded by Peraldonian soldiers.'

Now Blythe too could see the pale grey uniforms flickering through the trees. At his side, Lukas had drawn back the string of his bow. In the damp twilight he heard the faint whisper of the arrow's flight and one of the grey shadows cried out, collapsing forward into the undergrowth.

For a moment Blythe stood irresolute, his bow hanging slack in his hand. He had worn a grey uniform too, had lived and fought alongside these men. Lukas was watching him, as one of the other Peraldonians ran to help the injured man.

'Decision time, Phin,' he said gently.

A twig cracked behind them.

Three men, swords and knives in their hands, rushing at them, crashing through the undergrowth. Lukas seemed to vanish into the dark, fading into the shadows, moving round behind the trees. Blythe dropped his bow, swinging himself up on one of the branches overhead, swiftly clambering out of reach.

The air by his head fractured. A knife thudded into the branch beside him. He wrenched it out, thrusting it into his belt so that his hands were free.

He had underestimated, he thought. There were at least half a dozen of them.

He saw one of the soldiers below drop, an arrow in his back. And then, from the seashore, he heard Eleanor scream.

He edged along one of the branches, and jumped, tumbling the man beneath over onto his back. A brief tussle, a harsh jab with his fist, a knee in the groin and the man doubled up, gasping and helpless.

He turned to face the other, the knife in his hand, and flung himself forward, twisting at the last moment so that the man's sword became entangled in brambles. Together they crashed into the thorns, and he thought it would be all right, that he could just disable the man, like the other. Perhaps he might manage to avoid killing them.

A blow glanced off the side of Blythe's head. In a swirl of dizziness, he felt an arm round his neck, pulling him out of the brambles. Someone's boot slammed into his gut, a fist knocked his head back against a tree and then he heard, unbelieving, a familiar voice.

'Tobin!' The man in the thorn bush was yelling. 'Hold off! Do you see who that is?'

He was staggering to his feet, sandy-haired, freckled, an open, honest face, pale with shock. 'Tobin, for God's sake – !'

The man in front of him lowered his fist. He stared at Blythe.

'Captain Blythe!' He stepped back, stammering and confused. 'What are you doing here? I thought, we all thought, you were dead . . .'

Blythe looked at him, dimly aware that Lukas was not far away, arrow poised. And as he watched, catching his breath, the man called Tobin fell forward at his feet, his eyes staring with frozen disbelief. Lukas had not hesitated.

'Estan.' Blythe spoke to his old companion.

Lukas stepped out of the shadows, the bow poised. 'You know this bastard?'

'Yes. He served in my company, in the Warden's Watch.'

He was talking to Lukas, keeping his eyes on the Peraldonian. 'Go and find Eleanor. I heard her scream.'

'Look, what's going on here?' Estan's glance was flickering from Blythe to Lukas. 'What are you doing with Cavers?' He was aware of being way out of his depth.

Blythe looked him straight in the eye. 'Spying for Peraldon, of course, like Reckert.'

Estan believed him. He believed him. He drew his sword, turning his back on Blythe, making for Lukas with determination.

Blythe lunged forward, sliding the knife into the man's heart.

The look of sheer surprise on his face shocked them both. He died instantly, tumbling over in the brambles, speckling the leaves with scarlet.

For a moment, Blythe stared down at the body of his former colleague. He was shivering, suddenly. He rubbed his hand over his forehead as if tired.

He bent down and pulled out the knife, wiping it on leaves to clean it.

Lukas's bow was dangling loose from his hand. He was watching him. 'That wasn't easy, was it?' he said.

'No. None of it is easy.' His voice, unusually quiet, was harsh and bitter. 'We'd better go and find Eleanor.' he said.

Lukas nodded, and together they walked back across the sand to where the girl was lying.

Her head ached. A rough blanket flung over her, like once before, and sand beneath her fingers. She stirred, opening her eyes, and saw the comforting brightness of a small fire on the sand.

Ash was standing over her, as if on guard. She was receiving complicated waves of love and reassurance from him, coupled with something else . . . regret? She didn't understand.

Lukas and Phin were sitting together, leaning against Astrella on the other side of the fire. They were all right, talking quietly. And they were drinking.

She sat up, and pain shot through her neck and head. A quick movement and Lukas was beside her, helping her to rise, amusement and sympathy in his voice.

'Poor little Eleanor, you have had a rotten time, haven't you?'

She was glad of his arm for her legs felt like cotton wool. 'Is Reckert – ?' Her voice was like a rusty hinge. She sighed and then wished she hadn't. She didn't really need to ask. Looking into Ash's golden eyes she knew what had happened. He had done it. He had killed Reckert.

Lukas guided her across the sand, and she subsided weakly against Astrella, next to Blythe.

'They're all dead. All the Peraldonians.' Blythe's voice was empty of expression.

'The scurries won't trouble us either. They're useless without a Mage to control them. Look.' Lukas nudged a loose pile of sand by her feet. It melted under his foot, sliding aimlessly across the ground, dissipating into multi-coloured grains before reassembling as another formless heap. She watched it with disgust.

'You missed all the excitement,' said Lukas, bringing her a drink.

It was wine. She almost choked on it and looked up at him in amazement.

'They brought a boat with them,' he said, smiling. 'We can have a feast. If you're up to it, of course.'

She wasn't really, but it was good to sit on the sand and watch Phin and Lukas build a barbecue, roasting lamb and apricots, baking potatoes in the ashes. And later, when they had eaten and were watching the dying embers, Lukas began to play on the small flute he'd found in Reckert's boat; silly nursery tunes, some of which she recognised, some very strange indeed, and he and Phin laughed when she told them the words she knew.

The connections were so bizarre between her world and this. Both trivial and profound. The language, so idiomatic and familiar. The history and religion, so extraordinary, so unlikely.

And yet she remembered Sun gods in her own world: Apollo, Ra . . . there were probably others, but she had never been interested. And Artemis, of course. The Moon was so often associated with the feminine. Perhaps the same archetypes prevailed everywhere. Perhaps they were of such power, so overwhelming that they could not be contained in one world, and would recur over and over again, resonating through time and space.

Unfamiliar speculations made her headache worse.

It was so far away, her childhood, on the other side of time. And her parents, distantly affectionate, preoccupied by their own conflict, what would they be thinking? That she'd taken herself off on holiday, forgetting to write? It had happened before. They might not even notice at all, communications being so strained. Had time passed at all, back in her world? Or were people still playing round a bonfire, throwing glass into the air?

She leant back against the warm feathers and closed her eyes. There was no point in wondering. A light shone, beckoning her onwards, and all she had to do was to follow it.

It seemed so simple.

PART TWO

Chapter One
The Lake of Lallon

'I don't much like this.'

Surprised, Matthias glanced at his companion. Haddon was tightening the strap on his rucksack, avoiding the Mage's eyes.

'What's wrong?' Matthias asked. 'I can sense no danger.'

'It's Asta.' Haddon trudged on over the springy grass. 'Why did she fly off like that? Why wouldn't she stay?'

'The Arrarat always know best.'

The unfamiliar mountains were quiet around them. No birds sang, no sheep grazed on the steep slopes. The sky hung clear and cold over them, blue tinged with rose as the sun set over the far peaks.

They walked mainly in silence, Haddon carrying the heavier load, for Matthias was not yet quite recovered. He had not wanted Haddon to come. He knew it would be dangerous. But the other Mages had insisted and, in truth, he was glad of company.

It had felt like running out, leaving Stefan, Thurstan and the others to fend for themselves on Jeren. The Fosca attacks were coming without pause, and even with the Mages to help the loss of life was frightening.

'Attack!' Thurstan had shouted, slamming his fist down on the table. He was white with exhaustion, scratched and filthy, like everyone else. He had returned from the abortive mission to help the Cavers seething with anger and bitterness. The heavy seas had turned his small force of volunteers back, and he had to wait, in impotent fury, for the Cavers to reach Jeren.

He was glad to find that Eleanor had gone. It had at least

shown her capable of action. And in the company of Lukas Marling, perhaps she would not go too far wrong . . .

Blythe was a dead man as far as he was concerned. Renegade or spy, he was better out of the way. Practical as ever, Thurstan Merauld turned his mind to the situation on hand.

It was dangerous enough. The remaining Fosca were attacking without pause, exacting a spiteful vengeance for the death of so many of their kind in the Great Wave.

It was exhausting and horrifyingly wasteful of life, but Thurstan was burning with a fierce rage, and he carried the others with him.

'Why should we stay here like rats in a trap, waiting to be slaughtered? Let's get going, leave here and go and find the High Bloody Priest of Lycias!'

'We have no chance against Peraldonian defences.' Stefan Pryse, reasonable as ever. 'Such tactics always fail.'

'Lefevre is not at Peraldon.' They stared at her, the silent, despairing woman who had brought the news from the sewers of Peraldon. Selene looked down at thin hands, and spoke again.

'He is touring the Empire. The official reason is to ensure that everything is in order for the new Emperor. But there is a rumour circulating, that he has to find . . . something: that he is searching. He is travelling now.'

'Do you know the route?' Thurstan, immediately attentive.

She paused. 'Only in dreams . . . if you trust me, I could tell you . . .'

It had been vague at best, a series of half-remembered pictures and ideas. They had maps and charts and knew how to navigate. They were still debating the issue when the ceiling fell in and the Fosca were among them again.

Smisson died that time, and Martitia. Their centre lost, the Jerenites looked to Thurstan. Ruthless with anger and grief, he conferred with Stefan and the Mages and gave the commands.

There were enough boats to take all the Cavers and Jerenites. They would all go – although it was probably suicidal – because Jeren was no longer tolerable. And without the help of the little colony on Peraldon, getting food and supplies would be even more dangerous, even more difficult. They would pack up, all of them, follow Selene's route to the south, and attack the creator of the Stasis as he travelled.

In private conference later, Matthias fought another battle. Blaise's diaries again, revealing terrifying paths to power.

He offered to bargain for control of the dark. If it came to open warfare against Peraldonian forces, their hard-won ability to move in the night like cats might just tip the balance. And the Fosca could not function for more than a few hours at a time in the dark. Attacking Jeren, or the Cliff, they had always operated a shift system, returning south-east to sunny Peraldon to recharge flagging reptilian energy. Taking the dark with them into Peraldon would be a major advantage.

The other Mages had argued, fearing that the price would be high, but Thurstan merely nodded. 'How else can we hope to endure?' he had said in the end. 'What else is there for us to do?'

So here Matthias was, trailing up a mountainside on the other side of the Boundary, to a place mentioned both in the Scriptures and the Cabbala, with Haddon Derray as company, and a carved wooden staff as his only support.

He had no idea what the price would be. He only knew that there would be a heavy reckoning. The debt was already stacked high.

In crossing the Boundary Matthias had risked so much.

It would not have been possible without the Great Wave, battering with all the force of Astret's tide against the unmoving barrier of static time. That the Wave should move at all indicated the instability of the Stasis. And the Boundary, the limit of the area controlled by the High Priest of the Sun, would have to be shaken by such a manifestation of Astret's power. But that alone would have made no crucial difference, although it did set him wondering. The deciding factor was the secret held in Blaise's diaries.

Matthias suspected that Blaise himself had never recognised the message which emerged from that amazing and unwieldy collection of fact, theories, speculations and lore. He had been distracted by Reckert, Matthias realised now. Reckert had been a source of dissension and division between the Mages, subtly and cleverly diverting their energies with trivia.

But now Reckert was gone, and Matthias was beginning to appreciate the arcane significance of the diaries. A series of small, leather-bound volumes, covered with page after page of Blaise's uneven spidery handwriting. Because he had been blind, the writing was often untidy, almost indecipherable. There were gaps and ink blots. But the message was clear. No one item of information provided it; rather, if it was all taken together, taken as a whole, an answer was revealed.

It was not an easy answer, not comfortable or soothing in any way. Stark and inescapable, it would dominate his life.

That anything is possible, if the right price is paid.

The trick, of course, is estimating the price correctly.

Balance exists everywhere, both in life and out of it. Magic dangerously distorts the balance, which must then be redressed. The Stasis was the supreme example of this. Matthias knew that sooner or later, one day, Lefevre would have to pay. The Mage is always at risk, for the responsibility is his.

And he decided, watching the preparations for Thurstan's last-ditch, desperate plan, that he would welcome such a responsibility.

The edge of the Boundary lay only a few miles from the wrecked island where the Cavers had lived for so long. As they flew high on Asta, with their keen night vision Matthias and Haddon saw far below them the turbulent wash of the tide over untidy piles of rock. White foam crashed around the remnants of their home.

They continued northwards. For a while they flew up and down the edge of the Boundary, examining the blank opaque wall for some weakness, some flaw. Above them it met and mingled with the heavy clouds. The Cavers had attempted to fly over it in the past, but had never succeeded. The air became too thin and their Arrarat refused to continue long before reaching the top. For all they knew, there was no end to it. It seemed to go on forever, reaching far out beyond even the stars. An immovable barrier, dividing more than space.

It stretched down through the darkness into the waves below, deep into the cold ocean. Long ago, they had taken soundings to gauge its depth, but no rope was long enough. As far as they were concerned, the Boundary touched the bottom of the ocean bed and penetrated both sand and rock.

The Cavers had observed the action of the ordinary tide against it. Water was absorbed into it, losing all impetus, stilling until it no longer moved at all. Fish were imprisoned there, unable to swim forwards or back. They saw seabirds fly into it and become caught there between one moment and the next. No one knew whether they lived or died, suspended in unmoving water, hanging there in dim cloud, for nothing ever came back.

But this time Asta had encouraged their attempt. No longer was there the flat refusal of the Arrarat to fly further. They could try, she implied. It was worth trying . . .

The Great Wave must have made some impression on it, Matthias knew. Perhaps enough to make a difference. But how to take advantage of any such weakness, always supposing they could find it, was another matter.

Asta was heavily burdened by the two men. Matthias did not want her to get exhausted before they attempted the crossing, because he knew he would need her strength. He could not afford to spend long, indecisive, on this side. There had been no break in the wall, no weakness that they could see. There was no reason to delay, but he was still unsure what to do.

On what forces could he depend? The skills he had learnt, the knowledge absorbed, the intensifying power of his staff? And Asta herself, the vivid courage of a great hawk . . .

He knew what he had to do. Asta swerved round.

Ahead of them the cloud was dense. Matthias whispered a prayer under his breath, and tightened his grip on the spiral staff. He was holding it steady, forward over Asta's head.

And as they left the cool night air for the cloud of unmoving grey, he began to chant softly words both ancient and new, a potent mix of old lore and present intuition. One part of him was aware that his heart was thudding uncomfortably, that behind him Haddon was almost forgetting to breathe with tension.

He kept the stream of words going, prayers, incantations, formulae, quotations from the Scriptures, from poetry, from Blaise's diaries. Anything to keep the flow of thought going, to keep the mind free from the paralysis of fear. If he could keep his mind open and agile, they would have a chance.

Still they pressed on, and the grip of the Stasis became a physical reality all around them.

The cold fog began to drag at them with a physical force. The Arrarat's wings were starting to move sluggishly in the dense, deadly cloud. With a sudden shock, Matthias felt the bright strength draining away, like a fall from a great height. The wide perspectives were rapidly closing in, the valiant heart slowing. The power of the Boundary was tightening around them.

With terror, he felt his own thoughts becoming embedded in the difficult paths of immobility. The flow of words was ceasing, the pauses between each syllable hanging like dead weights on his mind. Slowly, slowly, his eyes turned to his hands, clenched on the staff.

Quick now, here, now – before it's too late.

Around them the living corpses of small birds were petrified in flight, wings outstretched. Behind him he knew that Haddon was straining to keep breathing, keep moving, keep watching.

The eyes of frozen birds stared at them, intelligence still gleaming there, receptive and aware, but incapable of response. A living hell of stillness, trapped in the instant between one breath and the next.

The quality of the imagination is the key to magic. Even the words were similar. He had researched once whether they were the same words, with the same root. They were not, but the principle held. There can be no magic without imagination.

The effort then, beyond the cloying grey mists, sharp and clear: the visualisation of themselves elsewhere, on the other side. He used every power he had ever acquired, heightened and strengthened by the force he snatched from the sentient life soundlessly wailing around them.

It was a ruthless and deadly process. He saw the last flicker of intelligence held in a gull's eyes flare before its final extinction. He saw anguish and hope die in the pale glare of a gannet, knew that a storm petrel had relinquished its last courage. Magic is indiscriminate. Rapacious and greedy, magic takes whatever it needs, grasping and clutching.

But the imagination is unfettered power.

With such forces then cradled between his eyes and the spiral staff, Matthias imagined the open skies beyond the Boundary, the wide night with the sweeping northern wind, the sea crashing below and other birds, flying free, with wild, unhampered grace.

It was the soaring birds that kept his mind open, the dancing counterpoint to the Stasis. As limbs turned to rock, as his heartbeat failed in the shock of the cold, the idea of flight, the essence of movement, carried him through.

The wind blew in his face. The great wings lifted and fell, and he heard Haddon laugh softly, incredulously, behind him.

They were through, and the mountains lay ahead.

It was exciting at first, thrilling to be the first through the Boundary since the Stasis began. Perhaps things really would change, perhaps there was real hope.

This was the home of their people, these cold northern hills and wide valleys. It had been so long, so lonely. What had happened to them, what had the Stasis meant to them?

Asta flew swiftly, lifting high to clear the vaulting crags and cliffs. The band of twilight gloom bordering the Boundary did not persist for long. Within only a few miles they were soaring through a grey, storm-filled daylight. They saw no one, no human habitation. It was not surprising. People had never colonised this bleak, wind-swept countryside before the Stasis.

They stopped at last, in a valley below the high ridges of the Carald Mountains. A break only for food they had thought, but Asta had immediately lifted away from them, leaping up into the dark, racing stormclouds.

Echoing through his mind, Matthias learnt of her regret, her sorrow at leaving them. He knew better than to question her decision.

They began to walk, along narrow sheep tracks, through boggy valleys, up the sides of steep hills, across ridges, beneath overhangs. The cold wind accompanied them, ever upwards.

'Is it far?' With another man, one could have taken it for weariness, or fear. But Haddon was stronger than most, foolhardy with generous courage.

Something was wrong.

A deep dread made Matthias stumble when they came to the crossroads. It was barely worth the name, the meeting point of two sheep-tracks, almost blotted out by the rough, short-cropped grass.

To the left, always to the left.

Let not your right hand know what the left – no, that was wrong. Let not your left hand know, always the left, the feminine principle of intuition, Moon-given, Moon-guided.

What right had men here? And yet only men had ever come this far, followed this path. He was only one in a long line of suppliants, and the Lady had always honoured this pact.

Come to the Lake of Lallon, said the Cabbala. Come to the Lake of Lallon, state your desire in trust and faith, and the Lady will grant your wish.

The air was cold about them, colder than he had expected even in these latitudes. Breath misted in front of his face. He pulled his thin cloak closer, momentarily regretting the impulse that had led him to leave his warm, Caver-made cloak with Margat. But hers had been lost in one of the attacks on Jeren, and he had not planned to be gone for long.

He wished, like Haddon, that Asta had not put them down so far from the top.

They trudged on, still silent, along the path over one ridge and then another, far out of sight of the valley below. As they went higher the grass became more sparse, and there were long stretches where they had to scramble over sliding shale and scree.

All the time the sense of dread grew. Was this the right thing to do? Last time they had tried to reach the Lady Astret, Lycias had answered their call. Matthias was not sure that he could bear to take that particular chance again, amongst so many other risks. Perhaps they should give it up, go back down the mountain, mount their Arrarat hawk and return empty-handed.

It was the only sensible thing to do.

It was the only thing he would not do.

His legs were on fire with the climbing, the scar on his thigh throbbing and painful. Haddon was in an even worse condition, gasping for breath, labouring, dragging far behind.

Something was wrong.

'Matt . . . I can't go any further.' Haddon stopped, sweat running down his broad face. He tried to take a step towards the Mage but his knees buckled and he fell to the ground.

At once Matthias was at his side, his cloak swirling about them both. 'This is not natural, not right,' he said rapidly, his hand on the other's pulse. It was racing, light and feverish, and his breath was still strained, his eyes clouded in the pallid skin.

'Go on . . .' Haddon managed to gasp. 'Leave me, I shall be all right . . .' Already his breath was coming easier, now he had stopped moving.

Matthias nodded, standing up. He took off his cloak, and put it over the man lying prone on the hard rock, muttering a sleep-spell softly, under his breath.

'I shan't be long,' he said, not knowing if it was true, talking meaninglessly to cover the approaching oblivion. 'Don't worry, I'll be back for you . . .'

He waited until Haddon's eyes closed, and then he turned back to the mountain, beginning to walk again.

A ward spell lay on this place. Human companionship had no place here. He would have to do it alone.

What had happened here? What had the Stasis meant in these lands?

What would be the price this time?

* * *

There was no glimmer of light reflected in the Lake, yet he knew it lived still. The sun had sunk low behind the mountain's edge, sending its dying rays glancing over the valleys below. But there was no light here, in the arena created by the mountain's last eruption, millenia in the past.

In deep shadow, beneath the encircling walls of black rock, the water seemed to swallow up light, bleeding it from the empty sky.

He thought he had never seen anything so evil.

He had not expected evil here, in this, the most ancient of the Lady's sacred shrines. It would go awry, his appeal, here. It would all go wrong, and he had no idea why.

He would have to find out.

Gradually, he began to edge his way down the slope towards the water. It was easier to sit back against the cold rock and slither, braking himself with hands and feet, his staff awkwardly balanced across his knees, than to attempt walking.

He tried not to look at the water, knowing it for an enemy. There would be time enough for that.

It was a long way down, the slope steeper than he had realised, and once he lost balance, rolling part of the way. The staff, wedging in the stones, broke his fall, and then he went more slowly, testing each movement before trusting his weight to it. He was tired now, and knew that he would make mistakes.

At last, he stood on the rim of the Lake, and looked out across it.

A deathly silence hung over it. He had not expected birds overhead, or fish moving in the water. But even the air was still here. No wind, no breath of life. There was no way to tell whether time was moving or not.

His own breath sounded raucous. With an effort he gathered his concentration, holding the staff steady, pointing out over the black water –

'Matthias! Matthias, Matthias . . .'

His name whispered low over the water broke his concentration. Too soon, and wrong, the sound moaned from the depths, stealing health and strength from him.

'Who are you?' he managed to say.

'Do you not know Me?' The whisper was riven with frail anger. 'Am I so forgotten? Astret, Lady of the Moon, is My name, but My power is fading, fading . . . I cannot help you now, Matthias, not here, not now . . .'

'What is happening?' Grief hung in the air over the still water. He shook his head. 'The dark –' he said, trying to remember. He could not afford to be distracted by the sorrow of it. 'We need the dark. Three days of it, just three days, to restore the Balance . . .'

'I cannot help you here, there is wrong here . . .'

The voice was dying, sinking below the level of consciousness.

Wildly, Matthias looked around. What wrong? What had happened here?

Black rock, black water sucking in light, and giving nothing back.

A shadow beneath the water, heavier than the water's black. He lost it again, moved round a little, peering into the depths of Lallon's Lake. Weed caught round something, holding, tugging at it, pulling it back to the silent deep.

'Astret!' he breathed. 'What have You done!'

'It was not I . . .'

He skidded, stumbling along the water's edge to where the weed shadowed beneath the surface. He saw it again, and then hesitated no longer, splashing out into the unimaginable cold.

It seemed to freeze around him, weighing him down, clinging to his limbs, catching at his movements. It made him gasp. It would sap his strength, take all his power. It wanted him, hated him. The sense of wrong, of evil, in the water was overwhelming.

Still the shadow wavered just beyond his reach. He plunged forward, losing his footing, beginning to swim.

The weed twined round his legs. For a moment he let it pull him down, holding his breath, and looked through the dark, opaque water at the shadow trapped there.

A woman. Long hair wreathing between weed and water.

Frantically he kicked himself upwards, fighting against the weight of water in his clothes. It took all his strength to struggle free from the drag of the lake. He surfaced, gasping. He had to get her out, and quickly.

He swam a little further out, trying to get away from the weed, but it seemed to clog the entire lake, and the cold became even more intense away from the shore. His hands were blue: the woman could not possibly be alive. He had to make sure.

He pulled his knife from his belt and, filling his lungs with air, dived. The water clung around him, surrounding him with malice. He had to dive deeply to reach her, fighting against the pull of the lake, diving again and again, slashing with his knife through the slimy clutching weed until she was free, while the cold sank into his bones. Choking, he began to pull her back towards the rock, knowing all the time that it was useless. She had to be dead.

She was not dead.

Gasping, he lay beached on the black rock and looked at her. With his Mage's sight he knew her to live, although she was blue with cold, and her breast appeared unmoving beneath the severe black dress. Water ran from her face and neck, fell from her fingers and hair, rolled from the soft mounds of her body.

She was very young. And there was something else.

Shivering, he pulled himself up, looking out over the water again.

'Three days, Astret,' he said, and his voice this time came stronger. 'Give us three days, and we'll break the Stasis for You.'

Silence. And then a sigh over the water. It was relief. The wrong had been removed.

'Take her from this place. If she lives, the price will be high, too high for you to pay alone. But you shall have your three days' dark.'

Then another sigh. 'Beloved . . .' Dying, across the water.

He was on his knees, soundless tears on his face, for he knew whom She meant.

Such loneliness, such sorrow. What healing could there ever be for a God eternally divided?

There should at least be peace.

He turned back to the girl lying at his side. She was still locked in that death-like sleep. Greatly daring in this place, he closed his eyes, holding the staff as a focus and spun a dream for her, a waking dream. Wrapping her mind in the shape of his imagining, safe, he took her body in his arms and looked up at the black slope.

A path lay before his feet, gently rising in a widening spiral away from the Lake. It had not been there before, hidden by the malevolence of the place. Now the path was waiting for him to take her away, waiting for him to take her from the Lady's sacred Lake.

It was completely dark by the time he reached the top, bone-weary and aching. His clothes hung dripping and clammy in the chill wind. Looking back, the Lake was lost in night. Forward, the hills fell away, silent and empty.

Only when he had begun the descent into the valley did the Moon shine down on him, illuminating his path. Only then was Her face reflected in the still waters of Lallon.

'For Lady's sake, Matt, what happened to you? Who is this?' Haddon had recovered, was running towards them as soon as he heard Matthias's step. His arms were outstretched to take the burden, but then he stopped, staring down at the young unconscious face.

'Who . . . who is this?' he repeated, his voice unsteady.

Matthias looked at him, shocked by something in his voice. He said nothing, but began to understand how the price would be paid. By others. By Haddon.

Chapter Two
Coronis

She awoke as the morning sun touched the dew. There was no movement, just the knowledge that he was observed. Haddon slowly turned away from the fire he was building, gently, so that she should not be startled. His hands fumbled with the wood.

Black eyes regarded him, unblinking, strong. She was beautiful in ways he had not expected, glorious in youth and wild power, and yet not arrogant, not brash at all.

He smiled. 'Hello,' he said. 'My name's Haddon.' He kept it simple, wondering if she would understand. 'My companion and friend is Matthias, one of the Three. He brought you out of the Lake . . . He's gone to get us some breakfast.'

Still she said nothing, so he went on trying to create an atmosphere of friendliness around her. He could not bear her to become frightened.

'I hope you're not cold. We only had one cloak between us, and that not Caver-made. We have a long way to go today, and would be glad of your company . . .' He stopped.

'My name is Coronis,' she said, after a pause. Her voice was low, quiet with the healing of water. He was absurdly glad that she understood, spoke the same language, spoke in a calm voice, warm as honey.

Further and further he fell.

'What happened, Coronis? What happened at the Lake?'

Just naming her gave him a thrill of joy. The sound of her name, the word encompassing the reality. She was really *there*, living, breathing, speaking to him and he knew that nothing would ever be the same again.

Black hair, black eyes, born of black water and rock.

Shot through with brilliance she was, black gleaming into silver, gold, peacock blue and turquoise. He could have cried, looking at her, for the perfection of it.

'I cannot stay here . . .' she said. In one smooth movement she was on her feet, black robe fluttering in the morning breeze.

At once he was beside her.

'Why?' he said. 'What is it? What are you frightened of?'

'My father,' she said, and whatever he had expected it was not that.

'*Why*?' It exploded on the calm mountainside.

'She is at risk,' said Matthias, returning. He was carrying three small trout, a fishing rod instead of the staff. He watched them both with doubt and spoke warily. Haddon must be told and quickly. 'She is with child,' he said. This was the other thing.

Haddon stared at her. It was not at all noticeable. She tossed her head and met his gaze.

'Yes,' she said. 'He is right.' The look she gave Matthias was hardly one of gratitude. 'I should not stay here. They will be coming to see that the sacrifice has been accepted.'

'You were – a sacrifice?' Haddon's eyes were dark with anger. Such things had been unknown before the Stasis.

'To appease the Lady. For the ill in our land.'

Matthias said nothing, cleaning the fish, setting a pan over the fire. The clouds were beginning to gather, a heavy sullen look in the sky. There was a storm coming.

They would have to take her. There had been no choice, really, since he had pulled her from the water, since Haddon had seen her. But this was getting worse all the time. A sacrifice to Astret, pregnant as well.

'What is wrong here, "the ill in your land"?'

Later, trudging down the mountain, Haddon had looked round at the quiet slopes, shadowed now by grey clouds. It seemed peaceful, and fertile. There were no trees, but it was high for them. Streams ran between bright grass, bubbling over dark stones.

The Arrarat still had not returned. And there were no other birds.

She had looked beyond the line of hills, up into the sky. 'Storm,' she said briefly. 'Storm and wind. Every day it comes. The sacrifice was not made, not accepted.' Her voice was empty of expression. 'There will be storm and wind today. You will see.'

They were walking down into the valley furthest away from Coronis's home. Matthias had said that the direction did not matter, that the Arrarat would come only when they were far away from the Lake of Lallon.

A shout far away over the hills. They swung round, and the girl gasped. A line of horsemen stood along a distant ridge, and as they watched began to thunder down the slopes towards them.

'My father!' she said. 'I think he will kill me for this.'

Haddon had drawn his sword, grim-faced.

'There are too many to fight,' said Matthias. 'We'll have to hide.'

'They've seen us! And where could we hide here?'

No caves, no trees, no shelter. Just bare, hilly countryside, the wind rippling across the grass, rain spitting around them.

They started to run, dodging away from the sheep-track round the edge of the hillside. Again, no shelter, just a cold wind-swept valley, open to all the elements. The girl was hampered by her skirts. She paused, looping them up into the waistband, looking not back towards their pursuers but up into the darkening sky.

Matthias noticed it.

He felt it too, the violence in the air. The wind scything through the valley held malevolence in its grip, ill-will in its icy breath.

'The storm!' he said, clutching her shoulder. 'What is it? What brings it?'

She stared at him, and at the back of those cool eyes he saw terror. 'The Stasis brings it, of course! The Stasis, for ever and always, the Stasis!'

And then lightning split the sky, thunder crashing overhead, and she nearly fell to the ground with the force of it. Haddon whirled her up into his arms, and ran diagonally across the valley floor, towards a break in the long line of hills.

Rain was now sheeting down, almost horizontal in the

power of the wind, and the air darkened. Matthias hurtled after them, black cloak streaming behind, at one with the torn rags of cloud blowing all around.

He knew this wind. It was the other side of the wind which brought Astret's wave to the Caves. This was Lycias's tempest, sent to harry the northern people who had been so loyal to the Moon. It was vindictive, crushing and punishing the countryside, a storm of brute, relentless force.

The tempest was dangerous enough in itself, a vortex of violence, but the worrying thing was that he could no longer tell where the riders had gone. Lycias was confusing his perceptions, distorting his awareness of danger.

Haddon cast him a glance of enquiry as he caught up, expecting him to know which way to go, but he could only shake his head.

The ground was sodden underfoot, the rain running over the grass in spiteful streams. Again the sky was shot through with flame and in the flash he saw Haddon's face, pale and stern, masked by glistening water. Raven hair fell over the girl's face. He was glad not to see those black eyes, complicating the storm.

Thunder, overhead, shaking the ground under their feet. Dark shadows suddenly in front of them, to the side, ringing them. Horses stamping, steaming in the rain, the jangle of the bits, the smell of leather. The black-cloaked riders, long spears held steady at their throats, surrounded them.

In one smooth movement Haddon had put the girl down and was sheltering her with one arm, his sword firm in the other hand. Matthias beside him, pushing the sword down.

'Not now, you fool!' he hissed.

'Who are you, stealing the Lady's sacrifice?'

The voice was deep, rough with anger, from a heavy figure mounted on a large bay. His face was in shadow, but the spear he held was pointed straight at them.

'It was a wrong sacrifice. The Lady needs no such rites.' Matthias spoke quietly and yet his voice carried clearly over the thunder that rumbled in the air.

'What do you know of it, stranger?' The word held loathing and mistrust. The other riders were edging forward, their horses stamping, shying in protest.

'Father!' The girl broke away and was standing crying words up at the man who had first spoken. 'He speaks the truth! The sacrifice was not accepted. The Lady would not take – me. The Lake would not take my life.'

Again the lightning blazed and Matthias felt himself shudder with the malevolence of it. 'We cannot stay here!' he yelled over the rising thunder. 'We must find shelter!'

For a moment the girl's father appeared to hesitate, and then the strong hands reached down with unbelieving gentleness and pulled her up to sit across the horse's shoulders, cradled in his arms.

A nod from him, and two other riders came forward, dismounting, allowing Haddon and Matthias to swing up first.

The wind howled with fury as they rode through the storm, sending rain hurling at them, bitter as gall. The horses galloped swiftly, sure-footed over the uneven, boggy ground. There was a long way to go.

Down rocky tracks, through steep gorges and into the lower valleys the riders fled, running before the storm, buffeted and bruised by its force.

It increased in virulence as they fled further from Lallon's Lake. The lightning seared through the air, aiming straight at them, and Coronis's father led them through strangely convoluted routes, doubling back, dodging and weaving from side to side.

Thick cloud masked the hills from their sight. They were running through a wilderness of wind and rain, fractured and tormented by the anger of the wild storm, and neither Haddon nor Matthias had any idea which direction they were following.

Just ahead of Matthias a rider was suddenly struck by the deliberate lightning, seared and burnt to death while thunder roared all around them. Charred rags and bones fell smoking to the ground and Matthias's horse reared up, terrified, nostrils dilating, eyes rolling.

They dared not stop to gather up the body. There was little enough left of it anyway. The panicked horse tore away into a shadowy forest, and for a moment the girl's father slowed down, leaning over his horse's neck, shouting through the storm to his companions.

'It's more direct, through the Forest . . .'

'Madness with this lightning, Ingram! The trees will catch it!' A thin-faced man, gaunt with fear, started off in the opposite direction. The girl's father caught his bridle in a movement too quick to measure, desperation in his eyes.

'Is it far, through the Forest?' Matthias asked the rider behind him.

'Two miles – maybe three . . .' A gruff voice, sour and unwilling.

Matthias turned to Ingram, cupping his hands to amplify his voice.

'I can protect us, if it's no more than three miles.'

'How?' Derision and disbelief in the one scornful syllable.

'Like this . . .' Matthias drew out his staff from beneath his cloak, and grasping it at one end, held it out to the storm, murmuring the words of summoning. He was not afraid to distort the balance now. There was so much already on his account.

With fury the storm hurled itself at the carved spiral, and became entrapped within it, the lightning caught in its whorl, blazing round and round, streaming into infinity.

'Now!' shouted Haddon, impelled by the look on Matthias's face. 'Through the Forest, while we've got the chance!'

Astounded, the riders whirled around and dashed towards the trees, the staff held high in Matthias's hand, high above their heads, right into the centre of the tempest.

He bought them time, and safety for the span of the Forest. Crashing through the undergrowth, pounding down the muddy paths, ducking under branches, Haddon watched his friend's face, waiting for the moment when he knew Matthias would collapse with the strain of it. The Mage's jaw was set hard, rigid with control, and the knuckles of his hand shone white in the dark dripping shadows. Haddon only saw his eyes once, and then looked no more, appalled by the raging fire of lightning contained there.

The Forest was devastated around them, trees falling

crashing into each other, fires flaring and smoking, the ground shaking. But none of it touched them, for Matthias held the storm steady over their heads, imprisoned, powerless in the spiral, and they were safe, galloping down the muddy paths.

As they burst through the trees onto the open plain, Matthias fell across the horse's neck, the staff caught in the folds of his cloak.

No one stopped. As the rain began to drench them once more, the thunder to echo overhead, they spurred their horses on, wildly racing across empty, broken plains.

At last, in safety, they reached the fortress.

Chapter Three
Ingram Lapith

The fortress-city of Bilith rose solid and strong from the wasteland of flattened grasses, heavy grey stone blocks of immense size reaching high up into the drenched air. The gates, swinging open as the riders approached, were of whole tree trunks, threaded through with steel. The walls were yards thick.

Within the walls a maze of narrow streets and tumbled houses was silent under the steady wash of rain, the shutters drawn and doors bolted. A small dog whined in an alleyway, scratching at a door, its coat dark and clinging with wet. All the time the rain poured down, turning the streets and paths into streams, the gutters into overflowing torrents.

Matthias was still unconscious, slumped against his horse's neck. He was taken with Haddon to Ingram Lapith's own home, a large stone-built house set deep into the fortress walls. Other buildings grew all around it, sprouting from its side, tumbling in irregular blocks, rooms over yards, sheds and stables jutting out into the street, doors on different levels, windows set narrow and dark between massive blocks. Heavy stone arches connected doors across cramped passages. It was impossible to see where one house ended and another began in the jumble of ponderous architecture.

Men ran out to take their horses, leading them away to the stables at the side of the house. Matthias was carefully carried upstairs and put to bed. A physician was called. In the anxiety over his friend's condition, Haddon did not see Coronis run through a doorway at the back of the house as soon as they arrived.

It was only later, when he learnt that Matthias was

suffering simply from exhaustion, that Haddon began to wonder where she was.

As it grew dark, the storm died away. It was always so, explained Lapith, briefly looking up from his wine. They were seated at a long oak table in the hall. Rushes covered the stone floor, and a roaring fire burned in the wrought iron grate. Weapons hung on the walls; axes, spears, knives and swords. Between them were bright tapestries, hunting scenes set in flowery woodland, eagles flying over mountain passes, square-rigged ships tossed on sapphire waves.

The wine was good, rich and spicy. Haddon leant back in the comfortable wooden chair, watching his host. Ingram Lapith was heavily built, wide shoulders rippling under the loose russet brocade robe. Grizzled hair was cut close to his head, and his eyes were black and unsmiling like those of his daughter.

'The storm comes each day,' Lapith said, frowning, 'between the hours of sunrise and sunset. Since the Boundary was set up it has always been so. The Storm hides the Sun from our lives and there is no peace anywhere. As it rages, so does the violence of our people . . . there is a lull in the War at the moment – a man called Javon is imposing some order. But things have not been easy, and the Storm augments every hardship.

'It was different today. I've never seen lightning or heard thunder like that before. A man was killed!' He stared blankly into the pewter goblet. It was plainly a refuge for him. Again he looked up at Haddon. 'You should not have taken Coronis from the Lake.' The words were wrenched from him. 'A sacrifice was necessary. The storm today was Astret's revenge, for a spoiled offering.'

'You're wrong.' A quiet voice from the stairs. Matthias stood there, leaning on the staff, his eyes intent on the older man. 'The Lady would not stoop to such pettiness.' He came forward and joined them at the table, sitting opposite Haddon.

'Pettiness?' Lapith scraped his chair back on the stone. 'That power was not petty!'

'No. But neither did it originate from the Lady. It was

Lycias's storm.' He held Lapith's gaze steady. 'Have any of you offended the Sun God? What has happened here?'

There was an uncomfortable silence. Matthias still looked only at Lapith, although he could feel Haddon's eyes on him.

'Nothing. Nothing that can be explained or excused. It is nothing to do with you.' Lapith's voice was expressionless, but then his hand clenched on the table. Matthias remained silent, waiting. This was complicated beyond imagining.

'Why should I tell you? You come here, from Lady knows where, waving one of those bloody staffs in the air, and expect us to lay ourselves bare before you! One display of power and you think we owe you everything!' Lapith's voice was raw with fear.

'You owe us nothing.' Matthias was still calm. 'I expect nothing. You need not say anything. But that storm was from Lycias, and this land is dedicated to Astret. Something has happened here.' He paused, watching the big man clenching and unclenching his hands on the oak table. 'You know what it is, don't you?'

A long silence this time, broken only by the crackle of burning logs in the grate.

'Coronis.' Lapith spoke so quietly that they could barely hear the words. 'With child. My own daughter, vowed to the Lady from birth, pregnant! Today's storm had to come from Astret!'

Matthias sighed. He knew better.

'The father?' His voice was also quiet.

Lapith shook his head. 'No one knows. She won't say.'

'What will happen to her now? Now that the sacrifice has been refused?' Haddon tried to keep his voice neutral.

'I don't know. It will be up to the Elders. She cannot remain in the temple, unchaste.' He crashed his fist to the table, glaring at Haddon. 'Don't look at me like that! Do you think I didn't try? Do you think I was glad for my only daughter to die? I would have taken the child in, cared for them both. They could have lived here, but the offence to the Lady could not be overlooked!'

'Have your Elders so forgotten our Lady's chief concern?'

Matthias's gentle voice held all attention, quelled all anger. 'Mistress of the Moon, Guardian of ebb and flow, life and death, new life is sacred to Astret. That is why the Stasis is so abhorrent to Her. A distortion of the seasons, of time itself, of life and death. The Lady would not require the death of a pregnant woman.'

'The Stasis has not meant that here. Distortion, certainly, of the order of society, of the weather. But we live and die as ever . . . What could I do?' The cry rang out, reverberating in the stone hallway. 'What other choice had we, when the storms raged every day, with ever greater violence, with no relief or rest? Our seers said that it was because of Coronis. I had no choice!'

Anguish creased his face, and he stood up, turning from them, the chair falling against the stone with a crash. He gazed down into the fire, his back to them, his voice curiously muffled.

'There is nowhere for her to go, with that child. She can't stay here. I am Archon, here. Upholder of Law.' His voice sneered. 'My role would be impossible, tainted by this disgrace.'

'If Coronis were married, would there still be disgrace?' Haddon was looking down into his wine, his face unreadable.

'It might be – forgotten. But who would take her now? She will not name the father, and as he has not had the courage to come forward, he would not be a fitting husband. What kind of man would desert her in this way!'

'Not I.' Haddon's words were almost inaudible. 'I will marry your daughter, Lapith, if she'll have me.'

'You? You don't even know her!'

'I will never love another.'

A log fell in the grate, the sparks flying, as Lapith turned to look at Haddon.

The younger man raised his head, meeting his gaze. Matthias thought he had never seen the square chin set with such determination, the grey eyes so steady. He dared not speak.

'I will stay here, and work for you. I will earn enough to support her and the child. I am not without skills . . .' He stopped. 'Lapith, I would marry your daughter, and live with her, here if you'll allow it, or elsewhere. I will never leave her.'

Something like a sob seemed to shake the older man, and once more he turned back to the fire.

'Do you know what you're doing? You'll bring up another man's child as your own? When you've hardly had any time to know my daughter?'

'I will love the child as my own. I will love Coronis to the end of my life. This I promise.'

There could be no doubting it.

Matthias closed his eyes in a kind of agony. A heavy reckoning indeed. Surely this will be enough.

'I will only marry you if you promise me one thing.'

Haddon had found her at last on a high tower, staring over the battlements to the west, over the dark distant hills where the sun had set. She was still dressed in black and her pale skin gleamed in the moonlight.

He longed to catch her in his arms, to hold her warm against his heart, to smooth the wild black hair with his hands.

'Anything. Anything, for as long as the world lasts.'

The reckless passion of his words brought her head up, looking at him at last.

'You don't know what you're doing,' she said coolly, echoing her father's words. 'Haddon. Promise me . . . don't ever ask who the father is. Don't ask me that. I would have to die . . .'

'Don't talk of death!' He could hold back no longer, incredulous joy in his heart. 'I swear it. I will never ask.' A pause, and he felt some of the tension leave her.

'Oh, Coronis . . .'

He took her in his arms, his mouth seeking hers, just as a man lost in the desert might lose himself again in the healing springs of water.

She was trembling against him, startled by this urgency. His hands were caught in her hair, twining it round and round, so that she could not draw back even if she wanted. She had no such intention.

It was a haven of strength, a place of sanctuary from the nightmare of her life.

And his lips were like fire, his hands the pulse of life. The ice in her heart, the ice that had seized her when her lover left, began to melt.

There would be no going back.

Matthias stayed for the ceremony, which took place privately the next day. Coronis was silent, eyes downcast, but her hand reached for Haddon's with something like desperation as the words were chanted.

They had decided to stay with Ingram Lapith, sharing his great house. Haddon would join the hunting riders of Bilith, would make his life with the storm-tossed people of the plains.

Matthias's Arrarat hawk, Asta, circled the violent air above the stone fortress, waiting for the Mage, and lightning darted all around her.

Matthias left in a rumble of thunder. He had The Lady's promise of three days' dark. He did not look back to Haddon, standing below with Coronis.

As he flew over the windy plains towards the mountains, to the Boundary he knew he could pass, to Thurstan and Stefan setting out to break the Stasis, he wondered what had happened.

Below him he could see the crater of Lallon's Lake, calmly reflecting the grey skies.

Why had it been so evil that night? Why the black stare in Coronis's eyes?

What doom was held in those eyes?

What price would have to be paid?

Chapter Four
Travelling

As Eleanor, Blythe and Lukas journeyed southwards the sky lightened until, with incredulous relief, they were travelling in full sunlight. Eleanor's faint luminosity had decreased as the brightness grew and although the beacon in her mind still echoed and enchanted just beyond vision, she was aware that the Moon's powers were negligible here. She could not trust flooding light to rescue her in this sunny land. She hoped she would not need it.

The Arrarat carried them over a maritime world, sandy islands set in deep blue sea, forested archipelagos, fertile lagoons. They began to meet signs of human habitation, the odd fishing boat, a peasant village in a quiet bay, wood smoke rising above a clearing. These they avoided as potential dangers. Eleanor was delighted by it, by the tranquil countryside, the trust and ease of their companionship, the gradual progress southwards.

Blythe too, was in some degree relaxing. They were passing through the coastal regions of Challet. It was a land he knew, a climate he enjoyed. As they travelled, the villages became larger, often surrounding castles or great houses. In answer to Eleanor's questions, he kept up a running commentary, raising his voice over the wind as they flew, his arms steady around her waist.

'That's the Isle of Klau to your right, a principality of little economic power, basically given over to elaborate ceremony. Prince Oliphant Lacroix runs it, with varying degrees of success, or so I've been told. The marching bands are good, but there's little else to recommend it.

'On the mainland over there – Oliphant's brother Bartholomew lives in the Castle Masquier. You can see it, over that ridge –' and indeed gleaming, crenellated towers dominated the horizon. 'Don't be fooled by the armed guard' – helmets glinted in the sun between the battlements – 'Bartholomew is easy-going, not at all aggressive. He'd rather hold a party than a tournament any day. Who wouldn't? I used to like him –'

Later that day in a sheltered forest glade, over a supper of grilled fish and soup, Eleanor questioned him further. He knew the area well, had relatives and friends throughout.

'You've been here before then?' Lukas, stirring the soup, was curious.

'Oh yes – all Peraldonians of the ruling caste are sent on a tour of the Imperial domain.' His voice was ironic. 'It inspires a due sense of awe and responsibility. No one could deny the power of such an empire.'

'No one's denying it – we just want to end it.' Lukas was looking abstracted, and Eleanor wondered if he was thinking of the Cavers. He never talked about them, since his brief account of Caspar's news, hurriedly snatched during that last night on Jeren. The earthquake, the final Saying, and the appearance of Lycias. Nerissa, terribly mutilated. And the Fosca, continually attacking. It had been a catalogue of horrors.

As with Blythe, the past was a forbidden subject. There were so many no-go areas with them both.

Not that she wanted to talk about her own past, either. It could not be more irrelevant to what was happening to her now.

As a diversion, she asked a question that had been gradually forming during the journey.

'I don't understand – how the Stasis works. Why is it that time almost does not pass at all for Cavers, and yet the further south and east one goes, the sun both rises and sets and there is day and night? It's not at all consistent, is it?'

'No, of course not.' Blythe sounded faintly surprised that she did not understand. 'It is complicated – my uncle, Hamnet Lin, once tried to explain it to me. It works like this because of the Boundary. Within the Boundary, time does not move at all. And the closer one gets to it, the more static is the weather and the way things grow and change.'

'The Boundary divides so much,' said Lukas. 'We tried very hard to get through, during the Banishment War. Blaise was particularly interested in that . . . At one stage, we thought he might do it, but something held him back. And no one else was powerful enough to attempt it. What happens on the other side of the Boundary is impossible to imagine. The lands dedicated to Astret may be quite outside the ordinary terms of the Stasis. They may not even share the immortality . . .'

'If not that, there will have been some other distortion or lack of balance . . . We may never know.' Blythe frowned. 'But the Stasis, as you see, is patchy and differentiated, and that's why here it needs a man of Lefevre's genius to sustain it. The only consistent thing about it is that we are all immortal, barring accidents.'

Immortal, barring accidents. Next morning, while Blythe was checking the traps, Eleanor went for a walk through the forest. Quiet and shady, it seemed friendly, almost familiar. Pink campion and bluebells underfoot, the fresh green of new leaves overhead. Spring, familiar and delightful. The pace of the seasons was regular and varied, a fine shaping to life, a rhythm, a dance.

But not for humanity. No spring in the lives of men and women under the Stasis. She sat on a fallen tree trunk and wondered if she, too, would now live forever. No ageing, no death. No crows' feet round her eyes, no thin grey hair or the ache of arthritis in her hands when it was damp. Was it such a bad thing? She looked at her hands, turning them over. When would she begin to realise that they were unchanged?

'What, no wrinkles yet?'

Lukas had an odd ability to read her thoughts. 'I'm twenty-two,' she said, and then a shadow crossed her face. 'At least, I used to be, before I came here.'

'It has very little meaning now, doesn't it?' He sat down beside her.

'Will I be – immortal – now, like you?'

'I suppose so. I can't think of any reason why not.' He brushed the hair from her face and carefully scrutinised her.

'No, no visible signs of ageing yet. How do your teeth feel? Any aches or pains?'

'It's not funny!' She paused. 'Lukas, do you think I'll ever get back?' Her voice sounded small.

His eyes were serious. 'I don't know, Eleanor. If we break the Stasis, anything might happen. Matthias – if he's still alive – would be the one to ask –'

'No one knows anything, do they?' she sounded bitter. 'It's all one mystery after another.' He put his arm round her, giving her a quick hug, as one might a child. For a moment she leant against him, relaxing.

But then she remembered, and sat up. 'What's going to happen when we get to wherever we're going, anyway? I don't know what I'm here for, what I'll have to do even assuming that we can find the Benu Bird. What is it, anyway?'

He stood up, moving away from her, his face carefully neutral.

'Matthias once told me that it was the First Principle, the breath of life which started it all, created the universe for Lycias and Astret to exist in. For us, too.' He was watching a kestrel hovering in the air high above the clearing. The blue eyes reflected the sky. It was as if he were part of the sky, for a moment as if its substance was shining through his eyes. Clear, open, promising an infinity of warmth . . .

He turned to look back at her and smiled, and suddenly she could not meet those azure, sky-ridden eyes.

'Knowledge for mystics, perhaps. Astret did not encourage speculation amongst her followers.' He waved to Blythe, crossing the clearing towards them. 'The Mages were always on dodgy ground with the Priestesses. Phin might know more . . .'

Later she asked Blythe the same questions. They had spent the day flying through the passes of an increasingly mountainous region. Sharp peaks jutted up into the sky around them. Some were even snow-capped, although at the level they were flying the air was warm.

They made camp in a deserted, rocky valley. The upper end of the valley was forested, and the river that ran through it was a boisterous cascade of flecked white and brown.

Lukas had been fishing in the river and there was fresh trout for supper. They had pitched camp on a ledge high above the river, a place both sheltered and difficult to see from the valley. Blythe was leaning back against a rock, idly flicking stones into the river below them. She thought how well this outdoor, energetic life suited him. Dark eyes gleaming in bronzed skin. But he was still distant, and rarely smiled.

Like Lukas, he had no real answer to her questions. 'But I do have a suggestion,' he said, looking up as Lukas joined them. 'How about making a slight diversion? Let's go and visit my uncle Hamnet. He lives not far from here.'

'I thought we had a task to accomplish,' said Lukas firmly. 'Something to do with following a light. Remember? We don't have the time for family calls.'

'Hamnet Lin lives in some state,' said Blythe, watching Eleanor. 'A well-appointed castle. The best food and wine – hot baths – clean clothes –'

'What is this?' Lukas was cold. 'How could you even consider it? What do you think we're doing here?'

'As you like,' said Blythe indifferently. 'But perhaps you should think it over. Lin, besides living in comfort, is a learned man, has made a study of geography and astronomy, and, so the story goes within the family, actually helped Lefevre set up the Stasis. If we approach him right, he might be extremely useful –'

'Lefevre's right-hand man? Help us? Phin, your wits are wandering!'

'I think you're right,' said Eleanor, looking at her dry, cracked hands, dreaming of smooth sheets and hot baths. 'We do need to find out more before we actually get there –'

'Where's all this urgency then?' Lukas was frowning at her. 'What about the instructions from Astret? Let's not delay. Phin'll be arrested as a traitor, you'll be an exhibit in a side show. At best it's all a waste of time . . .' He paused, and then looked at her in a way that seemed to cut the ground away beneath her feet. 'It's been fun, hasn't it, a glorified camping holiday, and no responsibilities? But Nerissa is probably dead, and so many others. My friends and family are dying. This is not a game. Have you forgotten?'

'No one's forgetting anything,' said Blythe calmly. 'But there's no point in blindly rushing into a situation about which we know nothing. We have a potentially friendly contact here – let's use him.'

'And after all,' said Eleanor, warming to her theme. 'Why was Blythe chosen by the Moon, given a light to follow? This uncle of his could be the reason why he's important.'

No, thought Blythe. My importance, if such it is, is quite different. I have to kill the Benu bird, this Bird of Time we're all trying so hard to find. And Eleanor knows nothing about that at all.

Aloud, he continued reasonably, 'I do think we need preparation, and also that Lin could, just possibly, be a powerful ally. But, more immediately, more practically, we need help to get beyond this point.'

'What do you mean?' Lukas was still angry. 'Further procrastination?'

'Not at all. Just south of here is an area we never visited on the tour. The countryside is hazardous, unstable, volcanic. And there are bands of outlaws –'

'I'd like to meet them,' said Lukas, 'being no great admirer of Lefevre's law myself. Shall we sing revolutionary songs, or will riding Arrarat be enough in the way of credentials?'

'These are not rebels, in the sense that the Cavers and Jerenites are. They have no legitimate grievance beyond the very fact of their creation. Do you really know nothing of Mavrud?'

'Come on, Phin, let's have it. What's so special about Mavrud?' Lukas leant back against rock, hands in pockets, waiting.

'There is a university here, a scientific establishment. My uncle's Observatory forms a part of it. But its main function, Lefevre's particular pride and delight, is the study and manipulation of form. He is obsessive, does not even trouble to disguise it.

'He is trying to recreate the race of which Lycias is the flower. Gods and goddesses who will be subservient to *him*. The ultimate in megalomania.' He looked at Lukas, a faint, ironic smile. 'He does not succeed,' he continued dryly.

'And the results of his failed experiments now roam the hinterland around Cliokest. I've never encountered any of them, but the natives hold these "Parid" as they're known, in considerable awe, not to say terror.'

'Why weren't they destroyed?' asked Eleanor.

'They are useful to Lefevre. He has many tools.' He threw a stone into the torrent below with sudden force, his expression severe. 'He created the scurries, too. You know that. I've heard that the Parid are a little on the same lines, able to hypnotise and confuse the senses. They have really very little to recommend them, like the Fosca.'

'Failed gods, did you say?' Lukas was fascinated. For a moment he forgot his impatience. 'With god-like powers?'

'You could put it like that . . .'

'Does it matter?' Eleanor's voice was both plaintive and bad tempered. Seduced by visions of warm beds and clean clothes, she was unwilling to waste time discussing mutant gods. Blythe ignored her.

'Of course, how you define "god" is crucial,' he continued. 'A being of supernatural and eternal powers is one attempt –'

'But it's not good enough, is it? If it can be defined it's not a god anyway. I would not like to attempt a definition of Lycias or Astret.' Lukas was thoughtful.

'Yes. And so Lefevre's attempts in this area will always fail.'

'It's a kind of sacrilege, wouldn't you say? The evil ambition of an evil man –'

'But it's not quite that simple. In a way, in the absence of an effective, active Emperor, Lefevre is regarded almost as a god himself in Peraldon. Immortal, all powerful, he provides the power for our cities, the beasts to transport us, the mercenaries to fight for us. He structures the worship of the Sun God, even understands the mysteries of Lycias's demand. He knows *why* the Stasis exists. After all, he did arrange it himself.' He was silent for a moment. 'That's why I'm going to kill him.'

'With your little bow and arrow?' The long mouth smiled in gentle mockery. 'If Lefevre's so clever, why does he allow the Parid to terrify his loyal subjects?'

Blythe shrugged. 'There are many theories. Some – subversives – say that they are necessary to ensure that loyalty. You Cavers are not alone in distrusting Lefevre. He uses the Parid to keep the good citizens of Mavrud nicely penned in.'

'He does not.'

A new voice, a sourness in the air.

Parid?

Chapter Five
Sharrak

As one, they spun round to find the source of that clear, light voice. A little way along the rocky ledge from them a shadow moved. As it flickered, the sunlight glanced over it and then became still, entrapped, held steady. For the briefest instant they all saw something shift and blend within a golden framework of light. Something shivered there between shapes. Then the mix of light and shadow became more opaque, taking on solidity, and the facsimile of a woman stood before them.

Her eyes were huge, sea-green and wide spaced, her face heart-shaped. Pale hair, longer than she was tall, flowed out into the still air, glinting in the sunlight. As it drifted round her, the edges of her face and figure became blurred, as if her essence were being teased out into the air.

Her hands were clasped together at her breast, her slim body clothed in wisps of summer light. Her skin was flushed with liquid gold, shifting and creeping as the sun touched it. She laughed.

It was an intolerable sound, sliding over the edge of sanity.

Lukas had not stirred, watching every movement, leaning still against the rock. His eyes scanned every line of the shifting shape, trying to discover how it existed. Blythe had moved back, a knife in his hand, blending subtly into the rocky shadows behind them.

Thoughtfully, the green eyes regarded them. The figure stood quite still, like a statue or waxwork, but all the time light was deflected over it, blurring outlines, destroying stability. Then it spoke again.

'It really is not a good idea to leave Lefevre's straight and narrow paths.' Its voice was soft, gentle, almost, but there were resonances, strange resonances Eleanor did not want to think too much about. The voice continued.

'You would be well advised to seek out civilisation in Mavrud. Men there would help you; Hamnet Lin, Despard Cles, Elfitt de Mowbray. You would find there comfort, good advice, clear maps. There is no need for you to trespass further through my territory.'

'Lurking behind a tree, were you, ears pinned back?' Blythe was sharp, unimpressed. It moved towards him, suddenly, almost too quick to watch, trailing rags of golden light.

'You have not been alone on your journey, you know.' One soft, white hand reached out to caress the curling dark hair on his forehead.

He jerked his head away. It had left a stain of gold over his brow. He rubbed it off, and grey dust fell from his fingers. It laughed again, small pointed teeth discolouring the sunlight.

'How do you think the birds flew to meet your arrows?' it went on, the curious voice fluent and easy. 'Why else did rabbits spring into your traps, if it were not my doing?'

'Rubbish. No help was needed, and we certainly received none.' He was ungracious.

Lukas was watching, amusement alight in the cerulean eyes. 'Do introduce yourself,' he invited cordially. 'A lady of the Parid, no doubt?'

'What else would it be?' said Blythe flatly. The denial of the creature's gender altered the character of its warmth; a surge of energy, dangerous as electricity, crackled in the air.

But still it smiled, pretty lips stretched wide. 'Yes, I have been called Parid, and it is true that Lefevre created us . . .'

'Go away! Get out, go away!' Eleanor's cry of revulsion was released by the charge in the air. She clenched her hands at her side, her loathing like a physical presence.

An unbidden memory had assaulted her, overwhelming the facile prettiness of the creature before them. She saw that soft golden glow as a parody of another pure, merciless light, remembered a different, cool voice saying, 'You are here for a reason –'

She would have shouted again, struck out even, but the

creature's hand extended and a drift of shadow fell from it, skimming through the air until it wrapped itself round her. Eleanor became dumb, trapped in a web of light, bereft of speech and movement. The heart-shaped head turned on narrow shoulders to watch Blythe, inching along the rocky ledge away from it.

It was laughing again, a clear, sharp sound, like a nail scraping over glass, and the sound swam towards him, imprisoning his limbs. He could not move, or even speak to warn Lukas, and it had shifted again with bizarre swiftness, darting along the rocky ledge towards him.

Lukas had not moved. He was still watching, wary, but oblivious to the signals Blythe was trying to send him through the paralysing web of sound.

Slowly the Parid brought its small, grinning head round to stare at Lukas. It was standing completely still only feet from him. For a moment there was a deadly silence enfolding them all, a silence of appalling potential.

And then he laughed at it, throwing back his head, and the quality of his mockery broke the concentration. Suddenly Blythe found he could move again. But before he could take advantage of the Parid's loss of control, it had shifted once more, sharply, too fast for eyes to follow, and there it was, only inches from Lukas.

Its elbows were folded in against its breast, hands up by its face in an attitude of prayer. It reminded Eleanor suddenly of some avid carnivorous insect. Lukas stood motionless, cool, sneering at that disturbing, innocent-seeming face with its wide eyes and curving mouth.

All at once there was a hiss, and an arrow flew out from the rock, from Blythe's bow, straight into the golden creature's heart. For one nightmare moment, the shifting strands of light around it were wrenched away and what was left was a sliding horror, carapace and claw, wing and jaw, small evil head grinning foolishly at them.

Almost immediately it reappeared, gathering the horror in, obliterating it under the wash of golden light. During that appalling hiatus Eleanor found her limbs released; without thinking she turned and ran headlong along the ledge away from the nightmare.

The sound of high laughter followed her; the ledge rounded a corner and then dropped into nothingness. There was only the cliff, stretching down to the violent river beneath, sheer up to the crags above.

'Ash!' she cried, heart thudding. 'Ash! Come to me!' She tried the curious, warbling Caver cry but it turned into a scream as the rock beneath her feet began to crumble. She threw herself back, pressing against the cliff, and saw that the whole cliff was shaking and fragmenting, trembling to the rhythm of the dreadful laughter.

She could not go back; she could not begin to consider Lukas or Phin, for that shifting monster inspired absolute fear in her, and the sound of its laughter still cut through the stability of the cliff top.

She gasped as the rock beneath her left foot turned to dust. Desperately she turned to face the cliff and, clutching with shaking hands, reached for the uneven cracks and fissures in its surface.

They held; and then the shivering of the cliff ceased. But the ledge had disappeared, and she could not see what was happening further along, round the corner. She clung, sweating, to the grainy cliff, and tried not to think of the space beneath. Cautiously she tried to find another foothold a little higher up.

She would have to try for the cliff top, some thirty feet above. It should not be impossible, given that there were no further earthquakes, for the rock was uneven and cracked, and there were plenty of handholds. But her breath was ragged with fear, her mind glancing away from each movement because it would keep her there, on the rockface.

Trying to think only how to escape, she began to edge her way upwards, kicking off her shoes, moving one limb at a time, trying always to keep three points of contact with the cliff. Both feet and a hand, or two hands and one foot, while the other searched for security.

She covered the first ten feet without too much difficulty. But then the character of the rock changed again, becoming crumbly and insecure. Twice a safe foothold disintegrated and she was left swinging, clutching with her hands. Dust choked in her mouth and nose, sweat dripped in her eyes, and her hair clung to her skin, getting in her eyes.

She dared not look down. She knew herself well enough to realise that it would be disastrous. She could hear the turmoil of the river below and the roar of a waterfall.

She dared not think of that monster, the malevolence of its smile, the nausea of its alternative shape. It would not want them to escape. It would follow.

She hardly dared move, because each move was a risk, a departure from safety.

She could not stay still, because she was quickly tiring.

She could only move on up, and take the risk.

Her hand slipped, scratched and bloody, and suddenly her left foot was also left hanging free. A physical pain in her stomach as it contracted with fear.

She saw, high above, a deeply fissured rock jutting out from the cliff.

She could not reach it, not just by stretching. But if she could swing an inch or two more, there would be a place to rest. She dared not think what the effort would involve. She wished she was brave enough just to let go. It would be over then. But she was not yet defeated by fear.

Pivoting on her right foot and left hand, she let herself drop back, towards the cliff, and on the rebound, reached with both hands for the rock.

She made it, both hands securely fastened round it. But her feet still hung free, all her weight dangling from her hands and fingers.

She scrabbled and scraped, kicking and skidding, trying to bend at the elbows, hauling herself up. Her arms were not strong, could barely sustain her own weight, let alone drag it upwards. Cramping her leg almost to waist height beneath her, she found somewhere to put her knee . . . Never use your knees, she dimly remembered someone saying . . . it's too limiting.

She had no choice. It took her weight, pressing painfully down onto the rock. Her hands were wedged in a crack above her head. For a moment she hung there, resting her face against the rock, and then started up again.

She was nearly at the top when she came to the overhang.

So tired, so exhausted by now, she faced it only with dread. It would mean hanging from her arms again. There was no way round it, for it ran along the top of the cliff as far as she could see in both directions.

For a moment she rested, in a position of comparative comfort, her head heavy against her knuckles, feet wedged securely in a deep fissure.

She would never have the strength for it, let alone the courage.

What else could she do?

The final assault, reaching up and out over the valley. If only her fingers were not so weak, her arms so feeble. It was not without holds, but she was low on strength. It was not a difficult route for an experienced climber; the overhang was not severe, or even very deep. Just a yard or so out, over a height of some four feet.

She could not do it. She managed to get halfway up it, wedging her feet into the cliff, clinging with damp hands to the many small cracks, but then it became impossible.

Could she go down a bit, move further along the overhang and try somewhere else? But the sound of laughter still soured her hearing, and she would have to look down to judge a descent. She was almost breathless now, trembling with exhaustion. It seemed to her anyway that the overhang was more severe, further along.

It was impossible to go up or down, and pointless to move further along. She tried to call to Astret, focusing her mind on the clear light gleaming beyond sight. It was untouchable, perfect and pure, a mockery of the dust and sweat all around her.

It was then that she began to hate. In extremis, clinging but immobile, strength draining like water from her limbs, she cursed Astret, cursed the power that had brought her to this point, cursed the cold clear light that had ruined her life.

The river rushed below; would she survive a fall? She was a good swimmer, but too tired now, and the water was full of rocks. She had no other option; her fingers were cramping, and there was nowhere else to go.

A furious surge of anger gripped her then. To hell with it. To hell with it all.

She wasn't going to die like this, feebly dropping from a cliff. Not yet. She stopped thinking about the drop, about how tired she was, how impossible it all was, and started methodically to scan the rock above her.

Inch by inch, while her fingers cramped and ached. Unimportant reactions.

And then she saw it, the narrow fissure to her left.

A scrabble with her feet, and relief as they found a small jutting rock. No time to relax, just an immense, ultimate effort, her hands reaching, and clutching, and then finding the small outcrop.

It was firm, big enough to hold, and strong.

It was easy then, just a brief struggle, and she was over the top, lying flat on the turf, sobbing with exhaustion.

She didn't see Lukas and Phin clamber up onto the grassy clifftop a little way along from her.

'Eleanor! All right?' Lukas was on his knees beside her, reaching out to help her up. She took a deep breath and sat up, pushing his hand aside. She tossed the hair out of her eyes, and rubbed sore hands on her dress.

'Yes, of course I'm all right,' she said sharply, although there had been no 'of course' about it. 'I did that!' she said, suddenly elated. 'I did that myself!'

Blythe had joined them. Nobody was going to waste time congratulating her. Blythe spoke quickly. 'It's gone. Suddenly disappeared, but I don't think we should hang around –'

As if in response, a glissando of laughter distorted the air around them.

The two men exchanged a quick look and began to run, dragging Eleanor after them. They fled away from the pervasive sound, away from the river gorge towards the forest at the head of the valley. In moments Lukas was ahead, long legs striding out, pounding over rough grass, Eleanor and Blythe close behind. The sound was faint behind them.

Then, just as they reached the shelter of the trees, without warning a blur of gold coalesced in the air around them. Eleanor skidded to a halt, eyes wide with fright. It was a cloud enveloping the entire valley, falling around them in a dense, silent shroud.

Soft and shimmering, it disguised every tree, every shape, a thick cloying blanket. Leaves, grass, sun and flowers all disappeared. It clogged the air they breathed, foul and putrid, deadened every sound, changing every perspective. Eleanor, close to Blythe, reached out for his hand, but Lukas, further ahead, was out of sight. The stinking cloud was all around them. There was no answer when she called out.

Eleanor and Blythe stood still, turning round, trying to identify where they were, wondering what to do. There was no point in running when all sense of direction was lost, and they needed to find Lukas. Blythe clasped his hands together over his mouth and called his name once, twice.

With a rush the gold around them retreated as if sucked away, leaving them in a clearing of some twenty feet, surrounded by tall shadowy trees. And then, again, the creature wreathed in golden light was there, the edges blurring and indistinct.

The fog seemed to grow from the end of its long, waving hair, flowing out in all directions, blotting out their surroundings, writhing round them strong as steel ropes. They could only see the turf beneath their feet, and the triangular face of the Parid, its mouth spread wide, stained with gold, avid.

It drifted towards them, leaving trails of mist, the essence of contempt. 'Now you have tired yourselves out for nothing. So stupid. Men were ever stupid. How could you imagine escaping?'

'Where's Lukas?' Blythe's voice was resolutely undramatic. Slowly the Parid uncurled one hand, pointing through the glimmering mist, and a tunnel appeared through it. A long way from them, enshrouded with gold, Lukas was slumped unconscious, hands flung wide and abandoned.

'Alive, don't worry. There will be something special for him later. A follower of the Lady Astret, here!' For a moment Eleanor thought she saw a flicker of expression on the blankly pretty face. It offered no reassurance. It could only be construed as lust.

'Now,' it said. 'Would you like to see what else I can be?'

Laughter still hung around the Parid but its shape changed, the golden light solidifying.

Its smile became the meaningless rictus on the face of a praying mantis, huge eyes and chinless jaw. Hard, serrated, thickened forelegs clasped in an attitude of prayer before it, and the rank body behind rose massively off the ground, rearing up on two of its back legs.

It was like nothing either of them had ever seen before, not spider, not mantis. Livid putrescent flesh gleamed through the cracks of the carapace, blood-swollen veins throbbing. Grey shrouds of trailing web fell from it, like stinking ribbons of skin.

Eleanor wanted to retch.

'My name is Sharrak. Look well,' it said, the voice still light and airy amidst the corruption of distorted flesh, 'for this is the legacy of Lefevre's power, should you choose to disobey.'

'Dear God,' muttered Blythe, and Eleanor put her hand to her mouth, shrinking back against him.

'*Which* God?' The monster moved closer, gently swaying on multiple legs. Blythe lifted his head, gazing directly into the blank, round eyes. He stared at it, considering.

'Lycias,' he said at last. 'The Brightening God, the Sun King.'

The monster was almost disappointed by his answer. 'Oh yes, very clever,' it said. 'You have the correct password to safety. I shall not harm you, although you may yet prove useful.' With a nod it enticed a cloud of gold to fall around him, pulling him away out of sight.

'But what of your friend here?' It swayed to one side, so that its head hung directly over Eleanor. 'Which God?' it repeated.

The only way would be to repeat Blythe's answer and buy safety. But she could not, a hard grain of obstinacy within herself forbade it. She would not acknowledge a god worshipped in this way. And then doubt arose, doubt she had tried to suppress.

For what was the alternative? The Moon? The legacy of a dream, an idea of light, a lump of cold rock in the sky. The flooding light no longer helped her, she was alone. She had reached the top of the cliff alone. The beacon burnt sullenly still in her mind, but it had brought her to this, had duped and deceived her, and who would help her now? She was caught in an alien world, with alien values and alien conflicts. It was nothing to do with her, nothing, nothing.

'Which God?' it asked for the third time.

'No God at all. There is no God.' And as she spoke it seemed as if this world's heart missed a beat, as if both Sun and Moon were momentarily extinguished, as if death lay claim to everything and anything.

The creature's head slanted sideways away from her with distrust and doubt. Revulsion and abhorrence were plain in its green eyes, and with a charge of power it stripped the stain of gold from her.

She fell to her knees, bereft of every support. Lukas and Blythe were held powerless, unable to help her, and this world with its warring, jealous gods was only a dream, a fiction in her mind.

'There is no God,' she repeated slowly, on her knees in the mud, as the mantis creature, and her friends, and the grassy, forested clifftop drifted away, leaving her in the desert of her own imagination.

Unbidden a voice spoke, coldly.

'What am I, then?' asked the Moon, driving shafts of ice into her heart.

'What am I, then?' asked the Sun, shrivelling flesh from her bones.

'Nothing and no one! You are nothing to me, and I am nothing to you!'

'You lie,' they said together, unified for once. 'Cheat and fool, you lie.'

And another smaller voice, within her own soul said, 'You can remain inviolate no longer. You must really choose now, and become involved. You are only half alive here.'

Eyes shut, hands over ears, she rejected with all her force these promptings, denied and redenied the claims of Moon and Sun, religion and love, magic and the unknown.

She might as well be dead.

Chapter Six
Carnival

'Can I get you a drink?'

'No, I must find my friends!'

'They're not here.'

'How do you know? Who are you?'

'A friend . . .'

No, you're not, sour old man with hook-nosed mask and tattered gaudy cloak. My friends are lost, lost in an empty forest with echoing pathways and deserted clearings.

She had found a track in the end, after hours of useless searching. She had blundered through wild roses, across ditches, into brambles and stinging nettles. She was tired, scratched, hungry and frightened.

She could not find the cliff or their old camp. When she called, the Arrarat failed to come. Lukas was captured and Phin lost. She wandered through the trees, crying their names, but no one answered.

As dusk fell she had come, exhausted and lonely, to the dirt track, winding through the forest. She followed it over a hill, always among trees, down a hillside, into a valley. Ahead the shapes of trees were outlined, spiky against a filter of coloured light, beckoning her over the next hill. People. She started to run.

Turquoise and amber, emerald and scarlet, pools of light shone on people, crowds of people, dancing and laughing along a path, crossing the dirt track winding down the hillside.

A party. Everyone was going to a party, and no one even noticed her.

The thin old man, with his stupid mask, had shocked her, staring at her between the tree trunks.

He did not know where Lukas and Phin were. She turned away, back to the crowds.

A party. Someone would know. In this vast forest, someone would know where her friends were. She crossed the clearing to where a man and woman were walking, exotic strangers in crinolines and breeches, wigs and spangled stockings.

Jewels flashed, scent reeked.

'Please –'

They looked her up and down, curiously, disdainfully.

'Who? Two men? A *monster*?' They passed on, murmuring with laughter.

The man with the hook nose had caught up with her, was holding out a goblet to her. She turned away.

She tried again, a group of young girls, skipping in time to the music.

'Oh no, no one like that . . . not here, not tonight!'

They disappeared in a cloud of jasmine and giggles.

He was still there, pale eyes gleaming through the narrow slits of the mask.

'What is it? Where are they going?' She spoke unwillingly.

'To the Carnival,' he said, 'Sharrak's festival . . .'

'Sharrak? Here?' Eleanor's voice rose in panic.

'Not yet.' His voice was cool and unworried. 'Later. At midnight, Sharrak'll come . . .'

'It's got Lukas!' Lukas, collapsed unconscious on the ground. Beginning to shake again, she turned back to the path, trying to see where it led.

'There's no hope for him, then,' said the dry voice.

The trees around were too dense in the dark, and the lights along the path too bright. It led up the side of another hill, and she couldn't see where everyone was going.

She was about to set off when he spoke again.

'Wait,' he said, and held his hands out to her. There was a goblet in one, full to the brim with dark wine. The other held a mask, the grey silk hood of a hare.

She stared at him, uncomprehending.

'If you're looking for someone, the mask will help. Only those with masks will move freely tonight.

'And if you're frightened, or nervous . . . this will do no harm . . .'

His voice was unexpectedly kind.

She took the mask with hands that trembled, and somehow found that she held the goblet too. It smelt rich, fruity and delicious, so she drank.

And was soon part of the crowd, her arm linked with a young man, golden cloaked, a scarlet top hat balanced over the mask of a bright cockerel.

'Have you seen my friends? . . . Lukas and Phin? Two strangers . . .?'

'Don't worry,' he said, stroking her hair. 'Do you like to dance? There will be music, later, fine music for dancing . . .'

'But I must find them!'

'But can you dance?' Through the mask he gazed at her with intensity. The question was more urgent than her anxiety.

'Of course,' she replied, crossly. 'But –'

'Come on, then!' And he began to run, pulling her hand so that she stumbled along beside him, until she found her balance and rhythm, and her feet began to skip, to jump and leap . . .

When she paused for breath, the man with the hook-nosed mask offered her more wine. He was always beside her, ready with a full goblet, just at her elbow, waiting. She frowned, but what use was there? She could not think what to do to help the others and everyone here was drunk. No one would talk sensibly to her.

There was music, spinning sound all around them, twining in the air, from groups of masked players, lutes and wind instruments, hand-held drums and bells, unlikely combinations of fiddle and voice, dotted along the pathway. People waltzed along one path, jived down another, skipped and lilted elsewhere.

At her shoulder again, the hook nose shining, the old man gave her more wine.

'Who are you, anyway?'

'Marial is my name. Music my trade . . .' From the folds of his velvet robe he brought out a small, golden harp.

Exquisite and fine, it gleamed as he held it up, and she reached out to look at it more closely.

'No!' Immediately he snatched it back, cradling it like a precious child. 'But you may listen, later,' he said, looking at her, a strange tremor of sadness in his dry voice. 'Later. At the Carnival . . .'

They were kind to her, in the Carnival forest. Banners and flags were strung between trees, lights blazing all around.

She was never left alone. Her partners were amusing, always courteous, sometimes disconcerting. Under the wash of wine her enquiries lost their urgency.

'Nowhere? A tall man, blue eyes, black hair . . .'

'No, not here. Oh, I can sing, too. Listen, do you know this one?'

A man with the face of an owl sat sadly at the edge of a stream and serenaded her in a reedy tenor voice. There was a buttercup-yellow youth who flung somersaults and cartwheels around her until, dizzy, she clapped with delight. A china doll lady popped marzipan cherries into her mouth, humming under her breath.

A ragged, beribboned fortune-teller hooted with laughter on seeing her palms and refused to tell her why. But she had lost her fear, released from anxiety for a few hours, dancing and laughing, singing and flirting, as if she had never knelt in the mud, denying God.

For what use was it, striving in that unknown war? For the first time here she was offered a brief respite, a chance to forget, sing and dance with companions who were resolute in ignoring anything at all serious.

There were tents, pavilions and kiosks, lined with coloured silken cushions, and every now and then she saw couples disappear under the awnings, moving with secret delight.

Delicious smells wafted through the air from other pavilions, savoury and sweet, roasting meat, warm bread, vanilla and orange. The music became more intense in one of the larger clearings, enticing the crowds to join together in dance – and so they did, stamping and skipping.

Eleanor's partner by this stage was a tall wispy man whose

gentle kindness was belied by an ugly vulture's mask. He had stroked her silky hare's ears and lightly kissed her hands before drawing her into the dance.

People capered around interlocking circles, constantly changing partners, getting faster and faster until, dizzy and breathless, they sought refreshment. During the course of her third such dance, Eleanor found herself clinging to a purple and yellow clown whose slow rich humour created a wild spring of laughter in her. She flirted and teased, danced and drank. And more or less deliberately put out of her mind what might have happened to Lukas and Phin.

She was enjoying herself, after all. It had been a long time.

Chapter Seven
The Web

As the night wore on, she moved along brightly lit paths, from clearing to grove, from avenue to glade, not realising that all paths led to one place. In the shadows, Marial drifted after her, filling her glass as it emptied, waiting. But she was travelling through a patterned maze, high on sensuous enjoyment, and thought nothing of it.

She barely noticed the Moon rising high above the trees, shining coldly on the tinsel gathering.

Dissecting light, sharp and austere.

The purple clown had found her again, crowing with delight. He was nuzzling at her neck, pushing the silk hood off, releasing the bright curls. Leaning against him, sighing as he stroked and caressed, she took no notice of the subdued murmur from the crowd, did not even look up when that murmur became a groan.

A groan of rejection, directed at the Moon itself. Giggling, she twisted round to face the clown and attempted to release his mask.

As she did so there was a sudden shout, a shriek through the night.

'Sharrak!'

She would have spun round then, but her hand was seized, pulling her roughly back.

'I'll play for you now!' said Marial, his eyes flashing with desperation behind the mask.

'No!' She tried to pull away, craning her head round to see where Sharrak was.

'Yes!' He was furious with intent. 'Listen now! Don't look over there, don't, don't . . .'

It was too late.

She looked, and every pleasure fell away.

Between two immensely tall trees, arching high over the clearing, was slung a spider's web. She had not noticed it, had not looked up towards the Moon. It might have been there all along, high above the silken pavilions and the laughing crowds.

Spreadeagled there, silhouetted in cold light, was the familiar figure of a man, tiny and doll-like in its vulnerability and distance. Icy with dread, wholly forgetful of the unmasked clown and Marial's golden harp, Eleanor pushed through the staring crowd to the foot of the web.

Crouching there, antennae waving, vacant eyes unblinking, Sharrak guarded its prey. The crowd stood back, at a self-imposed distance from the creature, hissing with thrilled, horrified expectation.

She knew it was Lukas. She had last seen him helpless in the mist. He was now conscious, but so far away that she had only an impression of the blood streaking down the side of his face, of his clothes hanging in rags. Strands of web held his limbs fast but his head was free. In a glint of azure he met her eyes. His message was unmistakable; glaring, he wanted her out of it.

'Come away, dear girl, there's nothing to be done . . .' Marial was still pulling at her arm, but she ran forward towards the creature, shouting in a voice puny and insignificant with fear.

'Let him go! Get him down, someone. You must let him go!'

'Must?' The mantis head regarded her and the stench of its breath almost drove her back. Sickening, she saw it smile, wavering between monster and gold-stained light. 'What does it matter to you?' it said, coldly. 'You don't belong here, you owe no allegiance to Sun or Moon. Why, you told me so yourself.' It swayed towards her, praying claws piously clasped.'Go away, little nobody, and leave us to our games.'

With a movement too fast to watch, it was suddenly off the ground and crouching in the corner of the web far below Lukas's feet.

'Get out, Eleanor!' He was shouting at her. 'You heard it. Get away from here, you can do nothing!'

And another voice, calm in her ear. 'Eleanor. Keep it talking, I'll get him down.' It was Blythe, unsmiling, bleak as ever, hooded in a wizard's black robe, unhurriedly unsheathing a sword from the fold of his cloak.

'No!' she yelled to the Parid, sudden hope in her voice. 'I won't go! And I do owe allegiance, to him!'

And as she pointed up towards Lukas, she realised that it was true.

'Parlour games.' Sharrak was contemptuous. 'People who owe allegiance don't go partying while their companions lie prisoner.' It began to edge along the web, gliding with ease over the golden thread.

How could she answer? She had indeed put her friends aside, had thoughtlessly flirted and danced, laughed and drank. Overwhelmed with guilt, she remained silent.

Still watching her, the creature slid smoothly up the web, over to where Lukas hung. For a moment, it was still, staring down at her, as if waiting for her to say something. Then, casually and effortlessly it buried its teeth in the outflung wrist before it.

Immediately it moved back, out of the silvery moonlight, as Lukas's body soundlessly contracted in a shudder of agony. Bright blood cascaded from his wrist, splashing down over the web.

The waiting crowd sighed. This was what they had come for, the point of the Carnival. The wild edge of danger, the thrill of horror after the fun.

Lost, dazed with grief, Eleanor was incapable of action. But Blythe, muttering under his breath, incomprehensibly, 'Not again!' sprang forward and started to clamber up one of the trees, reaching out onto the tacky, elastic web towards the Parid.

A moan from the crowd, their faces white, upturned to the high-strung web, the figures there outlined against the Moon.

'Come on, girl!' The sharp, dry voice at her elbow no longer offered wine and music. Marial was gripping her shoulders, roughly shaking her until she dragged her eyes away from the falling blood and looked instead at the knife he was holding out to her.

'Take it,' he said. His eyes were dark with nightmares, sunk deep in pale flesh. His mask had gone, and there was no comfort in the gaunt bones and bitter mouth.

'I'll help the black wizard,' he said. 'You get your friend down, and quick. There's too much blood there.'

Now it was dripping sluggishly onto the black grass beneath her feet.

Her heart was thudding and her breath came in uneven gasps as she raced across the grass and began to climb one of the trees.

She did not notice the scratches and grazes from the branches, or the vile stickiness of the web. All the time she watched Lukas, strung high above her, his head turned away from her so that she could no longer see his eyes.

It was difficult, moving across the web, for it stretched to irregular spans at every movement. Her feet plunged wildly, her hands clutched at stretching elastic and took her no further. She was sobbing with frustration and fear, lurching and swaying, trying to keep hold of the knife, trying to get to Lukas.

Marial, bright-chequered cloak trailing, was already high overhead, moving across the web above Sharrak. She was dimly aware of Blythe, close now to the bulk of the monster.

He had reached its legs; disdainfully, delicately, it flicked them out of the way of his swinging sword, and moved closer again to Lukas.

Trying not to think of those razor teeth, the blank eyes and stinking carcass, Eleanor concentrated on releasing Lukas's foot, slashing through the web. She tried to get further up, to free his uninjured arm, but Sharrak, with that sickening speed common to all insects, had darted round and was just behind Lukas's right hand.

Its teeth were only inches from the wrist, only an arm's length from her face. Eyes fastened on Eleanor, it hissed. 'Call them off. Or –' and its mouth opened, very slightly.

He'll die anyway, thought Eleanor, for the blood still gushed, staining the web. A spider's saliva can stop blood congealing, she remembered. It would flow, and flow, over the web, over the face of the Moon, until there was no more left . . .

The web lurched, and jolted.

Marial had slashed through the strong top strand connecting the web to the tree. With a snarl Sharrak turned towards him, agile over the sticky threads.

Quickly Blythe freed Lukas, pulling him away from the sagging web, hanging from one of the loose strands, gradually descending to the ground.

She wanted to follow them, to get away from the web and Sharrak, but she could not move. Her eyes were held fascinated by Marial's peril.

Shimmering and glowing the creature dissolved into a flickering kaleidoscope of shapes, all half-made and indistinct, faces and forms melting into each other. And as its instability wavered between ideas, dangerous, sparking energy darted down the web towards Marial. He screamed as glittering electric power seized him, the frail, old body twitching and jerking with impossible, cruel convulsions. He was strung there writhing like a fish on a hook, and the thin screaming went on too long, high and remote in the cold moonlight.

There was of course no hope for him, pinioned there in agony, or for the two men on the ground. No sooner had they fallen onto the grass, Blythe gripping Lukas's upper arm hard, quickly tying a handkerchief round it as a rough tourniquet, than the mob surrounded and overwhelmed them.

The crowd was dangerous now, high with excitement and blood-lust. People surged forward. In seconds Blythe was disarmed and Lukas separated from him.

Eleanor did not know what to do next. She could not bear to contemplate what was happening to Marial, and the mob below were howling for her, chanting and screaming.

A shape fell through the air, coloured rags fluttering in the moonlight. Marial, faint or dead, she didn't know which, released on a strand of web.

There was nowhere to go but down, for Sharrak was above. Blinded by tears she tumbled down through the sticky threads, clutching at loose strands to stop herself falling too fast.

At last she was on the ground again. No one touched her.

They stood around, staring through the slits in the masks, the painted mouths blank and expressionless. Silently they watched her struggle free from the remains of the web, and when she stood up, they took a step back.

They hated her. Through all the grief and exhaustion, she could feel it, tangible as iron. She did not care, stumbling through the path they cleared for her, trying to get to Lukas.

Marial was lying on the ground, stirring and groaning. She saw Blythe, taut with anger, held fast by masked men. And Lukas, half-fainting, slumped on the grass.

She ran to him and knelt down, pulling him over so that his head was in her lap.

'Don't die,' she whispered through her tears. 'Don't die – don't leave me –'

She didn't realise at first what was happening to Marial.

He was sitting up now, his head in his arms, his gaze averted from the Parid. It waited there, poised over him, avid claws twitching, wide eyes empty.

Its voice, when it came, was quiet, soft with menace.

'Marial, my golden harper, my pretty minstrel . . . why? Why should you turn against me? They deserve their deaths, Moon worshipper, traitor and nobody. But you, one of my own people, my own especial care!

'Have I not provided for you? Fed you, delighted you in dreams, enchanted you with carnivals and music? When did you ever suffer, thirst, go hungry? Did I ever neglect you? *Why* meddle in this?'

There was a long silence. Tears were streaking down the hollowed cheeks and then he met its gaze.

'She is young. Only that. The only young thing in existence . . .'

'She!' It spun round, stretched out one serrated claw, pointing to Eleanor. 'She is nothing! Less than any dream, she doesn't exist! A figment of some fourth rate magician's imaginings, that is all she is. An irrelevance, a lie, a cheat and a sham!'

True. Every word of it true, this world dissolving around her, the crowds, the monster, trees, grass and distant Moon, all receding. The desert of her imagining would reclaim her, pull her back out of this world, tease her out of feeling and thought, out of any possibility of hope.

Only one thing to hold her together, the weak clasp of Lukas's hand, the faint thread of his voice.

'It knows nothing . . . don't listen . . .'

She bent her head in shame.

Not far away, Marial spoke.

'We can't argue with you, or disobey. We only receive and give praise, and it is not enough. The music we make is arid. There is no new life, nothing honest and fresh. She is young. That is enough! It must be enough!'

'Eleanor –' Lukas's voice, barely audible, struggling for clarity. 'Call the Arrarat . . . try . . .' She looked round and saw where Blythe stood and caught his eye. Then, grasping at straws, she called once, twice, the low, baroque cry which summoned the hawks.

For a moment it seemed as if the entire crowd was staring at her and that a perilous limbo held everyone still. Then the air was filled with the heavy beating of wings, the air rushing and shaken by the speed of the birds.

They swooped once, black and silver, very low, and the crowd scattered back into the trees. Then, wheeling, they regained height, soaring high above the two giant trees, high into the face of the Moon.

Ready to dive, they hovered for the briefest moment. And all at once a pattern of golden lights sprang from the creature at the edge of the clearing and formed a mesh, a spider's trap over Sharrak's prisoners.

Looking up at it, Eleanor saw hundreds of minute spider-creatures, tiny replicas of Sharrak, running all over the mesh, strengthening and fastening.

There was time to run out beneath it. But Marial was injured, and Lukas could not move. She would not leave them . . . and looked despairingly across to Blythe.

She saw him come to the same decision.

The Arrarat hawks had swerved up and away from the net and now they flew higher, higher even than the cold face of the Moon. Dark there for one breathless moment, they hung still, before sharply pulling in their wings, plummeting like stones to break through the net.

'Don't –' she whispered, knowing that the attempt must fail.

The air whistled sharply overhead, and then the two great hawks were caught in the elastic net. It folded around them, swathing wing and feather in clinging, sticky thread. Strange fumes came from it, confusing the senses.

In seconds the birds were bound too tight even to struggle. Watching that bright strength crippled, emasculated, Eleanor was gripped by rage. What help could there be for them now, with the Arrarat captured?

Blythe pushed through the engulfing net to kneel on the grass beside Lukas and Eleanor. Briefly he looked at them, and then said softly, almost under his breath, 'We'll manage it yet, never fear,' as the net tightened and gripped them all.

Chapter Eight
The Well

Blythe was the first to wake, and after a glance around, drew in a sharp breath and closed his eyes for an instant.

He had noticed Eleanor, hanging as he was, arms pinioned, tied fast to a strand of web. Lukas, white, scarcely breathing, some distance away. They were both unconscious. There were other shapeless bundles wrapped in sticky web suspended around him, but he did not want even to think about them.

As for the stranger who had helped them at Sharrak's web – well, some yards below, a figure shrouded in grey strands hung from a single thread, a muffled harp trailing from one entwined hand.

He forced himself to open his eyes again and looked around. He shuddered.

They were in a dark chasm, hundreds of feet in diameter, lit by a pinpoint of light far above. The pit was criss-crossed, spanned by webs, some broken and hanging loose, others, newer, stretched tightly over an unimaginable drop.

There was nothing beneath them. At least, Blythe could see no end. The curved walls of the chasm gradually drew closer together, presumably to meet at some vanishing point, miles below. There was no possible way to measure the depth, unless something were dropped, an experiment he did not want to try.

He was also unwilling to spend time considering the other objects suspended over the drop. It was enough to realise that they were not the first prisoners in this well; other webs embraced skulls and vertebrae, ulnae and femurs, the bleached remnants of Sharrak's larder. Other corpses must have tumbled into the void as the web decayed. Blythe wondered how long it took.

He looked again at Lukas and noticed that the rough binding on his wrist was still holding, although the ominous red stain was slowly spreading. His pallor was devastating. He would not long survive that loss of blood.

As for the girl – but as he watched she began to stir. Thinking fast, he began to speak.

'Eleanor, it's all right, we're all here. Don't look down!' His voice echoed strangely in the profundity of the chasm.

She had opened her eyes, uncomprehending and blank, and he immediately tried to fill her thoughts with words, before she could register where they were.

'Lukas is okay, I can see he's fine, and neither of us is hurt – I don't know where the Arrarat are, but I'm sure –'

He gabbled on, as one talks to reassure frightened children, with meaningless, soothing sounds. 'The hawks will look after themselves – don't look down, look at me, Eleanor, at me!'

This was almost a shout, for he could see that panic was not far away. 'Take a deep breath, you're quite safe now, quite safe. Listen. This is a prison – look at me, Eleanor – we'll be all right as long as we keep still.'

'I can't – do anything else.' There was only the faintest tremor in her voice, but he could see the knuckles of her hands shining white with tension. Then he realised that his own hands were similarly clenched. With an effort, he relaxed them.

'What – is this place?' she whispered, still looking rigidly only at him.

'Sharrak's storehouse, I imagine,' he said bleakly.

'What – what should, I mean, what can we do?' Her eyes slid away from his face. 'Oh, Lukas! We must help –'

'At the moment, I don't think there's anything we can do,' he said carefully, trying to keep his tone light, trying to defuse her rising hysteria.

'It can't just leave us here!' she cried, and then fell silent for a moment. Then, 'Where's Marial? What happened to him?' She gazed round wildly as she spoke, before Blythe could distract her, and then fatally looked down.

A scream often produces an echo, even in a small space. This one rent both air and sense and rebounded with unflagging energy on, and on, and on, until the bones above and around them crumbled, falling, clattering, past them into the void.

Fine dust clogged eyes and mouth, sharp splinters caught in their hair and clothes, and the noise went on.

It was still echoing round them when they heard a sharp, snapping sound. One of the strands of web holding Lukas had broken in the chaos of sound and falling debris. His left arm suddenly hung loose, the blood sluggishly dripping once more. He was held only by two threads, one from his uninjured right hand, the other from his tied feet.

'Quiet! For God's sake, be quiet!' Blythe dared only whisper, but she had already stopped. 'Don't do that!' He didn't really need to say it.

Eyes wide, she was trembling.

'Lukas . . .'

'Is still with us. It's still holding, as long as we're quiet and don't start another avalanche.' He took a deep breath, willing his heart to steadiness.

'Understand,' he said. 'We'll be all right while the web holds, we've got time to think. Try to keep calm.'

There was a long pause as she tried to direct her mind away from the drop.

'Sharrak's storehouse . . .' She was struggling to regain some sense of order. 'Do you think – it – will come for us here?'

'Sooner or later. Let's hope it's later.' He was silent, considering.

'It's madness.' Her voice was small and quiet. 'For a time, when we were travelling with Ash and Astrella, I began to think that this world was real, somewhere where things really happened. I thought that my past was probably just a kind of dream, a boring, dreary dream. I want it back, now. I want ordinary people, and ordinary things to happen. A nine-to-five job in an office. Cars in traffic jams. Adverts. Pigeons on window sills. This is only a nightmare. It must be. I can't take it any more.'

'Tell me about it. Your world. I know nothing about you,

really. Who are your family, what did you do before coming here? Who are you?'

Anything to divert her. But she looked around again, at the echoing dark above and below, and at Lukas, deathly white.

He saw her shudder, and tears rise to the grey eyes once more. But she tried, haltingly at first and then more fluently.

It was more bizarre than he could comprehend, a catalogue of strange preoccupations and inconceivable machines. Her grasp of practicalities was at best incomplete. It was probably inaccurate, too. Suspended by fragile web over an unimaginable drop, she sounded both incoherent and foolish.

He concentrated on asking the right questions to keep the flow going.

'Your family, what do they do?' He felt more at ease when she spoke of her personal life, but even here she was sketchy, skating over what he guessed to be difficult relationships, uneasy truces. 'Do you live with your parents? Do you have a man, married or promised?'

She shook her head. 'I've had lovers, even lived with one for a while, but nothing really worked. I always wanted something different, some change . . . I was bored . . .'

Karis never had a chance to become bored, he thought. Though we did not grow old, we did not need change, then.

Silence fell as they contemplated wasted lives, and momentarily forgot their extremity.

They were not prepared for what happened next. A change in the temperature. Gold light drifted in from the side of the chasm. Sharrak, in its guise of shimmering beauty, floated along a rope of web towards them. Streams of light dribbled from its fingertips, running over the rounded lines of its limbs, bleeding into the dark air.

It was dazzlingly bright in the abyss, but the brilliance made the darkness pull back in revulsion. A faint sweetness hovered around it.

Eleanor's palms began to sweat. She remembered its other incarnation and nausea welled up. Her head began to ache with the pounding of her heart, the sickness in her stomach.

'Dearest . . .' The words were soft and lascivious. 'Not too uncomfortable, I hope. I like my guests to linger . . .'

It reached out over the void, with one long, gold-stained limb and pulled a skull from the clinging web. Blowing dust from it, the creature gazed consideringly into the empty eyes and then moved slowly along the web until it was next to Lukas. As Eleanor watched with fascinated horror, it held the skull in front of his closed eyes, and for a moment it appeared that the living man had vanished, had been swallowed by worms, stripped of flesh, leaving only a hollow framework of whitened bone.

For a moment time slipped. The present or the future? What was the difference, where did it lie?

Eleanor looked away.

'Beloved,' it said, amused. 'Don't wriggle or you may find . . .' Sharrak held the skull out and let it fall, spinning, a glimpse of bleached white through the dark. No sound marked its arrival at the bottom.

It looked down at the broken web at its side. 'Hardly worth repairing, is it? I feel your companion will not be with us for long anyway.'

It bent towards the unconscious face, opening its thin mouth in a kind of smile.

'No! You disgusting hag! Leave him alone, leave him alone!' Eleanor was crying with frustration and fury, struggling against the web, oblivious of the danger of noise.

The Parid sneered at her, a faint hiss coming from the curling mouth. Then, abruptly, it fell silent.

Someone had joined them. With shock they stared at the discreet figure of a middle-aged man, leaning against the jamb of a doorway cut into the far side of the well.

A flood of light streamed from the room behind him, framing him in silhouette, and it was difficult to see his features. He was slight, grey-haired, self-contained. When he spoke his voice was light and pleasant.

'You are indeed disgusting, you know,' he said to Sharrak. 'Uncivilised, this sort of thing.' He waved at the prisoners. 'Why bother, little sweetie? Aren't you fed enough?'

Sulkily it evaded his glance. 'Why? Do you want them?'

Like a whiplash, light flicked across the void from his hands and sharply struck it back to the other form. Glowering, the spider-mantis scuttled along the web, lurking just behind Eleanor.

'Well?' So cold, his voice, cold and empty. 'Who have we here? Collecting again, I see. But to what purpose? An explanation is due, my strange one.'

The Parid snarled. It spoke.

'Moon worshippers. Traitors, spies, strangers! You would rather I was kind, hospitable to them? They are outside the Law of the Lord. They are mine!'

'A triumph of deductive reasoning, my dear.' He was contemptuous.

'I know you,' said Blythe quietly. 'De Mowbray, Elfitt de Mowbray, Governor of Mavrud, Keeper of Cliokest.'

'We've met?' His elaborate attention was diverted. 'But how remiss of me! I don't immediately recall –'

'Blythe. Phinian Blythe. My uncle is Hamnet Lin. We met when I made the tour, long ago.'

There was a pause and even Eleanor, half-fainting with nausea at the Parid's proximity, felt a change in the degree of tension. It was as if matters were suddenly held in abeyance, while de Mowbray decided what to do.

The silence went on almost too long. Then, inexplicably, he said, 'We'll have to see about that,' and without looking again at them, stepped back into the warm light, Sharrak scuttling after him.

'Wait!' shouted Eleanor. 'Don't leave us here! Don't –'

The heavy door swung to, leaving the rock face blank and impenetrable.

She was openly crying now, tears falling unheeded down a white face.

'Why won't he help us? How can he leave us here?'

Angrily, Blythe looked at the surface of the rock, tracing the outline of the door. Shutting his mind to the pattern of Eleanor's misery, he studied the well, swaying in his bonds so as to get as many different perspectives as possible.

He thought there might be a way to open the door from their side. It was just possible. Among the shadows, Blythe could make out the door's outline. There was a narrow ledge in front of it, six inches or so of rock. There was also, to the right of the door, a small protuberance in the rock, more regular and balanced than the natural roughness of the surface.

'Phinian!' Eleanor had stopped crying. 'What are you planning?' Her voice was high with anxiety.

He answered her unspoken fear. 'We can't stay here, can we? Lukas needs help and soon. I never did like waiting.'

'What do you mean? What are you going to do?'

'I think we may be able to open the door from this side –'

'How on earth – ?'

'I'll have to get free first,' he said, as if in reassurance. 'It might not be possible, anyway.'

It would not have been possible, of course, but for the merest chance. In the fall of debris following Eleanor's scream, a shattered fragment of bone had wedged on the sticky webs round Blythe's wrists. And when he had experimented with momentum, swaying to get different views of the rockface, it had slipped down into his fingers. It was razor sharp, and although the web's elastic blunted pressure, it parted easily enough under the sawing splinter.

'Don't!' He could not, he must not. She could see the threads breaking. 'You're cutting the web that's holding you up too. You'll just drop!'

'No – I think not . . . it's round my feet too.' He craned his neck, carefully watching which threads were parting, calculating how long before the bonds broke. His fingers were beginning to cramp from the awkward angle of the cutting motion, but not enough to stop him.

'You'd leave me here!' She was frantic. 'Alone, you'd leave me and just *jump*! There's no chance, you know there isn't . . .'

'Better than being a spider's breakfast,' he muttered.

'That man, what did you call him – de Mowbray. He'll come back, he'll make it let us go . . .'

'Look.' He stopped sawing for a moment and looked at her. 'De Mowbray is Lefevre's man. If he has not yet realised that Lefevre regards me as a traitor, he soon will. He will not be disposed to help me out, or my companions. At best, I may have bought us a little time.

'Even if, by some miracle, he does decide to get us out of here, it will probably be too late, because Lukas will die soon anyway, and that thread' – he nodded to the web attached to the spinning, enshrouded figure of Marial – 'is fraying with every revolution.'

She had not noticed, had not even considered Marial's danger. The strands were indeed giving way; in a short time he would fall. She began to weep again in pity for Marial.

Blythe returned to his sawing.

After a while she started reasoning again, desperately trying to convince him that he should not risk anything.

He ignored her.

In the end, driven, she almost shouted at him. 'If you insist on suicide, go ahead, I don't care, but what about Lukas? What about Marial? What about *me*?'

The nub of the matter, the eternal cry, desperate and unlovely.

Again he stopped and looked at her. 'Do you remember when we first met? In that council chamber on Jeren, with that bloody barbarian waving burning twigs around?'

She nodded wordlessly. How could she forget?

'I knew then that you were fated to find – a way out. I recognised something in you, something I shared.'

He paused, swallowed, mouth dry at the recollection. 'It wasn't just that damn light in the mind, it was more than that. You also have lost everything, family, friends, familiar world. I don't know why it's significant, but I don't, can't believe that this is the end. It may be a dream, a delusion, but I know it for sure. This is not the end, Eleanor, for you or me.'

And with that the final strand snapped and his hand hung free, still clutching the shard of bone, and for a moment he spun over the abyss.

Now he was only attached by strands to his left hand and feet. There was no way of freeing his feet first, as he was stretched too tightly by the opposing ropes of web. Ignoring Eleanor's pleas, he concentrated on slicing through the web on his wrist. It parted almost immediately.

A calculated risk; would it be strong enough to sustain the shock? A dizzying, horrible drop as he swung head down, attached only by his feet. A sudden pull on his ankles as the thread stretched, and held. Breath gasped, and was not easily released, as he narrowly missed the far wall of the chasm in an erratic swing created by the change in weight.

Sharply, trying not to think of the void below, he convulsively jerked upwards, bending his knees and reaching out, grasping at the web above his feet.

He failed. He was now swerving, upside down, through a wide arc, just missing Lukas. The dark fetid air rushed against him. Again, an exhausting paroxysm of energy, and his fingers brushed the straining thread but failed to grip.

For a moment he hung there, shutting out Eleanor's cries, trying to still the swinging, trying to recoup some strength. Then he tried again, curling up like a spring and shooting upwards, denying gravity. With a gasp he caught the web, quickly weaving his left arm round it so that it took some of the weight.

He drew himself up, hunching close to his chest and started slashing at the remaining strands round his ankles. His fingers were slippery with sweat, his heart thudding with effort, not thinking what would happen if he failed.

The web parted: he hung loose from his left arm, his only defence against the drop. He swayed against it, altering the passage and depth of the swing by leaning sideways.

Gradually the speed and arc of the swing increased: the air began to whistle round him and the door in the rock face came slowly nearer to the high point of the arc. He felt suddenly a shift in the web round his left arm: it was giving way under the strain. Soon, it would break.

Praying indiscriminately to whatever God there was, he hurtled though the air to the doorway with its small ledge of sanctuary.

At the furthest point of the arc he leapt out and away to the side of the well. A brief moment of flight, unsupported over emptiness. Fingers reaching, straining, he clutched at the ledge. For a second he hung there, fingertips scrabbling for purchase against damp and lichinous masonry.

It crumbled under his fingertips.

He plunged down, down into the abyss.

* * *

There could be nothing worse than this, she thought. Terror and pain beyond her dreams had been exacted from her denial of the Sun and the Moon, the denial that a balance had to be maintained.

And now, surely, she was stripped of every arrogance. The tears that coursed heedless down her face were no longer for herself but for her friends, dead and dying, and for the death of the Cavers' hopes. For all her resistance, she had been drawn into their struggle, had become involved with them. But so easily had she been diverted, so easily seduced by trivialities!

If order were ever to be restored, it would not be through Eleanor Knight, who had wilfully wasted every opportunity, squandered every chance.

With the realisation that she had utterly failed and was utterly abandoned, doomed, she lost all fear. Nothing could ever be any worse than this.

So when, at last, the web holding Marial broke and he fell discarded into the chasm, she bequeathed him a requiem in tranquillity.

Soon after, Lukas was released into the void and something within her broke, shattered like glass falling through flame. She began to long for a similar oblivion.

When her own bonds, some incalculable time later, began to give, she felt only relief, for it would soon be over.

The realisation that her denial of Moon and Sun had meant nothing, and that all her actions had to be counted failures, accompanied her fall through the dark.

A rush of air, a kaleidoscope of black upon black overwhelming the senses, and she knew and felt nothing.

Chapter Nine
Lycias

Two men were dining elegantly at the top of a sun-lit tower far above a glittering sea. They talked civilly but with some constraint. Amber wine glowed in crystal glasses, but neither did more than sip.

A light vine-covered trellis shaded them from the heat of the sun; flowers, cream, purple and cerise, tumbled among the fragile leaves. Dappled light moved in the soft breeze.

A humming bird, entranced by the sweetness of candied peaches, hovered shyly just behind the older man's shoulder. Noticing, he pushed his chair back and to the side, allowing it to dart an uninterrupted path to the sweetmeat. There was no sound beyond the faint whirr from the bird's wings, and their own quiet conversation.

'But why leave? Surely it would have been better to stay?' He looked away from the humming bird back to his wine, avoiding the other's gaze.

'No. I think not.' His face shuttered and guarded, one could hardly discern the marks of shock and suffering so recently imprinted.

Phinian Blythe was clean, rested, composed, and if not precisely relaxed, at least self-contained. The memory of that heart-stopping fall had been defused by the care and courtesy he was now experiencing.

His situation was not really much less dangerous than when he was hanging in Sharrak's chasm. De Mowbray's questions were becoming increasingly searching.

'Lefevre knew that there was a disruptive element at work among the Cavers,' he said. 'He has many spies. He decided to send someone to work among them, undercover. If the Stasis was at risk, the Cavers would be a focus for the disruption. Astret would never use Peraldonians . . .'

He leaned back, calmly regarding the fine linen cuff of his borrowed shirt, wondering just how closely de Mowbray was in contact with Lefevre.

'They seem to have accepted you fairly thoroughly. Was it difficult?' de Mowbray smiled with sympathetic enquiry.

'Certainly not easy . . .' Remembering suspicion and violence, he paused. 'I don't know that I'm trusted even now. Definitely not by the Jerenites. And Lukas – is a natural rebel. He in no way followed the orthodox Caver line.'

'He is brother to Matthias, is he not?'

'I believe so.'

'That would explain the lack of the typical Caver's narrow vision. A promising student, Matthias. Lefevre was distressed when he returned to Sarant.'

'He trained under Lefevre?' Blythe looked up.

'Oh, not for long. He was one of the last generation to study on Peraldon. We met occasionally. He specialised, if I remember correctly, in Synchronicity. The science of manipulating events so precisely that echoes can be set up in alternative worlds. That's presumably how he managed to obtain the wild card.'

Conversation ceased for a moment while a uniformed manservant cleared away the dishes of fruit and honey and replaced them with strong black coffee.

Blythe looked out into the sunlight, enjoying the faint breeze, and wondered how Eleanor had coped with the fall and subsequent resurrection.

De Mowbray had had just enough time to consider the possibility that Sharrak's prisoners might be of more use alive than dead.

He had paused, back in the room beside the Well, watching the retreating shadows that were Sharrak. There was more to this than the Parid's hurt pride. A Caver, for God's sake, here. And the girl, from another world, Matthias's hand again. And he did remember Blythe, Lin's nephew. He would have to find out what was going on. It would be better not to kill them immediately. He stared at his hands for a moment and then gave the instruction.

A net, far stronger than web, was thrown across the chasm. Let them drop, he thought. It would be a salutary experience, would perhaps soften them a little.

Blythe had fallen only moments later.

They had been tended and healed in de Mowbray's efficient and sophisticated hospital wards, but were not allowed to meet. Blythe learnt only indirectly of Lukas's recovery and Eleanor's silence, and found himself urgently wanting to see them. This he disguised.

De Mowbray was in no hurry. Pouring coffee, he calmly extracted the tale of the flight from Jeren, constantly emphasising Eleanor's role.

Blythe played it down, realising that any unknown elements would be perceived as dangerous. It was not difficult. He drew a picture of her as feeble, spoilt, helpless and muddled, and hoped that de Mowbray's own interviews with her had reinforced that impression. It held, after all, more than a grain of truth.

'As it happens, I can't get her to say a word.' De Mowbray frowned in answer to Blythe's enquiry. 'The fall was no doubt traumatic. She'll probably relax after a few more days.'

'Would it help if I met her? It might provoke some reaction. You must have rooms where you could watch unobserved.'

'My dear Blythe, do you think I don't trust you? Of course you may meet her, and I wouldn't dream of eavesdropping . . .'

He put down his coffee cup. 'Shall we go?'

They strolled along graceful walkways, spanning the clear sky between the towers of the citadel. It was an agreeable path, scented air, the soft swish of the sea below, and clematis and wisteria lining the trellises overhead.

De Mowbray was civilised and undemanding, and Blythe found himself slipping back into the habits of a lifetime, the lifetime before the death of Karis. Such an easy life it had been, pleasant and enjoyable. Elegant pastimes, cultured conversation. Midnight balls, open air concerts, parties on the Ferry . . .

He stopped. It was all built on sand, he thought. Built on the grief of the Cavers, on the destruction of the Moon's power.

He looked sideways at de Mowbray. Neat and dapper, the Governor of Mavrud adjusted his cuffs and smiled courteously.

'Ah, here we are,' he said.

They stepped together into a deserted, brightly lit corridor, and at the wave of de Mowbray's hand double doors opened ahead of them.

It was a long, cool room, containing some twenty beds, jutting out from the pale green walls at regimented intervals. Plants bloomed at every empty bedside, vines wreathed around walls and ceiling.

De Mowbray nodded briefly to the solitary figure standing at the far end of the room by the window, and then bowed, withdrawing.

'Eleanor –' Quickly he crossed the ward towards her. She turned at the sound of his voice, and waited calmly. She was watching him as if she did not know or care who he was.

'Eleanor – are you all right?' He held out his arms to her, shocked by the mildness of her smile.

'Phinian. Yes, of course, quite all right.' She moved towards him, allowing him to hold her briefly. 'How about you? You weren't hurt?' She seemed a million miles distant, insubstantial as air. He didn't know what to do. Unhurriedly she disengaged herself.

'No, I'm fine. And Lukas is recovering too, they tell me.'

'Yes, I know . . .' She was vague. 'I've not seen him yet.' Thoughtfully she took a small sea-shell from her pocket, turning it over in her hands, sitting down in the chair by the window.

Blythe was not often at a loss for words, but he didn't at all know what to say next to her. She seemed perfectly content with the mere knowledge of Lukas's safety. It was almost as if she had nothing else to do.

'What's happened, Eleanor? What's going on?'

She raised her eyebrows. 'What can you mean? Nothing's "going on" as you put it. It would be nice to see Lukas though, don't you think? Get them to pull some strings or something. You seem to be well in here.' But she appeared to be only faintly interested, and Blythe didn't know what to do next.

He stared at the bright fall of her hair, the gentle grey of her eyes, wondering what had brought about such an alteration.

'You must tell me,' he said firmly. 'Something has happened, hasn't it?'

At first she didn't answer, but then she looked away, down at a small creamy shell in her left hand. She sighed. 'When you fell I, I – well, it was terrible. Terrible. And then, Lukas too . . . the worst thing ever. I couldn't bear it. I was glad when I fell . . .'

Simple words to describe a revelation.

'There was a blank, just black and empty as I fell, I can't describe it. Like a faint, I suppose.'

She paused. 'It was more than that, though. I don't know how long the fall lasted, can you remember?'

He shook his head, wordlessly, appalled by her coolness.

'I . . . had a dream. I think it was that. It must have been. It was a realm of fire . . . I found myself bathing there, in a realm of light and heat. It was like a sea. I could rest on the waves of heat swirling around, and yet it didn't burn or hurt in any way. Just warm, generous, loving comfort . . . holding me up, stroking me, reassuring . . .

'It was so beautiful too, as if the flames were flowers, everywhere, the scent was so lovely! There was no sun in the sky, it was just turquoise and azure, stranded with fire. And rainbow cascades of sparkling rain, fountains of cool water, there just to give a contrast to all the warmth . . .

'I thought it was heaven, at first. Quite literally, because I must have died, in that fall. In our world, hell is a realm of fire . . . but this was no hell, it was gentle, bright and glorious, and I loved it so! I wanted to stay there forever, it wasn't at all lonely, because all that warmth was the warmth of love . . . I thought that all that delight was for *me*, because I was so loved, so adored.'

She smiled with irony, but her eyes were blank.

'It wasn't all perfect; there was something odd there. Something nagging at me. I couldn't quite relax back into all that loveliness.

'And then I saw Her. The Moon.' She looked sideways at him, as if doubtful that he would understand. 'A woman, someone I met once before, in another dream. I knew then that this was a dream, because how else can the Moon, a lump of rock in the sky, be a woman?'

Blythe made no attempt to answer, a slight frown on his face. She struggled on.

'Martitia – Thurstan's mother, remember? – Martitia once said to me that imagination creates gods, creates everything. Our imagination, and that of – God. Whoever, whatever He or She or It is. That the Cavers see God in the Moon, means that It exists and acts through that form. God has to have a comprehensible face if It is to have any meaning for us. So God appears as Moon, as Sun – in my world as Man – whatever is appropriate. You know this.'

'It is one way of looking at it, certainly,' he said slowly, considering unfamiliar concepts.

'So, I met the Moon, in a firegarden, in a dream.

'She could barely exist there, She was fading, attenuated, almost transparent, in a kind of agony. She could hardly stand in all that warmth, and there was a dark cloak falling across Her face.

'When She looked at me, I couldn't bear it. When I first saw Her, long ago, I don't know if I can explain, She was so beautiful, so extreme, so ultimate that it was also unbearable, but not like this. Here She was almost like a skeleton, devastated, black eyes huge in a ruined face.'

She swallowed, turning over the shell in trembling hands, striving for clarity. 'She said that this place, this realm of fire, was Lycias's country, not Her's. That was why She was fading there. He was too strong, all around, and She could not exist in His presence. But She needed to talk to me, and it was only possible here because I wouldn't understand anywhere else. She gave me this shell, as a pledge.'

She held it out for him to see, delicate, flecked with brown, a thin spiral of loosely patterned cream and amber. A golden glow, mother of pearl, lined its inner surface.

'She said that people can only understand what God is in moments of ultimate trauma. At the extremities of human existence. Grief, joy, fear, ecstasy. Nothing else would do. Falling into that pit was an adequate qualification.'

She almost laughed. 'It doesn't make it easy, does it? Anyway, Her message was that we should go no further. She had directed us south because this is where we need to be to find how to release the Benu. And then, as She said that, HE came.' The trembling became shuddering, and she lifted her hands from the little shell as if to shield her eyes. 'There was no need for a sun in the sky because He was *there*, the centre of all that heat, burning with – laughter, or anger, I couldn't tell. I couldn't see Him for the brightness.

'He said, I could try if I wanted to find the Benu. That the Stasis would indeed end, the Boundary break, if I could release it. But that I would find the price too high, because what could I set against a God's love for a mortal? I don't understand this, what did He mean?

'The Moon was no longer there, eclipsed in every sense by Lycias. And I – I didn't understand, could say nothing. What words have I, to talk to a God?

'He showed me His face then, so beautiful He was, with such a terrible smile –' She closed her eyes momentarily. 'In His eyes, pure will. Implacable, eternal will. He left no choice anywhere. There is nothing I can do, now. Nothing at all, for ever.'

Silence. She half smiled, as if in apology, and turned back to the window, looking out into the clear blue sky, the golden sun calm and high.

She seemed to have forgotten him already.

He would not let her get away with this. Deliberately he drew the heavy curtains across the window, blocking out the light, and turned to face her.

'What of the Moon then?' he said, his voice harsh. 'What of this light we've all been following?'

'Have you still got it?' she looked at him curiously. 'Is it still in your mind?'

It wasn't, of course. It had disappeared when they had hung in Sharrak's lair, had deserted them as they dropped into the abyss.

'It's no use, you see,' she said. 'It was never strong enough to win against a God that powerful.'

Her voice was blank and final.

'I will not accept that!' Lukas's voice shattered the darkened stillness.

Turning, she saw his familiar figure in the doorway, tall and gaunt, silhouetted against the light from the corridor. He was wearing the dark Caver cloak over clean jeans and shirt.

'Not good enough, that, Eleanor,' he said, coming towards them. He moved slowly, carefully, as if unused to action, and his wrist was still heavily bandaged. But he was well enough, gripped by a forbidding fury she could not comprehend.

She looked at him uncertainly, and then back to Blythe, who stood silent, wary, expectant.

'How much of that did you hear?' he asked Lukas.

'All of it. At least I assume I did. From falling into the pit onwards. It was an interesting construction as an excuse.'

'What do you mean?' she cried.

'You've never really wanted to help, have you?' He swung round to face her. 'It's all just been a game to you. Given a little importance, a bright light to follow and to help you out, you thought you'd play along for a while, just as long as it suited you. And now it's become a real issue, now you've seen what we're really up against, you decide to give up. To run out.'

'You don't understand!' she said desperately. 'There's nothing we can do, however we try. Just think, how could we ever dream that we could set ourselves up against God? How could we ever have been so mad!'

'I really believed you could do it.' He spoke quietly, his face hard. 'When it became clear that the Moon had adopted you, when I saw that light blazing, and Fosca running, I really thought you could do it. It wasn't particularly easy, there were the horrors, Jocasta dying, and all those other deaths, Jerenites, Cavers, Phin's wife and child – all those deaths involve you, sweetheart, to a greater or lesser extent. Even with all that, I thought you could swing it. But now it appears that all those lives were wasted. You were never up to anything much.'

With whiplash force his words stripped her of all warmth and friendship, and left her destitute under Lycias's sun.

Blythe laid a restraining hand on his arm, shocked by Eleanor's pallor. Roughly Lukas shook him off, his eyes holding her immobile, trapped. 'What are you, who are you, what are you *for*, if not to fight this battle?'

'I'll tell you what I'm for!' She was passionate at last. 'To tell you to give up! Accept it! You are immortal, you have eternal life. Men had dreamed of it for years in my world, to avoid death and old age! You don't know how lucky you are!'

He hit her. Backhanded, with all the rage and despair of countless years of sorrow, across that empty face and spoilt mouth.

She fell soundlessly to the ground, the vase of flowers crashing to the floor around her.

Blythe sprang between them, shouting.

'Enough! Stop! What are you thinking of, what good can come of this?' He pushed Lukas back, holding him at arm's length, his back to the girl.

Lukas ignored him. He went on hurling words at her, seeming not to notice her cut lip and appalled eyes. 'I didn't leave Matt and Margat, Thurstan, all the others, for this, this *farce*! If you couldn't even see what was going on then, what immortality –' he spat the word, 'does to people, you must come from a bloody strange world, more alien than I can begin to imagine. Are they all monsters in your world, or are you unique?'

And then Blythe could take no more either, and lashed out suddenly, sending Lukas toppling onto a nearby bed.

A shadow moved along the wall over the floor.

Arrested, Lukas rolled out of the path of Blythe's swinging fist, and whispered, 'Scurry! Look, there!'

For a moment they stared at it. It was frozen against an empty locker, its body blending with the grain of the wood, the angles of its corners. Then Blythe dived at it, arms outflung, and for an instant it writhed in his grasp, mimicking his flesh, his clothes, a duplicate, diversified pattern of textures and colour hung on flexible folds of skin. It yowled with distress as he touched its clammy imagery and sent a shock fierce with electricity through his hands.

Cursing, he dropped it; a chaos of shape and colour, it sped to the door, Lukas crashing over furniture after it. It was too fast for them, and just as it slid away the door slammed shut in their faces, bolts heavily drawn across the outside.

'Damn!' Lukas hurled himself uselessly against the wood, and then leant against it, looking back at the Peraldonian. 'Now what? They'll know everything!'

Blythe stared round the room, its furniture awry, the still girl crouched by the window, the spilt water. 'Can you see any others?' he said to Lukas. 'I'd rather know if there are more spies here.'

Together they examined the room minutely. It was clear. Wordlessly, Blythe took Eleanor's limp arm, steered her to a chair, patiently dabbed at the split lip. She stared blankly at him, withdrawn and shocked. He spoke to her, but she didn't seem to hear. Eventually he stood up and joined Lukas, staring out of the window.

He was studying the drop below them, the smooth marble and sheer walls, the sparkling sea and jagged rocks below.

'I don't fancy it much that way,' he said, as if Blythe had suggested a quiet country stroll.

'No.' Blythe leant against the window sill, looking straight at Lukas and behind him, still motionless in the chair, the girl.

'That was a singularly stupid thing to do, even for a Caver,' he said coldly. 'Can't you tell shock, when you see it? You'd have done better to give her time.'

'Perhaps.' He was unrepentant. 'I don't think we can afford the luxury of time right now.' The irony of this did not escape him. The long lips curled. 'I am not going to give up here. I will not allow Eleanor Knight to give up either. She's no tool for Lycias.' He paused again, and looked at Phin for the first time. His eyes were serious. 'I think – we need to get out of here, before we discuss this further. I don't trust de Mowbray, for all his civilised ways.'

'Cavers never did appreciate civilisation. But yes, I agree. I would not like to have to rely on de Mowbray. He planted that scurry here, after all. He is Lefevre's man. And, of course, we are now his prisoners.'

'What about her?' Lukas nodded to the chair, not actually looking at Eleanor.

'I don't know. We'll have to give her time, as I said. She'll come round, if you try being careful for a change. What about it, Lukas?'

He shrugged, impatiently. 'It's not a tactic to use more than once. You know that.'

'Let's try and think this through without losing our tempers.' Blythe smiled slightly, although it was the last thing he felt like. 'She saw this light – and so did I. It has now disappeared. There can only be two explanations for this. Either the Moon has given up, lost the battle –'

'To hell with that!'

'Or – we don't need guiding any more. As the Moon said. Perhaps this is it. This is where we need to be.'

He spoke quietly, as if it were a secret. Then he knelt again by Eleanor's chair, and took her passive hand. 'Listen, Eleanor. You're going to be all right. I'll get you out of here, I won't leave you. You have nothing to fear from me, whatever it may look like. And remember this. Accepting failure is the worst thing of all. Nothing will be worse than what you feel now. You can choose a different path. You are free.'

Her eyes met his, aware once more. Moving convulsively, she put out a hand to reach him as he stood up, as if he were a lifeline.

'Don't go –'

'As I said before, this is not the end, for you or for me. Remember.'

He walked away, down the long ward to the double doors. They swung open as he approached, a line of guards outside, saluting as he passed through.

Lukas watched with amazement.

'Who *is* he? Whose side is he on?'

'He has his own battles to fight,' she said tiredly. 'I just – do trust him.' She had never sounded so lifeless before.

'Eleanor.' He took a step closer to her, and then stopped when she flinched, not looking at him.

'Immortality doesn't bring much in the way of wisdom, does it? I should never have said those things, or hit you. A classic case of becoming part of the problem not the solution.' She said nothing.

He tried again. 'It was nonsense for me to say it was your fault all those people died. You didn't ask to come here, how could you be responsible?'

'But I am.' At last she looked at him and he thought, this is what the Moon looked like in her dream. Dark eyes in a ruined face. 'I am responsible because I never once fully accepted what was happening here. I never realised, never even bothered to imagine, what immortality can do. We're not all monsters in my world, it's just me!'

He stood rock steady, watching, waiting.

'I know what you want,' she said. 'You want me to become involved just as you are, no hesitations, no doubts. But I'm not brave. I never have been. It's all too hard for me. I don't know what to do!'

'Oh my dear!' He ignored her shrinking back into the chair, moving swiftly across the floor towards her.

'Eleanor.' Again. Staring at her, dark against the window, willing her to look up.

At last she raised her head. His eyes, sky-bright, took her breath away with their intensity. His gaze held her steady, lending strength against the storm of emotion. As if wading through water, slow and heavy, she put out her hand to him and at once he reached out for her, gathering her up into his arms.

He held her tightly and, gradually, she began to relax against him. There was a curious half-smile on his face, the long mouth wry with self-knowledge, but she did not see that through the tears.

It was a moment of trust and forgiveness, and the conflict between them faded. The beginnings of a deeper trust would begin to grow, out of the ruins of rage and despair. It would be based on reconciliation.

It was not a bad foundation.

Chapter Ten
Cliokest

A whisper through the corridors, a shiver in the air.

'Lefevre! Lefevre's coming!'

The soldiers of Cliokest polished their swords, the priests in the Temple practised their chants, the cooks, skivvies, serving maids and waiters from the noisy kitchens braced themselves.

De Mowbray, in his room, sighed as the scurry departed, and ran his fingers through his hair. He needed help to understand all this, and although Lefevre's visit could not be worse timed in many respects, at least Lycias's priest would know what to do about his three unlikely prisoners.

He would almost certainly order their execution.

Blythe might be telling the truth: he might escape. De Mowbray was hedging his bets, playing the courteous host to Phinian Blythe. He had instructed scurries to watch him at all times, but hoped that the Peraldonian was indeed in Lefevre's pay, as he claimed. A trained soldier, Blythe would be useful to de Mowbray.

Lefevre would vouch for him. Or not.

The Caver was nothing more than a dangerously violent guerrilla. He would have to die. Perhaps it would be better to get it over before Lefevre arrived.

As for the girl . . .

An unknown quantity. From the scurry's account of her conversation she had given up. She was pretty enough. Perhaps he would find her a place on Cliokest, when she recovered. If Lefevre let her live.

Earlier than usual, this visit. Why was the High Priest coming this time? He had heard the official explanation, that Peraldonian territory was to be inspected before the new Emperor set out on his first tour. He did not believe it. Lefevre was unlikely to disturb himself for what would surely be a puppet Emperor. Could he be coming in response to his cry for help with the Parid? They were disturbing his dreams now, the shifting shapes of Sharrak, Lilith and Remule.

It was not easy, governing Lefevre's failures. He had needed the help of a qualified Mage to control them since the Stasis began. He wondered, not for the first time, what had happened to his old colleague, the Mage Gawne. He had been travelling in the northern territories long ago and had never returned. Marooned on the wrong side of the Boundary, no doubt. He had been adept at controlling the Parid. De Mowbray experienced a pang of envy. His own powers were at the most amateur level. But he knew enough to disguise his inadequacies, and no one realised that he was pushed to the limit by the Parid.

He took a comb from a drawer and straightened his hair. It would never do to appear less than immaculate.

Cliokest, his island fortress, would have to work late into the night to prepare itself for the High Priest's arrival. He would have a thousand things to organise and decide. Sharrak's captives were really a damn nuisance and a distraction. He had far too many other things on his mind. Sharrak had not taken kindly to his interference. Again, he longed fiercely for the services of a Mage.

He was not alone, however.

He sat up and rang the bell near his desk.

'Hamnet Lin,' he told his secretary, standing there. 'Send word to Lord Lin. I would be glad – no, I entreat him to honour us with his presence at dinner tonight. I know he will want to confer with the High Priest, tomorrow. Rooms will be prepared etc . . . His nephew, Phinian Blythe, is an unexpected visitor, and I feel sure they will have much to discuss before the festivities begin. May the Sun delight his life, etc, etc . . .' He looked at the neat little man standing at the door.

'Now, Greville. Don't waste time. We need Lin here. Now.' His voice, though soft as ever, had an unusual edge to it.

As the door closed, he leant back in the chair and regarded

the shining golden Mask of Lycias hanging on the wall opposite his desk.

The beautiful eyes, fine nose and faintly smiling lips seemed to mock his doubts.

'We shall see,' he said to himself. 'We'll see what's in the wind. At the very least, dinner this evening should be –' He smiled. 'Interesting.'

Standing on the highest tower of Cliokest, lifting his head, watching, scenting the air, listening for unusual sounds, Blythe tasted the flavour of de Mowbray's home.

Like a bizarre crystal the marbled towers and arches jutted out of the indigo sea. Turreted, crenellated, the walls were cream and gold, washed by sun and sea to gleaming brilliance. Russet tiles gave definition to the many different roof levels, pointed, conical, sloping, triangular and domed.

Small figures were moving far below him, in and out of the many courtyards, scrubbing and polishing, hanging awnings and flags, a mosaic of bright and active colour.

There was a causeway, broad and sandy, leading from Cliokest to the shore. Small boats were moored at its side, horse-drawn carriages and carts trundled along it, and he could just hear the bustle of shouting and conversation, the thumps and rattles as the carts were unloaded, the horses stabled, the passengers set down.

Graceful arching walkways joined the various towers and halls, and were flung further yet, high over the sea, supported by slim struts of metal. They reached far out into the mainland. There were guards stationed along these, and heavy gates at either end. Who used these portals, he wondered? Were they for Elfitt de Mowbray alone, to visit his appalling Parid?

The furthest of them spanned the calm bay, across the shore line and fertile valley to where an ugly tower jutted from a pine forest. Sharrak's lair, he thought. De Mowbray is in direct contact with the Parid at all times.

The tang of salt was clean and sharp. The waves lapped gently against the walls far below. The bay was calm and untroubled, peaceful apart from the bustle of activity in the castle.

It would be easy to feel comparatively at home here. De Mowbray had asked him to stay, to accept a commission in his guard.

'Peraldonian military training would be invaluable here,' he had said. 'It may all look peaceful, but there are certain difficulties . . .'

'The Parid?' Blythe had asked.

'Yes . . . and there are other factions. You have family in the region, Phin. Stay here with us . . .'

If one put aside the past, the legacy of grief, the hate and guilt that soured his every breath, then, yes, it would be a tempting offer. But just as the mountains rose, vast and jagged, their peaks lost in snow and cloud, casting long shadows over the calm bay, so did the evil of Lefevre loom heavy over his life.

There was no escape, no way out. He would have to see it through.

A voice, quiet and hollow, as Blythe strode through the corridors back to his room.

'The black wizard, I see . . .' A thin figure, grey and gaunt, a coloured cloak hanging in rags about him, stepped from the shadows. Old sad eyes looked at him.

'Marial! You survived!' Blythe moved to clasp his hand and then stopped, halted by the strangeness of the other's expression. His mouth was smiling, but the eyes . . . the eyes were black and tragic, and old. So old.

'How did you get away with it?'

'You see before you the latest addition to Lord de Mowbray's personal staff. I have been instructed to ensure your comfort. At your service, Captain Blythe.'

Marial bowed slowly from the waist, and Blythe knew that under the formal words despair was writhing within the man. 'Refugee from the wrath of Sharrak, rescued by a noble and gracious lord . . .' His mouth twisted, trembling on the edge of a moan. 'My reward and punishment. Look.' He moved his arms out from beneath his cloak.

He had no left hand. A greying bandage covered the stump. 'They took my harp,' he said, his voice still quiet, still hollow and expressionless. 'I didn't want to let go, but they made me . . .'

'Who?'

'The Parid. Remule . . . Sharrak . . .' He trailed off, eyes staring blankly ahead.

'De Mowbray stopped them. I belong to him now.'

He was only just lucid. He beckoned Blythe closer, his eyes scanning the wall beside them. 'The Arrarat . . . in a barn on the west side –' He shrank back, pointing with his good hand at the wall. A shadow flitted and froze there . . .

He gasped and shuddered, visibly trying to retrieve the shreds of control. 'I have been asked to inform you that your uncle, Lord Lin, will be dining here tonight. And . . .' he paused, directing his eyes once more to the shadowed wall. 'The High Priest of Lycias, Lord Lefevre, will arrive tomorrow. There are preparations to be made . . .'

He was too distressed to notice the shock in Blythe's eyes. He began to fish about in the folds of his ragged cloak, looking around as he did so.

'Dinner at eight tonight,' he said. 'Lord de Mowbray requests the pleasure of your company. Enjoy your meal, sir.' He held out his right hand, and Blythe took it. Another little bow, and Marial turned away, drifting like a dead leaf down the dark corridor back to the servants' quarters.

Later, in his room, Blythe emptied the little bag Marial had placed in his palm. A small blow pipe, such as a child might use, and three needle-sharp darts. And a glass phial, tightly stoppered. He smelt it, cautiously. A strong scent of herbs, concentrated and potent. Poison.

It was one way. He sighed, and slid the bag into his pocket.

He was glad he would be able to talk to Lin. He needed to know just what he would be risking in the path that lay before him.

Outside his room, with its rose-scented balcony and elegant furniture, across the bay and forested valleys, the mountains towered. A vast backdrop of rock and snow, they held the pretty bay and castle like a jewel in a casket.

In the sunlight the snow sparkled, far away. Bright and

dazzling like the mirrors of the cauldron it shone, reflected in the dark eyes of the Peraldonian standing, thoughtful, on the balcony. He was watching the flight of a bird dipping and soaring over the valleys, light and joyful. His mouth was straight and grim, his brow furrowed.

It was hard to imagine that he had once laughed, and loved.

Chapter Eleven
Hamnet Lin

The old man sitting alone in the guest apartments in the central wing of the palace was sweating, although the late afternoon was not hot. He looked down at his shaking hands and sighed. He wished he could have a drink. He could not cope with this. It was asking too much. Things were moving too fast.

The Stasis was at risk. Hamnet Lin, close observer of the path of Sun and Moon, had seen imbalance in his charts, chaos in his nightmares. Something irregular was occurring. The balance was no longer true.

Sacrifices had to be made, but not by Peraldonians. He was outraged by the chances now being taken. He had just learnt of Karis's death, that beautiful, laughing girl. De Mowbray had taken him aside on his arrival, and had briefly told him of the tragedy. 'Don't mention it to Phin,' he said. 'The trauma is still fresh . . .'

Up to this point only Cavers had suffered. That was their traditional role, one they had of necessity embraced through their foolish adherence to the Moon. But now the Stasis required the blood of Peraldonians, too. He knew Karis's death could not have been accidental.

Lefevre would know what to do, he comforted himself. He would have the answer. Thank God he was on his way.

De Mowbray was being malicious; gently smiling, he told Hamnet Lin all about his nephew's daring exploits with the Cavers. Undisturbed, Blythe watched the flickering candles, waiting. He knew that de Mowbray was trying to force a betrayal.

The dinner had started uneasily; Lin, plump and sweating,

drained his glass immediately, trying to blot out anxiety. He had clasped his nephew warmly, offering the triple kiss of close family relationship. His eyes were moist; for a moment Karis's name hung, unspoken, over them all.

'It should never have happened,' he muttered. 'Never, never. Things are going so wrong!'

'Tell us, Hamnet,' de Mowbray invited. They were seated at a table in his private quarters, overlooking the bay and mainland. The sun was setting, staining the sky red behind them, streaking the water with hectic colour.

De Mowbray had just lit the candles, and warm pools of light reflected on the silver dishes and crisp linen. Bowls of overblown roses stood at either end of the table, their petals dropping with elegance onto the cloth.

Lin began talking as if this were a continuing conversation.

'You see, I don't think you understand, I don't think you know *why* there is a Stasis!'

'The God chose immortality for His priest and people. Our great and good fortune.' De Mowbray was continuing to eat, unworried.

'But *why*? Why should He do so? Have you never thought, there must be more to it than that?'

'Yes,' said Blythe quietly. 'Yes, I had wondered . . .'

'Mariana,' said Lin. 'Do you know who Mariana is?'

'I seem to remember . . . didn't Lord Lefevre have a sister, when he first came to prominence in Peraldon?' De Mowbray looked up,. interested. 'Wasn't she at the wedding? The second wedding, Dorian and Therese. I'm sure that was Mariana. And didn't she cause quite a stir? There was some story about poor Therese being cast quite into the shade. I don't know what happened to her. She must surely have married. I imagine she lives retired somewhere –'

'I'll tell you what happened to Mariana.' Again, Lin drained his glass, and de Mowbray refilled it. He had dismissed the servants long ago.

'She was – is – the most beautiful woman in existence. If you had ever seen her, you might understand. There has never been a woman like that . . .

'The God – wanted her. Needed her. At the wedding she

was so pure. Faultless. It may seem unlikely, but He does not – just take. There is always choice. There must be. That is the essence.

'Lycias asked her if she would chose between Him and another, a mortal named Idas.

'Yes, I see his name is not unfamiliar to you.' A sharp glance at his nephew. 'You would not recognise in those empty eyes what he used to be . . . Mariana chose Idas. Not because he was in any way better, more handsome, more intelligent, more loving. None of those. How could he be more than a God? She chose him *because* he was mortal. Simply that. Because he would grow old with her, would understand and share her own mortality. Because, like her, he too would die one day. And she could not bear that the God would ever tire of her, as He surely would as time passed. She chose Idas.'

The candles wavering in the light evening breeze were the only movement around the table. The night was still and dark around the castle, the last rays of the sun staining the quiet sea.

Enthralled, they listened to a story never before articulated. Lin rushed on, terrified by the dangers of revealing such a secret.

'Lycias would not accept this. He asked Mariana if she would chose Him if she were also immortal.

'Of course, she said yes.

'He struck a bargain with her brother Lefevre. Immortality for all humanity, if Lefevre managed to entrap the Benu, the Bird of Time. Lefevre is – the first of all the Mages. He knows all their arts, the transforming skills, the theory of Synchronicity, the Twelve Rites: the greatest Mage there has ever been. He has wisdom unsurpassed, knowledge deeper than Time. With God-given power, he trapped the Benu. I don't know how, although I was there.' He shuddered. 'It does not do to remember that Rite . . . I still dream . . .' For a moment he closed his eyes before continuing.

'Frozen in a spiral of amber is the Bird of Time, so that Mariana should remain forever lovely for our Lord Lycias.

'That is the origin of our beloved Stasis, the benison of our eternal youth. It has its root in the great love of our

Lord – the prayers are right about that. That love, however, is for Mariana alone, not for us. What happens here is incidental. It is only a fiction, a consolation, our belief that the Sun God cares for us.

'The Stasis is maintained so that Mariana may eternally accept eternal love.'

There was a long silence. Then, unwillingly, Blythe spoke.

'What of the Lady Astret?'

'What, indeed?' Lin sighed. 'You will remember that the setting up of the Boundary bereft the Lady of effective power in Peraldonia. How can a God exist separated from Its believers? And you know why the Boundary was set up. The Moon is anathema to the Stasis; ever changing, waxing and waning, the Guardian of the Left-hand Path, the Secret of the Lady. She governs the cycles of life and death, the fertility and creativity of human imagination, the flux of existence. She is everything the Stasis is not. Lycias is Her implacable enemy.

'But Gods cannot die. She fights back all the time, insidious and compelling, and women become pregnant, and the Cavers continue to fight, and over and over again people are entranced by the mystery of Her silver light.

'It's better than the alternative.'

'What do you mean? What alternative?' De Mowbray's voice was unfamiliar with strain.

'If Lycias held total sway, time everywhere would be completely static. As in the Boundary. Imagine. The same instant forever. The God in timeless ecstasy, the knife in the wound, the mouth smiling, the wave breaking. It could all stop, now, just like that, if Astret were truly defeated. The balance must be maintained!'

'What would happen if the Stasis broke?' said Blythe.

The old man spread his hands, helplessly. 'No one knows. It would be the most terrible of risks. What I fear most of all, more even than a total Stasis, is that Lycias might take His revenge, as He did with Idas.'

The memory of Idas ached in Blythe's mind; like acid, corrosive and destructive, it had annihilated every loving impulse, every moment of laughter and joy. He no longer thought easily in terms of day to day life, of the possibility of happiness, because of Idas. Idas, Mariana's original choice.

'You know what Idas has become. The Lord God brought this about because Mariana had chosen him. He will not tolerate insult or rivalry. I for one cannot easily contemplate what will happen to us all, Peraldonians, Cavers, everyone, if Lycias decides we're at fault. For that reason alone I labour constantly, as does Lefevre, to maintain the Stasis, so that Lycias may love an immortal Mariana, so that we do not become frozen in amber like the Benu, or emptied of humanity like Idas.'

Again silence fell round the neglected table. Blythe had pushed his chair back, his face unseen in the shadow. Lin was still trembling, as if the telling had increased the pressure of anxiety. There was no relief in that story, no relief for any of them, caught in an uncontrolled Stasis.

'Why are you so worried, Lin? What's been going wrong?' de Mowbray asked sharply, trying to break the grip of fear.

'I don't know exactly. Undeniably, things are more unstable. It dates from the death of the Emperor Dorian. Karis becoming pregnant outside the calculation, dying . . . the escalating violence, the Fosca used without care or caution . . . it's all wrong. Thank God Lefevre is on his way. He'll know what to do.'

De Mowbray sighed, sophisticated and undisturbed, and clapped his hands, calling for more wine. Both men were relieved. It was someone else's responsibility, after all. They drank again, and began to eat, not noticing that Blythe remained wrapped in silence.

With the cheese, they began to discuss Eleanor and Lukas. Blythe had hardly touched the wine, knowing that any decision would be crucial, but even so he was not prepared for his uncle's reaction. With unconcealed excitement, Lin put his fork down.

'When did she arrive here? Exactly, to the hour!'

'I don't know the precise time, but it was presumably during the attack on the Ferry, about nine o'clock on the thirteenth . . .'

Why did they bother, he wondered. Time and dates to

give patterns to empty lives . . . the Cavers kept no such artificial scales.

'Oh God, yes, that would be it!' Lin took a long drink of the heady wine. De Mowbray leant back in his chair, regarding the fat old man trembling across the table.

'The Stasis, of course! That's when it all started to go so badly wrong. It was already unsteady by then, but after she arrived the balance began to swing the other way. The Moon was in the ascendant . . . You'll have to kill her, and that Caver, too. Better do it now, before the High Priest gets here. I can't imagine what you think you're doing, letting them live!'

'She's given up,' said Blythe quietly. This was worse than he had expected. 'She's too frightened to interfere any further –'

'The very fact of her existence is enough to distort the balance! Take my advice, Elfitt, get rid of her now!'

'It would be rather a waste,' De Mowbray smiled, looking down at his fine, elegant hands. 'She's not unattractive. I've no doubt I could find a niche for her somewhere . . .'

'Madness! And Lefevre here tomorrow! The whole balance is being upset, and it's so difficult, God, it's so difficult to maintain it! You've got no idea what it involves. That's why it needs a Mage of Lefevre's stature to control it!'

'What *does* it involve, Hamnet? Just what does Lefevre do to maintain the Stasis?' De Mowbray leaned forward, curiously watching his friend.

The old man pushed his plate away, and again drank deeply. 'Checks and balances, weights and measures . . .' The double chins wobbled against the starched collar of his shirt. 'You just don't realise . . . It's all a question of balance. Life and death. Cavers don't matter, because they belong to Astret. Their deaths are insignificant, outside the calculation; they share the immortality more by accident than anything. But because they keep fighting, keep causing the deaths of Peraldonians, Lefevre invented the Fosca. Did you know that? They fight for Lefevre solely to save Peraldonian lives –'

'Why, then, did they kill Karis?'

Blythe could not let this pass. He was standing by the window, his back to them.

'Because the Stasis is unstable. She should never have become pregnant! Something must have happened to the Benu.' Lin's voice was shaking with fear. 'Things like that should never have to happen, if the Stasis is being properly controlled.'

'Could Lefevre have lost the Benu?' This was crucial.

'I am very much afraid that that is what has happened. A theft, treachery . . .' De Mowbray stood up, moving to the door. 'They must die. I'll give the order,' he said. 'There is no other choice.'

'Stop!' Blythe swung round, dark eyes flashing at them. De Mowbray paused, his hand on the bell-pull.

'You object, Blythe? Why?' So cool, his voice, so calm.

'There's no need.' Blythe kept his voice level. 'She's an innocent, she has no idea what's going on.'

'That is questionable, at best. And the Caver is dangerous, you must agree . . .'

'Let him go. Back to his grim little rebels and their sad Moon Lady. They won't bother you again. The girl will probably go with him happily enough.'

'I can't risk it. Not after what your uncle has said.'

'You might at least talk to her! She may have useful information!'

'Are you indeed working for our noble Lord Lefevre, Phin, or have you another axe to grind? I would be sorry to think that you were taking a different path . . .' It was gently said, and Blythe replied in the same manner, biting back the words.

'Astret is defeated.' He shrugged. 'There is no other path. The Cavers are almost certainly wiped out, the Jerenites on their knees. There can be no necessity for these executions.'

'Phin, don't imagine that the Cavers and Jerenites are Astret's only supporters!' Lin was spluttering with passion, wine dribbling down his chin. 'The Riders of the Plains, the fishing communities of the north – if the Boundary fails, as it will if the Benu is free, then Peraldon will be under threat from all sides! But –' here he turned to de Mowbray, still standing by the door, his hand on the bell pull. 'Elfitt, I would appreciate the chance to talk to them, before they die. Phin may be right. There could be information of interest.'

De Mowbray paused, considering. 'Very well,' he said. 'There will be time in the morning. Sharrak can have them after that. We need not bother Lefevre with them.'

There was at least something for which to be grateful.

Chapter Twelve
Escape

Armed guards accompanied Blythe back to his quarters. He heard them stand to attention outside his door and below his balcony. He knew there would be scurries in his room, that his every movement would be reported. He had given too much away in his anxiety, and next day Lefevre would confirm him as traitor and spy.

Lukas and Eleanor would not be the only ones to die.

He stood at the balcony watching the lights of Cliokest winking all around him, reflected in the still waters of the bay. The light in his mind had disappeared, had vanished when he dropped in Sharrak's pit. He had taken it to mean that Astret was indeed defeated.

Lukas did not believe it. He had spent the long ages of the Stasis refusing to accept defeat. His anger with Eleanor earlier that day had been the explicit result of this refusal.

The Moon was rising over the horizon, gleaming in the cloudless sky. Would this pale clear disc be the only reminder of Astret's mystery for them all now? The harmonious dance of time, the flow of life and death, the rhythm of existence, with all its extraordinary variety, would it all be held sterile and meaningless as the cold unchanging rock in the sky?

There is grace in the pattern of life and death, he thought. Everything should be fluid, subject to change and alteration. To seize the moment, to grasp it, holding it back from change, is the essence of sterility.

There is grace in death.

Even in Karis's death.

A final act of giving, it had been. A transfiguration of death so that he might understand the nature of evil.

So that he might understand and rejoice in the warm generosity of her love.

One could not hold love still, entrapped in amber. One had to let it go, let it change and grow, and then there may be something real. Something of beauty. And if at first the grace is not recognised, it is not so surprising. After all, the caterpillar cannot understand the butterfly.

His hands lay loose on the window sill, empty and open.

Let it go. Let it fly free, love and life. As a bird soars, as the mind leaps in imagination, as love bridges the lonely distances.

The only power lies in freedom.

For a moment he did not see that there were figures on the walkway leading from the bay to Sharrak's tower.

The pale moonlight glinted on something, a flash of red gold moving slowly along the slender bridge.

Eleanor. A tall figure beside her, his arm around her shoulder. Armed soldiers in front and behind.

De Mowbray had lied. Lin would not be given a chance to talk to Lukas and Eleanor before they died, for they were going to die that night.

Calmly, without pause, he went to the wardrobe and changed into dark clothes, keeping Marial's gift near to hand. Then, before the scurries had a chance to report anything, he vaulted over the balcony, landing in the midst of the soldiers below, and began to run.

Alarms and shouting, the shriek of swords drawn from scabbards, chairs and tables overturned, running feet and flapping cloaks.

Silent as a cat, fast as winking, he dodged them all, skidding across the parapet to a sloping roof, sliding down it and then jumping, hands reaching for the gutter at the other side, high over the waves below.

It broke as he hung from it, lurching diagonally down, and he leapt again, using its plunging arc as a swing. This time a window sill held, and in moments he had both feet up on it, his hands braced against the frame, kicking the glass so that it shattered into the room.

A hail of arrows clattered around him, but too late. Glass

ripping his clothes, he was in a bedroom, running across rich carpets while a woman screamed, blundering into furniture, crashing through the door.

Stairs. More guards, so he used the blow pipe, primed long ago, dropping the nearest. He seized a sword from the slack hand and began to wield it, forcing them back, and then, when it seemed he would follow through his advantage of surprise, suddenly turning and running crazily down a side passage.

More men, bewildered and aggressive, and again he was through, hurtling down corridors, skidding round corners, doubling back, through doors, windows and skylights. There were long passages and sudden spaces, hallways and offices, and always he was one jump ahead, and men stared at him in surprise, even as the alarm bells rang.

Then his way was blocked more successfully, but his sword was true and strong, and his will adamant. He would not be delayed. He would not allow Eleanor and Lukas to die in that terrifying well. Reckless, heedless of death or injury, he exploded out into the night.

Silence. Had he really lost them, or was it a trap? He dared not stop running, and he knew where to go. Not along the walkway, there were too many guards there, but round the perimeter of Cliokest, to where a lofty barn stood, far away on the rocks jutting out into the sea.

To where the Arrarat waited, high on rafters, communing with unimaginable worlds.

Through the moonlit night he could just see the barn, its heavy wooden door barred, its windows small and shuttered. Uniformed men stood to attention outside.

Blythe was below one of the towers, standing on rock in the shadow, his feet washed by waves. He was gasping for breath after the run, leaning against the warm brick. With the power of Astret directing his every move, he called to them, borrowing the cry he had heard so often. It was almost lost in the soft sound of the sea all around. He waited, sweat cooling in the sea breeze, listening all the time for the sounds of pursuit.

There was a scream, suddenly tearing through the night.

Shocked, the guards ran to the door, lifting the crossbar, cautiously peering round it.

They could see nothing. From their hesitation Blythe knew that they were anxious and on edge. Two of them, swords drawn, went further into the black depths of the barn, and then there were shrieks, cries of agonised terror.

In a flurry of feathers and beating wings, two vast black shapes surged out of the door, slashing and clawing with utmost force at the other men, until they had all fallen, torn ragged by the hooked beaks and strong claws.

Violence transformed to grace, the Arrarat leapt up into the cooling air.

He could have wept with relief. With the Arrarat free anything was possible. He stood quite still, hearing the footsteps thundering through the building at his back. He had no need to run now.

Astrella wheeled off into the night and it was Ash who came for him, as he had come once before to save Blythe from the Cauldron.

With incredulous gratitude, he stroked once the ebony feathers at the neck, and the great hawk inclined his head, inviting him to mount.

He was not graceless now.

He could not understand the Arrarat's thoughts, but knew that the hawk would make straight for Eleanor. He held on, remembering the scene he had witnessed from his balcony, of Lukas and Eleanor on the walkway, hoping the Arrarat would understand and follow the lead.

Ash leapt swiftly from the rocks, following the path taken by Astrella. Stretching his wings wide, swallowing up distance with every beat, they sped across the bay towards Sharrak's lair.

His heart could have sung for joy. Would they be in time?

Lukas's arms were so strong and warm about her that the trembling was almost stilled. She felt his breath in her hair, a gentle murmur that the guard would not hear.

'Can you swim, Eleanor?'

Faintly, she nodded. Again, his voice, soft, and she could have sworn with the suggestion of a laugh in it.

'Dive?' Again she nodded. 'Brave girl. Now, a quick prayer to Astret that the water's deep enough. When I count three, up and over you go. Then stay deep as long as you can. I'll find you. Ho for the shore and freedom . . .' His arms tightened briefly.

There was only a short distance left before they reached the end of the bridge.

'One two three –' he said rapidly, and then his arms were no longer around her and she was jumping at the high sides, scrambling and clutching, kicking out at the man who leapt for her ankle, slithering out of his grip and over, falling in a chaotic heap.

Unprepared, she hit the water badly and lost all her breath. It was a barrier of cold iron. She gasped, under the wall of water now, and her lungs filled with salt. Terrified, threshing, she kicked helplessly and then her collar was seized and she was dragged spluttering to the surface.

'Thought you said you could dive?' Lukas, supporting her as she struggled for breath, coughing and choking.

They were beneath the walkway itself, far into the shadow. She could hear shouting above, and lights swung out over the water. No one had followed them. She wondered why.

The same thought had occurred to Lukas. He was turning in the water, looking all around.

'Socially unacceptable, are we?' he murmured. 'Where is everyone?'

There was laughter from the men above.

'To the shore, now!' She did not look round, did not follow the line of his sight to the black swirl of water approaching them across the bay, broken by triangular fins.

His voice terrified her. There was no possibility of disobeying. She stretched her arms out, reaching into the sea, swimming swiftly towards the narrow sandy beach ahead. She did not see the snapping teeth, the sharp fins and small eyes of the great sharks cutting through the water.

For a moment Lukas trod water, gauging their speed and numbers. He had no weapon, no defence. His cloak hung heavy with water from his shoulders. He took it off, holding it by one corner.

There was one shark, larger than the others, a massive scarred blue-black creature, pushing forcefully through the sea. If he could delay it a little, Eleanor would have time to get to the shore. The others were further behind. She would be safe before they reached her.

He tried the old talisman, calling the Arrarat. Astrella's summoning, out over the dark waves, over the sound of rushing water. Then he swam back until he was further under the walkway, waiting behind one of the struts.

It made straight for him, mouth hanging just a little open, pointed teeth meeting in a wide downward grin. He dared it, treading water to the side of the strut, one hand holding the ridged metal. And then the shark slammed at him and he jumped, pulling himself up and out of the water.

It surged after him, teeth gaping, but he had swung round the side of the metal ridge and its jaws met uselessly on air.

Just out of the water, he let the cloak swirl out, spreading wide over the surface, so that the fish below would not be able to see him. For a while the shark was bewildered, the fin's triangle cutting back and forth around the black water, and then it worked out what to do and swam directly into the cloth, brushing it aside.

His grip was failing on the smooth metal. Inexorably, he was sliding back down into the water. As it jumped again, he lashed out with his foot and caught it a glancing blow on the snout. Its teeth ripped through the leather of his boot, just furrowing the skin. He felt the blood warm against the cool water and knew it would bring the others.

Again he tried to pull himself up, wrapping both arms round the metal, bringing his knees and feet up, braced against it. It almost worked. He cleared the water, a couple of feet away from the swirling shape below. As he watched it appeared to swell, to change form, rising up from the water. A familiar stench struck him . . . Parid.

He looked back. Eleanor had reached the shore. And a dark hawk was swooping through the air towards her, Ash, the glorious ebony Arrarat.

Astrella would soon be here, but he was already beginning to slip again and the turmoil in the water below was boiling with energy. As he pulled the cloak away from the surface of the water, he saw rearing out of it, a shifting miasma of tentacles and teeth, swollen belly bulging, mouth gaping . . .

He inched further up the strut, forcing himself to hold on. A whistle of air and there she was, swerving beneath the walkway, hurtling fast and sure through the struts.

His hands were cramping, his arms on fire. He flung himself away from both sea and metal, launching himself into the air, trusting to skills lovingly learnt so long ago.

She caught him, as she had always done, one wing skimming, dipping into the water as she took the risk, and he was safe, his arms clasped around the warm grey feathers, the welcome and joy delighting his heart.

'Took your time!' he shouted across the dark air as the Arrarat hawks banked high away from the waters of Cliokest's bay.

A laugh from Phin, his arms secure around Eleanor.

'Ungrateful! Which way?'

'South!' He pointed to the wide range of mountains around the bay, and the hawks curved in their flight out beyond the line of the bay, out to sea, avoiding the highest ranges.

The night was warm and scented with sea and flowers. Once more they journeyed on, leaving the bright towers of Cliokest in its pretty, jewel-like bay, and the sharks all around snarled their disappointment.

The morning, bright, clear and calm, drew her to wakefulness. It was very early, the air still slightly chilled.

Eleanor rolled over and out of the shelter of Lukas's cloak, slung as a tent over her, as so often before. The others further away were still asleep.

For a moment she looked over to Lukás, wondering at the chances that had brought them together.

When Blythe had left them alone in that long room amongst the broken glass and spilt water, she had felt abandoned, in a state of utter despair and loneliness, thrust there by Lukas's words.

And yet, with the same vivid power, he had shown her

that an alternative existed. Commitment and love were to him inseparable. One step towards commitment would be enough: the world would be transformed, just as it had when Astret had met her in the centre of the shining labyrinth.

She was nervous, apprehensive of taking such a step; but as so often before, alternatives were falling away. She could no longer exist here and not be involved. That path was wrought with despair. She was also beginning to realise that she could not exist here without love. Perhaps they were the same.

Lukas had not touched her beyond the comfort one gives a child. She watched the loose curl of his long fingers on the sand and thought, perhaps, that it would not be long.

The Arrarat brought them fish for breakfast. There was driftwood for the fire and the air was crystal clear, sharp and delightful. The smooth sand glistened, tiny creamy shells defined by light, while the shallow sea, gently turning and returning, ceaselessly washed the sand.

They had flown through the night, swinging out over the sea, rounding the jagged headland. In the starry dark she had seen a fragmented coastline, deep fjords scattered with a thousand islands, mountains rising high around them.

The Arrarat had flown through the long drowned valleys and ravines, flying round, not over, the mountains, for the air was cooling and their clothes damp and thin. Always south, further yet from Cliokest, further into the unknown regions of Rassalt.

In the darkest hour of the night they had put down on a sandy beach. Staggering with weariness, Eleanor waited while Lukas and Phin rigged the cloak as a tent. It hardly seemed necessary, for the sky was cloudlessly clear. Lukas had joked, light-hearted and exuberant, and for once Phin replied in kind.

As usual, they left her alone to sleep. So often in the journey from Jeren, she had crawled into the shelter of the black cloak, numb with weariness, and was asleep before they joined her. In the cold and wet regions, further north, they had all stayed close together, trying to keep warm. As they travelled further south, both Phin and Lukas slept in the open.

She had fallen asleep immediately, as soon as her head touched the sand pillow.

After breakfast, watching the gulls over the water, Blythe told them about Mariana and how the Stasis began. His voice was calm and even, although she could not see his face clearly. Instead she watched Lukas, the fine long fingers idly tracing patterns in the sand.

As always, he was relaxed, the long limbs sprawled gracefully against sand and rock. There were shadows beneath his eyes, but the vivid azure gleamed with fascination as Blythe told them about Mariana's choice.

Dark-lashed, he looked from the patterns up to Blythe. Unfairly, the eyes were both candid and revealing, until one realised that in fact they betrayed only passion.

A passionate, unaltering obsession to end the Stasis.

'What will happen if we succeed? If we find the Benu and end the Stasis?' Eleanor found herself asking.

Blythe looked at her. 'My uncle, Hamnet Lin, is scared to death of just that. Lycias would take His revenge, you see.'

'Could it be worse than the Stasis?' Lukas stood up, looking out at the gentle sea and clear sky. He spoke again with his back to them, his voice sombre. 'No possibility of life or renewal. Ultimate loneliness for us all. There is no love, no peace, nothing natural and easy between people, nothing created, changing or growing.'

'There has been love . . .' Blythe, speaking so low that she could hardly hear him.

'But Karis died, didn't she?' The words sounded harsh, but the look in his eyes was one of anger. He had his own methods. 'Anything good, anything fine dies under the terms of the eternal Stasis. You know this, Phin! You don't need me to say it! What possible revenge could be worse?'

'You would risk it, then?'

'What do you think I'm doing here?'

Of course. He would risk anything to break the Stasis. It was partly love for Astret; she had seen him watching the Moon too often to discount that. But mainly it was an instinctive hatred for the iron forcing bands which lay round every relationship, round every part of Static life. The Boundary was almost the least of it.

'Eleanor.' Phin was looking at her. 'May I borrow Ash? For a few hours?'

'He is not mine to lend,' she said. She was learning. 'He will come if the cause is right. Where are you going?'

'To Cliokest.'

'For heaven's sake! Why?' She couldn't believe it.

'Because Lefevre is there. The architect of the Stasis will have arrived by now. I have unfinished business with him.

'You'll never do it alone.' Lukas looked at him. 'Want company?'

'No, Lukas. Not you. Your role is different –' He spoke slowly, holding at the back of his mind Selene's instruction. When the Bird is found, you must kill it. Let them find it first, he thought. And then he would follow that puzzling command. Or not . . .

Lukas was still watching him. 'What do you mean?'

'You have to find the Benu, remember? Eleanor's great quest, and yours, if you take your brother's advice.'

'I don't know what this quest is, now that the light has gone, and Astret said we should go no further, anyway . . .' Eleanor trailed off into uncertainty.

'Won't Lefevre have the Benu safe somewhere?' Lukas asked.

'Apparently not. The Stasis is unstable at the moment, and if Lefevre had control of the Benu there would be no question of instability.

Lukas smiled. 'Good, we must be doing something right.'

'It's not that simple. Astret could be totally defeated, with the Benu lost. This is an uneasy limbo until someone finds it.'

'A free-for-all? With control of the Stasis as the prize?'

'Yes. I intend to remove one of the protagonists, that's all.'

'If Lefevre does not have the Benu, why kill him, Phin? Revenge?' No one but Lukas would have dared to say it, she thought.

'Is that so wrong?' Blythe held his eyes. 'Isn't there rather a lot on Lefevre's account now?'

'Yes. Rather a lot.'

'You must be mad! You can't go back, Phin, they'll kill

you as soon as you set foot in the place!' Eleanor clutched at his sleeve.

'Marial is there.' He almost said something else, but stopped.

'If you have time to find him! Phin, don't go! Please don't go back!' She had never asked anyone to stay in her other life, she thought. No one had ever mattered enough.

He stood there on the sunlit beach, the light breeze lifting the dark curls, looking at the sea, undisturbed as ever. He was a million miles distant from her, and her hands still lay on his sleeve. She took them away. He said nothing.

'You can't stop him, Eleanor,' said Lukas, watching her, frowning. 'Take Astrella, Phin. Look, she's waiting for you . . .'

At the waters' edge, ruffling her soft grey feathers in the sun, Astrella stood patiently.

Blythe smiled, and bending, lightly kissed the top of her head. 'Have a little holiday, Eleanor,' he said. 'I'll be back soon.'

She stepped away from him, then. 'Goodbye, Phin,' she said.

Alone he walked across the sand to Astrella.

In seconds man and bird were no more than a vanishing point in the clear sky, and she turned away, back to Lukas.

His face was unreadable in the soft light.

'I think this is an island,' he said calmly. 'Shall we explore?'

Chapter Thirteen
The Beach

'Look at this!' Lukas's voice, triumphant. She crossed the dunes to join him on the remains of a long-deserted landing stage. The planks were rotten and uneven beneath her feet, stained green with water.

He was crouching at its edge, pointing into the depths. Carefully she pushed back her hair, staring down into the water. A shadowy shape hung there, smooth and dark.

'A boat!' he said, kicking off his boots, splashing into the water, reaching down for it.

'Idiot. You're soaked!'

'Eleanor! Just think, we could go fishing!' He was only half laughing, intent on rescuing it.

'That's your idea of a holiday?'

'Isn't it yours?' he answered, but he wasn't really listening to her reply, stripping off his shirt before returning to the wreck.

He was up to his waist in water, pulling at the boat, white skin gleaming in the sunlight, muscles rippling across his shoulders. He was covered in the scars of old wounds. The most recent, on his wrist, still showed red and vivid. He had been through so much, for so long. Ceaseless warfare, constant anxiety for the length of the Stasis. He had lived an alien, appalling life, on the edge of dangers she was at last beginning to understand.

How could he still smile, pulling a boat from water?

She stood up and moved away from the landing stage back to the dunes, wandering through the gentle, warm mounds.

It would be easy to get this all wrong, she thought. She should have joined him, of course, helped him pull the boat up. But she hadn't wanted to, paralysed by this sense of his strangeness. How ridiculous, after they had been through so much together.

But here there was nothing to do. No heroic venture, no decisions to take, nowhere to go. The light had gone from her mind, and she did not know what to do next.

They had followed the beach all round the island. Some three miles in circumference, it was little more than a large rock surrounded by dunes. A few scrubby trees grew around a small rainwater pool, coarse grass and small pink flowers she did not recognise. It was calm, warm, quiet and safe.

They need only exist in the sun and sea, sheltered by dunes, and get to know each other, waiting. She was terrified.

Take a holiday, Phin had said.

It was hot. Lukas was far away. She took off the silky shirt given to her on Cliokest, and then immediately put it on again. She couldn't handle this.

Crossly she kicked at the sand. A glint of colour caught her eye. She knelt down and picked up a small creamy shell, warm gold glowing from its intricate interior. It matched the one in her pocket. She had always liked shells. And sand castles. She used to be good at seaside holidays. She kicked off her shoes and hitched up her skirt, tying it up at one side.

She began to wander along the shoreline again, in the dreamy contented way common to all beachcombers, and started to collect shells.

The sandcastle was almost finished by the time Lukas came to find her. It was a splendid one, two moats, spiral towers and elaborate bridges. She had arranged shells in patterns all over it and was sitting back on her heels regarding it with satisfaction.

'Nice,' he said, coming up behind her. 'But the moats won't get filled here, the tide's going out.'

'I know. It's just a prototype. The real castle will be over there –' she pointed across the sand to a small sheltered bay between outcrops of rock. 'There's a rock pool there –' she said. 'We can use it to fill the moats, and there are plenty of shells for decoration.'

'We?' He was laughing. 'You want company in this

project? I thought we might get into some serious boat repairs. Or a real house. There's a cave set in the rock further inland –'

'And it feels just like home?' She smiled at him. His jeans were drying, his shirt slung round his waist, his feet still bare. He grinned at her.

'Not quite,' he said. 'But it might be useful for storing things –'

'What things? Food, clothing, bedding, cooking utensils, books . . . all the things we're so cluttered and burdened by, that so badly need shelter and protection?'

She held up her empty hands, and looked round at the deserted beach.

He joined her in laughter. 'Of course,' he said, 'we could have a summer house here on the beach, and spend our time making the said utensils and clothing to put in the cave. And then we'll construct whole cities of sandcastles, working our fingers to the bone all day long, until the sun sets –'

'And then what will we do?' She was on her feet, gazing up at him, breathless with laughter and relief.

For a moment he paused in mid-flight. A shuttered look fell over his face. 'Eat, drink and make merry,' he said, but the sparkle had disappeared and Eleanor felt suddenly as if the sun had gone in.

She turned and walked quickly back to the sea, pretending to look for shells, not looking back.

Jocasta had died, she thought. It was not that long ago. And there was the Stasis, destroying everything. And all his life of fighting and hardship. He had nothing to give her. She was only a nuisance, a means to an end. He stayed with her only because of Astret and Matthias.

Depression settled in and the soft murmur of waves failed to soothe. More out of habit than anything else, she began to gather shells again, filling her pockets, while tears blurred her sight, and loneliness ached in her soul.

Chapter Fourteen
The Bargain

Flying in low, at sea level, Astrella put her passenger down amongst the lonely warehouses on the northern side of Cliokest. Blythe slid off the soft grey feathers, expecting the hawk to take off straight away, but Astrella stood there, patiently cocking her head to one side in enquiry.

He looked around, one hand resting on her neck. They stood in an empty area between rows of large buildings. Passages radiated out from where they stood and dust hung in the warm still air. It was completely deserted, no sound, no movement.

Tall double-doors to his left led to a huge, silent store-room, filled with sacks of grain, shelves of bottled preserves, dried meats hanging from hooks. He understood then why Astrella had waited.

The traditional role of the Arrarat, taking food to Cavers. Smiling to himself, he emptied out two grain sacks and filled them with an assortment of food. He even thought to put in candles, found in boxes on a low shelf. Another room was stacked with barrels and wine bottles, so he put a selection of those into the sacks too.

He returned to Astrella, lashing the two sacks together, and gently set them over her neck, tying them to the leather strap. Briefly she rubbed her head against his hand and then with a rush of air leapt up into the midday sun.

He set off down the central passageway, back to the heart of Cliokest. He still carried the sword taken from the guard he had killed with the first blow-pipe dart. There were two darts left.

He moved silently, keeping to the shadows, but every now and then he noticed a shape shifting across the walls as they were distorted by the presence of a scurry.

Soon he would have a fight on his hands.

A shadow whispered past him; a sword shrieked from a scabbard and armed guards stepped out from a hidden alcove.

He swung round, but a door opened behind him, and there were more men there.

Hard eyes regarded him implacably. He wondered whether it was worth resisting when they stood aside, purple cloaks swirling in the sharpness of the movement.

Blythe felt a sudden dread, a drop in the temperature that robbed him of breath.

'Captain Blythe,' said a voice from the shadows, sending the air writhing from its sound. 'I am glad to see you safe. We have matters to discuss.' A tall figure stepped into the dim light and regarded him evenly. Paralysed, Blythe failed to move.

One of the guards moved forward and took the sword from his nerveless hand. Then there was another voice from the door at the side.

'You've met before?' De Mowbray was standing just inside, calmly watching.

'Yes,' said Idas slowly. 'We've met. I know Phinian Blythe. Intimately.'

Fool, thought Blythe to himself. He had been prepared for capture, had even waited for it, including it in his plan.

The terror he had discovered in Idas's power was as potent as ever. In his small prison he was sweating in anticipation of the next encounter. He had planned a simple, suicidal manoeuvre based on deceit and bribery. He would lead Lefevre on, pretending to have been swayed by his uncle's arguments. If that didn't work, he would use information about Eleanor and Lukas as bait. All he needed was a few seconds with his hands free in Lefevre's company.

Casually, Idas had scanned the outer surfaces of his mind, quicker than a body search, and had discovered the blow-pipe and darts. Although it had not gone deep, Blythe found his hands clammy at the memory of that brutal, raking assault. Time spent in Lefevre's company would be useless now, hands free or not. He had no weapon.

No potential bargaining counter. Nothing he could use.

To have your thoughts and memories stolen was the ultimate violation. He could not stand it again.

He sat in a small prison at the top of a high tower. No furniture; straw on the floor, a jug of water, a bucket. The only window was six inches square and set twelve feet above his head. The walls were solid blocks of stone, the door of wood so heavy that it didn't give, no matter how hard he kicked. Iron hinges, iron bars.

Somewhere, far away, he could hear the sea.

He knew the tower was high because footsteps ascended a long staircase when anyone came. Scurries brought food daily. Silently they distorted the tray, the door, the stone, whilst armed men stood impassive round the wall.

He had been there three days before the first of his visitors arrived.

Soft, springy steps one night, unlike the heavy tread of soldiers. A key turned quickly, quietly, in the lock and a bolt was drawn.

A flood of light and a familiar figure standing there, putting the lantern on the floor, the leathery face smiling, underlit by brightness.

'Oh God, Uther!' Unthinking, in an instant he had crossed the narrow tower, arms held wide. They embraced and then stood apart, regarding each other.

'Well, now,' said Uther. 'You're looking better than when I last saw you but I can't say I'm glad to find you here.'

'Uther, what happened to you?' Blythe was remembering the quay outside his home, the flooding light and Uther absorbed into brightness.

'A couple of sessions with Idas and they thought I was in the bag,' said Uther carelessly. When you looked into the eyes, you could tell, thought Blythe. Like a stain, the experience of evil cannot be disguised.

'I'm on Lefevre's personal staff now. There's irony for you.'

'What are you doing here?' Blythe had stepped back, watching the wiry figure, neat in purple and gold uniform.

Uther smiled. 'I've got keys,' he said, waving them. 'Shall we go?'

'A weapon would be useful . . .'

'Lord, man, what are you waiting for? They're all urgent to find the Benu. It'll be Idas for you before you know it.'

'What do you mean?'

'Why do you think you're still here, cooped up in a high tower? You're being kept on ice, until they've got the time to give you a thorough going-over. Lefevre thinks you know where the Benu is.'

'What? He's out of his mind!'

There was a pause. The well-remembered face gazed at him curiously. 'You don't know? You really have no idea?'

'What is this, Uther? What are you up to?'

'Don't you trust me?' The cry spanned years of comradeship and loyalty and for a moment Blythe almost pushed aside the growing doubt.

'Uther! For God's sake!' But he stood still by the wall, watching. Evil stains, he thought. Blythe knew it well, but somehow had survived, was still resisting it. Why should not Uther be the same?

'Get me a weapon, Uther,' he said. 'A knife, preferably . . . and then show me where Lefevre's quarters are.'

'Madness! You'll never get near him!'

'I'm not leaving Cliokest until he's dead.'

'Give it up, man. There's nothing for you that way. Let's just get out of here –'

'And go where?'

'To your friends, of course. They'll be wondering what's happened to you . . .'

'No. Don't you understand? I need to be here. I'm not leaving.'

'You don't want to find the Benu?' Already the little man was edging towards the door.

Blythe stood still. 'Uther. For the last time. For the sake of friendship. Remember Karis? And what our life was before she died? Get me a weapon and then I'll come with you. I've unfinished business here –' He stopped. The look in the steady grey eyes across the room was kind, as Lefevre had been kind.

'I haven't forgotten,' he said. 'The Lady Karis died because the Stasis was under threat. The threat that grew from the loss of the Benu. The only importance is to find it, so that the Lord Lefevre can govern the Stasis once more.'

'You too, Uther? Under the spell? God, what does it take to make people realise what the Stasis is?'

He was standing, impassive, by the door. 'Idas will come soon,' he said. 'Your uncle asked that I should be sent to try first. But now it will have to be Idas. And you really will have to tell them where the Benu is then. This would have been a better way.'

He picked up the lantern and left the tower. The key turned in the lock and Blythe was alone once more.

There had been scurries round the wall all the time. He could not have believed Uther, whatever he said, accompanied by scurries. He was Lefevre's man, corrupted by Idas to serve the High Priest.

In grief for a lost friend, he began to pace the tower. After a while he stopped, leaning against the wall, his head resting on crossed forearms.

Would it be his fate, too?

That night he dreamed of footsteps following him, matching his own tread. Echoing his movements and his direction. Going the same way, always the same, and no way out.

Idas's footsteps, they were. Trampling through his mind, through the hidden pathways of memory, looking for information he knew he didn't have.

In the morning, Phinian Blythe watched a spider drop from a shining thread down the wall from the window. He had no premonition of disaster.

It crept across the floor to where he sat against the wall, knees drawn up. Only then did he draw in his breath with shock, as the stink of putrefaction surrounded him.

A laugh, and then it was there, full sized, golden hair flowing out from the pretty triangular face, the web of light bleeding into the air around.

He was on his feet now, back to the wall, waiting.

'Well met, Phinian Blythe,' said Sharrak. 'I had not thought to see you again so soon. Perhaps you are wishing now that you had stayed in my well. I understand that Idas is coming for you . . .'

He said nothing.

'I have a bargain for you, Phinian. I will help you escape, I and my friends' – for a moment its form wavered, sketching, suggesting a tusked creature, a sinuous great fish – 'will save you from Idas. If you do one thing for me . . .'

His mind was searching around, trying to make sense of the flickering shapes before him, trying to work out what it could possibly want.

'Kill Marial,' it said, the warm voice flat and colourless. 'De Mowbray has taken him, but he's mine. My servant, turned traitor. Kill him for me, Phinian, and you shall have freedom.'

'Are you so powerless? Surely you can do this for yourself?' He could not understand the request.

The early morning sun, creeping in through the tiny window, showed its body opaque as clouded glass. Huge eyes swimming with sincerity gazed at him. He wished that it would not hold its hands clasped together under the chin like that.

Sharrak would not answer him. It stared at him, moving through the air towards him, gold dripping like acid from the soft hands.

He almost retched. 'I will not bargain with such as you.'

'Your choices are limited. Idas will destroy you, this time. You know it. There is no hope unless you allow me to help.'

'If you can get me out, you can deal with your own traitors.'

Another pause. 'You don't understand . . .' it said, frowning. 'Just believe me . . . One day, you may find out the truth. If there is anything of you left after Idas.'

He closed his eyes, blotting out the blurred, heart-shaped face in its corrosive glow.

Idas. All paths lead to Idas, Mariana's original choice. He would do anything to escape Idas. Almost anything.

He would rather Sharrak had asked for de Mowbray's death, or Lefevre's. Or even Idas's. Something heroic and difficult. But Marial, harmless, mutilated, tormented,

Marial who had tried so hard . . . Marial who trusted him (strange that it still mattered so much). It wouldn't even be difficult, physically. But how could he kill Marial, in cold blood? He was no paid assassin. It would be the most selfish of acts, born of cowardice.

He could not face Idas again. That was an absolute. To live with guilt, or to be destroyed in the stampede of evil over his soul?

He was already cursed with guilt. Since the day of Karis's death he had killed, and killed again. Innocent and evil alike, they had fallen to his sword, his bow, his touch. Would one more make so much difference?

He thought not.

'What guarantee will you give me?' he said, and it sighed, relief audible.

'There is no need of guarantees,' Sharrak said, the delicate mouth smiling, the small tongue running over the lips. 'You will not be able to kill him unless you are free. I have to get you out –'

'Don't you want a guarantee yourself? What if you release me and I don't do as you ask?'

A laugh. 'It's not a question of *honour*, Peraldonian. Don't you know that broken oaths exact their own retribution?'

And then before he could answer it suddenly reached out and clasped him, locking the soft lips on his, and he tasted rotting flesh, maggot-haunted disease, and blood, blood, blood.

He did not notice it disappear, vomiting helplessly into the straw.

It was too late; he had agreed.

Later that day they came for him. The armed guard manacled his wrists together and led him down the stairs, along the pretty passageways, to de Mowbray's quarters.

Three men stood by the window in a long drawing-room. His uncle, Hamnet Lin, dressed in that absurd frock coat and starched cravat, drinking dark red wine with steady concentration. Elfitt de Mowbray, self-contained, neat in his grey uniform, watching his arrival with detachment.

And Lefevre. Bleached linen robes, the sparse white hair fringing the domed skull, the jowls hanging loose and flabby.

There was the light of madness in his eyes. It had not been there before. But now the pale eyes ranged widely around the room, restlessly searching, always searching, while his hands pulled apart the petals of a rose, letting them fall all around him.

The eyes lit on Blythe with furious relief.

'Where is it?' he cried. 'The Benu! Where is it?'

The violence in Lefevre's voice cut through the quiet of the room. The soldiers stood back from Blythe, leaving him alone in the centre of the russet carpet.

'I have no idea.' He spoke gently, quietly, as if to a sick child.

Lycias's High Priest seemed to swell in the air, to grow vast and overwhelming as rage swirled around him. De Mowbray's brow was furrowed with doubt, and Lin drained his glass.

'I have tried everything!' Petals fell from his fluttering hands, falling through the charged air. 'When Dorian died and the Benu disappeared, I tried to correct the balance alone – impossible! The God demands, and demands! A new Sun Emperor, I thought, perhaps that would help, but no, there is no help, no mercy, no relief! I cannot find the Benu and my Lord is angry, so angry!'

He was vast now, filling the air above their heads, his eyes desperate and insane.

Blythe remembered his uncle's words, describing Lefevre. The first of all the Mages, used to the unseen arts. Mind manipulation, he thought. Lefevre is not really growing vast, surging through the air towards me, I just think he is.

It didn't make it any better, not when those pale eyes glittered at him and he could smell the sweat of fear.

'Oh yes, you know, Phinian Blythe.' The voice rose, cracking with wild hysteria. 'Why should the Arrarat have saved you? I knew then, when they took you from my cauldron, that the Benu had chosen you –'

'What have the Arrarat to do with the Benu, my lord?' De Mowbray, courteously, trying to defuse the insane violence in the air.

'Are they not aligned to the Moon?' Lin looked up from his wine, diverted.

'Fool!' Lefevre swung round to him, sweeping the glass from his hands. 'They are not the Lady's! They are creatures of the Benu, acting outside Moon or Sun.'

'Tell de Mowbray what the Benu is, Lefevre.'

Unworried, Hamnet Lin had taken another glass, was pouring more wine. His retreat was plain. 'I think he deserves to know.'

'Perhaps . . .' The vast figure had shrunk down again to human proportions, just an old man, balding, with strangely pale eyes. Blythe watched, fascinated, the dangerous surges of power.

'The Benu is the Word. The Origin, the context of the Universe, the breath of Life. The first principle, beyond which there is nothing.' Mercifully, his voice was calmer.

'Lycias, our noble Lord, though infinitely beyond our understanding, is still of this world, of this place. Unalterably connected with us, with our imagination and faith. The Benu is not. Lycias's motives and actions are in some measure comprehensible to us. The Benu is beyond comprehension. As one ancient definition puts it, it is not this, not that. But it does exist, and so everything else exists. It has been stolen from me, an act of treachery and betrayal. But you, Blythe, know where it is.

'It is too perilous, uncontrolled. It is chaos, choice, chance. It denies my power, and that of my Lord Lycias. You must tell me!'

'I know nothing about it,' he said.

'The knowledge is still hidden from you, that is all. You are fated to find the Benu for me, and Idas will unlock the key in your mind.' He turned as he spoke, beckoning to the gigantic, empty-eyed figure by the door.

Blythe had not seen him enter, in the excess of Lefevre's passion. But now he sensed the drop in temperature, the denial of warmth.

He began to shake. Sharrak, where are you?

Idas walked slowly to the centre of the room, and stood in front of Blythe. He wondered whether to try running, whether it would be worth hurling himself out of the window, or onto the soldiers' swords.

It was too late. Like a magnet, the weight of those empty eyes drew his gaze upwards. Frantically he tried to look away, at anything else, anything at all, but already he felt the emptiness reaching out for him.

Sharrak! What of our bargain?

Ah, God, here it comes, the brutal scalpel, laying bare the fibres of his mind, his memory, his soul.

His eyes were now locked in communion with it, and there could be no relief . . .

It withdrew, abruptly. 'Sharrak,' said the chill voice. 'It will try to help him –'

Released, for one second, he staggered, struggling for control.

Without thinking, his legs still shaking, his mind a jumble of horrors, numb, he ran for the window, jumping up onto the table. He skidded along it, crashing into the rose bowl, wine decanter and goblets. Wine stained the cloth, and his uncle screamed. The window was closed; not caring, he leapt, falling with force against the glass, shoulder first.

It shattered, and in a shower of vicious splinters he fell down, down, past smooth walls, other windows, down towards jagged rocks, down –

To be caught, cradled in a golden, silky net, Sharrak's web.

Gently it slanted down towards the ground. He rolled from it, unhurt, to stand on a narrow ledge of rock, his wrists still bound.

At once the net vanished. In its place stood Sharrak, shining with brittle triumph.

It smiled at him, waiting.

'You cut that fine.' He was still breathless with shock and relief.

It said nothing, and stood to one side, gesturing with one delicate hand to a small figure cautiously picking its way over the rocks towards them.

Marial.

Chapter Fifteen
Knowledge

'Quick! I've got access to keys, this way –'

'Marial –'

'This way, this way. There's no time to lose.'

Through passages and courtyards, to stop beneath a shadowed arch of stone. A bright window shone to one side. Marial knocked gently on the glass.

'Locked out, Sim. Lend us your keys for a bit –'

'Again? I'm surprised they put up with it.' A jangle of metal on the sill. 'Three minutes. Then I want them back –'

'Of course. Thanks, friend.'

Hurriedly fumbling through the bunch until the lock sprang open, his wrists released, the keys returned.

'What are you doing back here? I thought you'd made it –' The old eyes were watching him sadly in the dark.

He could smell rotting flesh just behind them. It was not far away, waiting.

With so much guilt, did one more death make any difference?

Unbidden, another memory. Selene, lost, lonely Selene, outside the Lock-keeper's house. Beware guilt, she had said. Don't indulge, the way is too long . . .

He looked down at the tragic, desperate eyes and knew it would be easy, the work of a moment.

He could not do it.

Sharrak would call Idas. Broken oaths exact their own retribution, it had said, but it would hardly need to rely on anything else. Idas would be more than enough.

Still, he could not do it.

'Go, Marial. Get back to your post . . .'

Doubt frowned in the thin man's eyes.

'Get out of here! I don't need you, get away from me!'

Still he wasn't moving. What would it take?

And then a cool, expressionless voice singing through the air, calling.

'Idas! Idas! To the north courtyard, to the gate-keeper's house, to the traitor! He waits for you there!'

'Come on!' He clasped Marial's good arm, knowing it was too late, and began to run.

There were two imperatives now. He had to escape Idas, but more urgently, he had to get back to Eleanor.

For he knew now where the Benu was. Hurtling through passages, Marial at his heels, he thought of the knowledge triggered by that fall from the window. Lefevre had been right, he did have the key to it all, and it no longer lay dormant in his mind, either. In that fall, wanting death, he had instead found knowledge.

Eleanor held the Benu in the palm of her hand.

A small, creamy, luminous shell, given her by the Moon in a dream landscape on the halfway line to death.

A firebird, caught in amber, trapped in an infinite spiral.

Running heedless through empty corridors, vast halls, dormitories, he remembered her sitting by the window, turning the shell over and over. An exquisite, fine spiral, lined with golden fire. Did she know its significance, he wondered? If she did, it was only in her unconscious.

Sudden dread almost struck him into immobility. He had left her on an empty shell-strewn beach, with nothing to do except concentrate on Lukas.

She would lose it, he thought. The Benu would be lost forever on that lonely seashore.

And still they crashed on through doors, across gardens, scaling walls, in a frantic bid for freedom from the gathering forces behind.

More by luck than judgment, they came to the stables. Horses in stalls, several saddled and bridled ready for the evening patrol, men standing round talking, about to mount.

They hung back in the shadows, wondering if it was worth trying to steal a ride. One of the men turned and caught sight of them. He raised his torch high.

'Who goes there?'

Before Blythe could stop him, Marial stepped forward.

The man laughed. 'It's de Mowbray's new clown!' he said. 'What are you doing out, old man? You're going the wrong way for the maids' quarters. No soft thighs here to warm your bed . . .'

'Have you seen it? My harp, a golden harp?' His voice was reedy and thin, carrying across the courtyard.

A chorus of ribald suggestions as to what he should do with the harp, all eyes turned to him. Gently, sadly, Marial protested.

It worked. Blythe had separated one horse from the others, and mounted. Suddenly he spurred it forward, through the cluster of men, leaning forward to scoop up Marial.

He nearly lost him, as one of the soldiers gripped the tattered cloak, but the rags tore and they were off, clattering through the passages towards the causeway.

Marial knew the way, but they never made it.

They had to cross a large courtyard, deserted between high, blank walls. The only exit was lined with soldiers, spears pointing forward at them. Blythe pulled on the reins, harshly bringing the horse round.

Other riders were behind them, swords drawn and ready.

Blank walls, windows too high. Stone and steel all around. Again he yanked the horse round, digging in his heels. Wildly it galloped forwards at the line of spears.

'Hold on!' he yelled to Marial, knowing it to be useless.

The horse gathered itself for the jump, and then they were upon the spears, falling, rolling, in a bloody chaos of limbs and weapons.

He tried to protect Marial, tumbling forward, but he couldn't find him in the muddle. He pulled himself to his knees, shaking his head to clear it, waiting for the order, the blow, the disabling injury. Nothing happened.

A soldier stood over him, sword drawn, a threat dying on his lips. As Blythe watched the man's face changed. He took one step and began to fall, collapsing forward.

There was an arrow in his back.

All around him, other soldiers were falling. There were arrows everywhere, some flaming, shrieking through the air. Clasping his arms over his head, he looked up.

Huge, graceful shapes swung in the sky between the walls of the buildings; the scything sweep of wings, the rippling of black cloaks, the swift death, arrow-sent through the dark air. Alien eyes and hooked beaks, pale faces, staring down from the backs of the Arrarat hawks.

Cavers were attacking, and no one knew what to do. They had never needed to defend themselves against flying creatures before. Soldiers ran, shouting in confusion.

Incredulously, in the flaring torchlight, Blythe took the sword from the dead soldier's hand. Still there was no sign of Marial. Had he managed to slip away in the chaos? He stood up, taking his chance with the arrows, and began to run.

More soldiers ahead, led by a tall, unmistakable figure. Cursing, Blythe turned again and the uncertain fiery light revealed a narrow gap between two of the buildings.

Soldiers blocked his way. With calculating skill he lunged at one and threw him off balance, pushing him onto the other's blade. One quick sideways slash, and the other collapsed too.

Heart pounding, he ran on through the dark.

Footsteps rang in the alleyway behind him. He was pursued – but by whom? Hope dying, he turned to see who it was, and then knew that his dreams had all been prophecies.

Cloak billowing with the speed of his running, Idas was fresh and untired. Blythe had no option but to run, and run again, away from the battle and the wondrous advent of the Arrarat, away from Marial, lost in confusion.

A nightmare labyrinth of passages and dead ends, was de Mowbray's citadel. He could not tell, plunging through unlit archways, whether he would meet an open square, a back yard, the sea . . . or a brick wall. He dodged into doorways, threw himself over walls, even pushed his way into houses, crashing through darkened rooms and spindly furniture.

He was listening all the time for the sound of the sea. Only at the shoreline would he stand a chance of finding the causeway, or Sharrak's walkway. To get lost within the city of Cliokest would be disastrous, with Sharrak and Idas on the loose.

He had to get to the mainland. Somehow, he had to find a way across those mountains, across the sea to that calm island, where Eleanor held the Benu.

There was still no moon; the only light came from the odd lighted window, the occasional torch thrust into a bracket. The heavy tread of Idas's feet was relentless, untiring behind him, more potent and terrifying than any dream.

He dodged once into a narrow doorway and Idas rushed straight past, only to halt and swing round, returning unerringly to Blythe's hiding place.

He was already gone. But in that brief pause in the rhythm of the pursuit, Blythe had detected the sharp tang of salt in the air. Taking a chance, he ran down a cramped passage, barely wide enough for a man, rounding the corner of a large house.

It was a dead end, with the sea lapping gently at its margin. Faceless buildings rose sheer on either side, the lighted windows high above his head. Idas's footsteps still sounded, not far away. Without a second thought, with barely a pang of regret, Blythe threw his sword far out into the waves, kicked off his boots and fell into the water.

After the heat of the chase, the sea was blessedly, wonderfully cold. He shivered in the first shock of it, and then, without the faintest idea which way to go, started to swim.

Weed snagged round his ankles at first, and he gashed a knee on submerged rock. Above the steady sound of his strokes in the water, the even rhythm of his breath, he could hear Idas disrobing. It was taking him longer because of the armoured breastplate and helmet. Blythe would have smiled, if he had had the energy, to think he would live to be grateful for Idas's armour. As the water swirled through his arms, he remembered something else.

Triangular fins, cutting through the bay.

Sharks.

Chapter Sixteen
The Boat

'Your turn,' said Lukas, leaning back, drinking more wine.

Eleanor stared thoughtfully at the chessboard traced in the sand between them. Their pieces were shells, varied, precise and delicate. A fire glowed just a few feet away, pigeons roasting on a spit.

The wine came from the sacks carried by Astrella on her return from leaving Blythe at Cliokest. There were biscuits, cheese, rice, fruit and vegetables. A comfortable, light and airy shelter was constructed from driftwood just beyond the high tide mark.

They filled the days in calm and peace with sandcastle building and boat repairs, each courteous and kind to the other, and Eleanor was numb with loneliness.

She was also not good at chess, and her initial advantage in teaching Lukas the game was swiftly surpassed by his sure grasp of tactics. In her other existence, she thought, she would have sulked. Now these losses were drowned in the greater failures of her life.

Wearily, she moved her castle and Lukas crowed with triumph, taking his move.

'There! Foolish girl, you're not thinking!'

'Is it checkmate?' She peered anxiously at the pieces.

'It certainly is,' he said. 'There's a forfeit tonight, your third loss in a row.' He stood up, stretching long legs, and prodded the birds on the spit, turning them over. 'Your turn to do a little hunting and gathering,' he said carefully, not looking at her. 'Come night fishing with me.'

'My skills are for architecture,' she said, waving at the beach around them.

Sandcastles reared at every interval, littering the smooth

sand with fantastic shapes. Bridges, towers, moats and walls, foursquare and crenellated, spiral and circular, some decorated with shells, others with weed, some bare and uncompromising. It was a city of castles, a maze of fortifications, built afresh in damp sand every day. She kept busy that way, inventing new structures, new designs, while Lukas renovated the little boat.

He watched her all the time, hesitating to interrupt. He hoped that enforced idleness would heal her, that undemanding companionship would give her the space to recover courage.

It wasn't working, although sometimes she laughed and teased. She was sinking further into depression. He speculated what the loss of the light in her mind meant to her. Had the obsession disappeared, too? What was the Stasis to her now? It was not an issue to raise. Not yet.

Quite apart from Matthias's instructions, and everything else, he felt a pang of simple compassion for her. She was too vulnerable for this commitment, he thought, and wondered again just what that fall into Sharrak's pit had achieved.

'There's nothing like night fishing,' he said, keeping his voice light. 'There's a kind of phosphorescence sometimes: it's very beautiful. Come with me tonight.'

'All right then.' She was listless and then seemed to regret her lack of enthusiasm. 'I'd like it very much, thanks.'

He poured more wine and they toasted each other before starting to eat.

The night was clear and calm as ever. Lukas suggested that she borrow his cloak, and gathered up supplies in case they were out for long.

He had repaired the nets and line, and the little boat was stabilised by a deep keel and a wide, oval shape. He had improvised lanterns to hang from stern and prow, and as the moon rose she helped him push it out into the warm gentle sea.

There was virtually no wind, so they used the two flat paddles he had made. At first they went in stupid circles until, laughing, she worked out what was wrong.

Then, noisily at first, singing the Skye Boat Song, inspired by wine, they struck out into the bay while the high mountains around them stood silent and massive under the moon.

They had not gone far before Lukas dropped the nets. He told her tales of fishing trips with Matthias and Haddon, of nights when the Moon had seemed so near, so hidden. He recreated for her a world of close, dependent commitment and companionship.

She looked out at the horizon, over the smooth glassy sea, for once enjoying the salty tang and complete peace.

She almost jumped when he put his hand on her shoulder, and when she looked up at him, smiling, he bent to kiss her.

A simple act, unpremeditated and artless, and yet they were both deprived of breath. He sat beside her in the prow and lifted his hand to her face. There were tears there suddenly, but she smiled still. His arms encircled her with an aching, unexpected passion and his lips found hers again, tasting her tears, bitter-sweet, salt as the surrounding sea.

'Eleanor –' he began, breaking away at last, thinking perhaps he should draw back, this was too soon, too far, too fast.

But she looked up at him with such intensity in her wide grey eyes that he could not continue. 'Don't let the Stasis spoil this, too,' she said steadily. 'Let's not hold back, because we have eternity. Let's choose, now, to be different . . .'

He saw the rise and fall of her breast, the moonlight shining on her hair, phosphorescence in the sea all around. She was framed in light.

They kissed once more, exploring now, more confident, and his hands stroked the soft curves of her body. In the light of the Moon her skin was silver, sprinkled with freckles, warm and smooth to the touch. He pushed back the fall of her hair and bent his head, running his mouth along the line of her throat.

At length he drew away from her and spread the cloak in the bottom of the boat, welcoming her to its safety.

There they began to learn each other's body, matched together in pliable, sinuous grace, rocked all the while in gentle motion on the calm, shining sea, under a benign Moon.

The urgency of desire caught them both by surprise, and

surprise itself hurled them further into the last mystery. Her need for him was overwhelming, the channelling of all her loneliness and doubt. And to him she was alien and beautiful, the actual and potential focus of all dreams, all hope. Tenderness was there too, and affection and humour. But more than that was transforming need, exigent and undeniable, welding them together into one compulsion, one joy.

In the end she lay in the crook of his arm, bright hair in disarray. She said nothing, for there was no need. He had given her an ultimate reason for existing, and in return she would make the ultimate commitment.

'We'll stay here forever, if you like,' he murmured, tracing the contour of her mouth.

'We'll travel on, if you want,' she replied, secure in the strength of love.

So they spent the rest of the night in each other's arms, water gently lapping, the fish curious at their bows, and the quiet Moon flooded the air with Her blessing.

Chapter Seventeen
Reunion

At first Blythe struck diagonally away from the citadel, hoping to avoid the jetties and piers that jutted into the sea. He was trying to get out of the range of the citadel lights. But beacons had been lit on every flat roof and balcony, illuminating the still swinging shapes of the Arrarat hawks, and light glowed all around Cliokest. It was easy for Idas to keep him in sight, although at a distance. Blythe was a strong swimmer, practised and fit, with powerful arms and chest muscles. But Idas was not quite human and did not know the meaning of tiredness. The gap between them narrowed.

Looking back into the blazing lights from the citadel, arms beginning to ache, Blythe saw the sleek head nearing and realised his mistake. It would have been better to take his chance amongst the shadowy struts of a pier, dodging and hiding. To alter his course now would in fact shorten the distance between them, so he kept going along the same line, praying he would soon come to the causeway.

There was no sign of it; and his breath was beginning to rasp with exhaustion. Then, as if on cue, a swirl of dark water ahead of him broke up the horizon. Forward to the sharks, or back to Idas . . .

He could turn and fight, while he still had some energy.

Worse than death, that would be. Thoughts flashed through his mind, for the scything fins were close now. At least the great fish would be quick.

He was hardly moving now, very tired, just waiting for the slam of jaws. The water felt heavy, viscous, thick around him. The salt smell of it was no longer clean, but rancid, sickly.

The fin swerved to one side, away from him. He felt the heavy water move around him as the fish passed him by, so close.

To Idas? Were they making for Idas? But even as hope gripped him, he saw another figure, wearily, doggedly ploughing through water, following him.

A faint cry over the water, a thin, desperate voice. 'Wait! Wait for me!'

Failing and frail, old sad eyes glinted for a moment in the moonlight, and then squeezed shut in agony as the shark ripped into him.

It was over in seconds, the water only briefly disturbed, the stain a darkening cloud on its surface.

Who would want the golden harp now?

He wished the fish would come for him too, but the fins disappeared off into the night, leaving him alone with Idas in the water.

There was nothing to do but swim on.

He pushed on through water, while his memory flinched away from that unnecessary death.

There was still a long way to go, but somehow the gap between Idas and himself had widened again. He forced himself on. He did not care now that his arms were on fire, his breath gasping, his movements slowing and weak.

At last, he saw ahead the dark quiet shapes of a fishing fleet. Perhaps he could lose Idas among the boats, perhaps he might even get one free: ideas crowded in on him.

He must be near the causeway, he thought incredulously, for why would a fishing fleet, silent and deserted, be moored far out to sea? An extra spurt of energy with limbs afire, and he was amidst the gently bobbing boats. He made for the nearest, a two-masted boat with a small cabin, and reached it with a final expense of strength. Grasping, he lunged at a trailing rope. His arms felt like jelly; he hung there, dismayed, exhausted, and then a strong arm under his shoulder hauled him up and over the edge.

'Well, and what have we here?' said a soft, cool voice. 'Friend or foe?' The irony was all at once familiar to Blythe. Collapsed in a dripping heap against the wooden struts of the boat, he closed his eyes, wondering how to handle it.

'You're always fishing me out of the sea, Thurstan,' he said through jagged breaths. 'I hope you won't regret it.'

'So do I.' The irony had abruptly vanished and a lantern was suddenly uncovered and swung, blinding, in his face. A smothered exclamation, and Blythe hissed, 'Put that out! I'm followed!'

At once the lantern was extinguished. He was roughly hustled through a door and down some steps into the crowded cabin.

One small lantern stood on the table, giving only a feeble light. The windows were heavily blacked out and the air was clogged with cigarette smoke and tension. The table was cluttered with glasses and wine flasks. Three men sat round it, looking at him with curiosity. Blythe recognised no one.

Quietly as ever, Thurstan stood at the door, golden hair glinting in the light. He held a short knife to Blythe's ribs.

'Gentlemen,' he said. 'Allow me to introduce to you one Phinian Blythe, Peraldonian soldier and renegade, last seen escaping from Jeren with Lukas Marling and the girl.'

An indrawn breath from one of the men seated at the table, a slight, dark, intense man. Thurstan held up a hand, forbidding speech.

'Where are they, Blythe? What have you done with them?'

'They're safe.' His breath had returned and with every nerve he was listening for sounds outside. 'Never mind that now. I'm being followed by Idas, Lefevre's general. Give me a weapon and let me go.'

'Why should we believe you?' The old question.

'Because it will be the worse for you if you don't. Idas is Lefevre's right-hand man. He's no friend to you, and like nothing you've ever met before.'

Still Thurstan didn't move, his hard blue eyes searching the other's face.

'Do you mind?' Abruptly Blythe leant over the table, ignoring the knife and poured himself a drink. He was shivering with reaction and apprehension.

'What are you doing here?' he asked. 'Are there more of you on the other boats?'

'We're all here,' said a tall flamboyant looking man, dark curls cascading over his shoulders. 'Cavers and Jerenites both – what's that?'

A distant scream wrenched through the air, swiftly followed by a crash and then more shouting.

'Idas is here,' said Blythe grimly. 'A sword, Thurstan? For old times' sake?'

Thurstan was already through the door, out onto the deck. A clatter on the table behind Blythe. He turned to see that the dark man with the powerful eyes had unbuckled a sword and thrown it down for him. He seized it and then looked at the other, impelled.

'I am Lukas's brother,' the man said in explanation, 'Matthias. I am responsible for the girl's presence here.'

'They're all right,' he repeated, pausing in the rush upstairs. 'It's still holding good –' and then he was out, out into the cool night air.

The sound of shouting and fighting tore through the night air. The violence was focused on a boat across the water, to Blythe's left. Someone there had uncovered a lantern which swung crazily over the water as the boat rocked and swayed.

The huge figure of Idas was there, black with anger, lunging and smashing into the three men who were trying to contain him.

As Blythe paused, trying to work out the quickest way to cross the maze of boats, he saw Idas pluck up one of the Jerenite guards, crushing him against the cabin, and then discarding him, broken, into the sea.

Another unnecessary death. Too many, now. In a surge of fury, Blythe ran, jumping from boat to boat, and in seconds had crossed the dark sea.

Thurstan was there ahead of him, watching the wildly threshing figure from behind a cabin. He was fitting an arrow to his bow.

'Wait,' said Blythe, pushing the arrow-head down. He was tired of fear, of letting others pay the price. 'This one's mine.'

'Don't be a fool!'

Blythe ignored him. Blocking Thurstan's view, he

stepped out from the cabin's shelter, looking down the narrow gangway.

'Idas,' he said, quietly. 'I'm here.'

A snarl as he spun round, surging over the deck towards him. An almost tangible sense of evil surrounded him and Blythe could have cried out.

'Hell and damnation!' Thurstan's voice behind him, shaken for once. 'What *is* it?'

Blythe stood steady, feet slightly apart, holding Matthias's sword in both hands. Idas was still carrying a heavy, iron broadsword, had swum after him all that way, carrying five feet of metal. Blythe tried not to think about it.

He leapt suddenly forward, ducking sideways under the reach of the long arm, and the sword splintered down into the deck at his side. With a grunt Idas recovered the blade and swung a massive fist, catching Blythe in the stomach, winding him. He fell gasping to the deck.

His only advantage was that Idas moved slowly. As he raised his sword once more, Blythe jumped up, braced against the cabin, thrusting his sword straight at Idas's heart.

The creature whirled to one side, and the sword caught harmlessly in cloth. He ripped it out and only then did Idas stagger back against the cabin. Thurstan had shot at him, and an arrow jutted from his shoulder. Black blood began to flow, and he roared with rage and pain.

Again Blythe ran at him, and this time he caught Idas off balance. They fell to the deck, swords threshing, limbs entangled in a chaos of blood and noise.

The watching men tried to approach, to help, but a wall of malevolent power cocooned the figures on the deck. Idas's will, locked into Blythe's mind, was beginning to enfold him in its dread embrace.

It fitted round his thoughts like a glove, plundering his soul, predatory and hungry, draining strength and decision. He was weeping as his life was defiled, his memories and loves distorted by the knowledge of evil. Sickness rose in his mouth at the violation, and he barely noticed the hands encircling his throat, squeezing and throttling.

He would have welcomed death then. As evil branded

itself deep within him his hands fell loose by his side, the sword clattering unregarded.

A woman's voice sang over the water, shining with clarity, shining through the brutality. The sound of sanity and peace, bright and loving in the dark.

A moment of breathless shock. The power of evil waned. Briefly, awareness flickered at the back of Idas's blank, fathomless eyes. His concentration wavered; in that instant, Blythe broke away, rolling out of his grip across the deck to where his sword lay.

Furiously, Idas's mind reached out for him again, digging its claws deep. In the memory of purity, Blythe found the ability to murmur two words.

'Remember Mariana?'

The creature howled, hurling itself at him in uncontrollable hatred. Blythe stood his ground, his sword braced.

The iron sword clashed, and he parried, jumping to one side. Again Idas thrust at him, and this time the force sent his own sword flying, his hands numb. He could feel that mind paralysing him, rifling through his thoughts, beginning again to catalogue his soul. There was little time left.

He spun around and kicked Idas's sword arm. The blade grazed against his shoulder, but he felt nothing. With desperation he flung himself forward, and again they hit the deck in a huddle. Somehow, in the fall, Idas's sword became caught between them, the point of the blade at eye level, slicing through clothes, cutting into skin and muscle.

Again the song, clear and vivid, diamond-bright in the night.

With one final effort, ignoring the pain, his foot braced against the cabin, Blythe pushed Idas over onto his back, the sword still wedged between them. To regain balance Idas's grip loosened for a moment; Blythe seized the handle of the sword and angled it up, away from Idas, falling forward onto it, hard.

The point slid smoothly, neatly, into the creature's throat.

Blood spurted; a bubbling cry, and he thrust again with

the sword, again and again, obliterating forever that tortured and tormenting consciousness.

Sobbing for breath he leant back against the cabin, his clothes sticky with blood, the sword hanging loose in his hands. Then he pushed himself to the rail and hung over the side, retching.

An arm round his waist, helping him to a seat, a flask of fiery spirit held against his lips. He drank, choked, and drank again. He looked up and saw Thurstan watching him, smiling lips, equivocal eyes.

'Are there any more like that?' He nodded to the sprawling body.

'No, thank God.' His voice sounded strained and unnatural. He took another drink, leaning back, blank with exhaustion.

'You don't know what a good turn we've done the world there,' he said at last, passing the flask back to Thurstan.

'You may be right, at that.' He paused, cool eyes searching the other's face. 'Been busy, have you, since last we met?'

There was nothing to say. Uncomfortably Blythe shifted, trying to ease some of the aches.

'Come on,' said Thurstan. 'Let's get you patched up.' He helped Blythe to his feet. Together they went to the cabin below, and didn't even notice the slight figure standing alone on a boat across the water.

She lifted her head, catching the faint breeze from the mainland, listening to the quiet. For a moment she thought that the scent of roses drifted through the air. Then she too went below.

Chapter Eighteen
Strategies

A knock on the door.

She had been waiting for him, had even lit the lamp, so that he should be more at ease.

'Come in,' said Nerissa, and the door opened. She heard him pause in the doorway and knew he was shocked. She didn't mind. She was used to it by now.

'Sit down,' she said. He moved slowly, as if tired, and she remembered that he had been injured in the fight.

'I hope you are not seriously wounded,' she said.

'Thanks to you,' he said. 'I owe my life and reason to your intervention.'

A Peraldonian accent. She should have expected it, that slow, unfamiliar drawl.

'That creature was an abomination. It could not be allowed to continue.'

'That's rather what I thought. But I was not effective alone.'

She waited. He hadn't come just to thank her, she knew.

'Lady Nerissa –' He sounded strangely hesitant, and she recognised that he was used to command, not petition.

Perhaps it was her appearance. She was thinner now, bones jutting sharply from papery skin, and she still scraped back her hair with the old impatience. It was white now, they told her. Scorched white. Sometimes she wore a scarf to cover the shiny red scar tissue where her eyes had been, but she hadn't bothered recently. It was of little importance. But still, perhaps he was disconcerted. She decided to be generous.

'How may I help you?' she asked.

'I wanted to ask whether you know a woman called Selene?'

'She was my sister.' She stopped for a moment. It was still difficult. 'She lived in Peraldon, with the colony there. You have met her?'

'Once. For a few hours. But you say "was"; I did not know she was dead.' There was a pause. Nerrisa wondered what had happened for those few hours to be of such significance.

'What was Selene's relationship with the Lady Astret?'

So that was it. The light, beckoning again.

'I cannot tell you without the consent of others,' she said. 'It is forbidden knowledge.'

'May I call those concerned?' He pushed back his chair and it grated, wood on wood. 'With your permission?'

She nodded, stiffly, and told him their names. He went to the door and spoke to the guard outside.

He sat in silence waiting for them to come, and she had no desire to disturb him. He would not welcome probing. There was a quality of grief in him that she recognised and respected.

Matthias entered first and swiftly listed the names of the others – Stefan Pryse, Aylmer Alard, Thibaud Lye, Thurstan Merauld, Powel Hewlin – so that she should know they were all there. Matthias was always thoughtful, courteous.

She waited until they were all seated and then said, 'I have been asked to explain something of Selene's relationship to our Lady. It is as much your concern as mine.'

They had come so far, she thought. How extraordinary it was that they should all be sitting round a table, talking to this stranger. Jerenites, Cavers and Peraldonian together. It had taken endless negotiation, she remembered, councils, committees, discussions far into the night, when they had first arrived at Jeren.

She had known little about the voyage there, the mountainous seas, the hardship and fear. It had been little better on Jeren, as she recovered her senses, with the ceaseless waves of attacking Fosca. She had lain in Martitia's own quarters and heard the screams, the clash of weapons.

There was a difficult silence, and then Matthias spoke.

'I think we must now learn to trust. I have no objection.'

'Selene is dead, after all.' Aylmer, precise as usual.

'How did she die?' The Peraldonian, so weary, so tired.

'She left Peraldon to tell us about the massacre of our people there. They were drowned, she said, like rats in a trap.' Only Aylmer could make it sound dry, she thought. 'An Arrarat brought her to Jeren, soon after we had reached there. She died in one of the Fosca attacks.'

'We lost over fifty people in two days.' Thurstan, hard and unforgiving.

'I am sorry.' The Peraldonian sounded genuinely regretful. 'The Lady Martitia – is she – ?'

'My mother was among those killed.'

Another pause, and then Matthias spoke. 'Selene was a person of unusual powers. A clairvoyant visionary, she did not disdain to send us information on more practical matters.'

'She spied for you?'

'Oh yes. Why so surprised? Did Peraldon really think that they were the only ones to dabble in espionage?'

'I had thought she worked for the Moon in a different manner.'

'A mystic, rather than a shabby dealer in secrets?' Contempt in Thurstan's voice.

'There is no single way of accomplishing Astret's purpose.' Nerissa's voice was sharp. 'That is surely one of the lessons we have had to absorb recently. That is why we are all here now, Caver, Peraldonian, Jerenite; warrior, magician and priestess. No single path is enough. We must work together.'

'But Selene would have had accurate leads from the Lady Astret?' The Peraldonian was still uneasy.

'What is it, Blythe?' Matthias sounded tense. Nerissa knew he would be leaning forward over the table, dark eyes intent and potent. He had grown in power, since returning through the Boundary. She thought that he was now stronger than Blaise had ever been. 'What do you know about Selene and Astret?'

'Tell me first what you're all doing here. What made you come to Cliokest?'

'We're besieging Lefevre.' Stefan's voice, slow and ironic. 'Hadn't you noticed?'

Then Matthias again, clear and passionate.

'Selene told us, before she died, that Lefevre would come here. You can perhaps reassure us. Was she right?'

'Oh yes, Lefevre is on Cliokest now. But this is of course madness. You have no hope at all against Peraldonian defences.'

'Under cover of darkness we are at an advantage.' Stefan again, reasonable and measured. 'We have the Ararat, and men used to the night. It is a risk, but there is no choice. A knife-edge existence we had at the Caves, and it was worse on Jeren. It is either extinction or attack.'

'I had hoped that another path would suffice, that we need not resort to violence –' Matthias, softly, musingly.

'Do you mean the girl? Eleanor?' The Peraldonian's voice held depths she did not understand.

'She is still an unknown quantity. Any difference she may make has little to do with us. We have to act as if she didn't exist; we can't wait for her to achieve a solution for us.' Matthias spoke with dogged realism. 'If she does do anything to help, well, that would be wonderful. And if nothing is achieved, at least we'll be no worse off.'

'This is all very well. But what will happen when the sun rises, and Lefevre and de Mowbray see this little fleet and begin to defend themselves? They'll call in the Fosca right away. You haven't a chance.'

'We are not defenceless.' She could hear the smile in Matthias's voice. 'The sun will not rise today. We have brought the Moon's own darkness with us.'

'What can you mean?'

'After the Stasis began, Lefevre and de Mowbray pursued occult paths, dangerous experiments . . . We studied in a different school on Sarant. Lore and rite, ceremony and ritual, we followed the Moon's own path of order and rhythm. And although we are powerless to reinstate Her to Her true glory, we can at least sustain the conditions for Her service.'

She heard Matthias lean back, felt the room still with concentration.

'We brought the night with us,' he said. 'The rain and the wind of the Caver world. We can hold the night in place for three days. We understand the dark. Our lives have been spent there. Peraldonians do not. And the Fosca angels are reptiles, needing sunlight to provide energy. After two days in the dark they will fail. We will be at a considerable advantage.'

She heard a chair scrape, and a rustle as the curtain was pulled to one side, and then quickly replaced. There was the sound of rain against glass. The Peraldonian spoke, unwillingly.

'All right. I'm impressed. But why didn't you use this before? Surely with that kind of power you could have defeated Lefevre long ago?'

'There is a price to pay,' Matthias said, honestly. 'It is a very great risk, asking this of the Moon. We had wondered about it before, but the Stasis was too strong. We were all held passive in its grip. But it is now unstable.' He paused. 'What did Selene say to you?'

'She told me to find the Benu.' He spoke slowly, weighing the words. 'And, if it was found, what to do then.'

'No one knows where it is!' Thibaud Lye, strong and determined. 'We've tried everything, but it's hidden from all human knowledge –'

She had to speak. It shone clear and bright in her mind, Astret's light, pointing to the Benu, pointing to the Peraldonian. 'Except you. You know where the Benu is, don't you, Phinian Blythe? Are you going to tell us?'

Another silence, and she held her breath.

'Yes,' he said. 'I'll tell you. And then I must go and find it, before it is irretrievably lost.'

A golden spiral of light hidden in a creamy shell. Held in unknowing hands, dropped lightly on a calm seashore.

Would he be in time?

An hour later, above the sound of the rising wind, a distant wailing drifted across the bay from Cliokest.

The sun had not risen. The wind brought rain with it, chilling and dreary. Aghast, disbelieving, the inhabitants of de Mowbray's citadel gave way to fear, wondering whether they would have to face an eternal night, assaulted by the Cavers and their Arrarat.

Trying to batten down their panic, they turned to Lefevre, the architect of their lives.

He sat alone and silent in the rich apartment he had been given, refusing to see anyone. Sometimes he paced the fine carpets, sometimes he ran his fingers through the petals of the roses which stood in bowls and vases on every surface, their scent disturbing the night air. His eyes were still restlessly roaming every surface, every hidden place.

But most of the time he sat at his desk, staring blankly at a small golden pendulum suspended there. It hung steady, still, from its frame. But every now and then the wind rattled through the hangings over the door and the pendulum shuddered, and nearly began to move.

De Mowbray was not so afflicted; he ordered soldiers to set up defences, checked supplies, set every spare man and woman to work constructing torches. Furniture and barrels were broken up to supply wood, oil and candles were requisitioned or confiscated, held for rationing.

The black sky overhead was different in quality from the usual night; it hung heavy, forbidding and sullen over the bay, and the rain that poured down brought no relief. Biting wind hurled round corners, cutting through comfort. The sea, churned and whipped into a frenzy, crushed the frail craft along the causeway against one another.

Amidst the noise of wind and rain, the violence of their fear, the people of Cliokest watched the dark, ominous shapes swinging high in the sky above them. But no one saw the little fishing fleet, now swollen by other unfamiliar vessels, stringing itself out across the bay.

They were beginning to realise that the party was over. They did not know how to live in any other way.

'You'll have to go now,' said Thurstan to Blythe. 'We can keep de Mowbray busy for some time, but not forever. Go and get the Benu. There's no need for you to wait here any longer.'

Standing on the deck, they were watching the Arrarat diving at Cliokest, flaming arrows cascading down. De

Mowbray had tried to send for Fosca reinforcements, but Stefan, skimming through the sky on Averre, had shot the Fosca messenger down. There would be others, they knew. Sooner or later someone would get through, and then there would be serious fighting, fresh, untired Fosca, the besiegers besieged.

'I know,' said Blythe. 'But if I'm to get there in time I'll need help. Can you spare one of the Arrarat?'

'I'll take you,' said Matthias, moving away from the other Mages. 'Asta can carry us both. I think . . . I need to see this through, Phinian Blythe. If you don't mind, I'll come too. I've left instructions with Aylmer and Thibaud. The night will prevail for another forty hours. We should go now.'

He called for Asta, and out of the dark a fast, grey-white hawk with piercing golden eyes settled on the deck beside them.

Blythe was glad to have company, glad not to be alone again. They took only their cloaks and weapons, for they would not be gone for long.

They could either take the route round the headland, out over the sea, as Blythe had before, or, more direct, they could ascend the headland itself, the narrow range of precipitous mountains and deep gorges. It would more than halve the distance to the island, but would require much from the heavily laden Arrarat.

Matthias decided to leave the decision to the hawk; she turned east and began to ascend, steeply, the dark mountains.

Chapter Nineteen
Nerissa

The scent of roses was exigent. She would have to accept the summons.

'Come, Oswald,' she said, pulling her cloak around her. 'Call your Arrarat.'

Pale and trembling in the chill wind, Oswald blinked nervously, and cupped his hands together over his mouth.

A flutter of wings out of the dark, and then Alta stood beside them on the deck.

'You are sure?' Nerissa asked, as he helped her up.

'You'll need someone to show you the way,' he said, 'and the others are all busy.' He pulled himself up behind her.

But still she paused. 'There's no need for you to risk your life,' she said, fairly. 'Alta can take me to Lefevre. You could stay here.'

'There's nothing for me here,' he said, with bitterness. 'Since Richenda . . . I'd like to come, Nerissa. Don't make me stay behind.'

So they took off, and flew high over the bay, avoiding the swirling Arrarat beneath them, until they were right over the highest central tower of Cliokest. Other Arrarat suddenly dived at one of the walkways from the tower, diverting the guard, and Alta put them down just behind it in the deep shadow. No one noticed.

There was a flight of steps up to the tower. Quietly, Nerissa and Oswald climbed them, and found themselves outside Lefevre's personal quarters. There were only two scurries on guard.

A quick look at Nerissa's calm, faintly smiling face, and Oswald went to the door.

Ignoring the scurries rushing down the stairs to get help, he took a deep breath.

And knocked on the door.

No sound; the door swung open on its hinges as Oswald pushed it, and they passed through.

She stood still on the threshold, absorbing the heavy scent of roses, disguising something else. He locked the door behind them and started the ceaseless thread of description that had kept her informed since the blinding.

'Two huge windows, ten feet high, more . . . window seats, a table to your right, roses everywhere. There's broken glass all over the place, careful where you tread . . . There's been a fire in the centre, the carpet's all rucked up. It's still warm. There's no one here.'

She put out a hand and caught his arm. She could hardly breathe for the weight of evil. 'We are not alone,' she said. Evil of that strength had to have a physical presence.

He started to move away from her, but she held him back. 'No. Stay here,' she said, wondering that her voice was so steady. 'Are the windows open?' She was shivering, a continuous tremor.

'A little, on the catch . . . oh no . . . Oh Lady –'

He had seen it, the evil thing, he had found it.

She was glad she had no eyes.

'Tell me,' she said, her hand firm over his. He was swallowing, trembling with something worse than cold.

'By the window, I thought it was a curtain at first . . . Nerissa, let's get out of here. Now.'

'Too late . . .'

Quiet and slow, the voice was light with innocence, dark with depravity. It took every sound ever uttered by men and women and used it. Used it all up, every sob, shout, cry, laugh, caress and song. Every sound was laid waste in that voice.

She wished she had no ears, hearing this.

There was no possible reply to it.

Oswald's ceaseless whisper again – 'It's blood! I thought it was material, but it's blood, everywhere, hanging all over it, dripping, falling to the floor –' Oswald was trying to edge back all the time, to the door. She did not blame him.

'Nerissa, High Priestess of Astret, Lady of the Moon's misguided ministry, barren, dull, blind Lady of all Sorrow . . .' The voice trailed on, defiling a catalogue of titles, and she waited for it to stop.

'There is a role for you,' it said at last. 'No easy death, if the Stasis breaks, no ordinary life if it endures. The Lord is eternally just –'

She heard it move, sharply, and something tumbled to the floor.

'It's dropped something, the body of a man, I think. The body's wearing a frock coat, or something, but it's all covered in blood. Blood, everywhere . . .' She had heard it thud dully onto the carpet.

Oswald struggled on, the words rapid with shock. 'Standing there, it's a man, or was a man, or a flower, petals, something that has been –'

'Lefevre,' said the voice. 'I have been Lefevre, once, High Priest of Lycias, Lord of the Sun's great victory, wise, all-seeing, governor of the balance, arbiter of justice . . . Now I am something else.

'As you will be something else. This is why I have brought you here.

'What do you see with blind eyes, Nerissa? People's thoughts, their emotions, their hidden desires? Shall I tell you the path our Gods have mapped for us, for you and me, for High Priestess and High Priest?

'Shall I tell you what you will see now, with blind eyes?' It paused. Although she heard the clamour on the stairs behind them, although she would have welcomed interruption, any interruption, to stop the voice, she knew it would have to be said, and that she would go on hearing the words until she died.

'You will see the future, Sad Lady of Sorrow. The future for us all, explicit in dreams, disguised on waking. When I was Lefevre, I knew it too, in part, but it was often obscure. You will not have that relief.

'It was my reward, for capturing the Benu. It is your reward for loyalty to the Moon, for opposing the Sun. I wish you well with it . . .'

She could smell the blood through the roses, the sweat of Oswald's fear, and the decay of her own hope.

'What are you, now? What is your reward for losing the Benu?' Still her voice was steady.

'My reward?' The voice rose, skittering at the wild edge of hysteria. 'I am the King of the Fosca now, Sad Lady, I will fly with the creatures of the Sun, and blood will be my only food, and hatred my only impulse. An easier fate, Lady of All Sorrow, past, present and future, than the fate awaiting you . . .'

A crash as the window was flung back, and cold air flooded the room. She heard wings, leathery wings and teeth snapping, and furniture falling, china breaking.

She smelt wet scales and rotting flesh, and then almost staggered as Oswald pushed her aside, running across the room. She heard his sword, wrenched from the scabbard, heard the voice laugh as the thrust was turned aside, heard his moan as he fell, and the other sound as he died.

The soldiers were at the door now, knocking, shouting. They were battering it; it would not take long to break down.

Across the room the window was swinging on its hinges, crashing back against the wall. The air was cold and bitter.

The Fosca King and the dark angel had gone, back into the black night.

She lifted her hands from her face, and looked out into the future.

Slowly, she walked across the room, past the discarded body, past the still warm ashes and Oswald, calm at last, and climbed onto the window seat.

She stood only for a moment on the sill, and then sighed, once, before stepping out.

She fell through the night, the Lady of Sorrow.

As rose petals fall, to settle amongst the dead.

Chapter Twenty
The Fosca King

'What's happened? Why isn't it getting light?' Eleanor took Lukas's hand as he stood at the sea's edge, staring out across the unrelieved, black water.

'The night . . . Astret's night. They have brought the night. It must be Matthias. There's no other explanation. He's taken the risk, he's dared to do it.'

'Then the Moon will be freed!'

'No.' His voice was sombre. He turned to look at her in the feeble light of the fire. She had never seen him so bleak. 'This is desperate. Maintaining the night is Matthias's last resort. We've reached the crisis.'

'We . . .?'

'I'm a Caver still, you know.' Gently he smoothed back a strand of hair, caught in the rising wind, fluttering round her face.

A faint stirring of panic caught her breath and, noticing it, he pulled her close, holding her tightly.

'What do you mean, what will you do?' Her voice was muffled at his chest.

'Eleanor . . .' he paused. 'I think it's more a case of what *we* are going to do.'

No, not again, not this again, her thoughts cried. Don't ask me, don't need me –

'Look,' he said, turning her round so that, her back against him, she was facing out along the water's edge.

A heavier shadow stood there, glossy, ebony, shining against the dull night. Ash, yellow eyes gleaming, waiting for her, promising freedom and love. Demanding courage and commitment. A further rush in the chill air, and Astrella settled on the damp beach beside him.

'Shall we go?' he said. For answer she turned again, and clung to him, heart racing.

'Can't we stay here?' Stay here and love each other, she thought, in peace and tranquillity, in this calm haven of joy and laughter.

She knew his answer without needing to hear his voice.

They gathered up a few belongings, a little food, weapons, and then stood in silence, watching the fire hissing, dying, in the rain, and the hawks waiting beyond.

'Where will they take us?' she said, her hand resting on his cloak, as if it were a talisman.

'The Arrarat know best.' Lukas answered her need, not her words. 'They would not come if they thought we would fail.'

He swore to love her then, through an eternity that had nothing to do with the Stasis, in a living blaze of warmth and passion, and she returned his vow in full. Sealed as one, forever, they mounted their separate and beautiful birds, and flew off, up into the unknown night.

It was like that first Caver night, cold, dark and wet, when she had first wakened on that dreary plain and Lukas had shouted at her.

Buffeted by irregular gusts of wind, Ash swooped and banked and Eleanor's cloak gave little protection. In minutes she was soaked through, teeth chattering, fingers numb. She leant forward, crouching over Ash's shoulders, trying to reduce wind resistance, trying to bury herself in the sleek feathers.

Every now and then she looked back over her shoulder to reassure herself of Lukas's presence. He was not far behind, and waved at her, a white hand and face gleaming briefly in the dark.

Where were they going? What would she have to do? At least she would not be alone, Lukas was with her. And at least she would not have to decide, for the Arrarat were now initiating the action. She trusted the waves of strength from Ash. She understood now that the deep resonances in his mind sprang from sources quite different from anything she recognised. He was prompted through other, greater, dimensions, by forces beyond light and dark, Sun and Moon.

There was something else, too, something desolate in his love, but she refused to recognise what it was. She knew that she only had to go along with him, she only needed to be passive.

She could not bear to acknowledge that Ash was telling her farewell. It was the cold, the wet and dark, that was making her feel so sad. The night was closing in around them, and she was beginning to shiver.

What was there to separate her from the rain and the black? Seeping alike into her clothes, her hair and her soul, it seemed that she too was purely a creature of the night, tossed here and there by its whim, alone, empty of significance. The night ran through her, water through a sieve, and whatever she was was lost in it, dissipated and fragmented . . .

And yet welding her fast to an idea of warmth and purpose was her love for Lukas. It was the only thing holding her together, the only meaning in her life. Without him she would not exist, lost between the night and warring Gods.

Ash was rising all the time as the fjords below gave way to mountains. Range upon range stretched away into the dark beneath them. As her eyes became used to the gloom she began to pick out the shapes of deep valleys, ridges and peaks. There was a biting chill in the air now, and the highest peaks were touched by snow.

She had thought they were too far south for snow. And yet, as she watched, the slopes beneath her began to film over with white.

Astret's night, she thought. Matthias has done this, Lukas's brother with the powerful eyes . . . How could they fail, with such strength on their side?

She buried her fingers deeper into the feathers and laid her cheek against Ash's warm neck.

It was not farewell. It could not be.

Surely they would not fail.

It wanted to find its own kind, to take its rightful place, but there was something else first. Wild exhilaration in its heart, the new-begotten creature flexed its untried powers, testing ideas and thoughts. Finding them all potent, all poised for the unleashing, it laughed.

The sound blended with the wind, echoed round the mountains.

It recognised the night of Astret and knew it for an enemy. But it was not in the least worried by the cold and dark, for the Sun it loved was infinitely more powerful than any trivial denial of light.

Much remained from the wreckage of Lefevre's mind. All the forbidden teachings and mysteries. All the knowledge of Mage and scientist, all the memory of its previous existence as High Priest. Only one thing was missing.

Humanity.

The fledgling creature was the Fosca King. It would take its throne in the Palace of Blood soon. But first there was something to be done. Something Lefevre would have recognised.

It had to find the Benu. Still the obsession sent the pale eyes scanning through the night, searching, endlessly searching. But now it knew which way to go. Its mystic and clairvoyant powers had revealed a beacon of flame in its mind. This was not the Moon's light. This flame burnt wildly, an explosion of light, and its heart was blood-red.

A thrill of anticipation from the Fosca King's mount. The reptile's fine radar, sensitive as a bat's, had found its prey, sensing the two Arrarat winging through the mountains.

Avid, excited, they hurtled through the air and then the Fosca King could see them too, far ahead through the snow-clouded night.

And a third Arrarat, coming from the north.

For a moment the Fosca King was surprised. It sent out a leap of imagination, touching the fringes of the future, to find out who it was.

The power was undeniable. A Mage, a familiar pattern of strength and knowledge. Matthias.

A surge of delight. A worthy adversary, this. It remembered Matthias from those far off days. Blaise's favourite, sent to learn the secrets of Synchronicity.

It would have liked to draw the battle out, to defeat Matthias in some formal contest of skill, but there was not time, now.

Three Arrarat and the Fosca King. It would not be difficult.

It had a bow, of course and other weapons, but it doubted that it would need to use them.

It started by creating a double. Itself, mirrored, imagined into reality, surging through the air far ahead.

The duplicate sprang into existence between the black Arrarat and Matthias's hawk. Both of them swerved sharply and the Fosca King saw the man behind Matthias fit an arrow to his bow.

Oh yes, it thought, excellent. A pleasing symmetry about this.

Let them destroy each other.

It remembered the man with the bow, someone with a part yet to play, someone within Lycias's design, Phinian Blythe, the traitor. Even better. It had released him once, in the grip of some strange premonition. Now it knew why.

He was drawing the string back. The Fosca King held its double steady, between Blythe and the girl on the Midnight Arrarat.

The arrow, the aim true and powerful.

It passed straight through the mirror image, straight on through the night, and found its home in the breast of the dark Arrarat.

The black wings fluttered briefly, and then the hawk plummeted to the mountains, the girl falling, the bright hair tossed into the night.

A shout from the grey Arrarat, the one carrying the man it did not know, and that too plunged down out of the sky, down to the mountainside.

A thrill of ecstasy flooded the Fosca King. The blood-red beacon was extinguished. It had succeeded in its task. Oh excellent, oh beautiful, oh fine . . .

It could find its home now, its Kingdom of Blood. There was no urgency now.

But before it turned away towards the east, where the Kingdom of Blood lay, it laughed and loosed just one arrow.

And the heavily laden Arrarat carrying Matthias Marling and Phinian Blythe abruptly lost height, skewering round in painfilled circles, falling onto the wasteland below.

The Fosca King watched it crash onto rock. Then it turned its nauseous mount, and disappeared off through the snowy air, and the unreal wraith fled after it, screaming through the night.

Chapter Twenty-one
Guilt

'Can't you help her?' Blythe to Matthias, examining Asta's wound by the light of a small fire, kindled through the Mage's power. The hawk was crouched on wet cold rock, her wing awkwardly outstretched, black blood dripping.

Wearily, Matthias straightened. 'If we try to get the arrow out she'll probably bleed to death.'

'She's in agony now.'

Matthias didn't answer. He was standing next to the bird, one hand resting on her acquiescent head, his face averted from the Peraldonian.

'Well, what shall we do?' There was still no answer. Frightened now, more than he had been even with Idas, Blythe gripped his shoulder and spun him round.

'What is it?' He was shouting. 'What's gone wrong?'

Dark eyes flinty hard, lines deep-etched, the smaller man took his time answering.

'Did you see where your last arrow went?' His voice was hard, unemotional, stripped of feeling.

'No – I thought it hit the Fosca – didn't it?' Again that fear, gripping at his throat.

'You shot down the hawk carrying Eleanor. You killed her Arrarat. She fell. She's almost certainly dead.'

No, he thought. It's not possible, this couldn't be my role, destroyer and murderer. Not again.

'But I saw it! The arrow hit the Fosca –'

'Did you see it fall?'

'No . . . Asta turned west. I'm sure I didn't miss!'

'Your aim was true. But that was no Fosca. A wraith, it was, an illusion. Your arrow passed straight through it. And Eleanor was just behind.'

This could not be true. But there was no doubting Matthias's words. He had no reason to lie. He did not actually say it, so Blythe's mind started the refrain.

Murderer, again. Consistent, like the Sun of Lycias, destroyer of Cavers, friends and relatives.

He stood on cold rock looking at the black night and despair filled his soul.

A heedless engine of destruction, always ready and eager to extinguish life and hope. Remember the arrow on the string, the string held in curved fingers, and remember its power, sending death through the air, death to all hope, death to one frightened, ineffectual girl. It had all been a crescendo of annihilation to that one moment, a preparation for that final act.

Numb, despairing, he hardly noticed the other man turn away from Asta, hardly noticed the kind eyes studying him.

'You could not have known,' said the quiet voice. 'You could not have known that it was only an image. One should not assent to appearance, you know. It is usually misleading. Take the Parid, for example.'

The gentle voice ran on, covering over the first shock of guilt. 'How do you think the Parid change shape so easily? They're not real, they are only a collection of hypnotic vibrations imprinted on formless matter.'

'You're wrong.' Blythe looked up, caught out of his daze of self-hatred. 'I saw one bite Lukas. There was blood; he nearly died.'

Matthias shrugged. 'They're capable of using weapons, of inflicting hurt, certainly. But the shapes they assume – what was this one? Snake? Bird?'

'Mantis. Or spider. A mixture.'

Matthias wrinkled his nose in distaste. 'How could you be taken in? Such things don't exist.'

'I've seen Lefevre's workshops. Mutation is the prevailing fashion. Think of the Fosca.'

'They're different, the products of interbreeding.' Matthias returned to Asta, stroking her patient head. 'I had not thought that the Fosca shared any of the qualities of the Parid. I did not know they could use wraiths, too . . . The Parid exist only by projecting images onto the observer's consciousness. The scurries are like that too. They are animated matter defined only by their background, or by the master who instructs them. They can be used as servants or spies by anyone with rudimentary skills, but the Parid can only be controlled by a truly powerful Mage. But neither of them have an enduring physical identity. Don't be deceived. One doesn't have to assent.'

Blythe watched the fire steadily, but his hands shook.

There was a long pause. Matthias returned to Asta, his hand stroking the stained feathers, looking into the clouded, golden eyes of the bird.

'You are strangely afflicted, my friend, aren't you? What other crimes lie on your conscience?'

Unable to speak, Blythe looked out into the night.

'If there have been other deaths, murders, betrayals, accidents . . .' Matthias went relentlessly on, 'if you appear to be responsible for so much, why are you still here?'

'Why didn't I end it long ago?' Unrecognisable, his voice seemed to come from the air itself. 'Too easy,' he said. 'Too tempting . . . And besides –'

'You have work to do?'

'Yes.'

'Even at the expense of more deaths?'

'Yes.' Quietly, almost inaudible.

'Even if it is all useless, if nothing will ever change, and the Stasis goes on forever?'

'Whose side are you on?' Blythe was shouting, pricked at last into an explicit betrayal of emotion. 'What are you doing?'

'Defining,' the Mage said gently. 'I need to know what you are, what you're made of.'

'I'll tell you what he's made of, brother mine.' An infinitely weary, infinitely bitter voice, out of the dark.

'Lukas!' Matthias ran to his brother as if to embrace him, but stopped suddenly, halted by the outstretched hand.

'Don't – touch me,' he said distantly. 'Phinian Blythe here, look at him –' He stopped suddenly, just outside the firelight, watching Blythe's face.

The words were running on again in Blythe's mind.

Look at you, remorse and anguish from every pore.

Simple to fathom, easy to understand. You do Lefevre's work for him. No one is as good as you are at wiping out Cavers. You've got a way with women and the old too; first make friends with them and then murder them. And as for the Stasis, why, you're the very prop and stay of it all, Lefevre's trusted ally and tool. Just as he promised.

The words ran on, a litany of guilt pouring through his mind, running through the paths trampled clear by Idas. Where there had been love and laughter was only guilt and despair. As Lukas came nearer, and Blythe saw his face, the brilliant eyes hollow with pain, the long mouth set hard and rigid, the words went on.

You can rely on the Peraldonian military for speed and efficiency. You even think it's not really your fault, that it's chance, the sport of gods. That way everyone else can feel sorry for you too.

In the firelight, Blythe saw Lukas's face masked, unfamiliar with grief. The tall, easy grace was gone. Only will held him upright, rigid with exhaustion.

'I can't find her, Phin –' he said, suddenly, breaking through the poison in his mind. 'I can't find Eleanor. I saw her fall – Ash's body is over there – but I can't find her. She's not there –'

Blythe caught him as he stumbled, guided him to a rock and wrapped his own cloak around him. Matthias brought a flask of spirit. Lukas pushed it away with impatience.

Matthias knelt, trying to make up the fire. They needed warmth now, and healing, all of them. This was disaster on an infinite scale.

In the wet slush the fire spluttered and smoked. He worked hard, trying to build it up.

At last Lukas raised his head. 'Where's Phin?' he said.

Matthias looked round sharply, at the dying bird, the feeble fire and deserted mountainside. But there was no sign of Phinian Blythe, and his sword and bow were gone.

Chapter Twenty-two
Phinian

Later the snow began to settle in earnest. In the artificial night, the outline of rock and mountain became blurred under the softening disguise of white.

In his headlong flight from the two brothers, Phinian Blythe had left his cloak, and all his baggage but the weapons. Cold, his breath icy before his face, he began by running, to gain both distance and warmth, but soon found that the gradient was too steep, the mountainside too uneven and rocky.

He was following no path, he had no plan. He thought it might be necessary to get to the top of the mountain; there was a challenge to be met, a fate to be decided, and no sheltered valley would suffice. What the challenge would be he didn't know. He rather hoped it would be death, unavoidable and final, but feared that it wasn't time yet.

He tramped up the slopes and along ridges, slipping sometimes in the snow, falling against rock. His soul was black with self hatred, black with guilt.

Eleanor. The one hope, the holder of the Benu. Lost, because of him. The structure of the Stasis maintained, the Boundary strengthened, because of him, just as Lefevre prophesied.

And on a more human level, the look in Lukas's eyes.

He had recognised the grief held there. He knew it well. He had felt the same, when Karis died. It was an enduring grief. There was no end to it.

He recognised madness in the voice in his mind, cataloguing his actions. But the accusations were not false; on the contrary, it was as if pain had brought clarity and understanding, had pointed out in relentless purity the shape of Lefevre's design.

As he stumbled over rock and sank in wet snow, his shirt wet through and chafing, he began to wonder if so much could really be laid at the door of one man.

Like a shock, blinding, so forceful that he stopped dead, knowledge burst upon him.

It was not Lefevre; a poor human pawn, no more significant than any other of them. More powerful in some ways, of course. But at the mercy of the gods, eternally used for sport. The phrase rang in his mind. They were all, Lukas and Eleanor, Cavers, Peraldonians and Jerenites, Fosca and Arrarat and himself, each and every one of them at the mercy of Lycias's will. Their petty battles, feuds and hatreds were as toys to the gods; they meant nothing, and were nothing beside Lycias's eternal design.

What were the words Matthias had used? 'One doesn't have to assent . . .'

He did not assent.

He would not allow this to continue. He would not be party to a divine obsession.

He stood still in the snow, the white-covered slopes of the mountain a wasteland around him, and stared up into the sky. Rage seared through him, lending strength to despair.

'Lycias!' He didn't have to shout. Amplified by rock, thrown about an arena of stone and snow, the name reverberated in the silence.

'Lycias! Cheat! Deceiver! Lycias, I know You!' He was shouting now, shouting at the heavens.

Recognition flared like light and he held his breath, knowing that the God had come. He could see nothing at first, the snow was untouched. But then he realised that it had stopped falling, that it was frozen into immobility. Time ceases where the God is.

'And I know you.' Slowly the voice embraced his puny resistance and flung it back at him, feeble, emasculated.

Blythe stood still, braced in the timeless moment.

'I defy You,' he said at last, and although his voice was faint, he did not falter.

Laughter spiced the air.

'With what?'

'I challenge You!'

'With what?' again, mocking.

'A wager!' Inspiration struck him. 'I wager You that – that –' He paused, every fibre attenuated, knowing that there was an answer here. Then, clearly, he knew what his challenge was to be.

Lycias spoke; and suddenly Blythe could see Him, a lonely, small figure standing far away across the empty snow fields. Far away; and His voice was whispered, and yet Blythe heard every word.

'I can destroy you. Your destiny is in My hands as this snow is, melting and dying. You are as insignificant to Me.'

'But my challenge is not! You cannot allow it to go unresolved!'

'Can I not?' Effortlessly the figure approached, stealing brightness from the snow, blinding and beautiful. Fear such as he had never before known made Blythe's knees weak. He could *not* bear Him to come closer, absolutely could not face the God's presence. But still Lycias approached and the snow wept at His step.

Blythe covered his eyes with his hands, so the sight would not force him to kneel. Then the God spoke again, not unkindly.

'I could so easily destroy you – and yet – and yet, I would be loath to do so. You have more courage than most, Phinian.'

At the warmth of the voice, Blythe felt helpless with love, with gratitude and adoration. It was as if all misery and hatred and guilt had faded away into healing. Nothing else existed but the God, brilliant and loving. All his grief was defused, trivial and irrelevant. He yearned to worship and surrender.

'Lefevre has failed Me. I need a lieutenant on earth and the Priest has become selfish and unreliable. Come to Me, Phinian, and let us be friends.'

'Lord . . .' A daze of glory swept aside Blythe's doubts; he opened his eyes.

Lycias stood only a few feet from him, in His most unthreatening guise of a small, delicate, fair-haired man.

Clean-shaven and fine boned, guileless blue eyes and a calmly curling mouth, He stood on snow. Glowing, shatteringly bright in the simple clothes of a Caver. He raised one hand and held it out to the man.

'A bargain, Phinian? Join Me, and you shall have every power on earth. Do My will and you will be able to bring prosperity and order to all . . . make amends to the Cavers, Phin, banish the Fosca, restore peace. It would be easy, with Me to help you. Let us set Time straight, together.

'Come. Take My hand.'

An irresistible invitation, and Blythe knew he would not resist. Could not. Gripped by the decision, he forced himself to look at the God again, but the brightness forbade observation. His eyes fell to the ground beneath His feet. Snow, frozen in the Static night.

It shone, grey beside Lycias.

It pulled him up short.

Would Blythe's own life appear soiled, too, in comparison? Working with the God, for the God, would not every human contact seem defiled and useless?

Was this why Mariana had originally chosen Idas, trying to avoid the trap of perfection? Was this why Lefevre had become so careless of life, so heedless of responsibility? For surely nothing could matter beside the gift of a God's love . . .

He didn't have to assent.

His voice cracked. 'My wager . . .' Where were the words coming from? He wrenched his eyes up to meet those of the God. 'My wager . . . that I will find the Benu. I will find it, and release it before You . . .'

The soft lips curled, and watching, Blythe knew, incredulously, that he had hit the central issue. He looked away again, unable to bear it.

'There is no need for us to race each other,' Lycias continued calmly, unruffled. 'Let us work together to find the Benu. Our first joint enterprise, Our first task . . . a noble one.'

But this was an irrelevance, and Blythe knew it.

He shook his head.

Once a wager is made, it hangs there in the air, unresolved

and exigent. It cannot be waived, avoided or nullified. A balance of power is called into question and the only way to answer the question is to test the balance.

Soft regret and no anger at all echoed in the God's voice. 'You could have become great, Phinian Blythe. Now there is only death and madness ahead for you. Poor man. Poor little man . . . what have you done?'

Once more Blythe dragged his gaze up to meet that of the God, and ice clawed at his heart. The eyes were kind as ever, but the curling mouth was wrought only with cruelty now.

It was a warning, in a way.

'The race is on,' said Lycias, 'and I *know* where the Benu is!' He laughed, and at the sound the mountain began to crumble beneath Blythe's feet, and shrieking, thundering, the world was tossed into a jumble of stone and earth.

Caught in the landslip – or was it an avalanche? – Blythe found himself in a tumbling chaos of snow, mud and rock down the slope, while the earth juddered and shook around him, roaring as its fabric was torn asunder.

Loose stones skipped and jumped, larger rocks rumbling and crushing. He tried to clutch onto something, anything to halt the downwards descent, but there was nothing solid or stable.

Bruised and cut, he curled his arms round his head, drawing his knees in to protect his body, and for a time rolled like that, scraping and scraped in the mess of mud and rock, always downwards.

One rock, larger than most, bounced off the ground and caught his arm, crushing elbow and wrist against the mountainside. Dizzy with agony he failed to protect himself; his ankle twisted, pitching him forward so that his head smashed into a rocky outcrop. In a mess of blood and dirt he was flung by the force of the fall into a small hollow beneath the outcrop, and there, sheltered from the worst of the avalanche, he subsided into a graceless, unconscious heap.

Chapter Twenty-three
Mariana

Eleanor shut her eyes against a familiar brightness. Was this a dream again? Or was it death? She knew this world, Lycias's creation, and didn't want to be here. Last time in this place, she had seen the Moon eclipsed and had lost all hope, when Lycias had revealed His power.

She shouldn't be here again. Lukas would be worrying. And what had happened to Ash? She sighed, and looked around.

Not a warm paradise of flowers and water this time, but a seashore, recalling the quiet island where she had lived with Lukas for that brief, halcyon time.

The waves were no more than small ripples over smooth golden sand, washing soundlessly and ceaselessly. The sun hung low and gentle on the horizon, tinging the glassy water with rose. There were no birds, no wind, no disturbance of the still calm. Sand as far as the eye could see in one direction, sea the other way. Nothing else.

She hated it, the clean sterility of the place. Deliberately she scuffed up sand with her shoes, kicking it into untidy heaps.

'Don't do that.' A cool voice behind her. Turning, she saw a woman she had never met before. Frantic disappointment pulled at her mouth because she wasn't the Moon.

Instead, a quite remarkably beautiful woman stood there, raven hair piled high on her graceful head, one or two curls tumbling onto her white shoulder. Her eyes were green and serene, her lips generous and smiling.

'Why shouldn't I?' said Eleanor crossly. Classic beauty always made her impatient.

'It's so perfect here, let's not spoil it,' said the woman, her voice warm and husky. 'But I suppose it doesn't matter. Look, you can hardly see it now . . .' She pointed to the sand. The heaps had blurred round the edges with damp and were now melting back into the level surface.

'Who are you?' said Eleanor. 'And where's Astret?'

'My name is Mariana,' she replied, 'and I don't at all know why you should be thinking of meeting the Moon here. It's not at all Her kind of place.'

'Mariana? You're Mariana? The Stasis began because of *you*?' She couldn't help it; her voice rose in surprise. 'How can you bear it?'

'Bear what? What are you talking about?' The woman seemed genuinely puzzled.

'What's happening – what the Stasis is doing to people!' Passionately, she kept kicking at the sand, avoiding the woman's eyes.

Gently she smiled. 'They're all right, aren't they? Living forever, no old age or death? It's nothing to do with me, anyway. It's not my fault.'

'That's what I used to think,' said Eleanor clearly, remembering. 'And really, I think I have less reason to feel guilty than you. Either way one can't avoid it.'

'Avoid what?'

'Involvement.' She was thinking of Lukas all the time, impatient with this limbo. 'You can't stand outside people's lives. You have to act.'

'I know! Let's make a sandcastle!' The woman hadn't even been listening. She knelt on the sand and began to pile it up with long elegant fingers.

'Is this what you do all day?' Eleanor was disgusted. 'I'd imagined something quite different.'

'He will be here soon,' she said. 'He's not usually away for long.'

And then all Eleanor's confidence evaporated, because she did not want to meet Lycias again. She knelt on the sand and began to pile it up because there was nothing else to do. Tears gathered in her eyes, remembering the sandcastle shore she had shared with Lukas.

Was this all she was good for, constructions that dissolved into nothing? She sniffed, and decided that regret and guilt were useless if they didn't lead to action. She would talk to Mariana, and build sandcastles, and sooner or later it would all change again.

The pain in his arm was making him feel sick before even thought returned. He kept his eyes shut at first in case Lycias was still there, smiling, incandescent. He concentrated instead on what was hurting.

The arm was so bad that bruises, aching head and wrenched ankle faded in comparison. He made a tiny, indistinct movement as he tried ease it, but a small rock dislodged from the ground beside him and bounced down the slope. He would have to know where he was, would have to deal with any immediate danger. Warily Blythe opened his eyes.

He was lying in a narrow depression, overhung by a large flat rock. It was balanced precariously on an unsteady heap of smaller stones. It was stable, for the moment. Snow was falling thickly, silently.

He was quite alone. It could be worse. He lay still, trying to remember, to order thought, construct plans, but the pain in his arm was distracting. He would have to look at it.

It seemed hopelessly mangled, unnaturally bent between elbow and wrist, splinters of bone jutting through bloody skin. His left hand was a shapeless mass, stained red with blood, blue with cold. Dirt and mud clogged the skin. Dispassionately, he thought that soon the pain would be overtaken by numbness, and didn't know whether that would be better or worse.

A frail anger stirred then.

You weight the scales, don't You, Lycias? Isn't it enough to be God? Must You cripple the opposition as well?

He tried to shift, to ease the pressure on his arm, but soon stopped, partly because the flare of agony made him dizzy, and partly because the overhanging rock grated on its support at the movement. It was close to falling, would crush him if it did. He was trapped.

Time passed. Somehow, it passed.

In a daze he heard Lukas's indrawn breath and tried to speak.

'Don't come closer . . .' His voice was harsh but faint. 'The rock will fall.'

'Right.' Lukas sounded both concerned and disappointed. He'd been looking for Eleanor, of course, Blythe thought, hanging on to the shreds of reason.

Cautiously picking his way over the slope, Lukas called to his brother. In moments they had planned and executed an efficient rescue, shoring up the rock from beneath while Matthias's staff propped it away from the ground.

Then, gently, carefully, they lifted him out onto the scree slope. Mercifully he fainted as soon as they touched him and Matthias made a rough splint, tying it up with strips torn from his shirt.

At length, Matthias sat back on his heels, brushing hair from his eyes.

'It doesn't look good,' he said. 'I don't know that the arm can be saved.'

'You must, Matt,' said Lukas, intense and furious. 'He's been through so much. And besides –' He stopped. How to explain a friendship built on such confusion and grief?

'I'll do what I can, of course,' said Matthias reasonably. 'But we need shelter, warmth, food, bandages . . .'

'End this night, can't you?'

Matthias lifted his eyes from the injured man and looked at his brother.

'I could – but what of Thurstan, Stefan and the others? This is their only chance. I'm not going to imperil them for one man.'

It was unanswerable.

'He won't survive out here for long.' Lukas was not arguing, only commenting. Matthias stroked the carving on his wooden staff, retrieved from its role as prop. 'I can – possibly – restore him a little, temporarily, while you go for help.'

'How? Take a gentle stroll down the mountain, a quick trot up the next and then a leisurely ramble down the gorge, over the plain, over the next range . . .'

'Lukas. Think. Isn't Astrella here?'

The bitter torrent ceased. 'Of course,' he said slowly. 'But, Matt, what about Eleanor? She's here somewhere . . . Matt, I must find her –'

'She's safe.' Faintly, clearly from Blythe.

'What do you mean?' Lukas was on his knees beside him, passion blazing. 'You *know* where she is?'

'No.' Blythe was striving for clarity. 'When I left you – I met Lycias . . .'

Lukas frowned with disbelief, but Matthias's hand restrained him.

'Try to explain, Phin. I have felt something of this. That avalanche – was not natural.'

'No . . . I challenged Him, to find the Benu. He reacted by trying to obliterate me . . .' He was light-headed with the effort of talking and thinking. 'She's either holding it or knows where it is . . . Lycias would not need to be so – vengeful – if she were of no account. Lukas – I'm sure, I know, she's alive.'

'Well, where is she?' He was shouting, but a light scatter of rocks around them drew him to silence.

Blythe had not noticed; an uneasy faint had reclaimed him. Nodding to his brother, Matthias bundled his own cloak round him, and with painstaking slowness they half dragged, half carried him out of the path of the rock fall to the snow fields at the side.

'You can do nothing else here,' said Matthias. 'I think Blythe is right. Eleanor must still be alive. Go and get help. I can keep him going – for twelve hours, I think. Get back by then.'

'I don't like leaving you here.' Lukas looked around the empty wasteland of snow, the stars lending it an odd silvery brilliance. Black rocks defined the shapes of the mountains all around, a plateau towering high just behind them. Clouds were beginning to creep across from the west, blotting out the stars, clouds heavy and dull with snow. The cold was intense, and he could see that Matthias was already shivering. He took off his own cloak, and gave it to his brother.

'We'll be all right,' said Matthias. 'I'll make a snow shelter. We'll be waiting.'

A rush of air overhead, and Astrella touched down on a

rocky ledge at the edge of the snowfield. She looked across at them.

'Lukas –' Matthias caught his arm as he turned to go. 'We haven't long. The crisis is almost here. Take care.'

'And you.' Uncharacteristically, Lukas embraced his brother and then stood back, regarding him with doubt. 'Look after Phin, won't you? I wish it hadn't been him . . .'

'It's not easy, is it?' Unconsciously, Matthias echoed his own words. He smiled, but his voice was serious. 'Lady go with you, Luke. Don't be late.'

So Lukas and Astrella took off, leaving his brother and friend on the icy mountainside.

'Mariana.' Kneeling on the sand, Eleanor began the final assault.

'Do you love Lycias?' It felt like blasphemy even mentioning it.

Mariana sat back on her heels, pushing a lock of hair out of her eyes. She was faintly flushed, her eyes gleaming, lips slightly parted. She looked glorious.

'He is the God,' she said simply. 'How could I not adore Him?'

'But do you love Him?'

'With all my heart and soul.'

'And is it returned?'

'He has stopped time for me. And His eyes shine when He looks at me.'

Eleanor traced a pattern in the sand with her forefinger, thoughtfully. She began to pile up, in the centre of the spiral, a number of small shells.

'Karis,' she said, counting, 'and the baby. Jocasta, Albin, Reckert and Estan. The Moon worshippers in Peraldon.' A handful scattered here. 'Cavers, over the ages. Arrarat, Peraldonians and Fosca.' The heap was overspilling the pattern now.

Mariana watched with reluctance, the rosy flush fading. 'What are you doing?' she whispered.

'These people are dead.' Eleanor was cold. 'And here –' she started another pile, more shells from her pockets, 'here are the people captured or fighting, in pain, tortured, suffering . . .' She began to pile it up. 'Uther. Nerissa. Marial. Niclaus and Letia, Fabian, Thurstan and Martitia.' Her voice faltered. Perhaps some of these had died and she didn't yet know it. Unsteadily her hand hovered over the pretty shells. She picked up one of them and held it out to the other woman.

'Idas,' she said. 'You knew him once, didn't you?'

Mariana's emerald eyes were wide with distress, her hand pressed to her lips.

'Idas? What's happened to Idas?'

'Stop!' A thunderclap of sound spun them around, open mouthed, to see Lycias standing there at the waters' edge, bright and beautiful, blazing with anger. 'I shall shrivel you now where you stand,' He said quietly and the words blasted the paintbox world to ashes.

They hardly noticed that the beach had vanished, that they were crouching now at the God's feet on the top of a snowy, bitter mountain.

In cold and fear Mariana surged to her feet, and ran straight to Lycias, to be caught and cradled in His arms. Over her head He smiled at Eleanor.

'There is nothing for you here, little one.' He spoke gently, the anger seeming to dissolve as He held His beloved. 'I can afford to be generous with you. What do you want? Your Caver lover, a return to your world, an easy oblivion? The choice is yours.'

The piles of shells still stood in the spiral now traced in snow beneath her hands. She was still holding one of them, a creamy, delicate cone. She began to tremble, though not with cold.

'Shall I help you decide?' said the God. 'Stand here with Me.' Conjured to her feet, she found herself crossing the snowy wastes towards Him.

Cold wind blew through her hair, and snow fell through the air all around her. There were stars still shining in the east, but their brilliance was like tinsel beside the Sun God.

'Look,' He said, and opened His hands to her, fingers spread wide, revealing in miniature a scene from another life.

Chapter Twenty-four
Eleanor

People danced to a rock band in a country house, people she thought she had forgotten, Lewis and Caro, Pat and Rob. She cried out in amazement and the scene grew larger, stronger, increased until it was all around her, thronging and noisy, blotting out the cold mountain.

Someone had taken her hand.

'Eleanor!' said Lewis. 'Where have you been? Why, your hair's all wet!'

She slowly put her hand to her head, and looked at the fast melting snow vanishing on her fingertips.

'Come on,' he said. 'I've got the champagne, let's creep away somewhere and have a ball!' His eyes, dark and kind, were frankly admiring. 'Oh, you're so beautiful tonight!' he said, enchanted. 'It's as if I've never seen you before. Oh, there are so many things for us to do together!'

'Eleanor!' Another voice, Mark's, slurred and friendly. 'Come and dance! Show us all up, there's no one like you when it comes to dancing!' He pushed through the crowds and smiled at Lewis. 'You can't monopolise her,' he said. 'We need her. Your turn will come later!'

And then Debs, her old friend and rival, took her arm, whispering confidentially in one ear, 'Nell, love, there's someone wanting to meet you over there, look –'

Turning, she saw across the room a tall figure, loose-limbed, long mouth smiling, coming towards her –

'Lukas!' she cried, and the scene spun and melted, lights, admiration, friends, music and warmth lost in a kaleidoscope of sound and colour, settling at last into the dark chill of the Caver night.

* * *

She staggered slightly as the boat beneath her feet rocked with the waves' motion. Cold wind blew snow around her; through the gloom she could just see Lukas's tall figure across the water, moving from boat to boat, still coming towards her, shouting her name.

Dark shapes wheeled overhead, darting, and arrows shivered into the deck by his feet. Other people were fighting too, around them, but she could only look at Lukas, her hand held over her mouth with dread.

As he moved, a Fosca swooped down, obscuring her sight, and all at once they were everywhere. Dark angels darted here and there, claws and teeth ripping and shredding, talons slashing through the falling snow.

Other men were shouting too, trying to manoeuvre the Caver fleet towards Cliokest. She thought for a moment that she heard Thurstan's voice, pressed as he'd never been before.

It was desperate, Cavers falling all the time, falling on the slippery decks, falling into the agitated, freezing sea. Boats were on fire, some abandoned, some sinking, and the cries of the injured filled her ears.

The citadel blazed with light and fire; people were screaming there, too, and the Arrarat diving from the sky to attack its ramparts were calling, wailing in the wind.

Lukas was getting close, but as she watched two Fosca attacked him at once, slicing through the air. He staggered under one blow which caught his shoulder, and, spinning, managed to plunge his sword into the reptile's breast. It was not possible to withdraw it smoothly; as he laboured, frantic and straining, the other Fosca crashed into him with a scream, and the creature's long talon disappeared into Lukas's body. In a convulsion of agony he arched backwards, blood showering onto the snow, and then lay still, limbs contorted, face down to the whitened deck. A sigh; the limbs relaxed, and a gush of blood melted into the snow.

It was over.

He was dead.

She had not screamed, could not. Frozen with shock, she even forgot to breathe. A voice somewhere was muttering over and over, 'Lukas, oh Lukas, oh Lukas –' and it seemed that the whole world was echoing her words, as if the falling snow already settling on the dear, familiar body was reiterating with every crystal the shock of it.

Her knees sagged; she knelt on the hard deck of the deserted boat and bitterness filled the world, denying all hope, all love, all peace.

Through this extremity came stealing oblivion, like a thief in the night. Just as the sandcastles dissolved in the sand, as the snow melted under blood, so the wild excess of her grief became blurred and indistinct.

A numbness washed over her, calm and forgiving. An unusual serenity began to flow, smoothing away thought and tears. Cool and sweet, till even feeling drifted away. She became lost in a void, where there was no identity, no emotion, no consciousness and no memory. Nothing.

The God's eyes, plunging deep into her soul, recalled her to herself.

'Come, little one,' He said. 'Choose. Your own world. Oblivion. Or Lukas.'

'He's dead!' Even the God was no longer bright beside this fact. Blankly she stared around at the barren snow-covered plateau, white rocks rearing into the sparkling black night. Lycias was only a few feet from her, Mariana staring just behind His shoulder, watching. She could not concentrate on them.

'Time – can be reversed,' said Lycias carefully. 'It has been controlled before. With the Benu, I could reverse time for you.' He paused, weighing words, calculating. 'You could live, with Lukas, eternally, on that calm seashore. Forever loving, forever joyful.'

'As I do,' said Mariana. 'It was my choice.'

'I want – Lukas –' She could think of nothing else. Lycias took a step nearer.

'If you give Me the Benu, you shall live with him in eternal love. I will alter time for you.'

'But I haven't got it!' At last she understood what He was saying. 'I don't know what you mean!'

'Eleanor!' Another voice, familiar, harsh with strain. She

looked beyond Lycias and Mariana, and blanched to see Blythe approaching across the plateau.

Supported by Matthias, his face was white, will burning like acid in his eyes. A bow was slung over his shoulder. Blood covered his left arm from elbow to hand, bruises stained the skin exposed by the filthy rags of his shirt. He limped, seemed faint; in extremis and yet upright, supported by the man at his side.

Matthias held him up with one arm; the other clasped his carved light-wood staff. Power gleamed from it in a haze and clung round the Peraldonian.

Through that power alone, thought Eleanor, is Phin remaining on his feet. It cannot last long. He will fall soon, as Lukas has fallen.

Tears blurred her vision.

'Eleanor!' Blythe was shouting now.

'Eleanor!' Lycias came closer, wary with tension. Mariana was still just behind Him. 'Give Me the Benu,' He said, warm with concern. 'You should not be so abandoned –'

And He held out His hand, safe and forgiving, and she nearly gave Him –

The shell. The golden spiral in her hand, the shell given her by the Moon so long ago, jumbled in her pocket, adorning sandcastles and chessboards, always somehow scooped up and put back in her pocket.

She stared at it, small and perfect in her hand, reverberating with gold. 'What do You mean?' she whispered.

'Give it to Me, and you shall have your lover,' said Lycias. 'Time will be reversed. I promise it.'

'He never lies . . .' said Mariana.

'Eleanor!' Blythe again, a frail thread of dissent. 'The shell, the shell holds the Stasis steady. Give it to *Him* and it will be meaningless eternity for us all. Don't give it up!' His passion was almost tangible, as was his weakness.

'Matthias –' she began, stumbling towards him over the snow. 'Lukas is dead. I saw him –' and again sobs halted both her words and her movement.

'You need not suffer like this,' said Mariana with compassion. 'Does your love mean so little to you?'

'Can you bear to let him go?' Lycias was warm with gentle enquiry. 'Of course, if it's not important –'

He shrugged, but still His hand was outstretched, inviting.

Lukas was everything to her, everything. Her previous life was a pale, fragile dream, a mere shadow with no power to hold, to enchant, to delight. And a future without Lukas would be useless, without purpose, a dreary wasteland.

For what purpose was there, except that they should love each other? And yet, even as she thought this, she knew it was not good enough.

Lukas's whole existence, his entire life was dedicated to ending the Stasis. He might have held her high, he had loved her passionately; but he would never have loved her so much as to forget the distortion of the Stasis.

He was in himself the negation of everything the Stasis implied: he was warmth and anger, energy and passion. She could not, would not deny everything she loved in him. She could not live with him for an eternity of love, reinforcing the Stasis. It would destroy them both.

'Lukas, and love, forever,' said Lycias, His eyes alight with fire.

'The Stasis – forever –' said Blythe, his voice like a thread.

'Throw it to me,' said Matthias quietly, hardly daring to breathe. 'Throw it to me. Now.'

In her cupped hands the shell lay calm, waiting for her decision, its secret light promising unimaginable worlds.

I have lost you forever, Lukas, she thought numbly, always and forever, whatever I chose.

But I can at least do this for you.

She threw it with all her strength, releasing it into the frozen air, straight to Matthias.

It flew high above their heads, high over the fiery, burning soul of the God, turning and turning, far higher than any possible throw could take it.

As it spun through the sky, its spiral centre unfurled. A spiral unfurling, the curls and curves unwinding, spreading outwards, spreading to cover everything.

Light streamed from its golden heart.

Small at first like a dove, wrapped in light, the hawk grew into ecstasy. The Benu, born of fire, spread its wings and danced among the stars.

Its voice conjured the air from around her. Its hawk song was extreme in beauty, wild with danger.

She gasped in the wake of its flight, floundering beneath its terrible glory, wrenched out of time into a foreign dimension, where there was nothing but flight and fire and song.

In that moment out of time, she heard Phin move. In a dream her eyes turned to him, fitting the arrow to the bow, holding it steady in his ruined hand.

Unbelieving, she saw him lift it, up into the fire and the song.

'You shall not!' Lycias crying into the wind, a flame of passion lost in the greater brightness.

Phin's voice, still and quiet, at the centre of the song. 'For Selene . . .'

And then the arrow, born of undaunted courage, soaring beyond the power of the Sun God, beyond any human grief, to sink deep into the breast of the golden hawk.

Screaming, shattering time, the Benu began to fall.

She staggered, watching, as glory tumbled through the sky, down . . .

To where Lycias stood, clasping His beloved, locked in the final embrace.

A passionate conjunction of fire on fire. In the sound of a thunderclap, the God of the Sun and the Bird of Time met, in total mutual destruction.

Conflagration and destruction.

The fire of annihilation.

The world exploded, blazing in terror.

Chapter Twenty-five
The Benu

A great rush of wind filled the fire-swollen vacuum.

Then, silence, falling like snow on the blasted plateau.

The night, black again all around.

She did not dare to move, discarded there.

Beneath her fingers, burning rock rapidly cooled. For a long time she lay there. The snow would begin to settle again soon, she thought. The Stasis was back in place, the Boundary intact, for the Benu had been destroyed.

It had all been for nothing.

A touch on her shoulder: Matthias. She expected to see him burnt, scorched, but he was untouched. Her own hands had no mark, although they had lain on red-hot rock.

'Eleanor –'

She could barely look at him, his dark eyes gleaming with unusual light. She brushed the hair out of her eyes.

'What now, Matthias?' Her voice sounded unfamiliar, empty of feeling. 'What now? I thought that for once I'd made the right decision. I tried to put something else first. I didn't think it would all go so wrong . . .'

'I don't know that it has,' he said, but she did not understand.

'And now Lukas is lost, too, for nothing.' True despair is a simple emotion, seeing the world in a pure shade of black. She would not allow herself to register the expression in Matthias's eyes.

'Why did Phin do it?' she said at last, her voice shaking. 'Why did he kill the Benu?'

Phin was there, beside her, wrapped in the strength of Matthias's staff.

'Because I promised I would,' he said, simply. 'It's not over yet . . .'

There was ash hanging in the air all around them, the grey dust of death. All that was left of the golden Benu, the brilliant God, and His beautiful beloved Mariana.

Facing a blank future, she remembered only an appalling past. The grieving would begin soon, she thought. She stood silent on barren rock. There was nothing else to do.

And a litany of hate sounded in the air.

'I shall have My revenge for this, Eleanor. Whatever happens, wherever you go, I will seek you out. You will never escape. There is no way out now . . .'

'Matthias!' In fear, she clutched his arm and he looked down at her. He had such kind eyes . . .

'Remember,' he said. 'The Gods are liars, too . . .'

And still he smiled at her.

Together they stood as the snow fell and under its feather touch the clouds of ash settled.

The clouds of ash settled, and the snow died away, and the smile in his eyes was so like Lukas's . . .

And there, waiting, stood the Benu.

It stood there, across the plateau, risen from ashes, its hooked beak fierce, its eyes blank and empty.

And the Stasis broke, crumbling like a fall of ash, as the Benu Bird looked at them with blind eyes, waiting.

It was waiting for Eleanor, unfurling its feathers, lifting its head as her Arrarat Ash would, wanting her.

'Go now,' said Matthias, his voice soft in her ear. 'Go, Eleanor. Take this chance.'

Phin was watching her and she remembered his words.

It is not over yet. For a moment, their eyes met in hope and friendship.

She turned away and crossed the blasted mountainside to the centre of power.

Unfurling its feathers, like Ash.

She put out one hand and then it cried out, a wild hawksong of fiery compulsion, and she touched it.

In that instant she was swept up into its flight, surging in a blaze of energy, up to the blue heavens.

Out of the world, out of the only reality she had ever cared about. Away from Matthias and Phin.

Away from Lukas. Forever and always, away from Lukas.

A tracery of fire scattered behind them, while sunlight washed around.

And a whisper in the air.

The Gods are liars, too.

A selection of bestsellers from Headline

FICTION		
BLOOD STOCK	John Francome & James MacGregor	£3.99 □
THE OLD SILENT	Martha Grimes	£4.50 □
ALL THAT GLITTERS	Katherine Stone	£4.50 □
A FAMILY MATTER	Nigel Rees	£4.50 □
EGYPT GREEN	Christopher Hyde	£4.50 □
NON-FICTION		
MY MOUNTBATTEN YEARS	William Evans	£4.50 □
WICKED LADY Salvador Dali's Muse	Tim McGirk	£4.99 □
THE FOOD OF SPAIN AND PORTUGAL	Elisabeth Lambert Ortiz	£5.99 □
SCIENCE FICTION AND FANTASY		
REVENGE OF THE FLUFFY BUNNIES Cineverse Cycle Book 3	Craig Shaw Gardner	£3.50 □
BROTHERS IN ARMS	Lois McMaster Bujold	£4.50 □
THE SEA SWORD	Adrienne Martine-Barnes	£3.50 □
NO HAVEN FOR THE GUILTY	Simon Green	£3.50 □
GREENBRIAR QUEEN	Sheila Gilluly	£4.50 □

All Headline books are available at your local bookshop or newsagent, or can be ordered direct from the publisher. Just tick the titles you want and fill in the form below. Prices and availability subject to change without notice.

Headline Book Publishing PLC, Cash Sales Department, PO Box 11, Falmouth, Cornwall, TR10 9EN, England.

Please enclose a cheque or postal order to the value of the cover price and allow the following for postage and packing:
UK: 80p for the first book and 20p for each additional book ordered up to a maximum charge of £2.00
BFPO: 80p for the first book and 20p for each additional book
OVERSEAS & EIRE: £1.50 for the first book, £1.00 for the second book and 30p for each subsequent book.

Name ....

Address ....

....

....